PRICES

Christina confided to her mother in a tense voice. "It's so wrong of Kyle to spurn my business the way she is doing. Having her take over from me one day has always been a cherished dream of mine." These last few words caught in her throat, and she had to steady herself before she could continue, "Oh, Mum, what's it all been *about?* What's all my hard work been *for*, if Kyle walks away?" Christina's eyes welled with tears and she averted her head, blinking.

Audra felt a pang of sympathy, and her heart went out to her daughter. In an effort to comfort her, she murmured, "But Christie, darling, you've derived a great deal of pleasure and satisfaction from your designing, and making a name for yourself in the fashion world has always been important to you, as well as the challenge. What you've accomplished, your staggering achievements and success— why surely these things must be gratifying to you . . ." Audra let her sentence trail off. She was incapable of finishing it. How hollow the words are, she thought.

I, and I alone, know what Christina sacrificed, what it cost her to create the business. She paid a high price, a terrible price . . .

ACT OF WILL

Barbara Taylor Bradford

ACT
OF
WILL

BANTAM BOOKS
TORONTO · NEW YORK · LONDON · SYDNEY · AUCKLAND

*This low-priced Bantam Book
has been completely reset in a type face
designed for easy reading, and was printed
from new plates. It contains the complete
text of the original hard-cover edition.*
NOT ONE WORD HAS BEEN OMITTED.

ACT OF WILL

*A Bantam Book / published by arrangement with
Doubleday & Company, Inc.*

PRINTING HISTORY
Doubleday edition published June 1986
*A selection of Literary Guild and Doubleday Book Clubs
June 1986*
Bantam edition / June 1987

*Grateful acknowledgment is made for permission to reprint lines
from "Happy Birthday to You" words and music by Mildred J. Hill
and Patty S. Hill. Copyright © 1935 Birch Tree Group Ltd.,
Princeton, N.J. Used by Permission.*

PRINTED IN THE UNITED STATES OF AMERICA

KR   0 9 8 7 6 5 4 3

PROLOGUE

~~~

Audra, Christina and Kyle
1978

PROLOGUE

Audra Crowther sat on the sofa in the living room of her daughter's Manhattan penthouse. She held herself tense and clenched her hands together so hard that the knuckles shone white as she looked from her daughter Christina to her granddaughter Kyle.

The two younger women stood in the middle of the room, their faces pale, their eyes blazing as they glared at each other. Their angry words of a few minutes ago still reverberated on the warm afternoon air.

Audra felt increasingly helpless. She knew that to remonstrate with them, to attempt to make them see reason, was a waste of time, at least at this moment. Each was convinced she was right, and no amount of persuasion would make them reverse their positions or endeavor to understand the other's point of view.

Even their clothes were like distinguishing uniforms, underscoring their intrinsic differences, further separating them: Blue jeans and sneakers for Kyle, the white Swiss voile shirt her only concession to style, the combination giving her an oddly vulnerable, childlike look, with her scrubbed face and long hair hanging loose. And for Christina, an expensive, beautifully cut dress and tailored jacket of matching raw silk, without doubt bearing her own couture label; the silver-gray of the silk the perfect foil for her chestnut hair shot through with reddish-gold lights, the gray also emphasizing her lovely smokey eyes which had always been her best feature. She was slender and impeccably groomed, not showing her forty-seven years in the least.

Tycoon versus student . . . role model versus rebel . . . mother versus daughter, Audra thought, smothering a sigh. Well, it wasn't the first time a mother and daughter were at odds with each other; that was an age-old conflict.

Suddenly Kyle broke the protracted silence when she

3

snapped, "And there's another thing, Mother, you had no right to drag poor Grandma into this debacle, drag her all the way from England, especially since—"

"I didn't!" Christina shot back. "It was your father who telephoned my—"

"Oh yes, go on, blame Dad," Kyle cut in, her voice scathing.

"But it *was* your father who phoned my mother," Christina protested. She appealed to Audra. "Isn't that so, Mummy?"

Audra focused her attention on her granddaughter. "That's quite true, Kyle."

Kyle tossed back her mane of black hair, then thrust her hands in the pockets of her jeans, her movements brusque, defiant. Her huge brown eyes, usually doelike and soft, continued to flash rebelliously. "I suppose he thought we needed a mediator. Well, we don't . . . there's nothing to mediate—" She brought herself up short, swung her long-limbed body toward Audra and gave her a half smile. "Sorry, Grandma, I don't mean to be rude, but you shouldn't have been forced to travel halfway around the world just because my parents have discovered they can't *influence* me, or *handle* me anymore." Kyle let out a laugh that was abnormally harsh. "You see, the trouble is my parents treat me like a child, Grandma. Anyone would think I'm nine years old, not *nineteen*, for God's sake, the ridiculous way they're carrying on."

Before Audra had a chance to comment on these strident assertions, Kyle pivoted to face Christina. Her voice rose shrilly as she rushed on, "Nothing will induce me to change my mind, Mother. *Nothing*. And *nobody*. Not even Grandma. I'm going to live my life the way I want. It's my life and no one else's. You and Dad can cut me off without a nickel. I don't give a damn. I'll get a job to support myself while I'm studying. I don't need any help from you!"

"Neither your father nor I has ever said anything about cutting you off," Christina exclaimed, furious that Kyle was even suggesting such a thing. "*Your* problem is *your* inability to discuss this matter intelligently. And *calmly*.

You fly off the handle every time we attempt to have a reasonable conversation with you."

"Listen who's talking! You're not calm either!"

Christina's mouth tightened in aggravation, but she tried to curb her increasing exasperation with her daughter. "That's not so surprising, is it?" she countered in her coldest tone. "I have built an enormous empire, an international fashion business worth millions and millions of dollars, and you're my only child, my *heir*. It's always been understood that you'd succeed me one day. Understood by *all* of us. Why, you're being trained with that in mind . . . and now, out of the blue, you announce that you don't want the company. I'm flabber—"

"No, I don't!" Kyle shouted. "Can't you get that through your head *yet*, Mother? I've been saying it for days! I'm not in the least bit interested in your stupid business empire! It can go to hell, *collapse*, for all I care! It's your problem, not mine!"

Recoiling, Christina drew in her breath sharply. She was as much stunned by Kyle's vehemence and manner as by her words.

Audra, registering shock, admonished swiftly, "Steady on there, Kyle."

Immediately, Kyle knew she had gone too far, and she bit her lip in embarrassment. Bright hot color blotched her neck, sped up into her smooth young cheeks. She glanced at her grandmother, so pale and still on the sofa. She saw the sadness and disappointment reflected in Audra's candid blue eyes, saw the gentle reproach on her sweet face. Discomfort tinged with shame swept over her. She recognized that she had discredited herself with her grandmother, whom she adored, and this she could not bear. She burst into tears and fled before she disgraced herself further, slamming the door behind her.

Christina stared at the door speechlessly.

She was mortified, enraged, and so taut her shoulder blades protruded through her thin silk jacket. "Can you believe this!" she exploded and took a step forward, obviously intent on following Kyle.

"No, no, let her go," Audra said firmly, pushing herself

up, hurrying across the room. She took hold of Christina's arm and led her back to the sofa.

Gently forcing her daughter down next to her, she went on, "There's no point in continuing this. You're only inflaming each other, and you know very well that the things we say when we're angry are difficult to retract later, and you must admit you're both overwrought at the moment."

"Yes, I suppose we are." Distractedly, Christina ran a hand through her hair, then slumped against the cushions, feeling miserable and frustrated. But after only a moment she jumped up, restlessly began to pace back and forth in front of the fireplace.

As she watched her, Audra's worry intensified. She had never seen Christina quite like this before—so agitated, with her temper so close to the surface and her patience so tightly stretched. Normally she was in control, no matter what the circumstance. But then her world had never been rocked as it was rocked now; and Audra knew, too, that Kyle's words, thoughtlessly uttered in the heat of the moment and without any real malice, had nevertheless been hurtful to Christina.

Wishing to assuage that hurt as best she could, Audra said in her most reassuring voice, "Kyle didn't mean it, Christie. You know, about not caring if the business collapsed. Of course she cares, and she does love you, dear."

"She has a fine way of showing it," Christina grumbled without looking at her mother, continuing to pace, her mind still fogged by the pain her daughter had inflicted.

Audra sighed and, understanding everything, remained silent. She settled back in the corner of the sofa, waiting for Christina to calm herself, relieved that the shouting had stopped. There was hardly any sound in the room now, only the faint murmur of silk against silk, as Christina's legs moved, the ticking of the brass carriage clock on a chest between the French windows, the muffled rumble of the traffic on Sutton Place spiraling up through those windows, standing wide open on this balmy day in the middle of May. She glanced toward the terrace, mottled with sunlight, blooming with greenery and flowering plants, absently wondering how well the pink azaleas would do out there.

Then she brought her eyes back to the interior, let them roam around. For a split second her anxiousness was diluted as she absorbed the loveliness of the setting awash with tones of peach and apricot and cream, the beauty surrounding her, enveloping her . . . the priceless art on the walls: two Cézannes, a Gauguin . . . the fine English antiques with their dark glossy woods . . . bronze sculpture by Arp . . . the profusion of flowers in tall crystal vases . . . all illuminated by silk-shaded lamps of rare and ancient Chinese porcelains.

What marvelous taste Christina and Alex have, Audra thought and experienced a burst of motherly pride in her daughter and son-in-law. This was not induced merely by the graciousness they had recently created in this room but was a genuine pride in what they were as people, for all that they had achieved in their life together. They had a harmonious relationship, and their marriage had only gone from strength to strength over the years, and for that Audra was thankful.

Her thoughts settled on Alex Newman. He was a gentle man, one of the most thoughtful people she had ever met. He had been like a loving son to her. How she wished he were here at this moment. He might not have succeeded in quelling the trouble which had erupted between his wife and daughter, but with his tact and good humor, and worshipping Christina the way he did, he always had a tranquilizing effect on her.

Audra turned her head, looked over at the carriage clock. To her disappointment, it was only ten minutes to five and Alex never got home from work before seven. On the other hand, perhaps he would arrive earlier today, since they were going out to dinner at eight. As she contemplated the evening stretching ahead, her heart sank. Unless there was a radical change in Kyle's disposition in the next few hours, it was going to be an awkward evening.

Now, as though she had zeroed in on Audra's thoughts, Christina said, "I don't much relish the idea of going to dinner at Jack and Betsy Morgan's, nice though they are, and so fond of you, Mummy. No, not with Kyle in this bolshy frame of mind."

Drawing to a standstill at last, Christina looked directly at her mother and smiled ruefully, her gray eyes filled with concern. For the first time she noticed the weariness etched on Audra's face and she bit her lip, frowning.

"You must be bone-tired and terribly jet-lagged, darling," she exclaimed. "How selfish we've been since you arrived yesterday! We haven't given you a chance to catch your breath. I'd better pack you off for a rest before we go out to dinner."

"No, not just yet, Chrstie. I'm all right, really I am," Audra said.

Christina crossed to the sofa, sat down next to Audra and took her hand. She held it tightly, looked into her mother's lined face, swamped by the deep and abiding love she felt for her. She shook her head and her smokey gaze was tender as she said, "Kyle's judgment might be cockeyed about some things, but she could easily be right about dragging you all this way, *needlessly*—" Abruptly she stopped. Guilt flooded through her. Her mother was seventy years old, almost seventy-one, and should not be exposed to their problems at this time in her life. She and Alex ought to be capable of dealing with their recalcitrant daughter themselves. Irritated at the thought of their ineptitude, Christina cried, "We haven't been fair to you, expecting you to cope with us and our mess when you could be at home pottering around in your garden, or going off on your little day trips to the seaside—certainly leading a tranquil life. You must think Alex and I are a couple of imbeciles!"

"Don't be so silly." Audra squeezed Christina's slender tapering hand, so different from hers, gnarled as it was by arthritis. "I'd come to you no matter what it entailed if you needed me, and even if I had to walk the three thousand miles to get here. I love you, Christie, and I love that granddaughter of mine, and Alex. I can't bear to see you all so unhappy."

Christina confided in a tense voice, "It's so wrong of Kyle to abandon her courses at the Fashion Institute and to spurn my business the way she is doing. Having her take over from me one day has always been a cherished dream of mine." These last few words caught in her throat, and she had to steady herself before she could continue, "Oh, Mum, what's it all been *about?* What's all my hard work been *for,* if Kyle walks away?" Christina's eyes welled with tears and she averted her head, blinking.

Audra felt a pang of sympathy, and her heart went out to her daughter. In an effort to comfort her, she murmured, "But, Christie darling, you've derived a great deal of pleasure and satisfaction from your designing, and making a name for yourself in the fashion world has always been important to you, as well as a challenge. What you've accomplished, your staggering achievements and success— why surely these things must be gratifying to you . . ." Audra let her sentence trail off. She was incapable of finishing it. How hollow the words are, she thought.

I, and I alone, know what Christina sacrificed, what it cost her to create the business. She paid a high price, a terrible price, really. That's why she's so emotional about it, why she can't stand Kyle's rejection of it now.

Having regained her composure, Christina was remarking in a more level voice, "The last two weeks have been sheer purgatory with Kyle, Mother. She's downright stubborn; her implacability astounds me. Unnerves me, actually. I've never met anyone like her."

Oh, Audra thought, *haven't you?* She threw her daughter a startled glance, but she wisely said nothing. This was not the time to start delving into ancient events; there was already far too much emotional turbulence in this family. And so adopting a positive manner, Audra said, "Kyle and I have always been such good friends since she was a child, and that's one of the reasons we decided I should come to New York, isn't it? Anyway, I promised to spend the day with her tomorrow. I'm sure she wants to unburden herself to me, and I am more than ready to listen."

"But you will *talk* to her, won't you? I mean as well as listen." Without waiting for a reply, Christina plunged on, "She pays attention to you, wants to please you. So you will make her see reason, won't you, Mummy?"

Audra nodded, although she had her misgivings, and
managed to say encouragingly, "Yes, I will, and somehow
we'll sort this out, Christie."

For the first time in days Christina felt a little of the
heaviness lifting from her and her tired eyes brightened.
She leaned into Audra, kissed her wrinkled cheek, then
rested her head on her mother's shoulder. "I'm so glad
you're here, Mam. You're such a comfort, and I know you'll
make everything come out right, as you always have."

Mam, Audra repeated silently. For years it had been
Mummy or Mum or Mother. *Mam* was the childhood
name. Hearing it now, suddenly, after all these years made
Audra flinch. It evoked so many memories, not all of them
happy ones. Then a rush of warmth and love filled her
throat and for a moment she could not speak. Automatically
she lifted her hand and stroked Christina's glossy hair. It's
true, old habits die hard, Audra thought, bending down,
kissing the top of her daughter's head. All that money, all
that power, all that fame, but she's still my little girl. I can't
stand to see her distressed in this way. But then there is also
Kyle, my only grandchild, and *her* unhappiness is insupportable. What a dilemma. Skating on thin ice between the
two of them. Oh dear God, wherever will I find the wisdom
and strength to help each one without somehow inflicting
hurt on the other?

Growing conscious that her daughter was waiting for a
response, Audra clamped down on her worries. "I can only
try to make things come out right for you, Christie," she
said softly. "I told you, when I arrived, that I'm not going to
take sides. Anyway, Kyle is correct about it being *her* life.
And she does have the right to live it the way she sees fit."

Straightening up, Christina nodded slowly. "Yes," she
replied evenly, "I know what you mean. But she's very
young and inexperienced, and she can't possibly know her
own mind. Not yet, at any rate." Rising, Christina walked
over to one of the French windows, stood gazing out at the
terrace. Then she swung around and gave Audra a penetrating look. "Rejecting my business out of hand is not only
foolish but irresponsible of her, wouldn't you say?"

"Well, yes," Audra felt bound to agree, yet she had the

need to defend her granddaughter, and could not help adding, "Still, Kyle is intelligent, as well as being a spirited and independent girl. And, you know, I also find her wise for someone her age." Audra paused, thinking: Well, in for a penny, in for a pound, and I might as well say it all. Taking a deep breath, she finished in her firmest manner, "I just want you to give some consideration to *her* needs, *her* desires, as well as your own. Promise me that you will."

Christina was startled, and there was a brief silence before she muttered, "All right . . . yes . . . I promise."

It struck Audra that there was a lingering reluctance in this promise. Slowly and very carefully, she said, "Once a long time ago, I told you that a child is only lent to you, Christina. Don't ever forget that."

Christina stared at Audra and the strangest expression crossed her face. She opened her mouth to speak and then closed it. She swung away, focusing her eyes on the terrace once more as she reflected on her mother's words.

Absently, Audra pushed a strand of silver hair away from her face and sat back, watching, waiting. She saw her daughter's shoulders droop in dejection, saw at once the pensive expression settling on her pretty mouth. Yes, she's remembering, Audra thought. And I've said enough for today. It would be wiser to let things rest where they are for the present.

Gripping the arm of the sofa, Audra pulled herself to her feet a bit unsteadily, exhaustion finally getting the better of her. "I think I will have a rest before dinner, perhaps try to get a little sleep," she said.

"Yes, yes, you should," Christina responded. She went quickly to Audra's side, put her arm around her shoulders lovingly, and escorted her out of the room.

Half an hour later Audra was still wide awake, much to her irritation. Try though she had to sleep, she was unable to do so. Christina had accompanied her to the guest suite at the far end of the penthouse, had closed the curtains, plumped up the bed pillows, and generally fussed until Audra had impatiently waved her out. Glad to be alone at last, Audra had undressed, slipped on a robe and stretched out on the bed. She had done so gratefully. Every bone in her body ached, she was debilitated by jet lag and her hands and knees throbbed painfully as her arthritis flared. But the moment her head touched the pillow, her mind had started to race.

Mostly Audra was worried that she had made a mistake in coming to New York. Might it not have been more prudent to refuse Alex's request and leave them alone to battle it out among themselves? And it *was* going to be a battle, Audra was quite positive of that. It would be a trial of strength. Christie would worry it through, refusing to let go, tenacious to the end; Kyle would dig her heels in, equally as stubborn and determined to win no matter what the cost to everyone involved. The stakes were so high neither of them could possibly act in any other way. Where was it all going to end? In disaster, she suspected. They couldn't both win. And the loser would be bitter and resentful.

I have to find a way to help them settle this, Audra now told herself; then with a stab of dismay she wondered how. If Alex, who was diplomatic and persuasive, had been unable to arbitrate their differences, then surely she would not be able to influence them either. I *must* find a way, she muttered.

With a sigh of weariness, Audra opened her eyes, acknowledging that sleep was going to evade her. The spacious bedroom looked as tranquil as it always did in the gentle light seeping in through the curtains. Usually the blue-and-white color scheme, elegant furnishings and opulent comfort engendered a sense of well-being in her. But these feelings were sadly absent tonight.

Audra shivered. The early evening breeze blowing in through the window came up off the East River. It was cool now and there was a sharp tinge of dampness in the air that seemed to penetrate her joints. Shivering again, she drew the quilt up over her body and reached for her pills. Putting one in her mouth, she washed it down with a sip of water, reminding herself that this was her third; the doctor had warned her not to take more than four in one day.

Sometimes she wondered about her arthritis, wondered

if her hard life had not contributed to her present
condition. Doctor Findlay said it hadn't, but when she
thought of the endless scrubbing and cleaning and washing
and ironing, the drudgery that had been her lot for so many
years, she could not help pondering. Well, those days had
long since gone. In her old age she had a life of ease.

As she put the tumbler back on the bedside table her
glance fell on the photograph standing near the cobalt-blue
glass lamp. Audra turned on her side, rested herself on one
elbow and gazed at it thoughtfully.

Three faces stared back at her. Christina's, Kyle's and her
own.

The picture had been taken last summer, in her rose
garden in Yorkshire. What a wonderfully happy day that
had been . . . her seventieth birthday. The weather had
been glorious, as the color photograph attested.

After a little tea party on the terrace, Alex had insisted on
taking this picture. In honor of the occasion and for
posterity, he had laughingly said as he had lined them up
near the old stone sundial, a few steps to the right of her
best hybrid tea roses.

Three generations, she murmured under her breath. But
we don't look as if we're related. We might easily be
strangers, as disparate in appearance as any three women
could be. And yet we are very much alike deep down
within ourselves.

Almost half a century ago I was told that I had an
implacable will, that I was relentless and propelled by a
terrible driving force within myself. I had been angry and
hurt. But it was the truth. And they have inherited those
characteristics from me . . . my daughter, my granddaughter. When Christina was a child, I committed an act
of will that changed all of our lives irrevocably. And then,
when she was a young woman, Christina repeated the
pattern, performed an act of will of her own that was as
powerful as mine. Now it is Kyle's turn . . . she is on the
verge of doing the same. And, as before, our lives won't
ever be the same again.

Audra sat up with a jolt, sudden comprehension flickering on her face. "I am to blame," she said aloud to the silent

room, and then she thought: If I had done things differently, things would be different now. Everything that is happening *now* harks back to when I was a young woman. *Cause and effect.* Every act we commit, trivial or important, has its inevitable consequences. It's like throwing a pebble into a pool and watching the ripples spread out . . . farther and farther, ever far-reaching.

Audra sank back onto the pillows and lay there, allowing herself to drift with her thoughts. They were centered entirely on Kyle.

Slowly the pain in her hands and knees began to ease, and her body grew warmer under the quilt. Audra closed her eyes at last.

Nineteen twenty-six, she mused drowsily . . . such a long time ago . . . but not so long that I can't remember what *I* was like then . . . when *I* was Kyle's age.

Audra
1926 to 1951

CHAPTER ONE

Today it was her birthday.

It was the third of June in the year 1926 and she was nineteen years old.

Audra Kenton stood at the window of her room in the Fever Hospital in Ripon, in Yorkshire, where she worked as a nurse, gazing out at the back garden. Absently she watched the play of light and shadow on the lawn, as the sunlight filtered through the leafy domes of the two great oaks that grew near the old stone wall. There was a gentle breeze, and the leaves rustled and trembled under it, and shimmered with green brilliance as they caught the sun. It was radiant and balmy, a day that invited and beckoned.

Matron had given Audra the afternoon off for her birthday. The problem was that she had nowhere to go and no one to spend it with. *She was entirely alone in this world.*

Audra only had one friend, Gwen Thornton, another nurse at the hospital, but Gwen had been summoned home to Horsforth yesterday. Her mother had been taken ill and she was needed. Weeks ago, Gwen had arranged to exchange her day off with one of the other nurses, so that she could be with Audra, celebrate this important occasion with her, and the two of them had planned a very special day. Now their elaborate plans were laid to waste.

Leaning her head against the window frame, Audra sighed, thinking of the empty hours looming ahead. Unexpectedly her throat tightened and she felt the tears gathering behind her eyes as sadness mingled with bitter disappointment trickled through her. But after only a few seconds she blinked and cleared her throat, managed to take hold of herself. Resolutely she pushed aside the negative emotions momentarily invading her, refusing to feel sorry for herself. Audra despised self-pity in others, considered it to be a sign of weakness. *She was strong.* Her

17

mother had always told her that she was, and her mother
had rarely been wrong about anything.

Turning away from the window, she walked over to the
chair and sat down heavily, wondering what to do with
herself.

She could read, of course, or do a little embroidery, or
even finish the sketch of the blouse she was designing, and
which she intended to make—when she could afford to buy
the fabric. On the other hand, none of these occupations
had any real appeal for her. Not today. Not on her birthday.

She had been so looking forward to the outing with her
friend, to enjoying a few carefree hours of pleasure for once
in her life. Audra had little to celebrate these days, and
festive occasions were a thing of the past, a rarity indeed. In
fact, her life had changed so radically, so harshly, in the last
few years, she hardly recognized it as her own.

It suddenly struck her that resorting to one of those
mundane hobbies, normally used to pass the time when she
was off duty, would be infinitely worse than just sitting in
this chair, doing nothing. They're poor substitutes, all of
them, for the plans Gwen and I made.

Audra had long since trained herself not to notice the
room where she lived in the hospital. But now, seeing it so
clearly illuminated in the bright sunshine, she became
painfully aware of its ugliness and lack of comfort. Having
been born into gentility, albeit somewhat impoverished,
Audra was a young woman of breeding and refinement. She
possessed taste in abundance, had strong artistic leanings,
and the austerity of the Spartan furnishings and institution-
al color scheme suddenly stabbed at her discerning eyes.
They offended her sensibilities.

Confronting her were walls painted a dismal porridge-
beige which ran down to a floor covered with dreary gray
linoleum. The iron bedstead, rickety night stand and chest
of drawers were notable only for their shabbiness and
utilitarian design. The room was chillingly bleak, intolerable at any time, but especially on this sunny afternoon.
She knew she had to escape its oppressive boundaries for a
short while, no matter where she went.

Her gaze fell on the dress lying on the bed, where she

had placed it a short time before. It was new. She had saved up for a whole year, putting away a shilling every week, in order to buy herself a present for her birthday.

She and Gwen had gone to Harrogate two Saturdays ago with this in mind. They had wandered around for several hours, mostly window-shopping and admiring the beautiful things they saw and which they knew they would never be able to afford. Audra filled with warm and affectionate feelings for Gwen as she thought of that day now.

Gwen was especially attracted to jeweler's shops, and Audra had found herself constantly cupping her hands and dutifully peering through glass at some bauble that had caught Gwen's attention. "*Oh Audra! Just look at that!*" Gwen kept crying, pointing to a brooch or a ring or a pendant. At one moment she had clutched Audra's arm fiercely and whispered in awed tones, "Have you ever seen anything like that gorgeous bangle, Audra! Why the stones could be *real* the way they sparkle like diamonds. It *would* suit you, Audra. Let's go in . . . it doesn't cost anything just to *look.*"

Audra had half smiled and shaken her head, not saying a word, and she had thought of her mother's jewelry, which had been much more beautiful than any of these tawdry imitations of the real thing.

Gwen's excited exclamations and urgent proddings continued a bit too long for Audra that afternoon, and she had eventually grown exasperated, had silenced her friend with a stern look and a sharp admonition to be quiet. Immediately regretting her shortness, she had quickly apologized to Gwen. And she had gone on to explain to her, for the umpteenth time, that *she* had no money to spare for frivolous items like brooches and bracelets and nonsensical hats and bottles of Devon Violets scent, which were just a few of the things Gwen constantly craved.

"You *know* I only ever buy clothes for myself," Audra had said, and had added, with a tiny rueful laugh, "and usually the most *practical* clothes I can find, at that, Gwen. Things I know will last me for a very long time."

And then, not ten minutes after she had uttered these words, Audra had seen the dress in the window of Madame

Stella's gown shop. She had fallen in love with it instantly. It
was a frock destined only to go to parties, a bit of airy,
gossamer muslin. Effectively draped on a stand in the
center of the window, it was the one piece of clothing
displayed. Next to it, accessories were scattered on the
floor: a picture hat of cream leghorn, a parasol of ruffled
cream silk and three long strands of pearls. All had
epitomized true elegance to Audra, but most particularly
the dress. It was highly impractical, obviously costly and
very, very beautiful. She had gazed at it for ages, not
knowing when or where she would ever wear it and yet
aching to own it just the same.

Even so, she had hung back, would not budge when
Gwen, shrewdly observing the expression of longing on her
face, had pushed open the door and insisted they go in and
ask the price. Despite Audra's reluctance and her adamant
refusal to enter the shop, Gwen had obviously had no
intention of being thwarted. She had taken Audra's arm in a
viselike grip and frog-marched her into Madame Stella's.

Although both girls had expected the dress to be
expensive, the two of them had been stunned, nevertheless, when they had learned that it cost three guineas.
Audra had made to leave at once. But the redoubtable
Gwen had restrained her, had somehow managed to
maneuver her into the fitting room before she could make a
graceful escape. Not wanting to create an embarrassing
scene in front of the saleslady, Audra had had no option but
to try on the dress.

It was the color that captivated her—a clear bright blue
that had reminded her of the delphiniums at High Cleugh.
She had not needed Gwen to tell her that it suited her to
perfection; she had seen herself in the cheval mirror.

Indeed, Audra had been momentarily taken aback by her
own reflection that afternoon. For the first time in some
years she had acknowledged to herself that for once she
looked quite pretty. Mostly she referred to herself as a Plain
Jane, which she genuinely believed to be the truth. But in
this she did herself an injustice.

Audra Kenton was not beautiful in the strictest sense,
but then neither was she plain. She was in a category

somewhere in between. There was a certain stubbornness in her well-defined face. This was reflected in the determined set of her chin and in her firm and resolute mouth, which was quite beautiful, however, when she smiled. Her best features were a faultless, creamy complexion, glossy light brown hair glazed with a golden sheen in the summer, and lovely eyes. In actuality, these were the most spectacular things about her. They were large, set wide apart, thickly fringed with golden-brown lashes and accentuated by finely arched brows. But it was their color that was so memorable and caused people to look at her twice. They were of a blue so deep and so vivid it was startling.

As Audra had stared back at herself in the mirror of the fitting room, she had not failed to notice how the blue of the muslin intensified their depth of color. She also saw that the "flapper" style of the dress was flattering and did wonders for her. Audra was small, only five feet two inches, and her lack of height was a constant source of irritation to her. Yet despite her diminutive size she was nicely proportioned, and the simple cut of the frock emphasized her pretty figure, whilst its short skirt, cut on the cross so that it flared out, drew attention to her shapely legs and slender ankles.

And so in the end, after some indecision on her part because of its price, and worried whisperings with Gwen, she had finally bought the dress. To make up the three pounds, three shillings needed, Audra had used her entire savings of two pounds twelve shillings, every other penny in her purse—which was all she had in the world—plus one and six borrowed from Gwen.

"Don't look so glum," Gwen had whispered whilst they had been waiting for the saleslady to wrap the dress. "It's worth every penny. Besides, it's about time you treated yourself to something nice."

There was no question in Audra's mind that the dress was the most beautiful thing she had owned since she was a child. And a memory had stirred, a memory of another time when she had come to Harrogate shopping—with her mother and Uncle Peter. It had been 1919, just after he had returned from the Great War. She had been twelve and he had bought her a pink party frock which had entranced her just as much as the blue muslin.

As they had left Madame Stella's, Audra had told Gwen of that particular trip and the pretty pink frock, had confided more about her past life, and Gwen had been agog and full of questions. Audra, who was reserved by nature, had nonetheless answered some of them, not wanting to offend Gwen by appearing secretive. Later, arms linked, they had taken a leisurely stroll along The Stray, the stretch of green common carpeted with lovely flowers which made a natural tapestry of brilliant color underneath the shady trees. Then Gwen had taken them to Betty's Cafe, the posh tearoom on The Parade overlooking The Stray, and had generously paid for them both, since Audra had spent all of her cash. She had also loaned her the money for her ticket back to Ripon, just as she had promised she would when Audra had been wavering in Madame Stella's. And Audra had reminded herself yet again how lucky she was to have Gwen for her friend.

At the end of their day's excursion, on the way to the bus stop, they had passed the Arcadian Rooms, where tea dances were held every afternoon in the Palm Court. Everyone knew that this was *the* place to go, the smart spot in town where the local swells foxtrotted and tangoed to the strains of Stan Stanton and His Syncopated Strollers.

Both young women had been itching to visit the Palm Court for weeks, and Gwen, who had learned the Charleston from her brother, had been teaching it to Audra in their off-duty hours. Audra had been astonished and thrilled when Gwen had announced she was taking them to a tea dance at the Palm Court on her birthday. "It'll be my treat, my birthday present," Gwen had said, beaming at her. "And you'll wear your new dress and everyone will admire you in it." The two of them had been bursting with excitement and anticipation as they had ridden on the bus back to Ripon, and they had been counting the days ever since.

But there would be no trip to Harrogate after all. No tea dance at the Palm Court of the Arcadian Rooms. No one to admire her or the new dress. Audra sighed. Earlier she had planned to wear it just for her own pleasure, although she had not been quite sure where she would *go* in it all by herself. But now she changed her mind.

Audra was nothing if not practical, and it struck her that it would be foolish to risk ruining it or getting it crumpled and soiled. Far wiser to save the frock for another special occasion, she reasoned. And there's bound to be one in the future, now that I have a friend like Gwen. Perhaps we'll go to the church Garden Fete in August, and then there's Gwen's birthday in September. We must celebrate that. Yes, something's bound to come up, she reassured herself, her natural optimism surfacing as it invariably did.

Audra was blessed with a sunny disposition and a cheerful personality, and it was these traits, coupled with her strong will and intelligence, which had saved her in the past. They helped her to cope with her problems in the most positive way. She never let her troubles burden her for very long, sought always to solve them with expediency. And if this was not feasible, she tried not to dwell on them unnecessarily.

Now she roused herself, took the blue frock off the bed and returned it to the clothes closet in the corner of the room.

After she had slipped out of her blue-and-white-striped nurse's uniform and put it away, she peered at the other garments hanging there, wondering what to wear for her walk in the country.

Although she did not have an extensive wardrobe, the clothes she did own were of good quality, and because she was fastidious, they were never anything but immaculate. For economic reasons, Audra made all of her summer clothes herself, and these were mostly lightweight dresses in the darker spectrum of colors; to her practical turn of mind these were guaranteed to wear better than the paler shades. Finally her hand came to rest on a navy cotton dress with a dropped waistline and a sailor collar trimmed with white. She pulled it out, found her black leather walking shoes with flat heels and began to dress.

Suddenly Audra thought of Gwen. How self-centered I'm being, she chastised herself. Here I am, concerned about my birthday, when Gwen has a sick mother to nurse. Audra wished she could go to Horsforth today, to help Gwen, but it was much too far to travel with only an afternoon free. Poor Gwen must be run off her feet, not to mention dreadfully worried, she thought. Then her face brightened as she adjusted the collar of her dress and pivoted to look at herself in the small mirror standing on the chest of drawers. Gwen's father was a doctor, and her brother Charlie was a medical student at Leeds University. Mrs. Thornton was in good hands. She would soon be well again, and Gwen would be returning to the hospital in no time at all.

As she left her room and hurried down the corridor, it struck Audra how truly attached she had become to her friend. Ever since Gwen had come to work at the hospital a year ago, her life had changed for the better, and it was much more bearable now. Until then none of the other nurses had ever attempted to be friends with her. Audra knew that this was mainly because of her background, her manners and her cultured way of speaking.

The other nurses thought she was stuck-up and unapproachable. But this was not true at all. It was her shyness that held her somewhat apart, prevented her from making the first gesture.

As if she had instinctively understood this, happy, laughing, gregarious Gwen had paid not the slightest attention to her reserve. Having singled Audra out as the one girl she wanted as her friend, she had persisted and had broken down the protective walls Audra had built around herself. Within the first week of knowing each other they had become inseparable.

I don't know what I'd do without Gwen, Audra thought, banging the front door of the hospital behind her. She's the only person I have in the world.

CHAPTER TWO

She had not intended to go to High Cleugh.

But before she realized it she was almost there.

When she had set out from the hospital, Audra had had no particular destination in mind. She had taken the road that led to Sharow and Copt Hewick, both small villages on the outskirts of Ripon.

There was no special reason for her to go there, other than that they were pleasant little spots; also, the route was picturesque, the surrounding landscape pastoral and unusually pretty at this time of year.

Arriving at Copt Hewick, Audra wandered slowly up the cobbled main street, thinking how well-kept everything looked on this hot June afternoon. The dainty gardens in front of the neat cottages were bright with nasturtiums and marigolds and dahlias; white lace curtains glowed behind sparkling windows; every doorstep was newly scrubbed, each step outlined with yellow scouring stone.

Glancing up ahead at the Blackamoor Inn, Audra noticed that it, too, was spruced up. Its white walls and black shutters had been treated to fresh coats of paint, and even the sign swinging over the front door appeared to have been artistically embellished with a few colorful daubs from somebody's paintbox.

Audra hesitated at the Blackamoor pub, which was at the juncture of several roads, wondering whether to take the main thoroughfare to Boroughbridge or the secondary side road that led to Newby Hall and Skelton. She chose the latter, although she did not follow the road to its end. Instead she veered off to her right when she was halfway down, favoring a narrow lane flanked on either side by drystone walls.

After only a few steps along the lane, she stopped dead in her tracks, immediately understanding exactly where her

feet were leading her. She half turned, wanting to go back
the way she had come. She discovered she could not.

High Cleugh drew her toward it like a powerful magnet.

With every step she took, Audra Kenton told herself she
was making a mistake, exposing herself to heartache,
especially today of all days, yet still she continued to walk,
almost against her own volition.

By the time she came to the bottom of the long, twisting
lane, she no longer cared whether she was being foolish or
not. She was conscious only of her yearning to see the one
place she loved above all others on this earth. She had
stayed away far too long.

She climbed over the stile set in the wall, jumped down
into the long pasture and ran through the tall grass. It
rippled and swayed like an undulating sea of green under
the light breeze which had blown up. Unexpectedly, a
couple of cows lazily lumbered across her path, and she
dodged around them, plunging ahead, her young face taut
with anticipation, her long hair flying out behind her as she
ran.

Audra did not break her pace until she came to the huge
sycamore tree at the end of the pasture. Upon reaching
it, she stooped down and stepped under its spreading
branches which formed a canopy of green, shutting out the
sky. She leaned her body against the tree, pressed her face
to its trunk and closed her eyes. She was out of breath and
panting with exertion.

After only a few moments, she began to breathe more
evenly. Slowly, she smoothed her hand over the tree, felt
the rough texture of the bark under her fingertips, and she
smiled to herself. This was her tree. Her place.

She had named it the Memory Place in her mind. For
that was exactly what it was—the place to remember them,
to relive the past, to recall the happiness and joy that had
once been hers and was no more.

Frequently they had come here together. Her mother.
Her brothers, Frederick and William. And Uncle Peter.
And when she was here at the tree they were with her
again, and her misery was vanquished for a brief while.

Audra opened her eyes, blinking in the cool green

darkness of the sycamore's shade, and then she moved out from underneath its branches. Circling the tree, she came to a standstill at the edge of the little slope that fell away to the banks of the River Ure just a few feet below her. Finally she lifted her head and gazed out across that narrow band of swift-running water to the wooded valley on the opposite side of the river. There it was, nestled in the palm of a natural dell set amidst the trees.

High Cleugh.

The small but lovely old manor where she had been born nineteen years ago today. The house where she had grown up, had lived for the best part of her life. Her beloved home until five years ago.

She feasted her eyes on it, struck as always by its simplicity and gentleness, which, to her, were the things that made it compellingly beautiful.

High Cleugh was an eighteenth-century house, long and low, with a fine symmetry that gave it an incomparable gracefulness. It was built of local gray stone and had many leaded windows that winked and glinted now in the bright sunlight. These faced out onto a terrace made of the same ancient stone; running the length of the house, the terrace was broken in the center by a very long flight of steps that sliced its way through lawns tilting to the river. Herbaceous borders, wide, rambling, grew beneath the terrace walls, splashed vivid hues against the dark stone and verdant grass.

But it was the massed delphiniums which caught the eye, entranced. These flourished in great abundance at the bottom of the lawns near the river's edge, their blossoms blanketing the ground with a breathtaking mixture of blues. Cobalt bled into a powder blue so delicate it was almost white, this tint giving way to cornflower, then a luscious violet-blue that in turn brushed up against lavender and the purple tones of belladonna.

Her mother's delphiniums . . . planted with such care and nurtured so lovingly over the years. Audra's heart clenched with a bittersweet mixture of pleasure and pain. Oh how she longed to be in those gardens once again! It would be so easy for her to slip over to the other side of the river. All she had to do was follow the path along the bank until she came to the stepping stones. These giant flat slabs, worn smooth by running water and time, stretched across the shallowest part, led directly to the copse adjoining the manor.

But she could not go to High Cleugh. If she did, she would be trespassing. Another family lived there now.

She sat down on the springy grass, pulled her knees up to her chest, rested her chin on them and clasped her arms around her legs.

For the longest time Audra stared at High Cleugh.

There was no sign of life. It appeared to slumber in the brilliant sunshine as if it were not inhabited at all. A peacefulness lay over the motionless gardens. Not a blade of grass, not a single leaf stirred. The wind had dropped and the air was warm and languid. There was no sound except for the faint buzzing of a bee somewhere nearby and the gurgle and spash of water rushing over dappled stones as the Ure wended its way below her.

Audra's gaze became more intense than ever. She saw beyond the exterior walls to the inner core of the house. She closed her eyes, let herself sink down into her imagination, remembering, remembering . . .

She was inside the house.

She stood in the hall with its apricot-colored walls and worn green-velvet bench and the palm in the pitted brass pot. All was shadowy, quiescent. She listened for a while to the stillness. Then she stepped forward, her footsteps echoing with a metallic ring against the marble. Slowly she climbed the staircase. It twisted upward in a graceful curve. She paused on the first landing. Her room was here. She went inside, closed the door, sighed with pleasure.

Familiar walls of the palest green surrounded her, reminded her as always of a summer sea on a misty Yorkshire morning. The polished wood floor gleamed like glass under her feet as she stepped up to her four-poster bed. She reached out, touched the tulips printed on the worn coverlet, traced a finger around their once-red petals long since washed out to the color of old rust. Burnt sienna it was called in her paintbox. She glided to the window, looked out across the Dales, heard the rustle of the curtains as they flapped about in the breeze. The scent of carnations filled the summer air. She turned her head, saw a cloud of pink petals in the blue willow-patterned bowl that stood on the oak chest. Their perfume drifted away, was replaced by a sweeter, headier fragrance. October roses lifted full-blown heads from the bowl, shining yellow against the blue. It was autumn now. The time of the harvest.

How well she knew the changing seasons of this house.

The air had grown chillier. The fire crackled in the grate. She felt the warmth of the flames on her face. Snowflakes fluttered against the window pane. The gardens were made of white-icing sugar.

She was no longer alone in the house.

She caught the sound of her mother's laughter, the swish of her silk gown as she joined her by the fire. The Beautiful Edith Kenton. That was how they always spoke of her hereabouts.

Sapphires blazed at her throat, on her cool white arms. Blue fire against that translucent skin. Hair the color of new pennies, an aureole of burnished copper light around the pale heart-shaped face. Warm and loving lips were pressed down to her young cheek. The smell of gardenias and Coty powder enveloped her. A slender, elegant hand took hold of hers, guided her out of the room.

Frederick and William waited in the hall, sang carols as they descended the stairs. Rowdy, loving brothers and devoted sons. Uncle Peter stood behind them in the entrance to the drawing room. He embraced her with his smile and ushered them all into the room.

She stood transfixed.

The room had acquired a magical quality this Christmas night. Its faded elegance had taken on a curious new beauty in the muted, golden light. Candles glowed on a sturdy little fir. Logs hissed and spurted up the chimney. Sprigs of holly decorated the paintings, draped the mantel, hung in great beribboned swags in front of the windows. Mistletoe fell from the cut-glass chandelier. Paper chains were inverted rainbows looped across the ceiling. The air was

*redolent with new aromas that assailed her senses. She
smelled pine cones and wood smoke and eggnog, and
succulent goose cooking and chestnuts roasting on the fire.*

They crowded around the fireplace.

*They sang carols and drank the eggnog from little crystal
cups and lifted the steaming chestnuts from their bursting
shells. And their laughter reverberated through the house.*

*Three red-felt stockings hung from the mantelpiece. They
opened them . . . she and Frederick and William. In hers
there was a treasure trove. An orange, an apple, a bag of
nuts and a new penny tied in a scrap of silk; a sachet of
potpourri, Pears soap and yards of silk ribbons for her hair
plus a box of Egyptian dates, lavender water and a book of
verse with the name "Edith Kenton" written on the flyleaf in
her mother's flowing script. Little things which had cost
nothing but whose value was priceless to her.*

Snowdrifts were banked outside the house.

*Sleet and bitter winds rattled against the window panes
and heralded the new year. The Christmas decorations had
disappeared. The house was hushed and desolate without
her mother's laughter. It was the time for Uncle Peter to go
away again. She saw the sadness on his face, and her
mother's eyes, blue like the sapphires she wore, were filled
with tears. . . .*

Audra's face was wet with tears . . . she had not
realized that she had begun to cry. She straightened up and
brushed her eyes with her fingertips, tearing her gaze away
from High Cleugh.

She lay down and buried her face in the cool, sweet-
smelling grass, then squeezed her eyes tightly shut as she
felt the sharp prick of tears once more. But now she did not
bother to suppress them; instead, she allowed herself the
luxury of weeping.

And she wept for those she had lost and for the past and
for the way things had once been.

Eventually her tears ceased. She lay there quietly,
staring up at the china-blue sky, absently watching the drift
of the scudding clouds, ruminating on her beloved family

and all of the things which had happened in the last few years.

CHAPTER THREE

Audra's father was a shadowy figure in her mind.

He had died in 1909, when she was only two years old, and her memories of him were indistinct.

But the images of her mother, and of Frederick and William, were potent and so very vivid to her the three of them might have been standing there, looking down at her lying on the grass. And Uncle Peter was as indelibly imprinted on her heart as the other three were.

How inexorably their lives and their destinies had been bound up with his.

Peter Lacey had died in 1920 whilst still a young man. He had been an officer in the British Army during the Great War, and had fought in the trenches of France, where he had been badly gassed in the Battle of the Somme. His lungs had been so seriously damaged that his health had never been the same, and that was why he had died. Or so they said at the time.

Audra's mother, the Beautiful Edith Kenton, had been inconsolable. She had followed him to the grave less than a year later, in July of 1921. She had been thirty-seven.

Frederick, Audra's elder brother, had told her that their mother's death was due to heart failure, but she had recently substituted *heartbreak* for the latter. Audra had come to believe that their mother really *had* died of a broken heart as she had pined away for Peter Lacey; since Audra had grown to young womanhood, she had come to understand their relationship so much better. They had been lovers, of course. There was no longer any doubt in her mind about that.

As a child Audra had never questioned his presence. He was their Uncle Peter, a distant relative of their father's—a third cousin, she had been led to believe—and he had been there for as long as she could remember.

After their father Adrian Kenton died of consumption, Uncle Peter had become an even more frequent visitor, staying with them at High Cleugh for a week or two at a time. Because of his business interests and financial affairs, he had returned to London at regular intervals, but he was never absent for very long. And whether he came for an extended visit or a brief few days, he never came empty-handed. There were usually presents for them all.

"Isn't it wonderful the way Uncle Peter looks after us," her mother had said once to Audra. "I am a great burden to him, I fear. He is such a busy man . . . but very kind and generous, and most uncommonly thoughtful. He *wishes* to take care of me, and of you and your brothers. He insists, and will not have it any other way." Edith had sighed, then smiled her shimmering smile. "He was devoted to your father, of course. That is the reason why he has made *us* his responsibility, Audra."

But it was not devotion to their father at all, Audra had come to realize. It had been adoration of their mother that had caused Peter Lacey to become their benefactor and protector.

Once she had come to understand the reality of their life together, Audra had accepted the truth about them, and she had never blamed or censored her mother and her uncle in her heart. They had been very much in love. He had also loved Edith's fatherless children and behaved as a father would toward them; he had taken care of the Kenton family to the best of his ability and his financial means. There had been a wife somewhere in the background, and two children, a boy and a girl; otherwise Edith Kenton and Peter Lacey would have married.

Audra and William had not comprehended the situation when Edith and Peter were alive, but Audra had lately come to wonder if Frederick had ever had his suspicions. After all, he *was* the eldest. He had been seventeen when Edith had died, and William fifteen, and Audra had just celebrated her fourteenth birthday the month before.

The Kenton children had been stunned and heartbroken

at the unexpected death of their mother, and disbelieving.
It had been sudden. And then, only a short hour after her
coffin had been lowered into the ground, they had suffered
another terrible blow.

They were so shocked they were unable to speak, when
they learned that Edith had died penniless, and that they
were not only destitute but without a roof over their heads.
High Cleugh was not their property as they had always
believed. It had never belonged to their father, in fact. He
had merely rented it from the owner—Peter Lacey. Peter
had permitted Edith to live on at High Cleugh, and without
paying rent, since 1909.

Apparently a codicil in his will had protected Edith after
his death—but not them. High Cleugh was to remain her
home for as long as she lived; after her death it must revert
to his estate. The annuity he had left her also ceased when
she died.

There was no separate provision for them, most probably
because Peter Lacey had not anticipated that their mother
would die at such an early age. Obviously neither had she,
despite her great sorrow at his passing, since she had not
left a will.

The three orphans were told all this by their mother's
cousin, Alicia Drummond. She had taken them back to her
house, The Grange, after the funeral service at St. Nicho-
las's Church and the burial in the adjoining cemetery in the
village of West Tanfield. She had hurried them into the
library, a cheerless room filled with gloomy shadows,
dolorous paintings and ponderous Victorian furniture,
where tea was to be served later. Aunt Alicia's husband,
Uncle Percival, her daughter, Cousin Winifred, and her
mother, Great-Aunt Frances Reynolds, had attended the
funeral and had joined them for tea afterward.

Although the Kenton children disliked the Drummonds
intensely, they held a certain affection for their great-aunt,
who had always shown a particular fondness for Edith, her
only niece, and the Kentons. And so they automatically
gravitated to the Chesterfield sofa next to her chair. Here
they aligned themselves in a row. They were a staunch little
trio, wearing their best Sunday clothes and black armbands

of mourning, sitting stiff-backed and controlled. Somehow
they managed to hide their sorrow behind expressionless
faces.

Aunt Alicia had poured tea from a Georgian silver pot,
and the maid had passed around the delicate china cups,
then offered them plates of watercress sandwiches and
caraway-seed cake. They were not able to eat a thing.

Audra was the first one to speak up, after Aunt Alicia had
delivered her devastating news about their impecunious
state. "What's going to happen to us? Are we to be sent to
the workhouse?" she asked in a small but curiously steady
voice, fixing Alicia Drummond with a penetrating stare.

Great-Aunt Frances, shocked, exclaimed, "Of course
not, dear child!" and then she reached out and patted
Audra's hand. She was a much nicer person than her
daughter, and she continued in a kindly tone, "I'm too old
to take you in, I'm afraid. However, you will all come and
live here at The Grange. Your Aunt Alicia and Uncle
Percival have very generously offered to provide a good
home for the three of you."

The Kenton children, with no other living relatives, had
been obliged to accept this offer, dubious though they were
about moving in with the Drummonds. After only a few
days at The Grange, they realized just how much they were
going to detest living there. The large Victorian mansion
was as cold and as forbidding as Alicia Drummond herself,
who was also a snobbish, bigoted, avaricious and crafty
woman. The house was run on ludicrous timetables; the
rules were rigid; the atmosphere was depressing and
unpleasant; the food, mediocre at best. The Kenton
children had been brought up with a great deal of love and
freedom by a woman who was also an excellent cook, and
they were shocked by life at The Grange.

A week after Edith Kenton's funeral, some of her
furniture and other possessions from High Cleugh were
sold at the auction rooms in Ripon, to pay for her funeral
expenses and settle her debts. At least, this is what her
children were told by their aunt. The best pieces of
furniture, a number of good paintings, and choice items of
silver were removed to the The Grange by Alicia Drum-

mond. "I shall be happy to store these things for you until you are old enough to have them," she had explained to the three young Kentons.

Despite the fact that this sounded reasonable enough to Frederick and William, Audra, who was far smarter than her brothers, did not trust the woman. And her distrust only increased when, several days later, she noticed her mother's things appearing in various rooms of her aunt's house. And so that night, when everyone was asleep, she had crept down the corridor to the room which Frederick and William shared. She had awakened her brothers, and, curling up at the bottom of Frederick's bed, she expressed her concern to them both, whispered that they must make an inventory of all of their mother's possessions which were now in this house.

William, who knew Audra was much cleverer than he or his brother, nodded in agreement. But Frederick blanched in alarm, afraid that they would be thrown out if they so much as put one foot wrong. "She'll take offense," he whispered back, frowning. "We can't do it, Audra. It would be throwing aspersions on her character—as if we think she's dishonest."

Sweeping aside his protestations, Audra hissed, "I'm sure she is, so we *must* do it. To protect ourselves. And what about Mother's jewelry? The sapphires in particular? Does *she* have those too, Frederick?"

Frederick shook his head vehemently. "No, she doesn't, and that I know for an absolute fact. But they *have* disappeared. I looked everywhere for them the day after Mother died, and to no avail. When I was searching her drawers, I suddenly remembered that I hadn't seen her wear them since Uncle Peter's death. She must have sold them, Audra, and used the money to help support us over the past year. It's the only possible solution."

"Why didn't you tell me about the sapphires before now?" Audra demanded in a low but fierce voice, throwing him a reproachful look.

"Because I didn't want to worry you," Frederick whispered back, and then his voice sank as he added, "But Aunt

Alicia does have Mother's other jewelry. She took the box
away from me . . . for safekeeping, she said."

Although she had faithfully promised Frederick she
would not do anything rash, and so risk incurring their
aunt's disfavor, Audra was determined, nevertheless, to
have her own way about the inventory. Alicia Drummond
did not intimidate her, but after thinking it through, she
wisely decided to wait for the right moment to introduce
the subject to her aunt. This presented itself much sooner
than Audra had anticipated.

On Sunday of that week, Great-Aunt Frances returned
with them for lunch after church services. And it was the
old lady herself who inadvertently gave Audra the perfect
opportunity. They were all seated in the dark and depressing library, where Uncle Percival proceeded to pour careful
glasses of sherry for the adults, when unexpectedly their
great-aunt brought up the matter of Edith Kenton's jewelry.

Out of the blue, she said, "I think Audra is old enough to
have something of dear Edith's, a memento of her mother.
Perhaps the cameo brooch. Please be kind enough to fetch
me Edith's jewelry box, Alicia." Aunt Alicia, tight-lipped
and sheathing her annoyance, did so.

Smiling at Audra warmly, the old lady took out the cameo
and pinned it on the front of her summer frock. "Take care
of it, child—it was a favorite of your mother's," she said.

Audra promised that she would and thanked her great-
aunt for allowing her to have it now. Then she shrewdly
seized the moment. "Frederick, William, come and look at
Mother's jewelry. You must have your share of it when we
grow up."

As her two brothers joined her at their great-aunt's side,
Audra exclaimed to Frederick, "Perhaps I ought to make a
list of these things, so that we can talk about them later and
decide what we'd each like to have. That's only fair, isn't it,
Frederick?"

There was a startled silence.

Frederick gaped at her, aghast, and bit his lip, knowing
what she next had in mind. William tried to hide his delight

in her audacity without succeeding; his eyes danced mischievously.

And then, before anyone could make a comment, Audra ran to the desk, found a pencil and scrap paper, and returned to her great-aunt's chair, where she pored over the box. At one moment, as she scribbled away, Audra looked up at the silver-haired old lady, and remarked in an off-hand manner, "Great-Aunt Frances, do *you* think I should also list Mother's furniture and her possessions which Aunt Alicia is storing for us here? You know, so that my brothers and I can divide everything else properly."

Great-Aunt Frances gave her a surprised look, and then she smiled slightly. "Well, Audra, you are a practical child, it seems. I think that's an excellent idea, especially since poor dear Edith did not think to make a will. This way the three of you can discuss the division of your mother's property at leisure, and make your decisions. Why don't you take an inventory next week, my dear?"

Audra nodded solemnly, camouflaging her triumph behind a bland expression. "Yes, I think I will, Great-Aunt."

In the days which followed this conversation, Frederick, quaking in his boots, had warned Audra that there were bound to be repercussions. *He* had noticed the calculating look in Aunt Alicia Drummond's mean little black eyes when they had all been in the library, even if his brother and sister had not.

But nothing untoward had happened in the end, and the long, hot summer had slithered into a cool autumn; then winter had come finally, and life at The Grange had continued uneventfully. And as miserable as the Kentons were in the unloving environment of their aunt's home, even Audra felt bound to agree with William, her favorite, that they were fortunate in one respect: The three of them were together. They had each other to love, and for companionship and consolation.

It was the week before Christmas that Audra chanced to hear a strange remark, one that worried her briefly; its true meaning was to baffle her for some time thereafter.

Late one afternoon, knowing that Great-Aunt Frances had come to visit, Audra went looking for her.

She was about to push open the drawing room door, which was already ajar, when she heard Aunt Alicia mention her mother's name in the most scathing manner. She did not catch what her aunt said next because Alicia lowered her voice. But Audra stiffened as Great-Aunt Frances suddenly exclaimed in a horrified tone, "You cannot punish the children for the sins of the mother, Alicia!"

Instantly, Audra's hand dropped from the knob and she quickly backed away, not wishing to hear any more, and knowing that it was wrong to eavesdrop anyway.

She crept down the dark passage to the back parlor, where she sat for a while, pondering her great-aunt's odd remark. Audra knew that it had to do with them—that much was patently obvious. But she could not fathom its meaning. *How* had her mother sinned? At once she told herself that her mother had not committed a single sin in her entire life. As young as she was, Audra was perceptive and she had long known that Alicia Drummond had always been jealous of her mother's classical beauty, her charm and her refinement. So much so, she had never lost a chance to demean Edith Kenton during her lifetime. Seemingly she could not resist doing the same thing after her death.

For the next few days Audra continued to wonder why Alicia wanted to punish them, but eventually she managed to curb her worry. She consoled herself with the knowledge that whatever punishment *she* had had in mind for them, their great-aunt had obviously found a way to put a stop to it.

But as it turned out, Frances Reynolds' words had apparently meant little or nothing. Certainly they had not been a deterrent to her daughter.

For in the end they had been punished.

Two months later, in February of 1922, Frederick and William were dispatched to Australia as emigrants, and Audra was sent to work at the Fever Hospital for Children in Ripon.

Their fierce protestations and anguished pleadings to stay together had made no impression. They were helpless in the face of their aunt's determination. And so, against their wishes and those of their Great-Aunt Frances, they had been forced to do as Alicia Drummond said.

It was a wrenching moment for the three young Kentons when Frederick and William took leave of their sister on that bitter winter morning. Before setting out for London and the boat to Sydney, they had huddled together in the front hall, saying their goodbyes, fighting back their tears.

Audra clung to William, whom she secretly loved the most. Emotion welled up in her, and her throat was so tight she could barely speak. Finally she managed, "You won't forget about me, will you, William?" And then she started to sob brokenly and her eyes streamed.

Swallowing his own tears, endeavoring to be brave, William tightened his arms around his adored little sister. She looked so young and vulnerable at this moment. "No, I won't. *We* won't," he said reassuringly. "And we'll send for you as soon as we can. *I promise*, Audra."

Frederick, equally emotional, stroked the top of Audra's head lovingly, and repeated this promise. Then her brothers stepped away from her, picked up their suitcases and left the house without uttering another word.

Audra snatched her coat from the hall cupboard and ran out. She flew down the drive, calling their names, needing to prolong these last few minutes with them. They stopped, turned, waited for her, and the three of them linked arms and walked on in silence, too heartbroken to speak. When they arrived at the gates, the two boys silently kissed Audra for the last time and tore themselves from her clinging arms.

Holding one hand to her trembling mouth, stifling her sobs, Audra watched them stride courageously along the main road to Ripon until they were just small specks in the distance. She wanted to run after them, to shout *"Wait for me! Don't leave me behind! Take me with you!"* But Audra knew this would be useless. They could not take her with them. It was not her brothers' fault they were being separated from each other. Alicia Drummond was to blame. She wanted to rid herself of Edith Kenton's children, and she did not care how she did it.

Only when her brothers had finally disappeared from

sight did Audra drag her gaze away from the empty road at
last. She turned back into the driveway and wondered,
with a sinking heart and a sickening feeling of despair, if she
would ever see her brothers again. Australia was at the
other end of the world, as far away as any place could
possibly be. They had promised faithfully to send for her,
but how long would it take them to save up the money for
her passage? A whole year, perhaps.

As this dismaying thought wedged itself into Audra's
mind, she looked up at that bleak, grim house and shivered
involuntarily. And at that precise moment her dislike for
her mother's cousin hardened into a terrible and bitter
hatred that would remain with her for the rest of her life.
Audra Kenton would not ever find it in her heart to forgive
Alicia Drummond for her cold and deliberate cruelty to
them. And the memory of the day her brothers had been
sent away would stay with Audra always.

The following afternoon, white-faced and trembling, and
fretting for her brothers, Audra had gone to live and work
at the Fever Hospital. Since there were no vacancies that
year for student nurses, she had been taken on as a ward
maid.

Audra Kenton's life of drudgery had begun. She was still
only fourteen years old.

She had been awakened at dawn the next morning. After
a breakfast of porridge, drippings and bread, and tea, eaten
with the other little ward maids, the daily routine had
commenced. Audra was appalled at the hardship of it, and
she, who had never done a domestic chore in her entire
life, had found that first day unspeakable. Balking at the
tasks assigned to her, she had asked herself despairingly
how she would manage. Yet she had not dared complain to
her superiors. Being intelligent and alert, she had understood within the space of a few hours that they were not
interested in the likes of her. She was inconsequential in
the hierarchy of the hospital, where everyone—doctors and
nurses alike—worked extremely hard and with conscien-
tiousness.

On her second morning she had gritted her teeth and
attacked her chores with renewed vigor, and she had

learned the best way she could, mainly by observing the other maids at work. At the end of the first month, she was as efficient as any of them, and had become expert at scrubbing floors, scouring bathtubs, washing and ironing sheets, making beds, emptying bed pans, cleaning lavatories, disinfecting the surgical ward and sterilizing instruments.

Every night she had fallen into her hard little cot in the maids' dormitory, so bone-tired she had not noticed her surroundings or the uncomfortable bed. She was usually so exhausted in these first weeks she did not even have the strength to weep. And when she did cry into her pillow, it was not for her state of being or for her mean and cheerless life. Audra wept out of longing for her brothers, who were as lost to her now as her mother and Uncle Peter lying in their graves.

There were times, as she scrubbed and polished and toiled in the wards, that Audra worriedly asked herself if *she* had brought this disastrous state upon her brothers and herself. Guilt trickled through her when she remembered how insistent she had been about taking those inventories of her mother's possessions. But generally her common sense quickly surfaced, and Audra recognized that they would have been punished no matter what. In fact, she had come to believe that Alicia Drummond had callously determined their fate on the very day their mother had died.

When Audra had been pushed out of The Grange and sent to the hospital, Aunt Alicia had told her that she could visit them every month, on one of her two weekends off, and spend special holidays with them. But Audra had only ventured there twice, and then merely to collect the remainder of her clothes and a few other belongings. For as far back as she could remember, she had felt uncomfortable in that appalling house; furthermore, she understood she was not welcome. Also, Audra's hatred for her aunt was another powerful reason for her to stay away.

The second time she went to fetch the last of her things, she had had to steel herself to enter The Grange, and she had made a solemn vow to herself. She had sworn she would never set foot in that mausoleum of a place again, not

until the day she went back to claim her mother's property.
And so, over those early months of 1922, as she had learned
to stand on her own two feet, she had kept herself to
herself. She had continued to do her work diligently, and
she had stayed out of trouble at the hospital.

If her daily life was dreary and lacked the normal small
pleasures enjoyed by most girls of her age, she nevertheless
managed to buoy herself up with dreams of a pleasanter
future. Hope was her constant companion. No one could
take *that* away from her. Nor could anyone diminish her
faith in her brothers. She was absolutely convinced that
they would send for her, that she would be with them in
Australia soon. Three months after Frederick and William
had left England, their letters had started to arrive, and
these had continued to come fairly regularly. They were
always full of news, good cheer and promises—and the
pages had soon grown tattered from her constant reading of
them. Audra treasured her letters; they were her only joy
in those days.

The hospital routine had scarcely varied during Audra's
first year. The work was hard, even for the strongest of the
girls. Some of them had left because their daily chores had
worn them down and inevitably demolished their interest
in nursing. Only the truly dedicated remained. Audra, with
nowhere else to go, stayed out of sheer necessity.

However, there was also something very special in Audra
Kenton, call it grit, that made her stick it out until she
could graduate to nurse's training. Small though she was,
she had unusual physical stamina, as well as mental energy
and toughness of mind that were remarkable in one so
young. Despite her youth, she possessed inner resources
which she was able to draw on for courage and strength.
And so she had continued to scrub and clean and polish
endlessly . . . run up and down endless stairs and along
endless wards . . . forever on her feet or on her knees.

The toil and monotonous grind of her days quite apart,
Audra could not complain that she was ill treated in any
way, for she was not. Everyone at the hospital was kind to
her and the other little ward maids, and if the food was
plain, at least there was plenty of it. No one ever went

hungry. Audra, plodding along and braced by her stoicism, would tell herself that hard work and stodgy food never killed anybody.

But by the end of the year she was looking to better herself. Her thoughts were focused on the day she would take a step forward and start climbing the ladder. She had been sent to work at the hospital against her will, but slowly, as she had mastered her chores, she had had a chance to look up, to observe and absorb. Gradually she had begun to realize that nursing appealed to her.

Audra knew she would have to earn a living, even if she went out to join her brothers in Sydney; she wanted to do so as a nurse. According to William, she would have no trouble finding a position in a hospital. He had written to tell her that there was a shortage of nurses Down Under, and this knowledge had fired her ambition even more.

It was in the spring of 1923, not long after Audra had commenced her second year at the hospital, that her chance came. Matron retired and a successor was appointed. Her name was Margaret Lennox, and she was of a new breed of woman, very modern in her way of thinking, some said even radical. She was well known in the North of England for her passionate espousal of reforms in woman and child welfare, and her dedication to the advancement of women's rights in general.

With the announcement of her appointment there was a flurry of excitement, and everyone wondered if the daily routine would be affected. It was, for, as was usually the way, a new broom swept clean and a new regime, in this instance the Lennox Regime, was swiftly instituted.

Audra, observing everything with her usual perspicacity, decided that she must waste no time in applying for nurse's training at once. From what she had heard, Margaret Lennox favored young and ambitious girls who wanted to get on; apparently she went out of her way to give them her unstinting support and encouragement.

Two weeks after Matron Lennox had taken up her duties, Audra sat down and wrote a letter to her. She thought this was the wisest tactic to use, rather than to approach her personally. Matron Lennox had been in a whirlwind of activity and surrounded by a phalanx of hospital staff since her arrival.

Less than a week after Audra had left the letter in Matron's office, she was summoned for an interview. This was brisk, brief and very much to the point. Ten minutes after she had walked in, Audra Kenton walked out, smiling broadly, her application approved.

With her superior intelligence, her ability to learn quickly, Audra swiftly became one of the best student nurses on the hospital staff, and earned a reputation for being dedicated. She found the new work and her studies challenging; also, she discovered she had a desire to heal and, therefore, a real aptitude for nursing. And the young patients, with whom she had a genuine affinity, became the focus of the love she had bottled up inside her since her brothers had gone away. . . .

Now, remembering all of this, as she lay in the grass on the crest of the slope above the River Ure, Audra thought not of her diplomas and nursing achievements over the past four years, but of Frederick and William.

Her brothers had not sent for her in the end.

They had not been able to save up the money for her passage to Australia. Things had not gone well for the Kenton boys. Frederick had had two serious bouts with pneumonia and seemed to be in a state of physical debilitation a great deal of the time. Apart from the problems with his health, he and William were unskilled and untrained. They had had a hard time scraping a living together.

She sighed and bestirred herself, then sat up, blinking as she opened her eyes and adjusted them to the brightness. Poor Frederick and William had had nothing but bad luck really. Their letters, which arrived less frequently these days, were permeated with defeat. Audra had all but given up hope of going out to join them in Sydney. She continued to fret and to miss them, and she supposed she always would. They were her only family, after all, and she loved them very much.

Her work at the hospital gave her satisfaction, and for this she was grateful, but it was not enough. Her sense of isolation, of not belonging to anyone, or more precisely, of not being part of a family contributed to the aridness of her life. Sometimes she found it unbearable, despite her treasured friendship with the devoted Gwen.

Audra stood up, then cast her gaze to the other side of the river.

The light had changed in the last few hours, and High Cleugh now looked as if it had been built from polished bronze stones. It was bathed in a sort of golden glow, appeared to shimmer like a mirage in the distance, and even the gardens had a burnished sheen in the rosy sunset. All of her life thus far—at least the best, the happiest parts of it—and her dearest memories were bound up with that old house. A rush of feeling swept over Audra, and she suddenly knew that she would never cease to yearn for High Cleugh and all the things it represented.

CHAPTER FOUR

Here they were, sitting in the Copper Kettle in Harrogate. She and Gwen.

Audra could hardly believe they were finally meeting after all these weeks. The two girls had not seen each other since the beginning of June. On this hot and muggy Saturday it was already the end of August, the end of the summer, and the first time Gwen had been able to travel from Horsforth for a visit with her best friend.

Even so, Gwen had not been able to make it as far as Ripon, and in her letter she had asked Audra to meet her halfway. Audra had agreed to this request immediately and had sent off a note by return post.

Now, flushed with happiness, Audra looked across the table and broke into a smile. "It's lovely to see you, Gwen. I've really missed you."

"So have I—missed you, I mean." Gwen's cherubic face,

covered with freckles and vividly alive, was filled with
laughter; it signaled her own pleasure at their reunion. "I
still feel ever so *awful* about not being able to spend your
birthday with you—" Gwen broke off, reached down for the
fabric shopping bag at her feet and proceeded to rummage
around in it. She pulled out a package wrapped in royal
blue paper and tied with scarlet ribbon.

With a gay flourish, Gwen handed it across the table to
Audra. "Anyway, this is your birthday present, lovey. I
never did get to take you to one of the fancy tea dances at
the Palm Court of the Arcadian Rooms, so here, I bought
you something instead."

"You didn't have to, you shouldn't have!" Audra protested, but it was easy to see she was thrilled to receive the
gift. It had been a long time since she had been given a
present, and there had been nothing on her birthday. Her
face lit up, and her bright blue eyes danced as she tore off
the ribbon and paper with the excitement of a small child.

"Oh Gwen! *A paintbox!*" Audra looked up and beamed at
the other girl. "How lovely. And how clever of you. I really
needed a new one. Thank you so much." She reached out
and took hold of Gwen's hand lying on the table, and
squeezed it affectionately.

It was Gwen's turn to look pleased. "I wracked my brains,
trying to think of something . . . something . . . well,
just right. You being ever so particular as you are. As it
happened, I was looking at that watercolor you painted for
my mother last Christmas . . . the tree reflected in the
pond at Fountains Hall, and it suddenly occurred to me.
The paintbox, I mean. I thought to myself, that's exactly the
thing for Audra. It'll appeal to her practical side, but it'll
give her pleasure as well."

Gwen sat back and wrinkled her pert, very freckled nose.
Her gaze did not leave Audra's face as she asked, "It will,
won't it?"

"Oh yes, Gwen, lots and lots of pleasure." Her eyes
widened and she nodded several times, as if to give added
weight. She lifted the shiny black lid and looked inside
at the small blocks of bright color. She repeated some of the
familiar names under her breath: *Chrome yellow* . . .

*rose madder . . . cobalt blue . . . jade green . . .
burnt sienna . . . crimson lake . . . Saxe blue . . .
royal purple . . . burnt umber . . . Malaga red.* Audra
loved the sound of the names almost as much as she loved
to paint.

It had been her favorite hobby since her childhood. Her
father had been a gifted artist, and his paintings had sold
fairly well, but then he had fallen gravely ill just as he was
becoming known. Adrian Kenton had not really had a
chance to make a name for himself before he had died. She
had inherited his talent—or so her mother had always told
her.

Audra closed the lid of the paintbox and raised her eyes
to meet Gwen's soft hazel-amber gaze. How pretty she
looks, Audra thought, so blond and golden from the sun.
Gwen's fairness and her flaxen hair, cut short in a halo of
curls around her head, added to the angelic impression she
gave; so did the pale blue frock with its big white Quaker
collar, which she had chosen to wear today. She reminds me
of a choirboy, Audra thought, and smiled at this analogy.
With her beautiful bosom and lovely figure, there was
nothing very boyish about Gwen Thornton.

Audra noticed that for once Gwen looked restrained in
her mode of dress. Usually she glowed and glittered with
all kinds of jewelry; necklaces and beads, earrings and
bangles and rings. Obviously she had made a big effort to
be both understated and dignified for this trip to Harrogate.
She wants to please me, Audra decided, and her warm and
loving feelings for Gwen soared.

Leaning forward, Audra said, "I'm going to paint a very
special picture for you, Gwenny. For your room at home.
Would you like a scene—the kind I did for your mother? Or
a still life, such as a bowl of flowers? Oh, I *know* what I'll
paint for you. The Valley Gardens here in Harrogate.
You've always said that's your favorite spot when all the
flowers are in bloom. Would you like that?"

"Yes, that'd be ever so nice. Thanks very much, Audra.
I'd treasure one of your paintings—Mum says they're
masterpieces. The Valley Gardens would look lovely on my
wall. So I'd—"

"Can I take your order, miss?" the waitress interrupted

rather peremptorily. She looked first at Gwen, then at Audra, her pencil poised impatiently above her pad.

"We'd like to have tea," Audra said pleasantly, ignoring her huffy manner and angry stance. "For two, please."

"A pot? Or the set tea?" the waitress asked in the same snippy tone and licked the end of her pencil.

Gwen said, "You oughtn't do that. I hope that pencil's not indelible. You'll get a purple tongue, and probably lead poisoning."

"Get on with you, I won't get no such thing!" the waitress scoffed disbelievingly, then gave the two of them a worried glance. "Will I?" she muttered and carefully examined the tip of her pencil. "Oooh bloomin' heck! It *is* indelible."

Gwen nodded solemnly. "I thought it would be. You'd better go and see a doctor immediately if you develop peculiar symptoms tonight, especially if they're at all like convulsions."

"*Convulsions!*" the waitress repeated in a shrill voice and turned as white as her apron.

Audra, taking pity on the young woman, said, "We're nurses and we know about these things. But I'm sure you won't get lead poisoning from licking that pencil a few times."

The waitress, appearing slightly relieved, nodded her head.

"You'll be perfectly all right," Audra reassured, and went on briskly, "Now about our order, I think we'd better have the *set* tea. I suppose that means it includes everything . . . sandwiches, scones, jam, clotted cream, cakes—all of the usual things?"

"Yes," the waitress said laconically. She brought the pencil up to her mouth, then dropped her hand quickly and edged away from their table.

When she was out of earshot, Audra stared at the merry-faced Gwen and shook her head a bit reprovingly. However, she could not help grinning at Gwen's gleeful expression. "You're incorrigible, Miss Thornton. And that really *was* a little mean of you. Why, you've gone and ruined that poor young woman's day."

"I jolly well hope I have!" Gwen cried with a show of indignation. "She's a right Tartar, that one, Audra."

"Perhaps she has bad feet—or a bad love life."

"I don't know what she's got. Yes, I do—a nasty manner, that's a certainty."

There was a small silence, and then Audra reached for her handbag, took out some coins and placed them on the table in front of Gwen. "Before I forget, this is what I owe you. The one and six I borrowed when I bought the blue dress."

Gwen was about to say it didn't matter, to refuse the coins; then she thought better of it. Audra was very proud and might even be insulted; and that Gwen could not bear. And so she picked up the money and said, "Thanks very much, lovey."

"I am glad your mother has recovered her health at long last," Audra said with genuine feeling. "I know these last few months have been very worrying for you, and such hard work as well."

Gwen let out a tiny sigh. "Yes, Mum's out of the woods, thank goodness. But I don't mind telling you, she's been a trying patient, Audra. Hard to keep in bed. The minute she felt stronger she wanted to be up and about." Gwen pursed her lips and sighed again. "Well, you know what Mum's like, a typical Yorkshire woman, very tough, who believes it's a crime to be ill. My father has finally convinced her she must take it easy, so that's all right then. But listen, Audra, enough of this . . . tell me *your* news. You didn't say much in your letters, except for boring bits and pieces about the *boring* hospital."

"There wasn't anything special to tell," Audra replied, amused at the eager and expectant expression which had suddenly appeared on Gwen's dimpled face. "Certainly nothing startling. It hasn't taken *you* very long to forget that Ripon's a sleepy old backwater, not a great big metropolis like Leeds."

Gwen giggled. "Course I haven't forgotten, silly. But what I meant was how're your brothers? What've you heard recently?"

"Frederick's health has seemingly improved. At least, so William wrote and told me. I was very upset with them both in June, though." Audra's face changed slightly and the light in her eyes dulled. "I thought they had forgotten all about me . . . and my birthday, but then their card finally did arrive . . . two weeks late."

"That's brothers for you, Audra, they're a bit daft at times," Gwen said swiftly, wanting to make her friend feel better. And it struck Gwen once more how sad Audra's nineteenth birthday had been. She vowed to make it up to her on her birthday next year.

Audra said, "Anyway, how are your brothers?"

"In top form. Jem's got himself a job as a copy boy on the Leeds *Mercury*, Harry's going to be apprenticed to one of the leading architects in Leeds, and our Charlie's flying high, feeling very chuffed with himself." A huge grin spread across Gwen's face.

Audra looked at her curiously. "Why is Charlie so pleased?"

"Because he got *very* high marks in his exams, Audra. Dad's really proud of him, and so am I. Anyway, old Charlie can't wait to get back to medical school now that the summer hols are just about over. Oh, and that reminds me, he asked to be remembered to you." Gwen's eyes took on a wicked twinkle and she brought her fair head closer to Audra's, whispered in a conspiratorial manner, "As I keep telling you, I think our Charlie really fancies you, Audra. And quite a bit, at that."

Audra blushed furiously. "Don't be silly, Gwen, of course he doesn't."

"He does too! He's always asking questions about you!" Gwen shot back with unprecedented fierceness, giving her friend a stern glare. "He's *definitely* interested in you, I just know he is."

"Oh" was the only thing Audra could think of to say, feeling flustered all of a sudden.

"Well, you could do worse, you know."

"Yes," Audra murmured, and then clamped her mouth shut as the waitress hove in view.

Much to Audra's relief the young woman headed straight for their table, carrying a laden tray. She began to unload the tea things with a great deal of fuss and clattering, and this naturally curtailed their conversation for a few moments.

Once the waitress had departed, she picked up the large brown pot and began to pour tea into Gwen's cup, remarking, "I suppose I could say *she's* just had the last word."

"Oh no she hasn't, not by a long shot," Gwen said with a sly little smile. "Wait until it's time for her tip."

CHAPTER FIVE

Gwen Thornton was an affectionate girl, open-hearted and generous of nature, and she genuinely cared for Audra Kenton.

From the first moment she had met her, Gwen had been drawn to Audra. She had recognized there was something very special about the delicate-looking girl with the extraordinary blue eyes and the shy smile that could dazzle at times.

Gwen had quickly come to understand what it actually was that made Audra stand out in a crowd. It was her background and upbringing. Coming from an ordinary, though solid, middle-class family as she did, Gwen knew that Audra's air of breeding was downright impossible to imitate. You either had it or you didn't. It simply could not be acquired. And it not only gave Audra distinction, but it explained her aristocratic aloofness, her manners and her self-assurance, which were bred in the bone.

However, Gwen admired and loved Audra for a variety of other reasons, all of which added to her uniqueness. She was a superior young woman in every way, one who was inordinately loyal and loving; she was also the most indomitable person Gwen had ever met.

Yet despite these commendable traits, Gwen could not help worrying about Audra sometimes. She chiefly worried because Audra was without a family. Gwen knew more than anyone how much this bothered Audra. She sorely missed her brothers, yearned to *belong* in the way she had when her mother had been alive. This was why Gwen went out of her way to make her best friend feel like a real member of the Thornton clan, to make her truly understand she was as much loved as her baby sister Jenny-Rosalie, and her brothers, Charles, Jeremy and Harry.

Ever since Charlie, the eldest, had shown an interest in Audra, Gwen had been encouraging him, endeavoring to foster a relationship between them. But from time to time, Gwen had had to admit to herself that the interest was a trifle one-sided thus far; and she sometimes wondered if her sweet but rather dull brother was the right match for Audra. But inevitably, Gwen managed to convince herself that he really was ideal. Certainly there was no question in her mind that Charlie was a good catch, since he was such an admirable young man, and one with an assured future. He would not stay a bachelor for very long, once he had qualified as a doctor, and he would make a wonderful husband and father. Gwen had always known in her bones that Charlie was cut out to be a family man.

And in Gwen's mind, the crucial word was indeed *family*. This was what Audra longed for the most, and so she was going to help her dearest friend acquire a family of her very own. And, of course, Charlie was the key.

All of these thoughts, which had frequently preoccupied Gwen during the past few weeks, had started to swirl around in her head again this afternoon.

She and Audra were now strolling through the beautiful Valley Gardens. Both girls were glad to be out in the open air, after being cooped up inside the noisy cafe.

Gwen cast a glance at Audra as they headed down the sloping path. She decided she would be very hard-pressed indeed to find a sweeter or prettier candidate for a sister-in-law. Audra looked particularly attractive today, wearing a primrose-yellow print dress patterned with primroses, and a straw boater with a yellow silk band and matching ribbons fluttering down at the back. The boater gave her a jaunty air, whilst the simple cut of the frock and its sunny color were flattering to her.

She might be small, Gwen thought, but she's quality through and through. And then, before she could stop herself, she said out loud, "Yes, good stuff in a little room." Gwen could have bitten her tongue off, instantly regretted repeating this comment Charlie had made about Audra, who hated any reference to her height or lack of it. She cleared her throat nervously.

Audra said, with a puzzled look, "Excuse me, I don't quite understand what you're referring to, Gwen."

Deciding it would be smarter not to mention Charlie, Gwen explained, "Oh it was just something my mother said about you—good stuff in a little room means that a small person often has a lot of wonderful qualities. Haven't you heard the expression before? It's very Yorkshire."

Audra shook her head. "No, I haven't, but it's a nice compliment."

"Yes," Gwen said, delighted that she had taken it so well, and tucked her arm through Audra's companionably. "And talking of Mum, she says I can have a party for my birthday, so I hope you'll come and stay with us at The Meadow, the third weekend in September. There'll be Charlie, Jem and Harry, of course, and I can invite a *few* friends. But only a few. 'Cause Mum couldn't cope with a big crowd after her illness. You *will* come, Audra, won't you? It wouldn't be the same without you."

"Of course I'll come. It'll be a lovely treat for me, and I always enjoy staying at your house. Thank you for inviting me."

Gwen laughed gaily. "You'll get to wear your gorgeous blue dress. *Finally*. Why, Audra, you'll be the belle of the ball. All the boys will be after you." Especially our Charlie, Gwen added to herself, and hoped he wouldn't be rejected.

Audra glanced up at Gwen, who was a few inches taller, and joined in her laughter. "*You'll* be the belle; after all it's your birthday party. But I must admit, I am dying to wear my new dress. And what frock are you going to wear, Gwenny?"

"Oh, I don't know. I'll find something suitable, I expect. Now, who else do you think I should invite?" Not giving Audra a chance to reply, Gwen hurried on, "I'll tell you

what, let's go and sit over there on that form and talk about
the party. You're so clever, Audra, I'd like your advice about
a few things. You know . . . such as what kind of food and
drinks to serve, and your suggestions in general. Come on,
lovey."

Gwen steered Audra in the direction of a park seat
positioned under one of the lovely weeping willows which
were planted throughout the Valley Gardens. Here the two
girls sat themselves down and brought their heads together.
They chatted animatedly about Gwen's twentieth birthday
party for the next half hour, covering all the different
aspects of it, planning the menu and the guest list.

Finally Gwen said, "Thanks, Audra, you've been a great
help. It'll be a nice party. . . ."

Audra turned her attention to the passersby, thinking
how smart some of the women looked, dressed in their
finery and out for a stroll before dinner at one of the swanky
hotels. They were obviously from London, judging by their
clothes, and were visiting Harrogate to "take the cure." It
had been a renowned Spa since Victorian times, and people
came from all over the world to drink from the variety of
the forty waters available in the Pump Room and visit the
hydros at the Royal Baths. Her mother had always loved
Harrogate for its elegance, and the Beautiful Edith Kenton
had called it a throwback to Victorian times and a more
civilized age.

Their mother had often brought them here for the day.
Audra recalled a memorable afternoon in 1911 when they
had come to get a glimpse of the queens of England, Russia
and Poland, who had all been visiting Harrogate on the
same day. Their Uncle Peter had been with them, and he
had lifted her up on his shoulders so that she could see
above the crowds. There had been lots of excitement and
flags waving and a band playing . . . Audra drifted along
with her remembrances of things past.

Gwen, however, was thinking of the future and wondering how to break her awful news to Audra. Earlier, she had
toyed with the idea of not saying anything, of writing a
letter at a later date. But Gwen knew that Audra, who had
so much integrity and was such a fair person, deserved

better from her than that. She decided there really was only one way to do it, and that was to jump right in, both feet first.

Reaching out, she touched Audra's arm tentatively, and said in an unusually subdued voice, "There's something I want to tell you before we go to the bus station for our buses. . . ."

Audra looked at her, instantly coming back to the present. "You sound very serious all of a sudden, Gwenny. Is there something wrong?"

Gwen swallowed and cleared her throat. "I've wanted to tell you this all afternoon, but I haven't known how to begin. Well . . . look, it's like this, Audra . . . I won't be coming back to work at the Fever Hospital. I'm ever so sorry."

Audra gaped at her friend, flabbergasted at this announcement. It was a bombshell, the last thing she had expected to hear. "Oh Gwen," she murmured, so softly it was a whisper.

Observing her closely, detecting the misery now flooding her bright blue eyes, Gwen cried anxiously, "Please, oh *please* don't be upset, Audra. *I'm* not going to *Australia*. I'll only be a couple of hours away, either in Leeds or Horsforth. We can see each other all the time, and listen, Mum wants you to come and stay for Christmas, like you did last year. And we'll be together on my birthday next month."

Audra, considerably shaken by Gwen's news, was only able to nod.

"You see, it's like this, Audra. Dad wants me to be nearer home, because of Mum's weak heart. He says I have to apply for a position at the Infirmary or St. James's Hospital, and until I get something at either place, I've got to stay at home with Mum. Dad's ever so set on it, Audra, I can't make him change his mind."

Audra, always sensitive to the feelings of others, heard the distress in Gwen's voice, and she smiled faintly and nodded. "I understand, Gwenny," she said. But her heart sank at the prospect of being all alone in Ripon. She felt as though she was being abandoned once more.

Gwen had a sudden idea. She exclaimed, "Look, Audra, why don't you apply too? For a hospital job in Leeds, I mean." She drew closer, took hold of Audra's small hand and was surprised how cold it was on this muggy day. She clutched it tightly, begged, "Say you will. Please, lovey."

"I'm not sure whether I should—"

"*Why not?*" Gwen demanded, her voice rising. "There's not one good reason for you to stay in Ripon."

Audra blinked and returned Gwen's hard stare, realizing immediately that her friend was absolutely right. She began to nod her head emphatically. "Yes, I'll do it, Gwenny!" And a smile broke through at last, expunged the sadness which had darkened her lovely eyes.

Gwen threw her arms around Audra. She hugged her tightly, bursting with happiness and filled with relief. The thought of leaving her beloved friend behind at the Fever Hospital had been more than the girl could bear.

CHAPTER SIX

"Matron wants to see you, Kenton," Sister Rogers said, drawing to a standstill, fixing a stern eye on Audra. "She did say *immediately*, so you'd better look sharp."

Audra, who had just finished taking a child's temperature, nodded. "Thanks. I'll go up at once."

Moving away from the bed, Audra glanced around at her young patients with her usual concern. The small isolation ward was occupied by children suffering from whooping cough, and she was worried about each of them on this icy December morning.

As she and the head nurse walked down the ward toward the door, Audra dropped her voice and said, "They're all a bit restless, especially the little one over there by the window. He's exhausted from the whoop, and he's not been able to keep his breakfast down because of his excessive coughing, and Doctor Parkinson is a bit concerned about him. Can you send a junior nurse in to keep an eye on him? And on the others, of course?"

"Don't worry about it, I'll stay here myself until you get back. I'm sure you won't be very long with Matron." A slight smile touched the head nurse's mouth and there was an unprecedented softening in her attitude toward Audra, and she remarked in a quiet tone, "Your diligence really is commendable, Kenton. You've turned out to be a good nurse."

These were words of praise indeed, coming from this most senior member of the nursing staff, who had worked herself up from ward maid and who was renowned as a disciplinarian. Audra, surprised, returned her smile and with a little burst of pride, she drew herself up to her full height. "Thank you, Sister," she said. "I do try."

Sister Rogers inclined her head and turned away.

It was a dismissal of sorts, and Audra crossed the front hall and ran up the wide main staircase, hoping that Matron had good news for her at last. After making the decision to leave Ripon and find a nursing job in Leeds, Audra had confided her intentions in the head of the hospital and had asked for her advice. Matron had given it and had generously offered to do everything she could to help Audra. Unfortunately, they had not been successful so far. It seemed there were no vacancies in any of the hospitals in Leeds or the surrounding districts.

Audra, however, was not overly dismayed about this situation, since Gwen herself had only just managed to find a place at Leeds General Infirmary. Lonely though she was at the hospital without her dearest friend for companionship in her off-duty hours, Audra remained cheerful and optimistic as she went about her duties.

For the past three months, Audra had held the firm conviction that something would turn up eventually, and now, as she came to a stop outside Matron's office, she wondered if it finally had materialized. She tugged at her cuffs to straighten them, smoothed her hands over her starched white apron, then knocked on the frosted-glass panel of the door. At Matron's bidding she went in.

Margaret Lennox sat behind her large, paper-strewn desk.

She was wearing the navy-blue tailored dress and small white muslin cap that signified the highest nursing rank in the hierarchy of every hospital, and she seemed more formidable than ever. But Audra knew from experience that this stern-looking woman had the kindest of hearts.

Matron raised her eyes. She smiled at the sight of Audra, who was a particular favorite of hers, and for whom she had a great deal of respect and not a little admiration. She was aware of Audra's history from the hospital files, and she never ceased to marvel at this girl's strength of character and inner fiber.

"Ah, Audra," she began pleasantly, "do come in and sit down. I have a matter to discuss with you."

"Yes, Matron." Audra stepped up to the desk briskly and lowered herself onto the wooden chair where she sat straight-backed as always, her hands clasped in her lap. Her wide blue eyes were riveted to the matron's face.

Margaret Lennox glanced at the letter in her hand, then put it down on the desk. "Well, Audra, I think I might have a position for you in Leeds."

A look of delight flew onto Audra's face and she opened her mouth to speak.

But before she could say anything, Matron lifted her hand and exclaimed, "Just a moment! Don't get too excited . . . at least not yet. I must explain that this is not the type of nursing job you've been looking for, Audra. It's not in a hospital, I'm afraid."

"Oh," Audra said. "I see," and her face fell.

"I know you're disappointed that I have not been able to get you situated somewhere appropriate," Matron went on in a sympathetic way. "However, I do think you should consider this private position, especially since you are so very anxious to move to Leeds."

"Of course I will, Matron."

"Good girl. Now, Audra, I have had a letter from a Mrs. Irène Bell, who is the wife of a well-known Leeds solicitor. She's looking for a nanny and has been in touch with me about finding a suitable candidate here at the hospital. Naturally, Audra, I thought of you at once."

Matron Lennox then went on to explain that she had originally met Mrs. Bell through her work with the suffragette movement before the Great War, and that they had remained friendly over the years. Then she continued, "I cannot speak highly enough of Mrs. Bell. She has many wonderful achievements to her credit, and I have a strong feeling you and she would be compatible. In any event, from what she says in her letter, it's not a difficult job. There is only one child to look after, a little boy of five years. The other three children are grown up, away at school I believe." Matron's brow lifted questioningly. "What do you think, Audra? Are you interested?"

Audra had been listening avidly, and she knew she would be foolish if she turned down this opportunity without investigating it further. So she immediately said, "Yes, I am, Matron."

Matron nodded, as though confirming something to herself, and said, "I am confident you can handle a job such as this with the greatest of ease." She sat back, brought her hands together and steepled her fingers, contemplated Audra over them for a few moments, before remarking: "You have such a wonderful way with children, I know you will do well as a nanny. But you are an *extraordinary* nurse, Audra, a true healer, and that's rare. Don't ever forget that you have this remarkable ability . . . one might even call it a gift."

"No, I won't," Audra said, flushing with pleasure. She murmured her thanks to Matron for her kind words and the confidence she expressed in her.

Margaret Lennox went on, "I did have special plans for you here at the hospital, Audra, and I had envisaged promotions coming your way quickly." She smiled at the young woman with obvious fondness, then lifted her shoulders in a small resigned shrug. "Well, there we are. . . . I for one shall be *most* sorry to see you go, if you *do* decide to leave, Audra. But, as I've told you all along, I would never presume to stand in your way."

"Yes, I know that, Matron, and I do appreciate everything you've done for me."

Matron half smiled, then finished in a more businesslike tone, "I will give Mrs. Bell a ring today and arrange for you to go over to Leeds for an interview. I'll let you know the details as soon as I have them. In the meantime, you had better return to your duties on the ward, Audra."

"Yes, Matron," Audra said, standing up. "Thank you again."

She was on her way to Leeds.

To meet Mrs. Irène Bell of Calpher House, Upper Armley.

Audra had the feeling that this was going to be an auspicious occasion. She laughed at herself under her breath. It was only an interview for a job after all. On the other hand, if everything went well there would be big changes in her life at long last. It might even be the beginning of a brand-new life.

This thought brought an extra spring to her step as she crossed the Market Place in Ripon, making her way toward the small country railway station on North Road. Audra's eyes sparkled with such radiant light, and there was such a glow on her fresh young face this morning, several people turned to look at her as she passed them by. But she did not notice this. Nor was she conscious of the weather. It was a harsh day, exceptionally cold, and the sky was sullen, laden with snow. But it might have been the middle of spring, for all she knew or cared, so intent was she in her purpose. She was also filled with anticipation and excitement. A week ago she had never heard of the Bell family, and now, here she was, journeying halfway across Yorkshire to seek a post with them.

What if she did not like the Bells?

At this thought her step faltered, but only for a split second. Stepping out as briskly as before, she told herself she would make a polite excuse and leave at once if the people at Calpher House did not appear to be suitable employers.

The ticket collector at the station gave Audra a cheerful greeting as he punched her ticket and handed her the return stub. He touched his cap politely, and she nodded in acknowledgment, then hurried down the platform where the Leeds-bound train was already standing, puffing out steam and whistling. She boarded it swiftly and went into the first empty First Class carriage she saw. She took a corner seat near the window with only a few minutes to spare before the guard blew his whistle and the train shunted out.

Audra soon began to realize that it was warmer in the carriage than she had anticipated. She pulled off her gray woolen gloves and unbuttoned her coat, then settled back, making herself comfortable for the journey.

Audra knew she looked smart today.

For her trip to Leeds she had chosen to wear her best gray Melton topcoat. Although it had been purchased in a sale and was already two years old, it was still fashionable, a wrap-around style with long, rolled lapels fastening at the hip with a huge button. Underneath the coat she had on a straight skirt made of gray wool and a matching gray jumper that came down over her hips. Together they created a slender tubelike effect, and she believed that this long line and her black court shoes with Cuban heels made her look taller. This pleased Audra, who was always trying to gain a few inches. Her only jewelry was her mother's cameo brooch, which she had pinned onto the front of her jumper, and her second-hand but treasured watch.

When Audra had been visiting Gwen in September, her friend had given her a cloche made of plum-colored brushed felt. "My worst buy ever!" Gwen had said when she had shown the hat to Audra. "It's like a pea on a drum. I look awful in it, but I bet it suits you to a T, lovey." Gwen had been correct. The cloche *was* perfect on Audra, and she had treasured the hat for a special occasion. In fact, she had not worn it until today.

But now she wondered if the hat was too frivolous for the interview with Mrs. Bell, and she opened her bag, took out her mirror. Her reflection reassured her at once. The cloche, which was very much the rage, gave her a stylish up-to-date look, and the rich plum tone of the felt added just the right touch of necessary color to her all-gray ensemble. Her clothes were definitely sober and dignified, and she felt sure she would make a good impression on Mrs. Irène Bell.

Audra repeated the first name under her breath. It was spelled in the French way and pronounced in the French way, and she thought it was a lovely name. As the train rumbled on through the Dales toward Leeds, Audra's thoughts stayed with the woman she was going to see; she began to review the few things she had gleaned about her from Matron.

It was Audra's understanding that Irène Bell was a successful businesswoman who had a strong intellectual bent and was something of a bluestocking. She was devoted to furthering the cause of women's rights and had always been a staunch disciple of the Pankhurst women who had done so much for female emancipation. According to Matron, Mrs. Bell was also a great admirer of Nancy Astor, the American married to Lord Astor, who was the first woman to sit in Parliament. Actively involved in politics herself, Mrs. Bell was seemingly a tireless worker for the Tory Party in Leeds, with many of her own political ambitions—especially regarding Parliament.

There was no doubt in Audra's mind that she was obviously an interesting woman, and one who was quite different to any *she* had ever met. Except for Margaret Lennox, of course, who was a true original, and whom Audra revered, even idealized.

Gazing out of the train window, hardly aware of the fields and hedges speeding by, Audra attempted to visualize Mrs. Bell. Since she had been a friend of Matron's for many years and had grown-up children, Audra reasoned she must be a woman in her middle forties. Instantly she was confronted by the image of a stern and somewhat severe person, perhaps resembling Matron and one who was a model of organization and efficiency.

Audra arrived at this last conclusion because of the tone of the letter she had received from Mrs. Bell earlier in the week. It was detailed and explicit, and her instructions for getting to Calpher House, Upper Armley, left nothing whatsoever to chance. It struck Audra, and for the second time in the last few days, that Mrs. Bell must be an exceptionally thoughtful woman, since she had sent her a First Class rail ticket instead of a cheaper one, as might have been expected under the circumstances. This was a truly considerate gesture, and one which certainly seemed to augur well for the future, at least to Audra's way of thinking. And she suddenly realized how curious she was about Irène Bell, and just how much she was looking forward to meeting her.

Punctuality was one of Audra's strong suits, and she always became agitated if she was late. Throughout the journey, she had glanced at her watch, praying that the train would be on time. Much to her relief it was. It pulled into Leeds City Station at exactly one minute to two, early, in point of fact, by sixty seconds.

Once she had left the bleak and grimy railway station, Audra was plunged into a whirl of traffic and pedestrians hurrying about their business. For a second or two the strident noise and the feverish bustle of the greatest industrial city in the North of England startled and overwhelmed her. The cacophony of sounds was a deafening contrast to the bucolic calm of sleepy, rural Ripon.

But since nothing ever fazed Audra Kenton for very long, she adjusted relatively quickly to her surroundings. After only a brief pause, she sucked in her breath, threw her shoulders back and brought her head up to a proud angle, ready and set to brave anything in this exciting new world awaiting her.

Tucking her handbag tightly under her arm, she walked purposefully across the road to City Square, where the statue of the Black Prince on his charger dominated the scene. She found the tram stop she wanted without any difficulty, and after a ten-minute wait in a small queue she followed the people ahead of her onto a tramcar going to Whingate. This was the terminus in Upper Armley where the tram turned around to go back to the city. Mrs. Bell had told her to stay on the car all the way to the end of the line.

Half an hour later, Audra alighted from the double-decker tram, which she had thoroughly enjoyed riding on, and she stood for a moment, looking around her with burgeoning interest. After all, she might soon be living here.

To her right was the tiny wedge of a park enclosed by spike-topped black iron railings and a neatly clipped privet hedge, which Mrs. Bell had said had the curious name of Charlie Cake Park. To her left was a huge red brick building, sprawling out behind a low brick wall, and she assumed this to be West Leeds Boys' High School.

Audra knew exactly which way she had to go now.

She began to walk ahead at a brisk pace, glancing at the scenery and taking everything in with keenly observing eyes. She saw at once that the village of Upper Armley was picturesque and that it had a quaint Victorian charm. And despite the darkly mottled sky, somber and presaging snow, and a landscape bereft of greenery, it was easy to see how pretty it must be in the summer weather.

Following Mrs. Bell's instructions, which she had committed to her excellent memory days ago, Audra hurried up Greenhill Road in the direction of Hill-Top, the area where the Bell home was located.

It was a nippy afternoon, very blustery, and she had to hold on to her little cloche as she struggled forward, buffeted by the wind that whistled down over the hill with icy ferocity. Audra was shivering when she reached the crest of the hill and drew to a stop in front of a pair of imposing wrought-iron gates upon which hung a large lozenge-shaped plaque. This was made of brass that had been rubbed up to a glittering sheen. It was inscribed with the name *Calpher House* in fancy scroll letters, and it told her she had reached her destination.

CHAPTER SEVEN

Irène Bell bore no resemblance to the image Audra had conjured up. The woman who walked toward her down the long stretch of luxurious Turkey carpet was tall, lissome, very smart, and she had the brightest, reddest of auburn hair. This had been cut in a sleek and fashionable bob, then shaped into a fringe above penciled brows and velvety brown eyes that shone with great brilliance. High cheekbones and a slender aristocratic nose were peppered with freckles; a rather wide mouth was outlined in scarlet lipstick.

Irène Bell was stunning, and she had an arresting personal style that stopped just short of flamboyance.

She took swift strides through the handsome blue and white living room, filled with antiques, where Audra stood waiting, and there was something reminiscent of the bold tomboy in her manner, the way she moved. In fact, her looks had a marked hoydenish quality; she also appeared to be much younger than her mid-forties. The red wool-jersey dress she wore underscored her intrinsic youthfulness with its long, loose-fitting bodice and pleated skirt, rather short, that swung around her splendid legs.

Audra, sharp-eyed as ever, recognized the dress at once. She had seen a photograph of it only last week in an old summer issue of *Harper's Bazaar,* which she had bought at the second-hand bookstall in Ripon market. It had been designed by a young French *couturière* called Gabrielle Chanel, who was currently all the vogue.

"Hello! Hello!" Mrs. Bell exclaimed, gliding to a stop, thrusting her hand toward her visitor. "So *very* pleased to meet you, Miss Kenton."

Audra took the proffered hand, then found her own being squeezed in the tightest of grips. "Good afternoon, Mrs. Bell. I'm happy to meet you, too."

Giving her a warm and winning smile, continuing to hold

her hand, Irène Bell drew Audra forward to the two huge
sofas which were positioned opposite each other in front of
the fireplace. "So very good of you to travel all this way,
Miss Kenton. And in this frightful weather. Yes, so very
good of you indeed. Do, *do* sit here. Yes, *yes*, next to the
fire. Warm yourself after your journey. Cook is preparing
hot chocolate. Cora will bring it up shortly. I *do* hope you
like hot chocolate. Would you prefer tea? Or coffee,
perhaps?"

"The chocolate would be lovely, thank you very much,"
Audra said, seating herself tentatively on the edge of the
blue velvet sofa. Her keen eyes rested on Mrs. Bell, who
sat down on the other one.

Now that she was seeing her close up, Audra realized
that she had not been wrong about Irène Bell's age after all.
She was definitely a woman in her mid-forties, but very
well preserved and exquisitely groomed. Although there
were tell-tale lines of age around her eyes and her mouth,
these were fine, hardly discernible; she had kept her figure
and there was no visible gray in her fiery hair, which was
natural, not dyed. And her vivacity, her energetic way of
moving and speaking with intensity and swiftness somehow
added to the impression of youthfulness she projected.

Intuitively, Audra knew that she was going to like this
woman, even though she had only been in her presence for
a few minutes. There was something open and easy, honest
and down to earth about Mrs. Bell, and Audra found herself
responding to her on a variety of levels. She sat back,
instantly relaxing, feeling suddenly comfortable here at
Calpher House. And she, who was usually so shy, so
reserved with strangers, was perfectly at ease with Mrs.
Bell.

Irène Bell crossed her long and elegant legs, and focused
her dark and intelligent eyes on Audra, assessing her, yet
without really appearing to do so.

She said in her light, gay voice, "In some ways I do feel
rather foolish, Miss Kenton. Asking you to come for an
interview like this. Matron Lennox gave you such a
wonderful reference, I actually thought of engaging you

over the telephone. Without even bothering to meet you personally."

Laughing as though at herself, her velvet eyes glowed with humor as she added, "But then I realized how unfair that would be to you, Miss Kenton. After all, it is important for *you* to like *us*. For you to *want* to live and work here at Calpher House. I knew I must give you the opportunity to come here and look *us* over."

Irène Bell laughed again, leaned back, rested one elbow on the pile of silk cushions, and continued to study Audra discreetly, not wishing to embarrass her. She was intrigued by the young woman who sat before her, who handled herself with such grace and dignity. Margaret Lennox had painted a charming verbal picture of her, and the Matron had obviously not exaggerated. Audra Kenton was smaller than she had expected her to be, even delicate-looking, but she was not terribly concerned about physical stamina. Strength of character, refinement, morality and a pleasant personality were her chief considerations when it came to selecting and engaging a nanny. This girl had every one of these qualities, and more, according to Margaret, whose judgment she trusted.

"Matron Lennox told me that she thought you and I would be compatible, Mrs. Bell, and she felt sure that I could handle the job here easily." Audra leveled her penetrating blue eyes at the other woman, and ventured, "But she *was* vague about it. Perhaps you would be kind enough to give me a few more details, Mrs. Bell."

"Good Lord, of course! I must fill you in, mustn't I? Well now, let me see. As you know from Matron, you would be entirely responsible for our youngest child. Our only son. Our three daughters are grown up. The eldest, Miss Pandora, lives at home. The younger two, Felicity and Antonia, are away at boarding school. Let me explain something, Miss Kenton. I go to business every day. I run the woolen mill I inherited from my father. I also have an exclusive ladies' gown salon in Leeds. *Paris Modes.* I'm quite certain you must know it."

Audra shook her head, looking regretful. "I'm sorry, I'm afraid I don't, Mrs. Bell. The only store I know in Leeds is

Harte's Emporium. I went there once with my friend
Gwen."

Mrs. Bell said, "My dress shop is not as large as Emma
Harte's store. But my imported French gowns *are* beginning to rival those she sells in her Model Room at Harte's.
But to continue: Because I am out most of the day, I need a
responsible person in charge of the nursery and the baby. A
person such as yourself. As to your accommodations here,
there is a lovely bedroom, large and comfortable, which
overlooks the gardens. It's on the nursery floor, has its own
private bathroom. You would have one day off during the
week, and every other Sunday. One week's holiday a year. I
would provide you with three cotton uniforms for summer,
plus a summer coat and hat. The same amount of clothing
for winter. Now, regarding the wages—"

Mrs. Bell broke off at the sound of a knock, and glanced
toward the door. It opened to admit a plump young maid,
who rushed forward rather too quickly, pushing a laden tea
cart in front of her.

"Ah Cora, there you are at last!" Mrs. Bell exclaimed.
"*Do*, please, be *careful*. Bring the cart over here by the
fire. This is Miss Kenton, Cora. Whom I sincerely hope will
be joining us at Calpher House. As the new nanny."

Cora and the tea cart came to an abrupt stop with a
rattling jolt. She stared at Audra, narrowing her eyes,
squinting at her. Then, as if she had decided she liked the
look of her, she smiled broadly, bobbed a half-curtsy.
"Please ter meet yer, Miss," she said, and proceeded down
the long stretch of Turkey carpet, handling the trolley with
a kind of dangerous abandon.

Audra inclined her head graciously and returned the
maid's smile. "Good afternoon, Cora," she replied, and
cringed as she watched Cora's perilous progress toward
them. She hoped that nothing would go crashing to the
floor, for the maid's sake.

Irène Bell dismissed Cora with a smile and a nod, lifted
the silver jug and carefully filled two large breakfast cups,
remarking, "We have a wonderful cook, Mrs. Jackson, and
the butler is Mr. Agiter. I believe you saw Dodie, the other

housemaid, when you arrived? Did she not open the door to you?"

"Yes, she did, Mrs. Bell." Audra rose and went over to the tea cart, took the cup of hot chocolate which was being offered to her.

Irène Bell exclaimed, "Do, but *do*, try one of Cook's hot Cornish pasties, Miss Kenton. They're delicious. And quite renowned hereabouts."

"Thank you." Audra placed the cup of steamy, frothing chocolate on the antique mahogany table next to the sofa, put one of the meat turnovers on a plate and returned to her place.

Taking a sip of chocolate, Mrs. Bell continued, "As I was about to say when Cora came in, your wages would be sixty pounds a year. This is an increase of ten pounds above what I paid the last nanny. Matron Lennox said it would not be fair of me to offer you anything less than sixty pounds. In view of your superior training at the hospital." Irène Bell now leaned forward intently. "Well, Miss Kenton, are you interested in taking the position, do you think?" A perfect, penciled brow lifted eloquently.

Audra was both startled and delighted at the amount of money she would be paid. She said, "I am interested, Mrs. Bell, very much so. However, I would like to meet your little boy before I finally say yes." Audra gave her a forthright look, and her sudden smile was one of sweetness and sincerity. "I'm quite positive I will like him, but I do want to be sure *he* likes *me*."

"What a lovely sentiment, Miss Kenton. And I'm over-joyed, simply *overjoyed*, that you're going to join our little family." Irène Bell's face, always mobile and expressive, now filled with a mixture of relief and pleasure. Her merry laugh echoed around the room. "I know the baby will take to you. How could he not? He's having his afternoon nap at the moment, but you shall meet him later. And before you leave, I shall show you around Calpher House. And introduce you to the staff."

* * *

The motor car slid to a standstill in front of the General
Post Office in City Square.

A moment later the uniformed chauffeur was opening the
rear door and helping Audra to alight. "Thank you so much,
Robertson," she said, giving him an appreciative little
smile.

"It's a pleasure, Miss. Good afternoon, Miss." He
touched the bill of his peaked cap and hurried back to the
driver's seat.

Audra swung around and took a step toward Gwen, who
was standing near the steps of the post office where they
had arranged to meet.

Gwen's eyes were out on stalks. Instantly recovering
herself, she rushed forward to meet Audra. Grasping hold
of her hands, she cried in a shrill, excited voice, "Well,
aren't we posh then! Rolling up in a fancy motor car.
Imagine that!"

Audra could not help laughing at Gwen's incredulity.
Then she explained, "Mrs. Bell kept me at Calpher House
rather longer than I expected. I started to get a little
nervous in the end. I didn't want to be late, to have you
standing waiting outside in the cold. So she sent me in the
car."

"That was nice of her!" Gwen exclaimed, obviously
impressed not only by the car but by Mrs. Bell as well. She
peered into Audra's face and demanded, "Well, did you
take the job then?"

"Yes, Gwen, I did."

"Oh, lovey, I am glad!" Gwen threw her arms around
Audra, hugged her tightly. Audra hugged her back, and the
two of them clung to each other, did a happy little jig and
then began to laugh uproariously.

Their frivolity was interrupted by a masculine voice,
which said, "They'll be sending the wagon for you two next,
the way you're carrying on like a couple of lunatics, and in
the middle of City Square, no less."

"Oh hello, Charlie," Gwen said, looking up at her
brother, who stood with his hands in his pockets, towering
over them both, surveying them through amused eyes.
"You're right on time, I see."

"Aren't I always." Charles Thornton grinned at his sister, then gave Audra a shy smile. "Hello, Audra," he said, unable to keep the look of adoration off his face. He thrust his hand at her.

Audra's heart sank at the sight of Charlie, whom she had not expected to join them for the evening, as he no doubt had. She had wanted to be alone with Gwen. They hadn't seen each other for several weeks, and they had a number of things to talk about, especially now that she had taken the job with the Bells.

"Hello," Audra responded in her quiet way, taking his hand, glad she was wearing her gloves. Charlie always had such clammy hands, even in the cold weather. In fact, he had a tendency to perspire, and whilst she knew he could not help it, Audra found this unfortunate physical trait distasteful. She liked Charlie well enough as a person, but she had no wish to have him as her boyfriend. This was Gwen's hope though, and she was forever pushing Charlie at her. Audra fervently wished she would stop doing it. Charlie Thornton was not her type at all. It was not that he was unattractive. He was tall, well built, with broad shoulders, very masculine really, although Audra suspected he would become flabby as he grew older. He had blond hair, a fair complexion and friendly gray eyes. His face, like his personality, was bland. Audra could not help thinking that he was soppy in certain ways, and most of the time she found him dreadfully dull. She supposed he was worthy in many ways, and yet instinctively she knew he was a weak man, ineffectual somehow.

Gwen volunteered, "Charlie's taking us to the pictures later, Audra. He's treating us. We're going to the Rialto in Briggate to see the new Mary Pickford picture. Isn't that nice of him?"

"Oh yes, it is," Audra was quick to agree and forced a smile.

Taking charge as usual, Gwen rushed on, "Well, don't let's stand here like three sucking ducks gawping at each other. We've an hour to waste before we go to the pictures, so let's toddle along to Betty's and have a nice cup of tea."

Audra and Charlie readily agreed.

It had turned even chillier and the snow that had
threatened throughout the day began to fall in small
fluttering flakes, settling on the ground. The light was being
squeezed out of the lowering sky as dusk descended
rapidly. Charlie took hold of the girls' arms and hurried
them across City Square in the direction of Commercial
Street where the cafe was located. As they turned into the
street, they all three stopped abruptly, staring into the
windows of Harte's department store, captivated by what
they saw. The windows had been dressed for Christmas and
they were dazzling in the gathering twilight, filled with
twinkling colored lights and glittering scenes depicting
various fairy tales. One window was devoted to Cinderella,
showed her arriving at the ball in her shimmering glass
coach, another to Hansel and Gretel, who stood outside the
gingerbread house, and yet a third paid tribute to The
Snow Queen in all her icy glory.

"How beautiful they are," Audra murmured, lingering a
moment longer than the other two, thinking of High
Cleugh and the glorious Christmases of her childhood.

"Yes, aren't they just," Gwen said, tugging at her. "Come
on, lovey, the snow's really coming down now. We're going
to be soaked before we know it."

Gwen tucked her arm through Audra's and kept up a
continual stream of conversation as they walked down
Commercial Street, living up to her reputation as a
chatterbox. Charlie, trudging along on the other side of
Audra, interjected a few comments, but Audra remained
silent—and reflective.

She was suddenly feeling uncharitable for having had
such unkind thoughts about Charlie, who was harmless
really and meant well. All of the Thorntons meant well, and
they had all been very good to her. Mrs. Thornton was
forever telling her to consider The Meadow her home, and
she had even turned the little box room at the end of the
second-floor landing into a bedroom for her. Mrs. Thornton
had insisted she keep a few clothes there, and when she
had visited Gwen in November, she had left behind some
toilet articles and a nightgown, which she would be able to
use tonight.

Next week she was coming back to Horsforth to spend
Christmas with Gwen, and she was well aware that the
Thorntons would make her feel like a part of the family,
truly one of them, as they always did. They had such a
wealth of generosity and kindness in them. And I'm very
ungrateful, Audra chastised herself. She knew how much it
would please Gwen if she were nice to Charlie, and so she
resolved to be pleasant to him, but without leading him on,
giving him the wrong impression. *He must not misunderstand*. That would be disastrous. And after the holidays she
was going to explain to Gwen, in the gentlest and kindest
possible way, that she was not looking for a husband.

CHAPTER EIGHT

It was a very cold morning. *Icy*.

Perhaps it *would* turn out to be the coldest day of the
winter after all, Audra thought, just as the gardener had
warned yesterday when she had been returning from her
walk. He had put down his wheelbarrow and looked up at
the sky, narrowing his eyes and sniffing, as if he had a way of
divining such things in this arcane manner.

And then he had made his prediction. "Yer'll be nithered
ter death termorra, Miss Audra. T'weather's coming in bad
from t'North Sea. Arctic weather, mark my words, lass."

She had never been to the Arctic Circle, but she did not
imagine it could be any colder than her bedroom at this
moment. It was freezing, and it seemed to Audra that her
nose, peeping over the bedcovers, had turned into an
icicle. An Arctic icicle.

She slithered farther down in the bed, hunching the
covers up over her shoulders, almost obscuring her face
entirely, reveling in the warmth of the quilt. It was filled
with the down of the eider duck, and Mr. and Mrs. Bell had
purchased a baker's dozen of these quilts when they had
been on holiday in Munich several years before.

Mrs. Bell had told Audra this when she had come to work

at Calpher House, had gone on to explain that the sheet
under the quilt was the only other piece of bed linen
required. Irène Bell had also cautioned Audra not to wear
her thick flannel nightgown, but to discard it in favor of a
cotton garment. Although she had nodded her understanding, she had not been absolutely certain that she really
understood at all. But later that night, at bedtime, she had
done as she had been bidden earlier in the day, and within
ten minutes of being in bed she had begun to feel a lovely
sensation of warmth permeating her whole body. The heat
generated by the quilt was extraordinary, something quite
amazing to Audra, and she realized that Mrs. Bell had been
correct about the cotton nightie. Anything else would have
been far too hot.

She smiled to herself now, remembering her first night
here, and then swiveled her eyes to the clock on the
mahogany chest as it began to chime. It was only six, but
this did not surprise her in the least. She was accustomed to
awakening at this hour. It was an old habit left over from
her years at the hospital in Ripon. Fortunately the routine
was not so rigorous here at Calpher House, and she could
stay in bed until seven, even a bit later if she wished.

Audra had truly come to cherish this dawn hour, when all
the family were asleep and no one was about except for the
servants downstairs. She thought of it as her own special
and private time, enjoyed the luxury of lingering in her
downy cocoon, without having the need to rush, idly
drifting with her diverse thoughts . . . and sometimes
daydreaming about the future.

And the future seemed decidedly rosy to Audra on this
December morning of 1927.

Certainly the years stretching ahead could not be any
worse than the five years which had preceded her arrival at
Calpher House, she frequently told herself these days.
Naturally optimistic, she always looked at things in the
most positive way, anticipating the best. She also expected
the best from people, despite her distressing experiences
with her Aunt Alicia Drummond. Burying the dreadful
hurt she had suffered at the hands of that inhuman woman,
she would remind herself that not everyone was cruel,

selfish or dishonest, that the world *did* have its ample share
of kindly folk. And the Bells and their staff at Calpher
House had helped to reinforce this belief in Audra. She had
been made to feel welcome from the first day, and she never
once forgot how fortunate she had been to find such a
congenial place to work.

It was exactly one year ago today that she had started
here as the nanny.

From the first moment she had stepped into this house,
Audra had felt as if she belonged here. It was as if she had
returned after a long journey to a place she had always
known. In a way it had been like coming home . . . home
to High Cleugh. It was not that Calpher House resembled
her beloved former home; as houses they were entirely
different in architecture and furnishings. What she had
found so familiar, had recognized with such clarity, was the
presence of love within these walls.

For the most part, it was the happiest year that Audra
had spent since her mother had died and tragedy had
struck their little family.

She fitted in well at Calpher House.

Because of her upbringing, her disposition and personality, everyone found her a pleasure to be around, and she was
popular upstairs and downstairs. The Bells were kind; the
servants treated her with a deference and respect that was
marked by friendliness.

After years of frugality and Spartan living at the hospital,
she was now surrounded by enormous luxury and comfort,
the likes of which she had never known even at High
Cleugh, where money for anything other than the real
essentials had been fairly scarce most of the time. All of
their pleasureful little extras had come from Uncle Peter.

The Bells were successful, affluent people and they could
afford the best. And because of Mrs. Bell's giving nature
there was an overabundance of everything.

Wonderfully delicious meals emerged from Mrs. Jackson's amazing kitchen, and Audra also got a chance to taste
such delicacies as *pâté de foie gras*, caviar and smoked
salmon. Crystal dishes of bonbons and nuts and Turkish
Delight were scattered across small occasional tables in the

elegant blue living room, for anyone to nibble on who wished, and even the everyday nursery meals could hardly be called *everyday* because of the way they tasted. Such things as steak-and-kidney pudding, apple dumplings, bacon-and-egg pie, Irish stew, and pork, beef and lamb roasts all had the most distinctive, mouth-watering flavors. As far as Audra was concerned, the cook was the first person to rival her mother in a kitchen; Mrs. Jackson was forever coming up with something extra-special to tempt their palates. Audra's favorites were Little Pigs of Heaven, a warm chocolate dessert that literally melted in the mouth; and Bandit's Joy, a hot potato dish flavored with honey and nutmeg that made a perfect accompaniment to saddle of mutton. She had asked Mrs. Jackson for the recipes for these dishes. On very special occasions, Mr. Agiter, the butler, had been instructed by Mr. Bell to serve her a glass of sparkling, ice-cold champagne. But she was already familiar with this wine, since it had not been out of the ordinary for her Uncle Peter to bring a bottle to celebrate her mother's birthday, or for Christmas Day at High Cleugh. She and Frederick and William had always been allowed one small glass by their mother.

Apart from the delectable food and vintage wines which seemed to flow without cease at Calpher House, there was a plethora of other things which added their distinctive touches to the sense of opulence that prevailed throughout.

Innumerable bowls and vases of flowers and exotic plants punctuated every room downstairs; the latest magazines and newspapers, current novels and other books spilled over large circular tables in the library, in Mrs. Bell's study and most especially in the family parlor where everyone seemed to congregate at night. Sofas and chairs were plump and inviting with piles of soft cushions, or they had their arms draped with fluffy mohair throws from Scotland, to be used on colder evenings wrapped around legs and shoulders.

Startled at first though she had been, and even a bit overwhelmed by all this luxury in one house, Audra had grown accustomed to it. Whilst it would be true to say that she enjoyed the comfort and the cosseting, she nonetheless did not consider it of any great importance in her life. The real reason she was happy at Calpher House was because her employers and the staff were all really good people who cared about others and their well-being.

These aspects of her job aside, it had been a fine year for Audra Kenton in other respects.

The letters which came from her brothers were much more positive these days, and were written in the same optimistic vein that had enhanced their earliest epistles to her. Frederick was growing stronger in health every week, and things had improved immeasurably for them. They both had good jobs in Sydney at long last. William was working in the circulation department of the Sydney *Morning Herald;* Frederick had become private secretary to an industrialist, a Mr. Roland Matheson, and Audra was happy for them, and proud of the way they had coped with their initial bad luck and daunting setbacks. And knowing they were no longer in difficult straits made her own continuing sense of loss and yearning for them that much easier to bear.

Then again, she and Gwen had been able to spend a great deal of their free time together. Mrs. Bell had kindly given her permission to invite Gwen to stay overnight at Calpher House on numerous occasions; she herself frequently traveled across to Horsforth to spend her day off with Gwen. Sometimes they took the tramcar into Leeds to browse in the stores and window-shop, and she was beginning to know the city well. Quite often they went to the picture house, and recently they had seen their first talking picture, *The Jazz Singer,* starring Al Jolson.

June had been a particularly happy month for Audra, mostly because of the attention everyone paid to her twentieth birthday. How different it had been from the previous year, when she had spent that very special day in her life entirely alone. Her brothers' cards had arrived from Australia not only in time but two days early; on the third, a small celebration was held in the nursery, with presents from the Bells and the staff at Calpher House.

And later that week, on Saturday, Mrs. Thornton and Gwen had given a party for her at The Meadow. There had been a splendid summer tea on the lawn. The table, covered in a white cloth, had groaned under the weight of all manner of lovely things—cucumber-and-tomato sandwiches, a Yorkshire pork pie, trifle, strawberries and cream, big pots of hot tea, plus an iced cake with the message *Happy Birthday, Audra* written on it in pink-icing sugar and twenty pink candles encircling the edge. And each member of her friend's family had given her a small but meaningful gift. After tea they had trooped inside for dancing to the latest records which they had played on Gwen's new gramophone. They had done the Charleston to the strains of "Black Bottom," "Ain't She Sweet," and "Yes Sir, That's My Baby," fox-trotted slowly to "Blue Skies" and "Among My Souvenirs," and everyone had enjoyed themselves that night.

Charlie had been present, along with his brothers, Jeremy and Harry, Mike Lesley, his best friend, and a couple of his chums from medical school. He was still attentive to her whenever he got the opportunity, even though she did her best to discourage him.

Once she had moved to Leeds the previous December and settled in with the Bells, Audra had spoken to Gwen about her brother. She had explained to her friend in the sweetest way that, as nice as Charlie was, he was not for her. She had asked Gwen not to encourage Charlie anymore. Gwen had said she understood and agreed at once to stop "fanning the flames." But Audra had seen the hurt in her friend's eyes, and she had quickly added that it had nothing to do with Charlie per se, that men in general did not interest her for the time being. She had then announced, and in a very firm voice, that she had no intention of getting married, of settling down, until she was thirty at least.

Gwen had looked at her askance on hearing this, had eyed Audra with a degree of skepticism, but she had refrained from making any sort of comment. At least until last month—November the fifth to be exact—when she had come to Upper Armley to join in their celebrations on Bonfire Night.

Mrs. Bell had told Audra she could invite Gwen to spend

the night at Calpher House, since they were both off duty
the following day. After one of the cook's extra-special
nursery teas and as soon as it grew dark, they had gone
outside for the lighting of the bonfire that Fipps, the
gardener, had made in the grounds. They had shared the
family's fun, watching the fireworks, waving the sparklers
which Mr. Bell had produced and eating piping hot
chestnuts and roasted potatoes pulled from the embers of
the fire. And then the two of them had gone off to the Guy
Fawkes Day party and dance at Christ Church Parish Hall
in Ridge Road.

Audra first saw the young man when everyone was
crowding around the huge bonfire outside the hall, gathered to watch the burning of the effigy of Guy Fawkes.

He was alone, standing near the porch, leaning against
the wall, smoking a cigarette. As he nonchalantly tossed it
to the ground, then stubbed his toe on it, he glanced across
at the commotion around the bonfire, noticed her, smiled.

Audra looked back at him and experienced a queer
sensation, one that was unfamiliar to her. She felt suddenly
faint and a little breathless, as if she had been punched.

His face was clearly illuminated in the glow from the fire,
and she saw that he was most arresting in appearance.

His dark hair, which came to a widow's peak above a wide
brow, was brushed to one side, parted on the left, and he
had dark brows, light-colored eyes. His face was well
articulated, sensitive, but it was the purity reflected in it
that struck her so forcibly, made such a strong and lasting
impression.

Their eyes connected. And locked. He gave her a hard,
penetrating stare.

She flushed to her roots, looked quickly away.

A moment later, when she and Gwen turned around to
go into the parochial hall, Audra noticed immediately that
he was no longer propping up the wall, and she filled with
disappointment.

Once they were inside, her eyes searched for him, but he
seemed to have disappeared. She waited for him to come
back, but he did not, and the dance fell flat for her after
that. As the evening progressed, Audra found it impossible

to tear her eyes away from the door for very long, and she
silently prayed that he would return. There was something
about him that intrigued her.

Although she was asked to dance several times and
accepted these invitations, for most of the evening Audra
sat it out on the long bench with the other wallflowers. She
was quite content to be an observer, watching the dancers,
in particular Gwen, who twirled around the floor with
various young bucks from the neighborhood, obviously
enjoying herself immensely. But Audra thought that none
of Gwen's partners looked half as handsome or as fascinating
as the dark young man who had so engaged her interest
earlier.

Audra had almost given up hope that he would make an
appearance again when he came barreling through the
door, looking slightly flushed and out of breath, and stood at
the far side of the hall, glancing about. At the exact moment
that the band leader announced the last waltz, he spotted
her. His eyes lit up, and he walked directly across the floor
to her and, with a faint smile, asked her if she would care to
dance.

Gripped by a sudden internal shaking, unable to speak,
Audra nodded and rose.

He was taller than she had realized, at least five feet
nine, perhaps even six feet, with long legs, and lean and
slender though he was, he had broad shoulders. There was
an easy, natural way about him that communicated itself to
her instantly, and he moved with great confidence and
panache. He led her onto the floor, took her in his arms
masterfully, and swept her away as the band struck up *The
Blue Danube*.

During the course of the dance he made several casual
remarks, but Audra, tongue-tied, remained mute, knowing
she was unable to respond coherently. He said, at one
moment, "What's up then, cat got your tongue?"

She managed to whisper, "No."

Glancing down at her with curiosity, he frowned, but he
did not bother to say anything further, appeared to be lost
in his thoughts or concentrating on the dance.

When the music stopped, he thanked her politely,

escorted her back to the bench, inclined his head, strolled off.

Her eyes followed him all the way to the front door. And as he walked out into the dark winter night, she wondered who he was and if she would ever see him again. She desperately hoped she would.

Later when she and Gwen were hurrying up Town Street, making their way back to Calpher House, Gwen suddenly blurted out: "Well, I must say, for someone who protests they're not interested in men, you were certainly mesmerized by that chap you had the last dance with. But I can tell you this, Audra, he's bad news. Oh yes, definitely, lovey."

Audra, startled, asked, "How can you say he's bad news? You don't even *know* him."

Gwen took hold of Audra's arm in her usual possessive way, slipped her own through it. She said, "I can tell just by looking at him that he's a real devil. I'm always suspicious of the pretty ones. *Very wary*. They generally end up breaking some poor woman's heart, lovey, maybe even two or three hearts, for that matter. You'd be much better off with somebody like our Charlie. And you know how *he* feels about *you*, lovey. *He hasn't changed*."

Audra said nothing. Gwen's remarks about the young man irritated and annoyed her. She considered them to be unwarranted and just a shade preposterous under the circumstances. Presumptuous, in fact, and for the first time in their friendship, she was put out with Gwen. The next morning, still rankling somewhat, Audra scrupulously avoided referring to the evening before, and she and Gwen did not discuss the young man again.

But Audra could not help thinking about him.

In the days which immediately followed the encounter, she kept recalling certain things about that night and about him . . . the way he had looked down at her, narrowly, speculatively, through the greenest eyes she had ever seen . . . the turbulent emotions he had aroused in her, feelings she had not believed really existed except in the novels on Mrs. Bell's shelves . . . his ineffable grace as he

had moved them around the dance floor . . . the true
classical beauty of his face, so unusual in a man.

Now, nearly two months afterward, Audra was still asking
herself why she never ran across him in Upper Armley.
Ever since the dance she had expected to do so, and she
never ceased to look for him when she went out and about
with the child who was in her charge. She was convinced
the young man came from these parts for she could
recognize the local accent when she heard it.

As Audra focused her thoughts on him, an echo of his
voice reverberated clearly in her head, and an image of his
face leapt before her eyes. And despite the warmth of the
quilt, she shivered unexpectedly and gooseflesh speckled
her skin. She wrapped her arms around her body, hugging
herself. She pictured his face close to hers on the pillow,
tried to imagine what it would be like to be kissed by him,
touched by him, held by him. Since their brief encounter,
the mysterious dark young man had haunted her, intruded
on her thoughts at the oddest times.

Presently Audra opened her eyes and endeavored to
quench the unfamiliar longings stirring within her. Until
she had met *him*, danced with *him*, Audra had never known
sexual desire, and of late some of the strange, new feelings
she was experiencing confused and frightened her, yet
excited her at the same time. She pressed her face into the
pillow, wanting to block out the memory of him, and
discovered, as she had so often in the past few weeks, that
she was unable to expunge the image of his face, his
unbelievable eyes. She knew she wanted him.

Turning onto her back, she lay very still, staring up at the
ceiling, her eyes wide, unblinking, and she wondered what
she would do if she did not run into him again. Dismay
gripped her, then instantly dissipated. Audra believed that
they *would* meet and that they would come to know each
other well. Very well indeed. She felt this in her bones.

A sudden clattering in the corridor outside her bedroom
pierced the early morning silence.

Audra started in surprise, then cocked her head, listened. She heard a stifled exclamation, then low unintelli-

gible mutterings, followed by the sound of feet clomping into the adjoining day nursery.

Audra knew that it was Cora going about her morning chores. She suspected that the housemaid had dropped the coal scuttle, which was not an unusual occurrence by any means. Cora, who was perpetually cheerful, had turned out to be a friendly soul, but she was also the clumsiest person Audra had ever met. A day did not go by without a breakage of one kind or another, and the culprit, sadly, was always poor Cora.

There was a loud knock on the door, and Cora's scrubbed and shining face appeared around it. "Mornin', Miss Audra."

"Good morning, Cora," Audra said, pushing herself up on one elbow, smiling in the half light.

"Is it all right if I comes in then, Miss Audra? Ter make t'fire for yer?"

"Yes, of course, Cora."

Cora's plump little body, encased in her pink-striped morning uniform, rotated across the room like a fast-spinning top. She dumped the coal scuttle and the ash pan down on the hearth unceremoniously, then spun over to the huge window. "It's ever so cold out this mornin', Miss. Arctic weather, so Fipps says. Aye, he says it's cold enough ter freeze t'balls off a brass monkey, that he does."

"Really, Cora!"

"That's what he said ter me, Miss."

"But you shouldn't repeat something vulgar like that, Cora," Audra reprimanded softly.

"No, I don't expects I should, least ways not in yer presence, Miss Audra." This was said somewhat apologetically, but, nevertheless, Cora threw her a cheeky grin as she hurried back to the fireplace. She asked, "And what are yer doin' termorra night then, Miss Audra?"

"Nothing special, Cora. My friend Miss Thornton is on night duty at the Infirmary for the next two weeks, so I won't be going to any New Year's Eve parties. I'll be staying here at Calpher House."

"Oh but Mr. Agiter allus has a party for t'staff, yer knows." Cora glanced over her shoulder, smiled with her usual engaging cheerfulness, added, "Yer were ever so shy last December, when yer first started here, and yer wouldn't come downstairs, but I hopes yer'll be with us this year, ooh I *do*, Miss Audra, ever so much."

"Yes, I will, Cora. Mr. Agiter has already invited me, and I'm looking forward to joining you all for a glass of champagne around midnight . . . to toast in 1928."

The child's name was Theophilus, Theo for short, and Audra had grown to truly love him in the year she had been taking care of him.

He was an odd-looking little boy, not exactly plain, but then neither was he fancy.

The first time she had set eyes on him, she decided that he was highly individualistic. This turned out to be true— and in many more ways than merely his appearance. Theophilus had a plump, perfectly round little face, not unlike a suet pudding, but his skin was pink and white rather than doughy or pasty in color. His fair hair, soft, silky, straight, had a way of flopping down over two sharply observing black eyes that resembled bright little chips of coal, and he was forever pushing it away with an impatient gesture.

It often struck Audra that these very dark eyes and the pale blond hair didn't quite go together, but then that was Theophilus. He seemed to be made up entirely of spare parts, each bit individually attractive if not specifically designed to go with the others.

Not matched up, are you, my little love? Audra murmured under her breath as she brushed his hair. His appearance usually preoccupied her for a few minutes before they went out, and this morning was no exception. She put the brush down, stepped away, regarded him critically, her head on one side. Reaching out, she straightened his tie, nodded in satisfaction, then bending over, she planted a kiss on his cheek.

"There you are, all ready!" she exclaimed, taking his hands in hers, helping him to jump down off the table. "And you're as bright as a new penny today, Theo."

He looked up at her through solemn eyes which were curiously wise and knowing for a six-year-old. "I hope the doctor also thinks that."

She bit back a smile of amusement, said, "I'm sure he will. Now, run along to see your mother, whilst I get my things together, and then we can be off."

"Oh yes, I had better do that. Before she leaves for Leeds. My spending money is due today." He set his face determinedly, marched toward the door in small but purposeful strides and disappeared into the corridor.

Audra watched him go, turned away, laughing to herself as she crossed the spacious and comfortably furnished day nursery. She had a few minutes to spare before following the boy downstairs, and she stood with her back to the fire, warming herself, thinking of her young charge.

Theophilus Bell never ceased to amaze and amuse Audra. He was a precocious child, although his precocity was not offensive. The cook said he was "old-fashioned" and this description fitted him perfectly. Audra was not a bit surprised he was the way he was—so serious and self-possessed. He had spent most of his young life with adults; even his sisters were much older than he. Pandora, who had married in the spring and moved out of Calpher House, was twenty-two. Antonia and Felicity, both now attending finishing school in Switzerland, were nineteen and eighteen respectively, and all three happened to be sophisticated young women who were well educated, well traveled and had been exposed to a variety of people and a great deal of radical thought in this house. And so they also were much older than their years, and, not unnaturally, they had had an influence on their small brother. The girls called Theo "the afterthought," and although Audra disliked this term, considered it to be rather unkind, she realized that there was a degree of truth in it. He had been born to Mrs. Bell when she was forty-two, long after she had expected to bear any more children, and, as she had said to Audra, "Theo just missed being a change-of-life baby, thank heavens."

Audra considered it a small miracle that the Bells had not fallen into the usual trap of pampering and spoiling Theo,

which so often happened to an only son who came to his
parents later in life and who was their pride and joy. He *was*
indulged occasionally, but this seemed to have little or no
effect on him, and he was not given to making excessive
demands on anyone, nor was he a temperamental child.

In actuality, Theo was a lot like his mother. Certainly he
had inherited Irène Bell's quick-wittedness, her intelligence and her studious nature. And if he was sometimes
unnerving in his forthrightness, he was, nevertheless, a
good child, very obedient, and he had never given Audra
one moment's trouble in the past twelve months.

Ten loud chimes, echoing through from the bedroom,
suddenly alerted Audra to the hour. Theo had been
suffering with a sore throat, and although he was better she
was taking him to the doctor this morning for a checkup.

Hurrying through into the other room, she glanced at
herself in the glass, smoothed one hand over her hair,
newly bobbed that summer, then went to the wardrobe in
the corner. She took out her heavy winter coat and hat, and
a thick woolen scarf and gloves in anticipation of the Arctic
weather which had apparently descended on them, just as
the gardener had predicted it would yesterday.

CHAPTER NINE

His name was Vincent Crowther and he was something of a
rebel.

He was born in the year 1903, at five minutes to midnight
on the twelfth day of June, in the middle of the worst
thunderstorm the new century had witnessed.

A lusty, robust nine-pound baby, he came screaming into
the world, fists flailing, face red and contorted, and giving
vent to such a fierce and angry display of temperament the
doctor told the midwife that the baby's tantrums were only
outmatched by the violence of the weather outside.

His mother secretly called him her Stormy Petrel
thereafter, and she was the least surprised of anyone when

her rebellious child grew up to be an equally rebellious man, one who was a maverick to boot and who always stood out in a crowd.

In a sense he was a natural star, one who drew others to him by sheer force of personality, dashing looks and more than his fair share of charm. Further, it did him no harm that he had what his father called "the gift of the gab."

The firstborn of Eliza and Alfred Crowther's eight children, Vincent boasted an almost girlish beauty as a child, but this turned into a masculine type of handsomeness as he matured. And there never was any question about his virility. It was like a gloss on him. In consequence, women fell at his feet swooning, and they had done so since he was sixteen. And he was well versed in their ways, was master of these love and sex games at a tender age. He was twenty-four.

His looks dazzled.

It was his coloring that was so sensational. The gleaming black hair and the black brows were in marked contrast to a light, creamy complexion and cheeks that held a tinge of pink like the bloom on a peach; he had cool green eyes, the color of light, clear tourmalines, fringed with thick black lashes. His eyes and his skin were the envy of his sisters—and most other women.

Matched to the striking coloring and handsome profile was a superb athletic body. He was exactly five feet nine and a half inches tall, well muscled, firm and taut and without one ounce of fat or flab on him.

Immaculate at all times, Vincent considered himself to be a bit of a dandy, loved clothes, wore them with flair and elegance. He cut quite a swathe wherever he went, especially on the dance floor, where his easy grace and good looks showed to such advantage.

He was his mother's favorite.

His siblings were aware of this. They were not jealous. In fact, they shared their mother's feelings about him to some extent. His brothers admired him; his sisters adored him.

Only his father treated him like an ordinary person.

Alfred Crowther loved his firstborn child, but he had no illusions about him. A former sergeant major in the

Seaforth Highlanders, Alfred was a veteran of two great wars, having fought the Boers on the African veldt and the Germans on the fields of Flanders. Subsequently, he knew men and their motivations, could read them well, and his own son was no exception. He had a great deal of insight into Vincent.

Alfred recognized there was a lot of devilishness in the boy, not to mention temperament and a good measure of vanity. He thought Vincent was too handsome by far for his own good. But, being a realist, Alfred knew there was not much point in worrying about this eldest child of his, who had been born with the looks of a matinee idol. Fretting would not alter these facts. The elder Crowther believed that what was meant to happen eventually happened. His fatalistic attitude could be ascribed to his Irish mother, Martha, who, when he was growing up, had constantly told him, "What will be, will be, Alf, sure an' it will. 'Tis *preordained*, I am thinkin', this life each one of us poor souls be livin' in this hard and cruel world."

Father and son were good companions. They enjoyed sharing a pint of beer, usually stopped off at the pub together at weekends, and often they went to race meetings in Doncaster and York, especially in the summer weather. However, despite a certain masculine camaraderie, there was not as much intimacy between them as might have been expected. It was his mother who was Vincent's confidante and friend. She always had been. She always would be—until the day she died.

His manifest physical attributes aside, Vincent Crowther was no dunce. In fact, quite the opposite was the truth. He was quick and intelligent; he had powerful analytical ability, which would serve him well later in life, and a retentive memory.

But coming from the working class as he did, he had left Armley Council School when he was fourteen and had found himself a job in one of the tailoring shops in Armley. He had quickly grown bored, mainly because his interests lay elsewhere. He was particularly drawn to building and construction and frequently wished he could have studied architecture.

After leaving the tailoring shop, he had a short spell laboring in the local brickyard, before finally finding an opening with a building firm. He was currently learning his trade; he liked working in the open air, drew pleasure and satisfaction from seeing each building take shape and grow and so fulfill the architect's original vision.

Sometimes Vincent told himself he was going to enroll in night school in Leeds, to learn draftsmanship, but he put this off, was always distracted by other more pleasurable activities. He was partial to dancing, and he had been a voracious reader when a boy, but otherwise he had no hobbies to speak of. For the most part, he spent his free time drinking with his cronies and could usually be found propping up the bar in the tap room of one of the local pubs, quaffing down pints or studying a *tissue*, the pink racing sheet that was published every weekday and was his bible.

He was engrossed in his *tissue* on this cold Saturday morning in late December, wondering which horses to back at today's Doncaster races. In particular he was concentrating on the runners in the one o'clock race, turning the salient facts over in his clever mind, considering the virtues and the weakness of the trainers and the jockeys as well as those of the different horses, and carefully weighing the odds.

Vincent was seated at the table in the center of the basement kitchen in the Crowther home at Armley, a tall, Victorian terrace house with two upper floors and huge attics under the eaves. The kitchen, with a big window fronting onto a patch of garden and yard, was a large yet cozy room; eminently inviting, it was comfortably furnished in the manner of a parlor, which was the custom in these parts.

The focal point in the room was the fireplace. This was actually a Yorkshire range, so called because it combined an open fire with an adjoining oven. The range also boasted an arm for supporting a kettle or a stew pot over the fire, and a boiler for heating water. All of these elements were built into the one unit which was about four and a half feet in height and the same in width.

The black iron range was surmounted by a heavy polished wood mantelpiece. On this stood a fancy chiming clock, two brass candlesticks, a tobacco jar, a rack holding Alfred's pipes and a container of spills. The hearth was encircled by a heavy brass fender that was cleaned with Brasso by one of the girls every Friday, and it glittered like gold in the dancing flames of the fire, banked high up the chimney back. Two green-moquette wing chairs flanked the fireplace, faced each other across a large broadloom rug patterned with blood red roses on a deep green background.

In point of fact, roses abounded in this kitchen. They were Eliza's favorite flowers. Pink and white cabbage roses entwined into garlands flowed down the wallpaper to meet scarlet rambler roses scattered all over the green linoleum; rose-patterned white china filled the shelves of a Welsh dresser positioned in a corner; pillows embroidered with yellow rosebuds marched across the dark green leather sofa set against the far wall.

It was a cheerful room with a gay and welcoming ambiance, and it was generally the center of activity, the heart of the family's home life. But this morning it was strangely deserted.

Vincent was alone.

He was glad to have quiet for once, to be able to pursue the serious work of picking out his potential winners in absolute tranquility, without the distracting racket often created by some of his brothers and sisters.

Taking a sip of tea, he continued to peer at the racing newspaper, frowning to himself in his concentration. He had been at this task for almost an hour, and at last he made several selections, wrote down the names of his horses on a scrap of paper, sat staring at the list for a moment. Slowly he nodded his head, satisfied he had made the best choices; then he reached for the packet of Woodbines.

He leaned back in his chair, sat smoking reflectively.

For no reason at all he suddenly thought of the girl. *Again*. She had a way of popping into his head when he least expected. He had met her only once in his life, but when he closed his eyes, he could see her face so clearly, and in such detail, he might have known her forever.

When he had first noticed her standing near the bonfire in the grounds of the Parish Hall, he had instantly and instinctively understood, and without the benefit of knowing her, that she was not the type of young woman whom a man played around with. *She was serious business*.

And since he was not interested in being serious with any girl, or of starting a relationship that would lead to the terrible bondage of marriage, he had fled, rushed to the White Horse for a game of darts and a drink with the lads. But just before ten o'clock he had run all the way back to the hall, hoping to have the last waltz with her.

How shy she had been, so stiff and unbending. Her manner and her attitude had put him off, and he had wandered out of the hall, discouraged and also baffled by her, asking himself why she had bothered to dance with him in the first place. She could have so easily declined his invitation.

But he had been unable to forget her.

Vincent sighed, took a long drag on his cigarette, blew smoke rings up into the air, watched them float away and evaporate as they did. And he decided that thinking about the diminutive Venus de Milo of the bright blue eyes and gorgeous legs was a hopeless waste of time. For one thing, she had apparently evaporated—just like the smoke rings. Ever since bonfire night, he had made a point of popping down to the church dances for a few minutes, looking for her, and he had kept his eyes peeled when he had gone about his business in Armley. He had never once run into her. Furthermore, none of the regulars who attended the church dances every Wednesday and Saturday seemed to know who she was. He had made innumerable inquiries about her for the past two months. The only bit of information he had been able to garner was that her busty blond girlfriend, also nameless it seemed, was a nurse at the Infirmary. Some good that did him. He knew he had about as much chance of ever meeting Blue Eyes again as a snowball in hell.

Perhaps that's just as well, he muttered under his breath. All I need is a *steady* . . . not bloody likely, I don't.

At this moment the front door flew open so unexpectedly and with such force, Vincent sat up with a jerk, looking startled. An icy blast of air blew right through the kitchen, chilling him. It brought with it Laurette and Maggie, two of his three sisters.

They had been to the co-op to do the weekend marketing and each carried two shopping bags filled to overflowing. They were bundled up in navy-blue winter topcoats, green-and-black tartan tam o'shanters and matching long woolen scarves. The cold wind had given them polished-apple cheeks, turned their noses into bright red cherries. Their eyes sparkled and there was such a gaiety and liveliness about them that they brought a delighted smile to his face.

"Hello, Vincent," they chorused, grinning at him.

"Hello, you two beauties," he responded, then exclaimed, "For God's sake, close that door, Maggie."

"Oh, sorry," the twelve-year-old girl said and pushed it with her foot. It banged so hard the frosted-glass panel rattled.

"Watch that glass!" Vincent cautioned and shook his head, mildly exasperated with her.

Maggie mumbled, "Sorry," and followed her elder sister to the counter near the sink, where she deposited her shopping bags of groceries.

Turning to face her brother, starting to unbutton her coat, Laurette said, "It's very quiet in here, Vincent. Where is everybody then?"

"Upstairs. Or out."

"Who's upstairs?" Maggie asked, always inquisitive. Shedding her coat, she flung it down on the sofa.

"Hang that up, young lady," Laurette instructed, giving her a sharp look.

Maggie pulled a face but she did as she was told. She pressed, "Who's upstairs then?"

"Our Mam. She's dusting the front rooms. And Jack, who's reading to Danny. Mam says he's got to stay in bed today—because of his bad cold," Vincent explained.

"I knew it! I just knew he wouldn't be any better!"

Maggie cried shrilly, rolling her eyes dramatically, showing exaggerated alarm. "I *told* Mam that. He coughed and coughed all night. Poor little Danny, he's always badly. But what can you expect, he's the runt of the litter." She continued to cluck sympathetically like a middle-aged matron of vast experience, then finished in a superior, knowing tone, "Change-of-life babies are often weak in health."

Vincent averted his head, biting down on his laughter. Maggie was a card. None of them ever knew what she would come out with next. His father said she was as old as the hills.

Laurette, however, was not in the least amused, and the look she gave her young sister was stern, disapproving. She thought Maggie was impertinent at times, that the girl saw and heard far too much for her age. But Laurette said nothing. She walked over to the coat closet and put her own things away. Then she took a cup and saucer out of the cupboard above the sink, joined Vincent at the table. She lifted the cozy, felt the pot, poured herself a cup of tea, added milk and sugar.

Vincent watched her all the while, his expression loving. He was concerned about Laurette's well-being at the moment. Just over a year ago she had married their first cousin Jimmy, but it had not worked out. She had come back home to live three months ago, much to his relief. He had believed that particular union to be doomed right from the outset, had never had much time for his cousin, whom he considered to be a bit of a wet rag.

Laurette was a sweet-natured girl, and at twenty-two she was the nearest to Vincent in age. They had always been very close. She was lovely looking with fair, wavy hair, a sensitive face and smokey gray eyes that were enigmatic and soulful. Tall, slender, she had a frame and a build similar to her brother's, but it was young Maggie who truly resembled him with her gypsy-dark hair, widow's peak and large green eyes that were a reflection of his. Olive, the middle sister, was more like Laurette to look at, but she too had dark hair, and she had inherited her mother's pale blue eyes. Olive, who was twenty, had married her childhood

sweetheart when she was eighteen, and she and her
husband Hal lived near by.

Maggie now joined Vincent and Laurette at the kitchen
table.

She stood next to her favorite brother, rested one hand
on his shoulder and with the other she slapped a packet of
Woodbines down in front of him, along with some loose
change.

"Here's your cigs, our Vincent. And don't smoke 'em all
at once either. Because I'm not going out again today. Not
for nobody, I'm not. Not even you. So there!" Flopping
down on the chair next to him, she threw him a challenging
look, added, "If you want to know, I'm fed up of being
everybody's blinking errand boy!"

He threw back his head and roared. "Aren't you the
tough little tiddler this morning. But thanks for getting my
cigs, love."

Laurette said, "I can't believe everybody went out
. . . on a cruel day like this . . . why, it's blue murder
out there, Vincent. Where on earth have they all gone?"

"Dad went to the barber's to get a haircut. Our Frank,
the aspiring equestrian, is at Hardcastle's stables, helping to
exercise the horses. And the learned Bill took his books
back to the library."

"I see." Laurette sipped her tea. There was a short
pause. Then she asked, "Olive's not been up this morning,
has she?"

"No, not yet."

"Oh, I am glad I haven't missed her. We're supposed to
be going to the old-time dancing tonight, and I want to
make my arrangements with her." Laurette paused and
smiled at her brother as an idea struck her. "Would you like
to come with us, Vincent?"

"I would!" Maggie interjected eagerly, swinging her eyes
to her sister. "Let me come with you and Olive, Laurette.
Please."

"No, you can't, you're too young," Laurette said. "Well,
Vincent, what about it?"

He shook his head. "No. Thanks for asking, though."

"But why not?" Laurette demanded. "You'd enjoy it. Come on, say you'll come with us."

He shook his head more vehemently.

Maggie cried, "Oh he doesn't want to go *there*, Laurette! It's too tame. He always goes to the *pub* on Saturday nights. But first he goes down to the Parish Hall and has a look round . . . giving all the girls the once-over, that's what I've heard. I bet that's why he stands in front of that there mirror over there, titivating himself for hours on end. I'm not surprised it drives our dad bats. He's vain, our Vincent is, and he fancies himself. Anybody would think he's a girl the way he looks in the glass all the time."

Vincent glared at her. "You're getting to be a right cheeky little bugger, do you know that, our Maggie?"

Maggie stiffened in her chair, shrieked, "You'd better not let me dad hear you call me that, our Vincent! Or he'll land you a clout that'll send you right into the middle of next week!"

"Huh! Fat chance of that!" Vincent shot back.

"Now you two, quieten down," Laurette hushed, scowling at them. She wagged a finger at Maggie. "You *are* getting too big for your breeches, and so you'd better watch it from now on. As for you, Vincent, you ought to know better than to swear at her. Mam doesn't like that either, you know."

"Aye," Vincent muttered, annoyed with himself for permitting the girl to get his goat in the way that she had.

Maggie, genuinely regretting that she had teased him, leaned across the table, peered into his handsome face, saw that it was cold and closed. She filled with chagrin, said softly, "I'm ever so sorry, Vincent, really I am." She reached out, squeezed his arm. "Let's be friends again. Oh and by the by, you said you'd give me something, for going for your Woodbines."

"If you're not careful, it'll be a thick ear," he growled.

"Well, I never!" Maggie gasped. "It's the last time I'll do an errand for you, Vincent Crowther. You don't keep your promises."

For a reason he couldn't explain he began to laugh. His eyes twinkled as he reached out, rumpled his little sister's hair. Then he pushed a sixpence toward her. "There you are, love, that's for your money box."

Maggie beamed at him. "Oh no, I'm going to spend it immediately. Thanks."

Vincent was thoughtful. After lighting a cigarette he murmured in a low tone, "Don't you think it's about time you settled things with Jimmy, Laurette? Went to see a solicitor in Leeds . . . about a divorce?"

"Yes, it is, and as a matter of fact, I have an appointment with a solicitor next Saturday. Jimmy's agreed to everything," Laurette said.

"Dad's going to be ever so pleased to hear *that!*" Maggie announced before Vincent had a chance to say a word. "He never did think much of that marriage of yours, Laurette. He says that's how idiots get born . . . first cousins marrying and having babies, I mean."

Laurette gaped at her. She paled and her soft gray eyes suddenly swam. She stood up unsteadily, rushed over to the door leading to the staircase, yanked it open. "I think I'll go and help Mam," she whispered in a hoarse voice and flew up the stairs.

Vincent was furious with Maggie and he turned on her angrily. "Will you never learn, lass? Your mouth's always open and your foot's always in it, for Christ's sake!"

"What have I said *wrong* then?" Maggie wailed. "And anyway, our dad *didn't* like her marrying Jimmy Wells."

Vincent sprang up, his anger spiraling. He looked down at his youngest sister in dismay. It took all of his self-control to keep his hands off her. He wanted to shake her until she rattled. Finally he said, "You know as well as I do how upset Laurette's been because she didn't get pregnant."

Her defiance fully intact, Maggie declared, "Well, if what Dad says is true, it's a good job she didn't, and that's a fact!"

Vincent lifted his eyes to the ceiling, groaned out loud. "Old wives' tales . . . our Dad's out of date, living in Dick's days." He strode across to the closet, took out his overcoat.

Maggie cried, "Where are you going, Vincent?"

"Anywhere to escape you."

CHAPTER TEN

Vincent saw her through the window of the pet shop.

For a moment he could not believe his eyes.

He stood staring, transfixed. And then he cupped his hands around his face, pressed closer to the glass. Oh yes, it was her all right. As large as life, looking at budgies. Then he noticed the child standing next to her.

Vincent's heart took a dip to his boots.

Was she a married woman? No, that was not possible. She had not been wearing a ring at the dance. And she was certainly too young to have a child as big as the one accompanying her. No, the boy was most likely her brother. And she was probably buying him a budgie, just as he himself had decided to buy his little brother Danny a pet of some sort. That was the reason he had directed his steps toward the shop in the first place.

Well, Vincent thought, standing here isn't going to get me anywhere, so I might as well go inside. His hand went to his tie automatically, and he straightened the knot; then, taking a deep breath, he opened the shop door.

The tinkling of the bell caused the girl to glance over her shoulder. At the sight of him her eyes widened. Seemingly she was as astonished as he had been a moment before.

Vincent smiled at her.

She smiled back, her face dimpling.

He thought her smile was quite the most dazzling he had seen in a long time. Encouraged by her pleasant reaction, he strode across the shop.

She turned around to face him, watched his progress in her direction with quickening interest.

As he drew to a standstill in front of her, Vincent saw the expectant look in her eyes. He took off his hat, stood holding it in his hands. He smiled again, said, "Excuse me . . . I wonder if you remember me?"

"Why yes, of course I do. We had the last waltz at the Parish Hall . . . on Bonfire Night. And I must apologize for not thanking you for asking me to dance that evening. You must have thought me very ungracious."

She was a lady. He stared at her, startled, and momentarily flustered. His voice fled and so did his nerve. Why would a girl of her obvious breeding be interested in the likes of him? he wondered, clutching his hat all that much tighter. A feeling of enormous disappointment trickled through him. *She* was beyond *his* reach. Oh yes, most assuredly she was. And just as she had been tongue-tied at the dance, now it was his turn to be struck dumb, and he felt like a ninny.

There was an awkward silence.

It was the child who broke it. He asked, in a shrill little voice, "What's *your* name?"

The girl exclaimed sharply, but in a low tone, "Now, now, that's most rude of you. Mind your manners, young man."

"It's Vincent Crowther," Vincent said swiftly, grabbing this opportunity. He was surprised that his voice sounded so normal, and this helped to restore his diminished confidence. He glanced down at the boy and grinned at him, thankful for his presence.

The child turned his small bright face up to Vincent's, thrust his hand toward him, announced, "And I'm Theophilus Bell of Calpher House, Upper Armley."

Vincent shook his hand, endeavoring to match the child's enormous solemnity as he said, "I'm very pleased to meet you. And if you don't mind me saying so, that's quite a mouthful of a name you've got, by gum it is, lad."

"It means *beloved of God* in Greek," Theophilus explained, puffing out his little chest importantly. He gave Vincent a shimmering smile and added, "But you can call me Theo for short."

"That's right nice of you. Thanks very much, I will." Raising his head, Vincent now directed his gaze at the young woman. He cleared his throat, and having entirely regained his composure, not to mention his cool cheek, he gave her his most engaging smile. "Well," he said, "you know my name. Can I have the honor of knowing yours?"

"Yes, of course you may, Mr. Crowther. It's Audra Kenton." Her smile was warm and as friendly as his had been, and she offered him her hand.

Vincent took it in his, was surprised at the firmness of her grip, the strength in her hand as she shook his. Such a small hand it was too, just as she herself was small and delicate. He held on to her hand for longer than was necessary, unable to release it as he gazed into her clear, very bright blue eyes, which reminded him of cornflowers. Unexpectedly, he thought: *I cannot let this woman go. Never. Ever. I want her for the rest of my life.*

He was appalled at his thoughts.

He blinked, finally let go of her hand, glanced away, and he was struck at once by the irrationality of his feelings. The mere idea of marriage was absurd, and to this woman it was positively ludicrous. She was different. Special. A lady. And one who would hardly be interested in *him*, a bricklayer learning his trade. She was obviously a relation of the Bells, who were local gentry, posh folk with pots and pots of brass and lots of clout in the neighborhood. These facts aside, marriage was not a part of his present plans; he had a lot of living to do before tying himself to a woman's apron strings. That was a mug's game. Why, he wouldn't even be twenty-five until June.

All of this had flashed through Vincent's head in a matter of seconds, and now he wanted to run out of the shop immediately, to escape before it was too late. But to his own irritation he discovered he could not move. He was rooted to the spot. Suddenly he felt uncomfortable, ill at ease with himself and, therefore, with her, and he began to twist the brim of his trilby in his hands.

Theophilus tugged at Vincent's coat, piped up, "We're looking for a budgerigar, Mr. Crowther. What've *you* come to buy?"

Thank God for the boy, Vincent thought. He said, "Well, I don't rightly know, if you want the honest truth." Giving his entire attention to the child, he stooped down, confided, "You see, Theo, I came to get something for my little brother. He's four. But I didn't think to ask him what he'd like before I left the house. So now I'm stuck, sort of. You look like an experienced young man when it comes to pets. Maybe you could make a suggestion or two."

"Mmmm. Let me think a minute." Theo nodded his head sagely, pursed his lips, adopted an expression of great concentration. He swung his observant eyes around the pet shop, leaned into Vincent and said, "It's a bit difficult really, making a proper suggestion, I mean. There's not much to choose from, you see."

Vincent burst out laughing at the boy's blunt words. "You'd better not let Mr. Harrison hear you say that. He thinks he owns the best pet shop in Armley."

"And he does, since it's the only one," Theo replied, grinning, looking inordinately pleased with himself.

"Little boys are meant to be seen and not heard," Audra remarked. But this was the mildest of chastisements. Laughter bubbled up in her throat and her eyes danced. She glanced at Vincent, then shrugged her shoulders. She murmured, "What can you do?"

Vincent said, "He's a right rum 'un, he is that."

Theo's beady black eyes, swiveling between the two of them, settled on Vincent, who obviously fascinated him. He said, "I think you should buy your brother a budgie. At least Mr. Harrison has a big lot of those to choose from. Come on, Mr. Crowther, let me show you." He plucked at Vincent's sleeve. "What's his name? Your brother, I mean."

"Danny." Vincent allowed himself to be led over to the many bird cages which lined one wall of the shop. He and the boy stood regarding them with interest, and after a moment, Vincent said, with some admiration, "I'll say this, Theo, they are beautiful."

Now Audra joined them. Vincent was instantly conscious of her coming to a stop next to him. He was troubled by the emotions she evoked in him, by the strong physical attraction he felt for her. He wanted to take hold of her hand, lead her out of this shop, go with her somewhere so that they could be alone. He wanted to crush her in his arms, to make love to her. His longing stirred within him and he felt the heat rise up into his face and he swallowed hard, tried to concentrate on the birds.

Presently, Audra said, "Theo wants that one over there,

on the right, Mr. Crowther. The one in the green cage. What do you think? Do you like it?"

Vincent could only nod.

Theo said, "Audra's buying it for me, Mr. Crowther."

"Aren't you the lucky little lad," he managed to mutter.

"Yes, I am. Go on, Mr. Crowther, pick a budgie for Danny. They're easy to look after. You don't have to walk them like a dog and they don't cost a lot to keep in food. They don't eat much."

"True," Vincent agreed. He was in control again, and he exchanged an amused look with Audra.

Theo pressed on relentlessly, "Now just look at this one! What a pretty bird. I bet Danny would like it. And it's a lovely example of the Australian parakeet . . . greenish yellow body, bright blue on the cheeks and tail feathers, and brown stripes down the wings."

"*Parakeet*," Vincent repeated, sounding baffled. He frowned at Theo. "I thought these were budgies."

"They are. But the budgerigar comes from the parrot family, and there are three hundred and fifteen species of colorful birds in that family," Theo told him proudly, enjoying airing his knowledge. "Lovebirds, lories, cockatoos, cockatiels and macaws, to name a few. I wanted a parrot. I was going to teach it to talk. To say rude words. But you have to be careful when you buy parrots. Because of psittacosis. That's parrot fever, and it's an infectious disease that *people* can catch. It's a bit like pneumonia. Anyway, Mr. Harrison doesn't have any parrots in stock. That's why I'm getting a budgie instead. But one day I *will* own a parrot."

Looking at the child in amazement, shaking his head, Vincent said, "For a little nipper you're certainly a mine of information, Theo. That you are. You sound as if you've swallowed an encyclopedia. *Is* that where you get all of your facts from then?"

"Oh no, I get them from Audra," Theo explained. "She's very clever, you know, and she's taught me a lot since she's been with me. My mother says she's the best nanny I've ever had. If you don't wish to get Danny a budgie, you could buy him one of those canaries over there. *They're*

from the finch family." Theo drew Vincent's attention to the
other birds, and continued, "They're pretty too, but the
best thing about them is that they actually *sing*. I know
Danny would like to own a canary. You'd have to teach him
to sing, though. The canary, I mean, not Danny."

"Yes, I understand," Vincent said absently. *Nanny,* he
repeated to himself. She was the boy's *nanny,* for God's
sake, not a posh relative of the Bells after all. She was one of
their employees. Of course, that did not alter the facts one
iota. Audra Kenton was still a lady. But a lady who worked
for a living. Impoverished gentility, he decided.

Perhaps she was not beyond his reach after all. Vincent's
hopes soared.

The three of them walked up Town Street together.

Vincent carried the bird cage for Audra. They had bought
similar budgerigars in the end, but Vincent had told Joe
Harrison to hold his until he returned for it a bit later in the
day. And then he had asked Audra if he could escort her and
the boy back to Calpher House. She had said yes. Hoisting
the bird cage in one hand, he had opened the shop door
with the other and ushered her out, grinning from ear to
ear, and congratulating himself on his luck this morning.

Now they walked along at a steady pace, side by side and
in step, not speaking but comfortable in the silence drifting
between them. Theo frisked ahead like a happy little
puppy.

Although it was almost noon, the weather was still quite
raw, but the wind had died away and it was a shimmering
kind of day and crystal clear. The sky, so high and vast above
them, was cerulean, cloudless, pristine, and bathed in the
silver light of a cold winter sun.

It's turned out to be magnificent, Audra thought, looking
about, smiling with pleasure. A tiny burst of joy surged
through her, filled her with a lovely inner warmth. A day
like this made you realize that anything was possible in life.
Anything at all.

Vincent breathed deeply, took a lungful or two of icy air,
feeling healthy and robust, as he always did in this type of

bright and bracing weather. He stole a surreptitious glance
at Audra, thinking how smart she looked in the gray Melton
coat and the plum-colored cloche, and then he realized how
proud he was to be with her—and to be seen with her in
Town Street, the main thoroughfare in Armley and as busy
today as it usually was on Saturdays.

Before they reached Calpher House he was going to
invite her out, Vincent now decided, even though he was a
bit nervous about doing so. If she refused him he would feel
like a damned fool; on the other hand, if he didn't ask her
he would never know. He wondered where to take her if
she did accept. That was a problem. Perhaps he should
bring her to their New Year's Eve party tomorrow. No, that
wouldn't work. The poor girl would be overwhelmed by his
boisterous family. Besides, on their first date he wanted to
have her all to himself. He began to rack his brains for a
suitable place to go.

Audra, also lost in her private musings, felt as though she
was floating, so buoyed up was she. For two months she
had held on to the belief that they would meet again. But
when he had walked into the pet shop, she had been
completely taken aback. Initially. And then, within minutes, it had all seemed so natural. She knew it was meant to
be. The awkwardness she had experienced at the dance was
no longer in evidence, and she did not feel in the least shy
with him. Quite the contrary, in fact.

He was even more handsome than she remembered and
as well dressed as he had been at the dance. He was a
charming young man with a pleasant personality, and the
way he had behaved with the child had only made her like
him all the more. Audra smiled. *Like* was a funny word to
use. It hardly described her feelings. She had fallen in love
with him in the pet shop.

She looked up at him through the corner of her eye. He
was the only man for her. The only man she would ever
want.

Vincent glanced down as she was looking up.

Their eyes met and held for a brief moment. He smiled
at her lovingly. She smiled back, a little tremulously. A very
intimate communication passed between them at this
precise moment, and they both caught their breath, staring

at each other. And then, fully understanding what had been conveyed without benefit of words, they instantly averted their faces, stared ahead, walked on in silence.

After a short while, Vincent finally spoke. He said, "I hope you don't think I'm being nosy, but how long have you worked for the Bells then?"

"A year," Audra replied. "As a matter of fact, Mr. Crowther, it's exactly one year ago today that I started my job at Calpher House. That's why I bought Theo the bird. As an anniversary gift."

"They should be giving you presents," he said gruffly before he could stop himself. And then for a reason he could not fathom, he experienced a small stab of resentment toward the Bell family.

Audra had caught the odd, disgruntled tone, and she eyed him curiously, for a moment puzzled. But then she smiled at him prettily and said, "They did, Mr. Crowther. At breakfast this morning."

"Well, that's good then, isn't it. I'm glad." He cleared his throat rather loudly and went on, "You don't come from these parts, I can tell that by your voice. You don't speak with a Leeds accent. So where are you from?"

"Ripon's my hometown, and that's where I lived until last year. Have you ever been there, Mr. Crowther?"

"Yes, I have, to the races. It's a lovely spot." His green eyes gleamed with mischief. "And lucky for me, I don't mind telling you. I've always managed to win a bob or two at Ripon races, and there are some nice pubs there too."

Audra nodded. "Yes. And you're from this area, aren't you, Mr. Crowther?"

"Oh aye, I am that. Armley born and bred, that's me. And listen a minute, would you mind calling me Vincent? I keep thinking you're addressing my dad every time you say Mr. Crowther."

Audra laughed. "Of course I will, and you must call me Audra."

"Done," he cried and came to a sudden and abrupt stop. He took hold of her arm and gently broke her stride.

She stared up at him, frowning.

Vincent said, in a rush of words, "Will you go out with me

tonight, Audra? I'd like to take you someplace nice. Maybe into Leeds, to go dancing. Say you will. *Please*." He flashed her his most winning smile and held her with his eyes.

She said, "I'm afraid I can't. You see I have—"

"You don't have to bother explaining," he cut in, sounding huffy and hurt. "I understand." A tinge of pink crept up into his face.

"No, you *don't* understand, Vincent," Audra said firmly. "I was about to say that I'm working tonight. But I would like to go out with you on my next evening off. Really I would."

"Oh," he said, momentarily thrown off balance. He recovered himself instantly, beamed at her. "That's all right then. And when *is* your next night off?"

"This coming Wednesday."

His face fell. "Not till then. Oh dear. Well, never mind. But it'll have to be the church dance that night. How do you feel about going there?"

"I'll enjoy it . . . with you." She offered him a small smile, suddenly feeling shy.

Vincent gave her a long look. "Yes," he said, "so will I, Audra."

They began to walk again.

Within seconds they were at the gates of Calpher House, where Theo stood waiting for them. When they came to a standstill, Vincent turned to Audra and said, "I'll meet you here at the gates on Wednesday, at seven sharp."

"But you don't have to trouble yourself, Vincent. Really. I can find my own way to the Parish Hall."

"*No*. I wouldn't want you walking down there alone."

"Very well then," she said.

He handed her the bird cage.

Theophilus said, "Goodbye, Mr. Crowther. I hope I see you soon. Then you can tell me if Danny liked his budgie."

"I'll do that, Theo. Ta'rar, lad."

Vincent swung to Audra. With a faint smile he raised his hat and was gone.

Audra watched him walk down the hill in long, brisk strides. He turned once, saw her and waved. She waved back. And then she took hold of Theo's hand and led him up the drive, only vaguely listening to the child as he chattered away.

As they drew closer to the house, Audra lifted her eyes and looked at it, thinking of the happy times she had spent here in the past year. And then some deep instinct told her she would not be living at Calpher House for much longer.

Today is the beginning, she thought. The beginning of my life with Vincent Crowther.

He is my destiny. I am his.

They were married five months later.

Some people were astonished; others were not.

The wedding took place at Christ Church in Upper Armley on a sunny June Saturday, a couple of days after Audra's birthday and one week before Vincent would celebrate his.

The bride wore blue. It was a simple yet elegant afternoon dress of crepe de chine, which she had designed herself, cut and sewn with the help of a seamstress from Paris Modes, Mrs. Bell's exclusive gown shop in Leeds. Her cloche was of blue silk swathed in chiffon; her court shoes with Louis heels were of gray suede, as were her elbow-length gloves. She carried a bouquet of pink roses, lily-of-the-valley and stephanotis.

Gwen Thornton was Audra's bridesmaid and Laurette Crowther her matron of honor.

They were dressed in identical frocks of dove-gray crepe georgette overprinted with yellow roses, cloche hats of stitched gray silk, and their posies were of yellow roses.

As they fussed and hovered around her in the entrance hall of Calpher House, Audra thought how truly lovely they looked, both so tall and fair, so young and fresh, and she was proud to have them as her attendants.

Mr. Bell had graciously offered to give her away, and so it was on his arm that Audra walked down the aisle of the beautiful old Anglican church with its Norman architecture and magnificent stained-glass windows.

It was when the organ music swelled and the strains of the hymn "O Perfect Love" reverberated through the high rafters that Audra's throat tightened. Her eyes filled with tears and she ached for her brothers. But knowing she could not permit herself to break down, she took control of herself. She lifted her head higher, looked toward the altar where Vincent was waiting with his brother Frank, who was his best man.

The love illuminating his face, the genuine admiration in his eyes were comforting, reassuring, and she thought how wonderful he looked in his dark blue suit, which was brand-new, the crisp white shirt and silver-gray silk tie.

Within seconds of drawing to a standstill at the altar, Mr. Bell stepped aside. Vincent took his place. His presence and the vicar's kindly expression instantly dispelled the feelings of loneliness she had experienced a second before.

The Reverend Baxter's words seemed to wash over Audra . . . for better or for worse . . . for richer or for poorer . . . in sickness and in health . . . forsaking all others. Of course she forsook all others. How could she ever want anyone but Vincent? The idea was quite unthinkable.

Before she realized it the ceremony was over.

They were married. She was Mrs. Vincent Crowther.

She walked back down the aisle, this time clinging to the arm of her husband as the organist pumped away enthusiastically and Mendelssohn's "Wedding March," joyful, thunderous, filled the church.

She and Vincent lingered on the church steps for only a few minutes, to have their photograph taken, greet his family, friends, the Bells and Matron Lennox, who had traveled over from Ripon for the occasion.

And then, amidst lots of laughter and a deluge of confetti and rice, they dashed to the car waiting at the church gates. Vincent's Uncle Phil drove them to Calpher House, where the champagne wedding breakfast was being given by Mr. and Mrs. Thomas Bell.

Sitting very close to him in the back of the motor car, Audra smiled up at her young husband and then glanced down at the gold band on her finger. She had not thought it possible she could ever be so happy.

CHAPTER ELEVEN

The moonlight had transformed her into a silver statue.

She stood near the window, motionless, staring out toward the sea, one arm resting on the sill, her body held at an oblique angle, turned inward to the room, her face in profile. It was the white satin nightgown, a mere wisp of a thing, that caught and held the light from the full moon, and in the duskiness of the room it had taken on the sheen and color of pure silver.

There was something ethereal and illusory about her as she stood there unmoving. Unobserved, Vincent regarded her from the doorway, unable to tear his eyes away from her, wanting to prolong this moment, to etch this image of her on his mind and his memory.

She did not seem real to him at all, and it was as if she was part of some dream he had dreamed long ago and was dreaming again. He felt that if he moved or spoke, the scene would shatter and then evaporate, as all dreams did, and that she would be lost to him for all time.

As he gazed at her his longing for her shot through him, and in the same sharp and urgent way that it always did when she was near him. He never wanted a woman as much as he wanted her. When they had arrived here at the Victoria Hotel in Robin Hood's Bay late on Saturday afternoon, he had been unable to restrain himself. The pent-up emotions, the desire constantly suppressed and held in check for the past five months, had exploded the minute they were alone in the suite. He had taken her to bed at once, before they had even unpacked.

In five days they had hardly left the suite.

He had become the inspired and skillful teacher, enjoying and reveling in this role, she the attentive and ardent pupil, eager, so ready to please. After the first couple of days, she had begun to overcome her modesty and her shyness with him, and now she was very much at ease with

him in their lovemaking. She accepted everything and
without question, her adoration of him written all over her
face. He had been overjoyed to discover that his tender and
blushing virgin had a deeply ingrained sensuality, just as he
did himself, was thrilled that her ardor was now beginning
to match his.

Oh how he loved her, this warm, willing young woman
who was his now . . . and forever. His woman. His lover.
His wife.

The knowledge that he possessed her in every way was
like an aphrodisiac, and just looking at her brought him to
searing heat. He fastened his eyes on her slender yet
shapely figure, so fully revealed to him through the flimsy
texture of the satin that clung to her body in such a
provocative way. She was small-boned and finely wrought—
but beautifully curvaceous. Her bosom was high, taut
under the satin. He could see her nipples standing out
sharply.

Heat raged through his loins, and in his groin there was a
dull ache. Suddenly he had an enormous erection. He
could not remember being as hard as this ever before, not
even in the past five days and nights with her, she who
charged him up more than any other woman ever had.

He took a step forward. His movement disturbed the air.

She swung her head toward the door, saw him, faintly
smiled.

When he reached her side, Vincent took her face in his
hands and, tenderly so, looked deeply into her eyes. They
were inky black in the dim light. He bent forward, kissed
her brow, her eyes, her cheeks and tasted the salt of her
tears.

Startled, he drew back, stared at her in bafflement.
"Audra, whatever is it, love? Aren't you happy with me?"
His erection went down.

"Oh Vincent, yes, I am. Of course I am." She drew closer
to him, put her arms around his back, rested her head
against his smooth, bare chest. A deep sigh rippled through
her.

"Then what is it? Why are you so upset?"

"I'm not upset, truly I'm not." She nestled closer, hoping

her body movements would reassure him. She loved this man so very much, with all of her heart and soul and mind. She did not want him to misunderstand her tears.

Slowly, she said, "I was standing here, waiting for you, admiring the beauty of the sea in the moonlight, when all at once I thought of the endless, endless miles of ocean stretching from here to Australia. And quite suddenly I did miss William and Frederick so; it was like a tight pain in my chest, a terrible constriction. I felt very sad, and I longed for them to be here in England. Somewhere. Anywhere. It didn't really matter where, so long as they were under the same sky as me . . . and then I thought of my wedding, and that's when I started to cry. Oh I do wish they'd been there, Vincent, that they had seen us get married." She sighed again, but it was a light sigh and one that was barely audible. "There was a moment in the church, just before the vicar married us, that I felt utterly and completely alone. It was awful."

"Yes, I understand," he murmured gently, stroking her hair, pressing her closer to him. "Of course you missed your brothers, wanted them at your wedding, it's only natural." He kissed the top of her head. "But the instant we were married, you were no longer alone, Audra. And you'll never be alone again. You have me now."

"I know I do, Vincent. And you have me."

"I'll never forget the way you looked on Saturday morning in the church, Audra. Not as long as I live, I won't. You were so bonny in your blue frock. You should always were blue; it does suit you, love."

He felt her smile against his chest. He knew that her sadness was trickling away, and he was glad of that.

She said, "Vincent . . . tell me again . . . you know, the things you said last night."

He chuckled softly. "I said a lot of things last night. What *things* in particular do you mean?"

"Why you married me."

"Because I love you."

"And why do you love me?"

He laughed, but quietly.

"Tell me," she persisted in a low, whispery voice, and she trailed her fingers across his shoulder blades.

This made him shiver. Instantly he wanted her.

"Because I love the look of you, the sound of you, the touch of your hands. I love the way you feel under my hands. I love every part of you. Oh Audra . . . *love*." He tilted her head back, kissed her throat, her soft yielding mouth. The blood rushed through him. His desire for her was rampant.

She responded to his kisses ardently. When he moved his lips against hers she opened her mouth slightly so that his warm, loving, probing tongue could enter, rest against hers. His embrace tightened perceptibly, and he kissed her more deeply, passionately, and their teeth grazed.

Audra shifted slightly so that their bodies melded together. Moving closer to him, she felt his hardness against her stomach through the thin fabric of the satin nightgown, and she shivered involuntarily. A fierce and sudden heat began to throb at the core of her, and the shivering intensified as she anticipated what would happen next, thought of the way it felt when he took her to him. The first time they had made love, on their wedding night, she had been apprehensive when she had seen him standing naked before her. But he had loved her with such care and tenderness, and so exquisitely, the pain had only been a few moments of sharp discomfort and now they fitted each other perfectly.

Unexpectedly his kisses ceased.

Stepping back, Vincent slipped the thin straps of her nightgown over her shoulders, pulled it down past her breasts. It slithered to the floor unaided, lay like a gleaming pool at her feet.

Again Vincent gazed deeply into Audra's eyes, his love for her spilling out. He lifted his hand, stroked her cheek. After a long moment he dropped his eyes and kneeling down in front of her, he rested his head against her stomach and his arms went around her. Pressing his hands into the small of her back, he slowly smoothed them over her buttocks, moved her body slightly, adjusted her stance to suit him.

She trembled under his touch, and her desire for him
swept through her. Her blood raced, her heart beat rapidly
and her skin tingled in anticipation. Reaching out, she
stroked his hair, then let her hands fall onto his shoulders,
where they rested.

Covering her stomach with light, fluttering kisses, he
continued to stroke her back, her buttocks and her thighs.
Then he leaned away from her ever so slightly, rested on his
heels, brought his hands around onto her stomach, still
smoothing and stroking her skin. Finally, his hands came to
a stop in the soft silky coils of fair hair that covered the
mound between her legs. Slowly, with infinite care, he
parted the tender petals, touched the tiny folds of warm,
moist skin that protected her womanhood.

He kissed her navel and her stomach. They were long,
slow, lingering kisses, and all the while his hands played
amongst the musky folds, touching and seeking. At last he
brought his tongue to join the quest. He began to nuzzle
her, kiss her, and as he did he heard the soft moans in her
throat. She gripped his shoulders, straining toward him,
and he brought her to the edge of ecstasy.

He stopped abruptly, pulled away from her.

She caught her breath. Her eyes flew open. She gaped at
him.

He took hold of her wrist quickly, firmly, pulled her down
onto the floor with him. Impatiently, he kicked off his
pajama bottoms, stretched out next to her on the carpet,
wrapped his body around hers, held her close to him.
Wanting to possess her though he was, he wished to
prolong their loving for a short while.

Lifting himself up on one elbow, he glanced down. Their
eyes locked in a gaze so filled with passion, so intense, so
searching in its depth of feeling it seemed to sear them
both. Vincent thought he was seeing into her very soul.
Her face overflowed with her abiding love for him and her
yearning. And looking into those clear green eyes, Audra
saw the burning desire in them and the wonderment and
the glitter of bright tears, and her heart clenched and she
reached up to touch his face.

It was Vincent who finally broke the contact. He found it

unbearable, suddenly, to look at her in this manner, so moved was he by her and so choked up with feeling.

Now his glance swept over her body stretched out before him.

How translucent she looked in the moonlight streaming in through the open window. She resembled a piece of perfectly sculpted marble, except that no cold stone was she. She was warm and desirable flesh and blood. How lovely her breasts were, pearly tinted, rounded and smooth, and her nipples were upright and hard like little bursting May buds, deep rose in color.

"Oh Audra," he breathed. "My Audra. You're so beautiful."

She half smiled, lifted her hand, smoothed one finger along his lips, then traced an outline around his mouth in the shape of a bow.

He caught hold of her hand, kissed the palm, then bent over her, brought his mouth to the cleft between her breasts and kissed her, enjoying the fragrant smell of her young sweet skin. Presently, he cupped his hand around her breast, began to fondle the nipple. It sprang up, grew more taut and erect than ever under his caressing fingers. Audra let out a little gasp of joy as his mouth came down on her other breast.

She cleaved to him, ran her hands over his back, then up onto his neck, and she twined her fingers in his crisp dark hair.

"Oh Vincent, Vincent, I love you so much," she whispered hoarsely.

On hearing his name, this endearment, he pulled away from her, moved rapidly. He braced himself above her on his hands.

There was no reason to wait now. He could not wait.

He took her urgently, needing to be joined to her, needing to make them as one. He shafted deeper and deeper, luxuriating in her total embrace, one that enfolded him in warmth and love and made him feel complete in a way that he had never felt except with her.

Oh yes, how he did love her . . . this lovely girl he held in his arms . . . his beautiful wife. She was his. They were made for each other, belonged together. And oh how he fitted into her so well.

Slipping his hands under her body, he lifted her closer to him, clasping her tightly, plunging in and out. And she thrust herself up to meet his long and thrusting strokes. Her arms clung to him, and she matched his fervent loving with an urgency of her own.

He cried out in his rapture, called her name over and over, all the time clutching her to him as though never to let her go. He knew he could not control himself much longer, that he was on the verge of exploding. He thought he might be blacking out. He seemed to be pitching forward from a great height . . . falling, falling, falling.

"Oh, I'm ready," he gasped against her burning cheek. "Oh Audra. Take all of me. *Now*."

"Oh Vincent!"

She arched her body toward his in the way he liked, meeting his passion, accepting it with love, offering him her passion in return, showing no restraint.

Wave upon wave of pure joy washed over her, and she thought she was drowning in her pleasure and his. Suddenly she was gripped by an uncontrollable trembling, and she crested upon the soaring waves, and as she did she felt an immense shuddering pass through him, and they were united in their shattering release. And then he fell against her, lay exhausted in her arms, and she stroked his hair, rested her head on his, feeling exhausted too and overwhelmed by her emotions.

Eventually Vincent roused himself. "I'm too heavy," he murmured against her throat.

"No, it's all right. Anyway, I like to feel the weight of you on me," she whispered. Then she shook her head. "Why on earth am I whispering?" she wondered out loud, speaking in her normal voice.

"I've no idea. And God knows why we're lying here on the floor." He began to chuckle.

"What's so amusing?"

"I am, love. For months and months all I could think

about was making love to you in a nice comfy bed, and now that we have one in the very next room I ignore it, choose the floor instead. Can you beat that!" He pushed himself up on one elbow, moved a strand of hair away from her face. "Anyway, it's all your fault."

"Why?"

"Because you're a little temptress, that's why. There you were, standing by the window in the moonlight and my heart did somersaults. I couldn't resist you. I had to have you. Right here on the floor, no less." He chuckled again. "There's no two ways about it, you do get me going, make me feel hot, love."

Audra made no response, glanced away.

Vincent sensed her sudden shyness, her embarrassment.

That was the curious thing about her . . . she was a mass of contradictions, he had discovered. From the moment he had made her his on the first night of their honeymoon, she had been a generous and giving partner, questioning nothing, doing as he wished. Yet in the aftermath of their lovemaking, she never wanted to discuss the pleasure they had just shared; nor did she like it when he made mention of it. He had noticed that she invariably fell into an extraordinary reticence. A veil went down, shutting him out. He supposed her attitude sprang from her upbringing, her breeding. It was all right to do it, but not to talk about doing it, when you were a lady. Well, no matter. Such things were not really very important in the long run. She was his and he did love her so.

Pushing himself up off the floor, Vincent gave Audra his hand, hoisted her to her feet. After smothering her in a huge bear hug, he found her nightgown for her, slipped it on over her head, then pulled on his pajamas.

"I don't know about you, but I'm famished all of a sudden. Let's have a picnic on that bowl of fruit." As he spoke, he went over to the table and picked it up.

"What a good idea," Audra agreed. "I'm a bit hungry myself."

Wrapping his other arm around her, Vincent walked her into the bedroom. They installed themselves in the middle of the large double bed, where they sat cross-legged, munching on big red juicy apples. A minute or two later, Vincent returned to the adjoining sitting room and retrieved the half-finished bottle of wine he had ordered from room service with their dinner. He carried it back to the bedroom with two glasses, which he filled. Handing one to Audra, he joined her on the bed once more.

After propping a pillow behind his back, making himself comfortable, he lit a cigarette, said, "Tell me some more about High Cleugh, about when you were little."

"Goodness, you are insatiable, and my past is not especially interesting," she replied with a light laugh. "Besides, it's your turn."

He made a face. "There's not much left to tell . . . you know all about my boyish adventures with my friend Redvers Buller." He winked at her. "I can't believe you want to hear about them again, and the scrapes we got into, the canings we got from the headmaster. It's boring stuff."

"But you're such a good raconteur, Vincent."

"Well, I don't know about that, love." He drew on his Woodbine, blew a smoke ring, flashed her one of his cheeky boyish grins. His dancing green eyes glistened as he leaned forward, pinned them on her. He cajoled, "Go on, Audra, let's hear about your mother and your Uncle Peter . . . the Beautiful Edith Kenton and the dashing army captain. I must admit, the two of them intrigue me."

"Aha, you're a true romantic, Vincent Crowther."

"I am?" He sounded doubtful.

"Yes." Audra smiled. "I could tell you about the mystery of my mother's vanishing sapphires, if you like?"

"Your eyes are like sapphires, do you know that?" He gave her a soulful look and blew her a kiss.

"Do you want to hear this story or not?"

"Yes."

As she began to speak he settled back, sipped his wine, listening to her attentively. Vincent was as fascinated and as impressed by Audra's background and family as he was enamored of her. And so not unnaturally he loved hearing about her childhood, and in particular he loved the sound of her melodious voice as she spoke of those days with such love.

CHAPTER TWELVE

"Close your eyes," Audra said, "and keep them closed until I tell you to open them."

"Okay," Vincent said, promptly doing as he was told.

Audra looked up at him adoringly. Her happiness knew no bounds today. She reached for her husband's hand, drew him across the grass, saying, "It's all right, there's nothing in your way, just step out as you normally would."

"That's what I *am* doing."

Audra smiled. "It's just a few more steps," she said, guiding him forward. She gripped his hand a little tighter as she told him, "Turn your head toward me, to the left a bit more."

Vincent did as she instructed.

"Now!" Audra exclaimed.

He lifted his lids, blinked for a second or two in the bright morning sunlight, then brought his hand up to shade his eyes. He squinted slightly against the brilliance, trying to focus.

"Look, over there, near the trees . . . in that dell," Audra was saying.

He followed the direction of her outstretched arm. His breath caught in his throat. "*That's* High Cleugh," he said in the strangest of voices, and stared in astonishment at the old manor house.

"Yes." Audra glanced up at him, frowning in concern. "You sound so surprised. Are you disappointed? Don't you think it's as beautiful as I made it sound, as I described it?"

"Oh, I do, I do," he was quick to reassure her. "But it's so big, Audra, and it looks ever so grand. I'd no idea. I mean I just never imagined it was that kind of house, you know, a *mansion*." He was unable to disguise the awe in his voice. It was obvious he was impressed.

Audra squeezed his fingers. "It looks a lot larger than it actually is, Vincent."

"Maybe so, but it's bigger than anything I've ever been used to, lass. And those gardens, Audra. Why they fair take my breath away, they do that."

Audra beamed at him. "My mother planned and planted them, and those are her delphiniums down near the edge of the river. Whenever I see delphiniums, I always think of her and of High Cleugh."

"I can certainly understand why, love."

"If you look down the river a little bit, over there to your right, you'll see the stepping stones I told you about. That's where we used to cross the river to come up here for our picnics . . . to the Memory Place. Of course, it wasn't called that then. I only gave it that name afterward—" She broke off, glanced away, and there was a hint of sadness in her voice as she finished, "You know, after *they* died, and after my brothers were sent away from me."

"Yes," he said, putting his arm around her shoulder comfortingly.

She looked up into his face, gave him a small smile.

He smiled back, all the while scrutinizing her closely, hoping that coming here had not upset her unduly. Days ago, when he had asked her to show him High Cleugh on their way back to Leeds from Robin Hood's Bay, he had not stopped to think that this might stir up memories that would make her sorrowful. After all, she had agreed so readily, even eagerly. But now Vincent could not help wondering if his forcefulness had been misplaced; perhaps he had been thoughtless. Her vivid cornflower eyes looked suspiciously moist to him.

Vincent cleared his throat. "Are you sure you want to have our picnic here, Audra love?"

"That's what I'd thought. It's so pretty, and there's such a lovely view for miles around. Don't you want to stay?" she asked, sounding worried, as always wishing to please him.

"Yes. Anything you say is all right by me."

Leaning forward, he kissed her cheek, then strode over to the sycamore tree. A few minutes before, he had deposited two brown-paper shopping bags under the spreading branches; he carried these back to the top of the slope above the River Ure, where Audra had remained standing. Taking a large tartan blanket out of one of them, he shook it out, spread it at her feet.

And then, with a great flourish, he did a sweeping bow in front of her, bending low in the manner of an old-fashioned cavalier.

"My cloak for your comfort, m'lady, and pray do be seated so that we can partake of our repast," he said, adopting an exaggerated upper-class accent.

Laughing vivaciously, her eyes sparkling with delight, Audra offered him a small curtsy in return. "Why, Sir Galahad, my grateful thanks indeed." She lowered herself onto the car rug with her usual grace of movement.

Joining in her laughter, Vincent flopped down next to her and remarked, "I must say, it was nice of the hall porter at the Victoria Hotel to arrange this food for us, wasn't it?" As he spoke, he began to take small packages out of the other shopping bag.

"Yes, most kind," Audra agreed, helping him in his task. "Oh look, the hotel chef put in some lovely Scotch eggs," she exclaimed, unwrapping the grease-proof paper, showing him the hard-boiled eggs encased in sausage meat.

Vincent eyed them. "Well, they look as tasty as anything me mam could make," he said, his mouth watering. "And I've just come across a little bag of pickled onions and a slab of fine Wensleydale cheese." He flashed her a huge grin. "We might as well dig in, Audra. Oh and here's your bottle of milk, pet."

"Thank you, Vincent."

They were both hungry after their long drive from Robin Hood's Bay on the East Coast, across the sprawling North Yorkshire Moors and down to Ripon. And so they said very little as they munched on the delicious tidbits in the picnic lunch which had been provided by the hotel.

It was an exceptional June day.

The sky was bright blue and filled with sunshine. The lightest of balmy breezes rustled through the trees, but there were no other sounds except for the faint gurgle of running water, the occasional trilling of the wild birds and the rushing and fluttering of their wings as they flew up into the sparkling summer air.

Neither Audra nor Vincent ever minded these silences
which frequently fell between them. In fact, they found
them companionable, enjoyed them as much as everything
else they did together. They were content to simply be in
each other's company, knowing that they did not always
have the need to make forced conversation. There was an
ease between them; it had been thus since the beginning of
their relationship in January.

Audra studied him surreptitiously.

It was the twelfth of June, and he was twenty-five today.
But he looked much younger to her. Perhaps this was
because of his fresh complexion, the tan he had acquired in
the last few days. Although they had been ensconced in the
hotel suite for a good part of their honeymoon, the time
they had spent outdoors had been put to good use. They
had walked a lot, and when she had ventured up onto the
precipitous cliffs to paint watercolors of Robin Hood's Bay
from that vantage point, he had insisted on accompanying
her. He had read his newspaper, studied his racing form
and then stretched out next to her, sunning himself.

Suddenly Audra wondered what Vincent would say if she
told him that she had not enjoyed her wedding day very
much. In point of fact, she would not have enjoyed it at all if
he had not been present. Audra laughed under her breath
at the ridiculousness of this thought. Obviously, without
Vincent Crowther there would have been no marriage in
the first place.

He had enjoyed his wedding, though. All aspects of it,
too. Smiling, laughing, shaking hands, he had been comfortable with everyone. So much so, she had been struck
quite strongly by his carefree manner. He was positively
nonchalant; he might have been the lord of the manor at
Calpher House. Not that his behavior had been offensive to
the Bells or anyone else—only enviable, as far as she was
concerned. For she had experienced great unease most of
the time, although she had endeavored to hide this behind
a gracious demeanor, a bright smile carefully glued into
place.

From the outset, she had sensed strange undercurrents
at the reception. Vincent had been unaware of them.

To begin with, there had been a certain awkwardness between the Thorntons and the Crowthers, and she had watched this develop into veiled antipathy within the first hour. Her internal discomfort had spiraled into distress, and she had found herself growing quieter and quieter with everyone; Vincent, full of bonhomie, had simply grown more expansive.

At one moment, she had gone into the Bells' elegant dining room looking for Vincent. Here Mr. Agiter, Cora and Dodie had been serving the breakfast buffet, a wonderful selection of good Yorkshire fare and other tempting delicacies from Mrs. Jackson's well-stocked larder. Instantly, she had noticed Gwen and Charlie huddled in one corner, heads together, looking conspiratorial. Just as she was about to turn away, she had observed them fasten their eyes on Vincent, who was on the far side of the room talking to Irène Bell. They had stared at him, daggers drawn.

If looks could kill, he'd drop dead this very minute, Audra had thought, and gooseflesh had sprung up on her arms. Averting her face, she had hurried over to join her husband, had taken hold of his arm almost protectively.

After chatting with Mrs. Bell for a moment or two, she had then excused them both to her former employer, explaining that she wanted Vincent to become better acquainted with Matron Lennox. Still holding on to his arm, she had led him out into the hall. She had felt sick inside. And dreadfully hurt.

She had been relieved, even glad, to leave for their honeymoon as soon as it was possible to do so politely, without giving offense to the Bells. They had been exceedingly generous, and she did not wish them to think she was unappreciative. Naturally, Vincent had wanted to stay longer, he being the social animal that he was.

Audra shifted slightly on the tartan rug, stretched out her legs in front of her and reached for a piece of the Wensleydale cheese, nibbling on it absently, trying to dismiss thoughts of Gwen. She found she could not.

Her best friend disliked her husband.

That was the sad truth, and it troubled Audra a great deal. Unfortunately, Gwen had taken a dislike to Vincent

months before she had actually met him—her words on
Bonfire Night still echoed in Audra's ears. It was all because
of Charlie, of course. Gwen had condemned Vincent
without bothering to get to know him, simply because he
had been chosen instead of her brother.

How immature Gwen is being, Audra thought. She was
disappointed in Gwen; she had certainly expected better of
her friend. Having cherished their friendship from the day
it had commenced, she was upset that it was threatened.
But it was Gwen, not she, who was putting it in jeopardy.
She loved Gwen; she did not want to lose her. But she also
loved her husband. If she and Gwen were going to continue
to see each other, Gwen would have to be more amiable
with Vincent. He came first now. And Vincent, being
oblivious to the girl's dislike, was always friendly and cordial
to her. In Audra's opinion, he should have received better
treatment from her old friend.

Swallowing a sigh, Audra leaned back on her elbows,
thinking hard. She must find a way to show her how unfair
she was being. Audra did not want Gwen to be a casualty of
her marriage. She was going to talk to her about this as soon
as possible. I shall have to be diplomatic, Audra thought,
and immediately began to rehearse what she would say.

For his part, Vincent was ruminating on High Cleugh.

Ever since they had arrived on the slope, he had been
stealing glances at it. The old house was now in his direct
line of vision across the river, and he felt a compulsion to
bring his gaze back to it time and again. And as he did, he
could not help thinking of the little cottage he and Audra
had found in Upper Armley and which they had rented a
month ago.

When they had stumbled on it, quite by accident one
day, he had considered them most fortunate. The cottage
was sturdy, in good repair, and in a location convenient to
his work. But suddenly it had lost its appeal. How small and
insignificant it was in comparison to High Cleugh, where
his wife had been born and brought up. What he was
offering her was so much less.

Swiveling his head, he gazed at her appraisingly and with
a flash of unprecedented objectivity. How pretty she was in

her buttercup-yellow dress, fresh and desirable in every conceivable way. And she had so many laudable attributes. He was convinced she was going to make him the very best wife. Although he was never given to much introspection, Vincent sank down into his thoughts, contemplating Audra.

If the circumstances of her life had been different, she would never have been permitted to marry him.

This unanticipated thought shook Vincent to the core. The fact that *her* family would have objected to her marrying *him* had never occurred to him before, but now that it had, he knew he was absolutely correct in this assumption, and this knowledge depressed him. He suddenly remembered his mother's dire words. "Asking for trouble, that's what you are, my lad," she had said. "If you marry her, you'll rue the day." Laurette had been against their marriage too, even though she liked Audra a lot. "You're from two different worlds," his sister had said when he had challenged her about her views. "It's not going to work. She's a lady born and bred."

In an effort to convince Laurette that this did not matter, he had told her about Audra's hard life as a ward maid, the drudgery of her demanding work as a nurse at the Fever Hospital. She had gaped at him, incredulous. "Don't be such a fool, Vincent. What's that got to do with anything! Her breeding and her gentility will always be part of her. She's different from you and me, from *us*, and believe me, that *difference* makes a big difference."

Always quick to flare up at the slightest thing, he had flown into a temper and stormed out, bristling with anger. And he had been put out with his favorite sister for weeks. Vincent had a strong mind of his own, and so he had gone about his business, done as he had seen fit. And he had seen fit to marry Audra despite the opposition from his family, which she knew nothing about.

Vincent was still convinced that his mother and his sister were wrong. Surely it was of no great consequence that he and Audra were from different backgrounds. They loved each other. That was all that counted, wasn't it?

Audra, her eyes on Vincent, sensed a change in him. She said, "Are you all right? You look a bit funny."

"Oh I'm fine, love," he said, then laughed somewhat shakily.

"You looked quite troubled a moment ago. Are you sure nothing's bothering you, Vincent?"

He forced a bright smile. "Never felt better," he exclaimed and thought to add, "I'm sorry that this is the last day of our honeymoon, that it's over."

"Not quite." She kissed his cheek, gazed into his face, loving him with her eyes. "We've still got the whole of today and this evening in Harrogate. We'll have a lovely dinner for your birthday at the White Swan. It's a pretty hotel; you'll enjoy staying there."

Audra sat back, tipped her head to one side, went on, "Even though our honeymoon will come to an end tomorrow, our life together is only just beginning, Vincent. Think about that . . . and I know we're going to have a wonderful life, you and I."

"Yes," he said, relaxing.

Audra suddenly grew animated and talkative, and there was a new vivacity about her as they finished their picnic. She spoke to Vincent at length about their future and was full of enthusiasm for all the good things she believed it held in store for them.

CHAPTER THIRTEEN

"Do you see anything that belongs to you, Audra?" Vincent asked, swinging his alert green gaze around the drawing room of The Grange.

"Those two oil paintings on either side of the French windows and the watercolor on that side wall," she said, "they're by my father. If you look at them closely, you'll find they're signed 'Adrian Kenton.'"

Vincent strode across the floor, peered at the two beautiful landscapes and then at the still life, and nodded his head. He pivoted to face Audra, who hovered near the fireplace. "What else is yours?"

"Most of the wood pieces in here . . . the inlaid chest next to the door, these two small Sheraton tables, and the console over there—oh, and the Meissen clock on it. There are two Chippendale-style chairs, but those must be in another room. She also has my mother's Georgian silver tea service, some smaller pieces of silver and three more paintings, but only one of those is by my father." A confident smile struck Audra's mouth and she patted her handbag. "I have my inventory in here, and the one for the jewelry, so I'm well armed—" Audra stopped, focused on the door as it opened.

Vincent did the same. He was riddled with curiosity about the woman he was going to meet. He had heard a few things about her from Audra, and he did not like what he had heard.

Alicia Drummond paused on the threshold.

Vincent, observing the middle-aged woman with quickening interest, thought: *Narrow.* Everything about her is narrow. Eyes, nose, mouth, face and body. He did not even question that she was narrow-minded as well; he had already surmised *that* from Audra's comments about her.

Audra, who had not seen her relative for almost six years, was startled. She decided that Alicia Drummond had not only aged considerably in this time, but looked as if she were ill. The woman was drawn, haggard even, and excessively thin, and her stony black eyes were sunken into their sockets. Wispy gray hair was pulled back into a bun, and she wore a drab brown silk dress that was unbecoming.

Closing the door behind her, Alicia walked into the room with her usual sedate stiffness. She said fretfully, in her high-pitched voice, "Hello, Audra. When you wrote to me two weeks ago, you didn't say you'd be bringing someone with you. I expected you to be alone. I was surprised when the maid told me you were accompanied by—" She surveyed Vincent, her eyes filling with curiosity and speculation, and finished, "Your young man." It came out sounding more like a question than a statement of fact.

Audra said briskly, "Good afternoon, Aunt Alicia. I would like to introduce my husband to you. This is Vincent

Crowther. Vincent, this is my mother's first cousin, Alicia
Drummond."

Alicia, rarely at a loss for words, was momentarily
speechless. *Husband,* she thought, utterly amazed. This
smartly dressed, good-looking young man was married to
plain, little Audra. It hardly seemed possible.

Stepping forward, Vincent thrust out his hand. "Pleased
to meet you, Mrs. Drummond."

"How do you do," Alicia responded, her cold eyes
weighing him up. Vincent spoke nicely, and there was only
the merest trace of the broad Yorkshire accent in his
vowels, but Alicia caught it. Working class, more than
likely, she commented to herself. Well, that explained
everything.

Waving a hand airily, in the direction of the sofa, Alicia
murmured, "Do sit down, both of you." She herself
perched on the edge of a chair and gave her attention to
Audra. "Why didn't you let us know you were getting
married?"

Ignoring the question, which she considered to be
ridiculous under the circumstances, Audra said, "We spent
our honeymoon at Robin Hood's Bay, and as I knew we'd be
passing close by on our return to Leeds, I thought it would
be a good idea to come and see you. I wanted Vincent to
meet you, since—"

"I'm glad you did."

"Since he'll be coming back next Saturday. With a van,
to—"

"A *van.*" Alicia sounded perplexed.

"Yes. He'll be coming to collect my things."

"*Things?*"

"Yes, my things, Aunt Alicia. Or perhaps I should say my
mother's things, which have belonged to me since her death
and which you have been . . . *storing* here."

"Gracious me, Audra, don't tell me you're planning to go
to the expense of hiring a van to come all this way—from
Leeds, you say?—to pick up a few odd bits of valueless
furniture."

"Valueless," Audra echoed, giving her a sharp stare. "I
wouldn't say that."

"Oh I would. They're not worth much."

"Whatever they're worth I want them. I wish to have my mother's things around me. Besides, they belong to me—and have for a long time."

"It seems to me that a couple of old tables hardly merit such enormous effort," Alicia scoffed. Adopting a scornful expression, she swung to Vincent. "Imagine hiring a van to come and pick up a few sticks of furniture. Audra is being ridiculous, in my opinion. What a waste of money. I'm sure you agree."

"Audra wants her things," Vincent said quietly but with great firmness. "And anything Audra wants I'm going to make sure she gets."

"Quite," Alicia sniffed, looking down her nose at him.

"There's the matter of the jewelry, Aunt Alicia. I will take that with me today," Audra announced.

Alicia opened her mouth, immediately closed it, conscious of the grim determination glittering in Audra's eyes, the implacable curve of her mouth. "I'm not sure the jewelry is here," she improvised. "If I remember correctly, my mother took it to her house for safekeeping."

"You're not *sure*," Audra repeated. Her expression hardened. "I would think you'd be scrupulously careful with other people's possessions. I'm also rather surprised you didn't get in touch with me yourself weeks ago. You knew I'd be twenty-one at the beginning of this month, that I was coming of age and was therefore legally entitled to what's mine." Audra's laugh was soft but knowing. "Actually, there was no good reason why I shouldn't have had my mother's things years ago. My—"

"You weren't married years ago," Alicia cut in, sounding defensive. "What would you have done with the furniture? Where would you have put it?"

"I'm talking about my mother's jewelry," Audra exclaimed. "And I was about to say that my former employer, Mrs. Irène Bell, said exactly the same thing only a couple of weeks ago. Both she and Mr. Bell were amazed you hadn't been in touch with me early in May, to find out what I wanted to do about my possessions. Mr. Bell's a solicitor, extremely well known in Leeds, and he's very conscious of legalities, all that sort of thing." Audra let her narrowed blue gaze linger on the other woman pointedly.

Alicia flushed, grew uncomfortable under this fixed and probing scrutiny. Ever since she had received Audra's letter, she had been put out. She was reluctant to relinquish the girl's valuables and had been scheming to keep them. But now Alicia was reconsidering her moves. She had no desire to become entangled with a solicitor, or with this husband, who looked as if he could turn difficult at the slightest provocation. Striving to hide her irritation, Alicia stood up. Clearing her throat, she muttered, "There is the possibility that my mother spoke about removing the jewelry to her house, to look after it for you, but that she never got around to doing so. My memory's not what it used to be, I'm afraid. It could still be here. Perhaps I had better go upstairs and check."

"Yes, that would be wise," Audra said.

Alicia hurried out, cursing Audra under her breath. She had not bargained for solicitors and husbands. The girl had caught her off guard.

The minute they were alone, Vincent said in a quiet voice, "She's a right crafty devil, that one."

"I know, and she's trying to steal my things," Audra murmured, also keeping her voice low.

"Don't worry, I won't let her. Anyway, I bet she's afraid you'll bring Mr. Bell down on her if she does anything wrong. I noticed the way her face changed when you mentioned he was a noted Leeds solicitor."

Audra sat back on the sofa, glanced around, disliking this room as much as she disliked the entire house and those who lived in it. She thought of the cruel things Alicia Drummond had done to her in the past, and a coldness settled over her heart like a hoarfrost. Unexpectedly, an image of her brothers saying goodbye to her as they set out for Australia leapt into her mind and with such vividness she stiffened. Then that awful sense of loss gripped her. She snapped her eyes shut, wondering if she would ever be free of this distressing feeling. Surely she would. After all, she was no longer alone. She had Vincent. He was her family now. Opening her eyes, she swung her head to look at him.

He met her gaze, noticed the bright blueness of her eyes dulling as a sadness crept into them. He squeezed her hand, said, "This place upsets you and it gives me the willies. Let's scram as soon as you've finished your business with the old battle-ax."

Audra nodded.

The two of them sat together on the sofa in silence, holding hands, waiting.

It was not very long before Alicia Drummond returned, carrying the wooden jewelry box. She brought it straight to Audra, thrust it at her with forcefulness and in rather a rude manner. "Here it is," she snapped. "No doubt you want to check, to make sure nothing is missing. And quite frankly, I would prefer you to do so. I don't want to be accused of misappropriating your property—at a later date."

There was no response from Audra.

She sat staring down at the box on her lap. How familiar it was. It had always stood on the dresser in her mother's bedroom at High Cleugh. Sometimes, when she had been a child and playing at dressing up in her mother's clothes, she had been allowed to dip into it, to take out a pin or a brooch or a pendant to wear for a while.

After a moment, she raised the lid, filling with relief now that she had these most personal things of her mother's in her hands at last. She began to sort through the items in the box, fingering each one lovingly. She thought of her mother's elegance and grace, smiled to herself as innumerable memories flooded her, touched off as they were by the different pieces.

She picked up her mother's engagement ring set with three tiny diamonds and gazed at it. My mother wore this for most of her life, Audra thought, and now I shall wear it. She slipped it on the third finger of her right hand, and as she did she experienced a sense of deep satisfaction. She felt as though the ring brought her mother closer; it was like a link to the past. And this pleased her.

Audra had no need to refer to the inventory, since she knew it by heart. The jewelry was intact. Nothing had been taken. And whether or not Alicia Drummond had been wearing it all these years was suddenly beside the point. The box and its contents were now hers, and rightfully so, and this was the only thing of any importance.

Placing the box on the sofa between her and Vincent, Audra opened her handbag and took out the other inventory. Directing her gaze at Alicia, she said, "This is the list of my mother's furniture and silver and paintings which are in this house. I'll leave it for you to look over later. Vincent will come back with two of his brothers next Saturday morning to collect everything. At about ten o'clock. I hope that's convenient?"

Mortified, Alicia could only nod.

Audra placed the piece of paper on one of the Sheraton occasional tables, and went on, "In the meantime, I thought we could take my father's paintings with us today. We have the motor car and they'll fit nicely in the back."

Wanting to be finished with the business and to get Audra away from this depressing house, Vincent sprang up, interjected, "I'd better start taking them off the walls." He glanced at Alicia, explained, "I know which pictures were painted by Audra's father; she already pointed them out to me."

Alicia Drummond thought she had turned to stone.

She could neither speak nor move. She simply gaped at Vincent, watched transfixed as he removed one of the oils, leaned it against a chair, then walked over to the other one, reached his hands up for it.

It was then that something cracked in Alicia Drummond. Years of rigid self-control fell away. "Don't touch my painting! Don't you dare touch it!" she cried, leaping up, rushing across the room, all semblance of dignity evaporating. She grabbed Vincent's arm roughly, peered into his face, shouted with mounting rage, "Don't you dare touch any of my paintings!"

He was flabbergasted at her words and her behavior. He shrugged off her hand, stepped back, swiveled his eyes to Audra on the sofa. They exchanged looks of astonishment.

Audra was on her feet swiftly and hurried across the floor. "They're not your paintings, Aunt Alicia. They're mine," she said in a firm but reasonable voice. She wondered if the woman had lost her senses. "Unless you've forgotten, my father painted them. And they always hung at High Cleugh. They are part of my legacy from my father, and my mother, and I—"

"Your mother!" Alicia screamed, whirling on her. "Don't you mention your mother to me. She was nothing but a whore!"

Audra gasped, recoiled.

Vincent could not believe he had heard correctly.

"Here, watch it," he exclaimed. "Don't you talk like that to my wife. I won't stand for it." He drew closer to Audra, slipped his arm around her and glared at Alicia. "Where do you get off, calling Audra's mother such a terrible thing?"

"Don't you like the word *whore?* Then pick any name you prefer . . . trollop, slut, harlot, strumpet! They all fit her. Because that's what she *was*. She took him away from me, she stole my darling Adrian." Alicia's shrill voice now turned into a wail. Near tears, she rushed on, "He belonged to me. We had an understanding. We were to be married. Until she set her cap at him, turned his head, inveigled him into her bed with her wiles and her fancy ways." The words choked in her throat. Alicia began to take gasping breaths, holding her hand to her chest as if in pain.

Audra was so appalled, so sickened by what she had heard, she could only stare at her relative in horror. "So that's what it's been about all these years," she said finally, shaking her head in disbelief. "*Oh my God!* My brothers and I were punished merely because you were *jealous*. How despicable, to tear us apart when we were children just because of something as futile as that. And when my parents were already dead, when the past no longer mattered. You are a foul woman, Alicia Drummond, foul. As for you and my father—" Audra paused, took a deep breath. "I hardly knew my father, but from what I've heard about him, Adrian Kenton was a fine and sensitive man. I don't believe for one minute that he could have ever been interested in the likes of *you*."

Filling with disgust, Audra turned away from the woman. She said to Vincent, "Please take down the other paintings by my father and then we can go."

Vincent did as she asked.

Audra walked over to the sofa, picked up her handbag and the jewelry box.

Additional restraints, self-imposed over the years, began to snap inside Alicia Drummond. And all of the ancient hatred she had harbored for Edith Kenton, and which had not abated even in death, rose up in her. It seemed to congeal in her face, which was contorted into an ugly mask.

She scurried across the carpet to Audra, leaned close to her face and cried, "Adrian Kenton was not your father! Not your father, do you hear? You're a bastard. *Peter Lacey's bastard.* She was carrying on with him when Adrian was still alive. My poor darling Adrian, having to bear witness to that."

Audra took a rapid step back, shaking her head from side to side frantically, denying the woman's words. "It's not true! It's not true!" she cried.

"Yes, it is," Alicia hissed. "Your mother was an adulteress and you are a bastard!"

"And you are a liar, Alicia Drummond!"

Vincent knew he must act immediately.

He seized hold of Audra's arm and almost dragged her into the entrance hall. Pivoting on his heels, he sped back to the drawing room, grabbed the three paintings he had taken off the walls, then swung to Alicia Drummond.

She stood in the middle of the room, twisting her hands together in agitation. There was a febrile look on her face and a wildness in her eyes. He thought she had gone quite mad.

He said, "I'll be back next Saturday for the rest of Audra's stuff, and everything had better be in good condition—*or else.*"

"How dare you threaten me!"

"I'm not threatening you; I just want you to know that I mean business. And the law is on our side; think on it, Mrs. Drummond."

Audra was standing where he had left her in the hall, clutching the jewelry box to her chest. Her face was white and she trembled.

"Come on," he cried, "and get the door please, love, my hands are full."

"Yes," she said, trying to throw off the sense of shock she was feeling, hurrying after him to open the front door.

Once they were inside his Uncle Phil's motor car and driving away from the house, Vincent breathed a lot easier. As he came to the gates at the end of the long driveway, he slowed, eased the car out onto the main road to Ripon. He drove in this direction for a few minutes, wanting to put a bit of distance between themselves and The Grange; soon he brought the car to a standstill, parked under a tall hedge.

Audra and he turned to face each other at precisely the same moment.

Vincent had never seen her looking so pale, and she hugged the wooden box as if she was afraid someone was going to wrest it from her. But at least she had stopped shaking. His heart went out to her as he stared into her eyes. They were awash with hurt. He wanted to make her feel better but was not sure how to do so.

He said softly, "It's all right now, love. And you don't have to set foot in that bloody awful house ever again."

Audra nodded. "Yes," she said.

There was a small silence as they continued to look at each other.

Eventually, she asked in a low voice, "You don't think it's true, do you, Vincent? You don't think that I'm . . . illegitimate, do you?" Her lip began to quiver and her eyes brimmed.

"Oh I don't! I don't!" he exclaimed, his vehemence echoing loudly in the confines of the small car. "You said it yourself and right to her face . . . she's a liar."

"But why would she make up something so awful, something as despicable as that?"

Startled by these questions, Vincent now looked askance at his young wife and said, "Audra . . . *love* . . . you're not daft, you *know* why. She spelled it out to you." His voice changed, grew much harder and sharper. "She's a bloody old cow, bitter and spiteful. Not only that, she's crackers, if you ask me. Off her rocker, that one. I wouldn't be surprised if they cart her off one day, put her away in a padded cell."

"Yes, perhaps you're right," Audra said slowly, wondering if he really was. Her eyes turned reflective as she ruminated on Alicia Drummond. The woman was wicked, wasn't she? *Evil.* Madness might not be involved at all. Audra's mind automatically swung to her brothers, and she sighed as she thought of them, remembering their years of hardship and worry in Australia, and her own problems and loneliness after they had been sent away. The shocking thing was that none of it need ever have happened. It had all been so unnecessary.

"Are you all right?" Vincent asked.

"Oh yes," she murmured, "I was just thinking . . . people can be rotten, can't they?"

"Aye, lass, they can," he agreed, then reached out, touched her arm lightly. "Try and relax . . . nobody's going to steal the jewelry box."

Audra half smiled. She loosened her grip on it, let it rest on her knee, and after a moment or two she remarked, "Well, I suppose we'd better be getting along. We can't sit here all day."

"Okay . . . but where to, Audra? Do you still want to go and see your great-aunt? Or shall we forget it and make tracks for Harrogate instead?"

There was a fractional hesitation on Audra's part; then she said, "I think we should go and see her. She *is* expecting me, and I want you to meet her." Audra gave him a reassuring look. "She's nicer than her dreadful daughter, I promise you."

"Just point me in the right direction."

"We're not very far away, as a matter of fact. Drive down this road, for about ten minutes, until we come to Cobbler's Green on the right-hand side. That's where we turn off. Bedelia Cottage is at the bottom."

Neither of them spoke as Vincent drove along at a steady

speed, and it was only after they had turned into Cobbler's Green that Audra said, "It *could* be true, you know."

Instantly understanding what she meant, he answered quickly, "Maybe it could, but I wouldn't spend any time worrying over it, if I were you."

"Why not?"

"Because you'll never know the answer. Your mother is the only person who could have told you the truth, and she's dead."

"She might have confided in Great-Aunt Frances; I told you before, they were close."

"You're not going to ask the old lady, are you?"

"Well . . . well, yes, I may."

But in the end, Audra did not ask her great-aunt anything at all.

From the moment they arrived at Bedelia Cottage, it was easy to see that the old lady was very frail indeed. Even though it was late afternoon, it was still a lovely day, sunny and warm. Nevertheless, the windows were tightly closed and she sat in front of a huge fire in her cluttered parlor, a silk shawl draped around her withered shoulders, her hands outstretched to the warming flames.

Audra led Vincent through the maze of Victorian furniture and bric-a-brac, the long-forgotten smell of the room immediately assailing her. The dry, dusty air held a hint of overripe apples, furniture polish and potpourri, as it had for all the years Audra had been coming here as a child. And when she bent to kiss the wrinkled cheek, she caught a faint whiff of moth balls mingled with lavender water and peppermints and she felt a rush of affection for Frances Reynolds. Sudden nostalgia took a grip on her, held her in its spell for a few moments.

Her great-aunt was overjoyed to see Audra after such a long time, and to meet Vincent. Surprised though she was that Audra had appeared with a husband, she took to him at once, or so it seemed to Audra. She chirped away like a small bright bird, smiling at them benevolently. From time to time she nodded her head and patted Audra's hand, and as she did she plied her with innumerable questions about her life.

Audra, equally glad to see her great-aunt, answered her as best she could, all the while observing the octogenarian closely. She looked as delicate and as translucent as the paper-thin china cups they were drinking tea from, and Audra thought that if she breathed too heavily on her the old woman would shatter. Silver-haired and slight of build for as long as Audra could remember, there was a new fragility, a brittleness about her, and Audra wanted to wrap her in cotton wool.

Old bones, old flesh, soon to turn to dust, Audra reflected silently, and a little shiver ran down her arms despite the warmth of the room. Audra's intuitiveness told her that she was probably seeing her aunt for the last time. Frances Reynolds was very, very old now; her life on this earth was coming to an end. It was then that Audra also knew that it would be quite wrong to start probing into her mother's past. That would be too upsetting to this gentle old lady, who had so adored her mother, who was always so affectionate toward her and who had made Vincent feel so welcome.

And Vincent is correct in what he said, Audra now thought. Only my mother knew the truth and she has taken it to the grave. It suddenly struck Audra that it would besmirch her mother's memory to start talking about adultery and questioning her own legitimacy.

And so she remained silent.

They spent almost two hours at Bedelia Cottage, and it was only when they made motions to leave that her great-aunt mentioned Edith Kenton.

Peering at Audra through ancient eyes, she said in her whispery voice, "When my darling Edith died, Alicia removed all of her papers from High Cleugh. But I took them away from her, because I wanted to keep them for you, Audra, until you were grown up."

Frances Reynolds paused, smiled slightly and shook her silvered head. "Ah, dear child, you are looking so eager, but I'm afraid there is nothing of great importance amongst your mother's papers. Some old letters, her birth certificate, her marriage lines, a few old photographs, nothing much else."

Audra's face fell; then she said, "But I want them anyway."

"Of course you do, my dear, and that is why I kept them safe for you all these years." She glanced at Vincent. "The papers are in that attaché case over there on the floor. Could you bring it here, please?"

"Right away," he said, leaping to his feet. He was back in a moment, offered it to the old lady.

"No, no, give it to Audra; the papers belong to her, Vincent."

"Thanks," Audra said, taking the attaché case from him. She noticed that her mother's initials, "EWK," were stamped in gold on the front between the locks. She snapped these open, peeped inside, touched the papers on the top, then decided to examine everything later, in the privacy of their room, after they arrived at the White Swan Hotel in Harrogate.

"Thank you very much for keeping the papers for me, Great-Aunt Frances, I'm most appreciative."

The old lady smiled and nodded. "I know you were going to see Alicia," she said in her weak voice that slightly quavered. "I presume that you did so and that you collected your mother's jewelry."

"Yes," Audra said and paused awkwardly, afraid to say anything more than this. She glanced across at her husband.

Vincent came to her rescue. "Everything was fine, and I'll be driving over with my brothers and a van next week, to get the furniture and the rest of Audra's things."

The old lady beamed at him and a satisfied, almost triumphant look entered her eyes. She reached for her cane. "Come along, the two of you, let us go into the dining room. I want you to choose a piece of silver for your first home."

CHAPTER FOURTEEN

"Please, Vincent, you have to get up," Audra said, shaking his shoulder.

He shifted his position in the bed, turned on his back and opened his eyes, blinking in the filtered light coming in through the filmy curtains. "Why?"

"Vincent, you know very well why," Audra exclaimed as lightly as possible, trying to sheathe her annoyance with him. "Gwen's coming to supper."

"*If* she shows up."

"It was my fault last Sunday," Audra said hastily, "I got the dates mixed up."

He threw her a skeptical look, said nothing.

"*Please*, Vincent," she begged, her voice rising, "please get up."

His answer was to reach out and catch hold of her wrist. He pulled her down next to him, wrapped his arms around her and hugged her. He whispered against her cheek, "Come to bed with me for half an hour."

Audra struggled against him. "I can't, you know very well I can't. There isn't time."

"You mean you don't want to," he said and let go of her at once.

Rising quickly, Audra stepped away from the bed and looked down at him, pursing her lips. "You're being terribly unfair."

"Oh no I'm not. You've turned cold on me lately."

She flushed. "I haven't. You always pick the wrong time!"

He swiveled his eyes to the alarm clock on the bamboo night stand. "What's wrong with four-thirty on a Sunday afternoon. It strikes me it's the perfect time."

"We're expecting a guest."

"Ah yes. La-di-da Miss Gwen Thornton." He pronounced the name with acerbity, added, "I don't know what you see in her, why you run after her."

"I don't run after her!"

"Yes, you do. I'm beginning to think you prefer her to me."

"Don't be so ridiculous," Audra exclaimed, staring at him in total astonishment. "You know that's not true." She felt a sudden surge of anger toward him and went on crossly, "Anyway, I'm not in the mood to . . . come to bed, to make love, not after your behavior these past few weeks."

"*My* behavior! What the bloody hell are you talking about?" He sat bolt upright in the bed and glared at her, his brilliant green eyes flashing as his temper flared.

Audra shook her head, very slowly, swallowing her exasperation with him, suddenly comprehending. "You just don't *know* what you *do*, Vincent, do you?"

"What do you mean?"

"Oh Vincent, *Vincent*, you're impossible. And you make me so mad at times. For one thing, I'm getting impatient with your performance every Sunday at lunchtime. You go off to the pub with your brothers, think nothing about strolling in well after two o'clock, having promised to be back by one at the latest, and then you turn nasty on me because lunch is spoiled . . . as if that were my fault."

"I didn't turn nasty today."

"Yes, you did. Actually, alcohol doesn't agree with you at all; it brings the worst out in you, makes you belligerent and touchy."

He was about to ignore these criticisms, since she had lately developed a habit of carping, but changed his mind. "Don't start giving *me* a lecture," he snapped. "I don't like it. I'm a man, not a kid. I've always gone to the pub on Sundays, ever since I was eighteen, and I'm not going to stop now. Not for you or anybody else. And anyway, everybody goes to the pub on Sundays; it's an old English tradition."

Only with the working class, she thought and instantly hated herself for even thinking this; she despised any kind of prejudice in others. She said, "There's something else . . . you left me alone to mark time at your mother's *again* last night, whilst you went off carousing in the pubs with your brothers—"

"It was our Bill's birthday," he cut in indignantly, all of his defenses going up.

"That's true, and I don't begrude it when you celebrate a special occasion of that kind. But it wasn't Bill's birthday last Saturday, or the Saturday before, *or* the one before that, when you also went off on your own."

"You didn't have to stay at my mother's last night. You could have gone to the old-time dancing with Laurette. After all, she invited you."

"I'm not married to Laurette, I'm married to you."

He sighed heavily and his mouth tightened in aggravation. "I hope that doesn't mean that I've got to be tied to your apron strings twenty-four hours a day for the rest of my life, because, believe you me, I won't be."

Audra bit back the retort on the tip of her tongue, asking herself why she was bothering to argue with him at this particular time. Gwen was due to arrive within the hour and she wanted the atmosphere in the house to be tranquil. All she needed was for Gwen to think there was some sort of trouble between them.

And so she walked to the bedroom door, said softly, "I still have a few chores," and ran downstairs before he could say another word.

Pushing aside her worries about the recent changes in their relationship, she busied herself in the parlor-kitchen of their four-room cottage in Pot Lane. After covering the deal table in the center of the floor with her best lace cloth, she took out several pieces of the beautiful china service the Bells had given them as a wedding present, and went about setting the table for supper.

Once she had finished she glanced at the grate in the center of the Yorkshire range, wondering whether or not to light the fire yet; these September nights soon turned cool. On the other hand, it was still sunny. Thinking of the weather reminded Audra that she needed fresh flowers for the center of the table and for the console in the tiny sitting room next door. She hurried across to the work table next to the sink under the window, found the scissors in the drawer, took the flower basket off the set-pot and went outside.

The cottage did not have a name, only the number thirty-eight painted in white on its green door, and it was one of three in a cul-de-sac behind The Towers in Upper Armley. Each house had a small garden, but Audra's was the most flourishing and resplendent because the previous tenants had cultivated it well over the years. Also, she had tended it diligently herself since they had moved into the cottage in June, and had made some new plantings and other improvements.

The last of the summer roses were full blown, tipped heavy and luxuriant heads down to the dark earth, and as Audra bent over the bushes, she breathed deeply of their scent. It was rich and sweet, and just a little heady, and it made her feel slightly dizzy. She began to cut the roses with great care, not wanting to destroy the fragile blossoms by knocking any of the petals off. She selected mostly from the pale yellow and pink blooms, since these seemed to be fading faster than the others.

"You've no idea how bonny you look, love," Vincent said from the doorway of the cottage.

She glanced up.

He flashed her one of his most beautiful and winning smiles.

She smiled back, understanding that he now wished to make amends. "Thank you," she murmured. Rising, she picked up the flower basket, walked toward him down the flagged garden path.

His eyes did not leave her face. When she came to a standstill in front of him, he put his arms around her affectionately and led her inside. After closing the door and taking the basket out of her hands, he drew her into his arms, kissed her deeply and with growing passion.

Audra responded, held on to him tightly, returned his kisses. And she did so willingly now, all of the resentment which had been building up falling away from her suddenly, unexpectedly. She thought: I love him, he loves me, and that's all that matters really. We'll work out our differences. Somehow we will.

After a moment he stopped kissing her, tilted her face up to his, looked down into her startling eyes. It seemed to

him that their bright cornflower blue had turned to the
deeper hue of the violet, and as always they reflected her
innermost emotions. His own gaze was intense, searching.
"Do you have any idea how much I want you at times?" he
asked finally, in a hoarse voice.

"Yes." She hesitated, then whispered, "I feel the same
way."

Vincent smiled to himself, knowing how difficult it was
for her to articulate such things. Trailing a finger down her
cheek, he said, "Perhaps Gwen won't stay too late?"

"No, I don't think she will. It's Monday tomorrow."

Vincent leaned closer, murmured in her ear, "Let's make
a date to have an early night, Mrs. Crowther."

"Yes, let's."

He hugged her to him, then released her. Swinging away,
Vincent walked over to the front door. "I'll be back in time
for supper."

Surprised, she asked, "Where are you going?"

"To my mother's."

"*But why?*"

"I promised Frank I would help him to fill in his military
papers. . . . Dad's finally given him permission to join the
army, and he's very excited, our Frank is. You know how
badly he wants to get into a cavalry regiment and go out to
India. Can't say I blame him, either. Not the way things are
in this bloody country right now." He made a face. "So
many men on the dole and more being laid off work every
day."

Audra held herself very still. "You're all right at Varley's,
aren't you? They're not having problems too, are they,
Vincent?"

"No, no, of course not." He smiled reassuringly. "We're
in the middle of building that ruddy great house for old
man Pinfold and his missis. Anyway, don't *you* worry your
little head about such things; that's my job, as the man of
the house." He blew her a kiss, flashed his cheeky grin.
"Ta'rar, love, I'll see you a bit later."

CHAPTER FIFTEEN

"So you did get a sofa. *Finally,*" Gwen said, stepping into the little sitting room from the parlor-kitchen.

"Yes," Audra replied, following sharply on her heels, frowning at her friend's back.

Gwen marched up to this piece of furniture, which stood in the center of the room facing the fireplace, and promptly sat down on it. She crossed her legs, settled against the cushions and made herself comfortable.

Audra hovered in front of her, studying her face intently. It was bland, as always, and innocent enough. And Audra knew at once that Gwen had not meant anything mean or unkind by the remark, even though the way she had said *finally* had sounded a trifle catty, as if she thought they hadn't been able to afford one before.

"We bought the sofa two weeks ago," Audra volunteered in her usual quiet way. "We'd been looking for that particular style for quite a while, since before we were married, actually."

"Oh, had you," Gwen said and swung around, brought her face closer to the back of the sofa, the three strands of cheap beads rattling as she moved. She sniffed the material. "Mmmm. *Leather.* Very nice too, Audra. I must admit, I do like the genuine thing. Nothing imitation for me, either."

Audra bit back a smile, walked over to the fireplace. She was amused by the incongruity of this last remark, in view of Gwen's penchant for fake jewelry. Always dripping in it, and a walking advertisement for Woolworth's, she had really outdone herself today. She was bedecked in a curious assortment of colored rhinestones and paste; none of it matched, and she glittered like an out-of-season Christmas tree. But that's my Gwenny, Audra thought with a rush of real warmth, her deep affection for her friend surfacing. She just wouldn't be the same without her beads and bracelets and dangling earrings; they're her trademark, and I don't suppose I would change her, even if I could.

Still smiling, Audra reached for the Swan Vestas on the mantelpiece. "It seems to have turned a little chilly," she said, crouching in front of the grate, striking a match. She brought the flame to the paper and wood chips and went on, "Are you sure I can't get you a cardigan, Gwen?"

"No, thanks very much, lovey, I'm all right. At least I will be now that you're getting the fire going." Gwen smoothed her hand over the skirt of her brilliant red silk dress, explained, "I should have worn something warmer than this, I suppose, but it's brand-new and I wanted you to see it. Do you like it, Audra?"

"It's a lovely frock and it really does suit you," Audra answered truthfully. She stood up, glanced approvingly at her friend.

Gwen preened; she patted her blond hair. "And what do you think of my new marcel wave?"

"I like it, and as a matter of fact I'm considering having one myself next week. Now, shall I make us a cup of tea? Or would you prefer a drink perhaps?"

"I wouldn't say no to a glass of sherry."

"I think I'll join you." Audra went to the hutch cupboard in the corner of the room, took out a bottle of Amontillado and two glasses, carried them to the mahogany console table which stood against the back wall.

Swinging her head, looking over the back of the sofa at Audra, Gwen remarked, "And while we're handing out compliments, let me pay you one. You've made this room look really nice, you have that, Audra. Your father's paintings are beautiful, especially that one over the fireplace, and this furniture of your mother's—well, it looks ever so handsome in here. The place does you proud, lovey."

Audra beamed at her. "Thanks, Gwen, and I am glad you like it. The room's small, of course, but that makes it cozy and comfortable, don't you think?"

Gwen nodded, then let her eyes roam around. "And what did you say the name of this funny green on the walls is?"

Audra laughed. "*Eau-de-Nil.*"

"What a strange name." Gwen made a face.

"It means water of the Nile in French, and it's a very popular color at the moment . . . in fashion, I mean."

"Oh is it. Fancy that. Well, you always did keep up with the latest trends in clothes, lovey, didn't you? I keep telling Mum that you're *the* expert on fashion and styles and fabrics and all that kind of thing. I hope you realize how much I value your advice. Yes, you've got the best taste of anybody I know." Gwen accepted the drink from Audra. "Thanks, lovey," she said.

The two women clinked glasses, and Audra stepped up to the fireside, sat down in one of the Chippendale-style chairs which had belonged to her mother. "I'm glad you think so—that I have taste, I mean."

Gwen smiled at her. "And where's Vincent then?"

"He went to his mother's, to help his brother fill out some papers. But he'll be back in time to have supper with us."

Gwen took a sip of sherry, not trusting herself to speak.

It seemed to her that Vincent was always rushing off to his mother's house, on some pretext or another, but she did not dare say this to Audra. Ever since their tense discussion on the subject of Vincent in July, Gwen had been scrupulously careful not to make any critical remarks about him. She had soon realized, on that hot summer day when they went to tea at Betty's Cafe in Leeds, that she was perilously close to losing Audra's friendship, and this had both distressed and alarmed her.

Audra was extremely important to Gwen, and so nowadays she kept a tight rein on her tongue at all times. But privately she believed that Vincent Crowther was not good enough for her friend, and nothing would make her change her mind. There was something about him that did not sit right with Gwen Thornton, although she would have been hard-pressed to pinpoint what this was, if asked. She thought of him as being emotionally dangerous, and her instinct told her he would make Audra extremely unhappy one day.

She wondered, yet again, why he was constantly trotting off to his mother's, if that was where he really had gone, and then dropped this thought. She was delighted he was not at home. This afternoon she wanted Audra to herself for a

while. She had something important to tell her and she
preferred to do so without Vincent being present. He could
be very opinionated. And he expressed those opinions
without being asked.

Conscious of the growing silence, Audra leaned forward,
peered across the dusky room. The twilight had come down
early today, and the only light emanated from the fire.
"You're very quiet, Gwen," she remarked. "Are you
troubled about something?"

"No, no, nothing's wrong," Gwen was quick to say. She
too drew closer, and let her voice sink low as she added, "I
don't want you to tell anyone, not even Vincent, but I'm
thinking of getting married."

"How wonderful, Gwen dear!" Audra cried, and then her
brow furrowed in puzzlement. "But I thought Mike had
another two years of medical school? You told me in the
spring that he wouldn't be able to afford a wife for a few
years."

"Oh but it's not Mike I'm thinking of marrying."

In the dimming light Audra could see that Gwen looked
very pleased with herself, and this further perplexed her.
"But you told me you were in love with Mike Lesley, and
certainly the two of you have behaved as if you were in the
past year . . . you've been like a couple of love birds in
fact," Audra said, "so what's suddenly happened to change
all that?"

"Don't be so dense, Audra," Gwen said with a light
laugh. "Obviously I've met someone else."

"Who?"

"It's someone you know—well, sort of—but you'll never
guess in a million years," Gwen declared, her voice echoing
with glee.

"No, I'm sure I won't, so you'd better tell me."

"*Geoffrey Freemantle.*"

Audra was flabbergasted.

She opened her mouth, then closed it without uttering
one single word. She simply gaped at Gwen in disbelief.
Taking a deep breath, she said at last, "You don't mean
Doctor Freemantle? The one who was at the Fever
Hospital for a while . . . you couldn't possibly mean *him*."

"Why couldn't I?" Gwen asked with sudden huffiness. "Of course I mean him."

"*Oh.*" Audra put her glass down on the Sheraton table a little unsteadily. She was staggered. If ever a man was wrong for Gwen Thornton, it was Geoffrey Freemantle. He was cold, arrogant, sarcastic and a snob. Good-looking, yes, in a stiff, formal sort of way, and from a wealthy family, too, but he was a pompous and disdainful man, older than Gwen by about fourteen years. Audra found herself filling with genuine dismay and concern. It was hard for her to visualize the gay, laughing, fun-loving Gwen with such a stuffed shirt, who believed himself to be superior to the rest of the human race.

"Is that all you're going to say? Just *oh* and nothing else?" Gwen's voice held a new tremulous quality and her feelings were obviously hurt.

"No, of course it isn't," Audra said, reaching out, squeezing Gwen's arm. Pushing an enthusiasm into her voice which she did not feel, she added, "I'm very, very happy for you, Gwen, really and truly I am. But I must admit to being a bit taken aback, since this was the last thing I expected to hear today. How did it all happen? Do tell, Gwen."

Mollified to a certain extent, Gwen said in a cheerier voice, "Well, after Geoffrey left Ripon, he went up to Northallerton, but he wasn't particularly happy there, so he transferred back to the General Infirmary in Leeds this past spring. Anyway, we kept running into each other in the corridors, and we remembered each other from Ripon. He was always very friendly with me—" Gwen broke off and giggled. "He finally asked me out at the beginning of July. And after one date it happened—just like that!" She snapped her thumb and fingers together, and the glass rings flashed in the firelight.

"It's been a bit fast," Audra commented, very softly.

"Yes, it has . . . just like you and Vincent."

Well, she's had the last word there, Audra thought and said, "How do your parents feel about it?"

Gwen's face immediately underwent a radical change and she bit her lip, looking worried and troubled. "To tell you the truth, Audra, I'm ever so upset with Mum and Dad. They don't seem to have taken to Geoffrey one little bit, and they're not pleased. Course, I think that's because Mike has been such a close chum of our Charlie's for years, and they always hoped I'd marry him. But what can I do? Geoffrey's the one for me, oh yes, he *is*, lovey."

"So you've made up your mind, Gwen?"

"Oh yes, I think so . . . no, I *know* so. And he's quite a catch for me, really he is." Her face began to glow again, reflecting the imitation jewels around her neck, and she appeared to swell with pride. "We've been looking at houses in Headingley, and I think we've found just the right one. It has a dining room, a lounge, a study, and five bedrooms, perfect for when we start a family. Next week, Geoffrey's taking me to Greenwood's in Leeds, to pick out an engagement ring, a *diamond* engagement ring, and the announcement will be in the Yorkshire *Post*."

"Have you fixed a definite date?" Audra asked next. She forced a bright smile.

"Not exactly, but Geoffrey wants us to be married in the spring, because he's taking me to Paris for our honeymoon, and he says you should only ever see Paris in the spring— for the first time, that is. He's going to fit me out with lots of new clothes too, in Paris, and we're to stay at the Ritz. Can you imagine *that!* And then we'll go down to the Riviera. Geoffrey says mimosa time in the south of France is very beautiful and not to be missed, and we'll be spending a whole week at the Negresco in Nice. It's a very posh place, you know, but then, so is the Ritz."

Gwen finally paused, leaned forward eagerly, fixing her eyes on Audra's face, seeking a reaction.

Audra simply smiled.

Clasping her hands together tightly, Gwen's expression of excitement now changed to one of awe at the glamorous prospects facing her in the future.

"Once we've settled in the house in Headingley, which I'm *certain* we'll buy, Geoffrey is going to leave the Infirmary and set up in private practice. He's going to take consulting rooms on Park Place in Leeds. He aims to be a fashionable doctor, treating the local gentry and society

women, and he'll be very successful and rich and I'm going
to help him all I can. We'll entertain a lot, for one thing,
give elegant dinner parties and luncheons, and that's why I
need lots of new clothes. Geoffrey wants me to look very
smart."

Audra could only nod, since her dismay was increasing
and she did not know what to say. The fake stones Gwen
was wearing, glittering so brilliantly in the lambent flames
of the fire, held her attention. For a split-second they
seemed real, looked like emeralds and rubies and sapphires
and not bits of Woolworth's glass. The jewelry will be the
first to go, she suddenly thought. He'll make her get rid of
it the minute they're married. Audra felt a stab of sadness
as she pictured Gwen stripped of all her silly garish baubles
which were worthless, yet had always meant so much to
her.

Poor little Gwenny, Audra thought, now endeavoring to
visualize her friend after *he* had worked his transformation
on her, after *he* had dressed her and groomed her and
turned her into the kind of Mrs. Geoffrey Freemantle *he*
wanted. In her mind's eye she saw a curiously stiff, cold
woman, that had nothing to do with Gwen Thornton. But
then none of the things Gwen had been saying had much to
do with the girl she knew so well and cared so much about.

Getting to her feet, Audra went and snapped on the
small lamps standing on the Sheraton side tables flanking
the fireplace. Then she hurried over to the console,
brought back the bottle of sherry and refilled their glasses.

Knowing Gwen was waiting for some sort of comment
after her graphic recital, Audra murmured, "Well, it all
sounds wonderful, very wonderful indeed."

After this statement there was no holding Gwen.

Audra realized this when she returned to her chair and
offered her friend the warmest of smiles—and her undivided attention.

Always a chatterbox, Gwen talked nonstop for the next
half hour about her impending wedding, Geoffrey, his
parents, the honeymoon and the life they would lead
afterward, and without drawing breath.

Leaning back, sipping her sherry, Audra merely nodded occasionally, aware that she would not be allowed to get a word in edgewise. But she did not really want to; neither was she listening very closely.

Her thoughts were centered on Geoffrey Freemantle. It was patently obvious to Audra why he wished to marry Gwen Thornton. She was much younger than he and was a beautiful blonde with a curvaceous figure, who had a vivacious, outgoing personality plus a loving nature. So all in all she was most desirable in every way; she would be to any man. Also, since she was a nurse and the daughter of a doctor, her background was ideal for an ambitious physician, and unquestionably Geoffrey Freemantle was that. Yes, Gwen could not be anything but an asset to him.

What truly bothered Audra was Gwen herself. Why on earth would she want to become *his* wife? He was the antithesis of Mike Lesley, and whatever Gwen now thought about Mike, Audra was aware that she had been genuinely smitten with Charlie's closest chum. There was only one answer: Gwen wanted Geoffrey Freemantle for everything he represented and all the things he could give her— prestige, position, money.

Instantly, Audra tried to dismiss these uncharitable thoughts and yet deep down inside herself she was convinced she was right. Not once in the entire time Gwen had been speaking about Geoffrey Freemantle had she mentioned that most crucial word, *love*. How can a marriage work without love, Audra wondered. Perhaps she ought to talk to Gwen about that. Immediately she decided against doing so, remembering how much *she* had resented Gwen's gratuitous comments about her own marriage.

Anyway, perhaps I'm wrong, Audra told herself. Maybe she does love him. And then, much to her astonishment, she thought: But loving a man doesn't necessarily make for happiness, does it?

CHAPTER SIXTEEN

Later that evening, toward the end of supper, Gwen flashed Audra a conspiratorial look. "Shall I tell Vincent my news?"

"Why not?" Audra said, laughing, aware that her friend had been bursting to let him in on her secret all night.

"What news?" Vincent asked, glancing from one to the other.

"I'm getting engaged next week," Gwen announced, then sat back in the chair, beaming and looking pleased with herself.

"Well I can't say I'm surprised." Vincent leaned over and kissed her cheek. "Congratulations, Gwen, and you ought to have brought Mike with you to supper. I like him, he's a straight bloke, and you've made a good choice for yourself."

There was a small silence.

Gwen said quickly, "Oh but it's not Mike I'm marrying."

"*Not Mike*," Vincent echoed, sounding startled. "Well, I'm blowed! And I thought you two were as thick as thieves. So you've found somebody else then."

"Yes."

"Cut up, Mike is, I'll bet."

Gwen's throat tightened and she discovered she could not speak. She simply nodded.

"Yes, I can well imagine how he's feeling." Vincent gave Gwen a very hard stare. "Mike thought a lot about you, Gwen, he did that."

Gwen said, "I know he did and I cared for him too, but obviously not enough, if I could fall for another man."

"And who's the lucky chap then?" Vincent asked, wondering how she could pass Mike Lesley up for someone else. Mike was very special and, now that he thought about it, the kind of man he would like for his sister Laurette.

"His name's Geoffrey Freemantle," Gwen was saying, giving him a bright, confident smile, "and he's a doctor at

Leeds Infirmary. But he's originally from Harrogate and that's where his parents live."

"And when did all this happen? I mean we were all together with Mike at the end of June, so it must've been in the last couple of months, right?"

"Yes, Geoffrey first asked me out at the beginning of July, but I've—"

"All a bit *quick*, Gwen, isn't it?" Vincent broke in peremptorily, and not giving her a chance to respond, he hurried on, "Marriage is a tricky business, you know, so I hope you're really sure about this chap. What I mean is that I *know* for a fact that Mike is the genuine thing, a really fine upstanding man, so I hope this new bloke is just as . . . *okay*. I wouldn't want you to be making a big mistake—a *terrible* mistake, Gwen."

Gwen's mouth tightened in annoyance and she glared at Vincent, bristling. How like him to express his unwanted and unasked-for opinions. She exclaimed coldly, "It just so happens that I've know Geoffrey for a long time—since I worked in Ripon. And as I pointed out to Audra earlier, you and she hardly had what I would call a lengthy courtship. Besides, it's none of your business, so there!" She sat back in a huff, still glaring at him.

"Oh excuse me, I'm sorry I spoke," he muttered and puffed hard on his cigarette, looking annoyed.

Audra could see they were heading for one of their little tiffs, and she exclaimed, "Now you two, stop this, don't spoil a lovely evening. Anyway, I have something to tell you both—a little news of my own."

Vincent swung to her, his brow lifting quizzically. "What news, love?"

"I've taken a job and I start in two weeks."

Vincent's jaw dropped and he stared at her in astonishment.

Gwen, equally surprised, cried, "What *kind* of job? *Where?*"

"At St. Mary's Hospital, here in Armley," Audra explained. It was her turn to look pleased with herself, and she rushed on enthusiastically. "And as a nurse, of course. Mrs. Bell introduced me to the matron there, and I'm looking forward to it immensely. It's a challenge, since I'm going to be on the Maternity Ward."

"Whatever made you *do* such a *stupid* thing?" Vincent demanded furiously, his green eyes blazing, an angry flush spreading up from his neck into his face. "I don't believe I'm hearing you right!"

Audra was so taken aback at his extraordinary outburst, she was momentarily thrown off balance. And then she sat up straighter and retorted, "I don't think it's stupid! I think it's very *smart* of me! After all, I've had a very good training and it's a pity to waste it. Matron Lennox has always said that nursing is a real gift with me, so why shouldn't I put it to good use? Not only that, I *want* to work."

"Well, you can forget it! No wife of mine is going out to work and that's that!"

His temper was boiling very near to the surface, and he shook his head with vehemence. "My God, Audra, what are you thinking about? How could you do such a thing? I can just hear my mates talking, sniggering behind my back because my wife has to work to help support the household."

"But that's not the reason I want to work!" Audra exclaimed.

"Maybe not, but that's what they'll think. Just you remember that I'm the man in this house and the bread-winner and that *I* wear the pants and make the decisions, not you." Glancing at Gwen, he appealed to her by saying, "I bet *you're* not going to work after you're married, are you? Will *you* continue to be a nurse at the Infirmary?"

"No, I won't," Gwen answered softly. She looked at Audra apologetically, reached out, touched her arm. "I'm sorry, lovey, but I'm afraid I *have* to agree with Vincent. He's right, really he is. Anyway, why would you want to go back to nursing in a hospital? It's such demanding work and the money's not much."

"Look, I want to use my skills and be *useful*." Determined to stand her ground with Vincent, Audra threw him a fierce look. "And why does it matter what people think? You're being absurd—"

"I refuse to discuss this any further, Audra!" he interjected. "The matter's closed!" He brought his fist down on the table much harder than he had intended, and the dishes rattled.

"Vincent, don't be so stubborn!" Audra was so infuriated by his attitude and his behavior that she could barely contain herself. "Being married to you doesn't mean that you can control me, make me do as you say. I would like to have a career in nursing, and it's my right to—"

"There you go again, Audra," Vincent laughed sarcastically. "It's Mrs. Irène bloody Bell talking, not you. I don't want any of her women's rights and suffragette nonsense in my house, lass, and you'd better not forget that!"

Audra sucked in her breath, took a hold of herself. "Oh Vincent, you're being so very unfair," she murmured, softening both her voice and her manner. She took hold of his hand, hoping to placate him, wanting to get her own way ultimately. "You're misunderstanding everything I've said."

He gave her a cold sulky little glance, made no response.

Laughing somewhat self-consciously, Gwen looked from Audra to Vincent, then said, "I don't like to see the two of you quarreling in this way. Come along, kiss and make up."

Knowing that Vincent would do no such thing, and wishing to curtail the quarrel because of Gwen's presence, Audra pushed back her chair and rose. Putting her arm around his shoulder, she brought her face down to his and kissed him on the cheek.

"All right, you win," she said softly. "I'll go to the hospital next week and tell them that I can't take the job." But she was merely making a gesture for the sake of peace and quiet. She did not mean one word she said, and she had no intention of giving in to him.

CHAPTER SEVENTEEN

The marriage that had begun with an intense physical passion in the heat of the summer had a winter frost on it by December. And the passion had cooled considerably.

Vincent and Audra were frequently at loggerheads in the latter part of 1928, and certainly the tranquility that had initially reigned in the little cottage in Pot Lane had given way to constant bickering and stormy quarrels.

The odd thing was that they were very alike in many respects, and this was actually part of the problem. Both were stubborn, strong-willed and independent-minded. In consequence, they were forever locking horns. Then again, each believed the other was wrong and therefore at fault. They were young and unable to make allowances for normal human frailties; neither could they compromise, which might have helped to lessen the tension between them.

Vincent, who was too self-involved at this time in his life to see much beyond his own desires and interests, had very little real understanding of Audra.

And surprisingly, she, who usually had so much insight into others, was rarely able to read him accurately because she was so subjective. In fact, Audra's view of Vincent Crowther would always be blurred and off-center, influenced as she was by emotions of the most powerful kind.

Audra was generally in a turmoil about him and filled with conflicting feelings. There were times when she believed she loved him to distraction, others when she was convinced she had nothing but hatred for him. Vincent, as it happened, felt exactly the same way, and he was often as confused about Audra as she was about him.

Another stumbling block in their relationship was their newly acquired habit of arguing violently about almost everything. They were suddenly incapable of discussing any subjects in a quiet and rational way, so that neither of them ever really knew what the other *truly* thought or felt.

And their mutual ambivalence about their marriage, and their dissatisfaction with each other, simply grew.

Sometimes they were able to make up in the darkness of their bedroom, drawn to each other—almost against their own volition—by the strong physical attraction they shared. But these occasions were growing rarer because their problems intruded more and more, and also because Audra, in particular, brought her anger to bed with her.

She had been holding a number of grudges against Vincent since September, and the one thing which rankled the most was his adamant refusal to let her return to nursing. She had reasoned, cajoled, argued and pleaded, in an effort to bring him around to her way of thinking. But Vincent had remained as unbending as he had been on the night of the supper with Gwen.

In the end, Audra had been the one to give in, suddenly understanding that if she defied him and took the job at the hospital, he would leave her. And very simply put, life without Vincent Crowther was quite inconceivable to her, whatever their difficulties might be. Therefore, she had allowed his wishes to come before her own, telling herself that her marriage was far more important to her than a job. Somehow she had managed to wear a cheerful expression most of the time, one that did nothing to betray her feelings of disappointment and frustration at his obstinacy.

But when Audra had gone to Calpher House to tell Mrs. Bell what had happened, her eyes had filled with tears and her unhappiness had tumbled out unexpectedly.

Irène Bell had been sympathetic, as she always was toward Audra, and she had done her best to comfort her. And whatever Mrs. Bell had thought privately about Vincent's attitudes, she had wisely kept her opinions to herself. "Perhaps he'll come around," Mrs. Bell had said encouragingly, giving her a hopeful smile.

But Audra knew he would not do so. It was not in Vincent's nature to reverse himself. Or to admit that he was wrong. Similar though they were in some ways, Audra did not share these particular characteristics with him. She was always able to recognize when her judgment was flawed or when she had made an error.

As she hurried down Pot Lane, on this raw afternoon early in December, she was telling herself just how wrong she had been. Wrong to marry him in the first place, and certainly wrong to stay with him as she had, forever wavering about what to do, forever indecisive. She should have packed and left the minute everything had started to go askew in August.

Well, she had done that now. There was no turning back.

She tightened her grip on the small suitcase she was carrying and clenched her teeth, thrusting out her determined chin. The decision had been made. *Finally*. She had walked out on Vincent Crowther and she had no intention of returning.

Deep down inside herself Audra knew that she still loved Vincent. She supposed she would always love him. But she had come to the realization that love was not necessarily enough to sustain a relationship. A couple had to be able to live together in harmony if a marriage was going to be successful. Seemingly she and Vincent could not do that. They were tearing each other apart with angry, hurtful words that were sometimes hard to retract later.

Last night they had had a particularly violent quarrel, their worst yet and one that had left her shaken and despairing.

An hour earlier she had been ironing the last of his shirts in the kitchen-parlor when suddenly she had put the flatiron down on the trivet with a bang, instantly understanding what she must do. She had quickly tidied away the ironing things, changed her clothes, packed a suitcase, then taken her meager savings and left the cottage.

As she had turned the key in the lock, her eye had caught the number thirty-eight painted on the green door and she had stared at it, had felt a strange pain in her chest. And then an immense sadness had fallen over her and she had leaned her head against the stone reveal of the door, closing her eyes, thinking of the past few months here. Simple and ordinary though it was, this humble little house was a palace to her. It was her first home of her own, and it contained not only all the things she owned in life but in a way her very life itself. Certainly her dreams and expecta-

tions for the future were sheltered within its walls. She had
believed that these would come to flower here with
Vincent, that they would start a family of their own, build a
good life together. But that was not meant to be—or so it
seemed to her.

Audra had cut off these thoughts, not daring to let her
mind run on in this manner. After slipping the key under
the doormat, she had picked up her suitcase and almost run
out of the cul-de-sac and into the lane.

And now as she headed in the direction of Whingate tram
terminal, she was still trying to push aside that sadness, as
well as the awful depression that had descended on her. But
the feelings lingered. Her dreams were shattered, her
hopes were flattened and the sense of loss she had lived
with for years loomed, enormous. She had lost again. Lost
her husband, lost their life together, lost her future.

Audra's step faltered, and for a split-second, as she
hesitated, she almost changed her mind and went back to
the cottage. But something inside her said *no;* she plunged
ahead determinedly.

The weather, which had been nasty all through the day,
had turned ominous.

There was a pewter-colored glaze on the sky and the
surrounding landscape was bleak and bereft of color. It was
like a painting in *grisaille* with its many tints of gray, and
the stark and blackened trees stood out in relief, were like
pieces of metal sculpture silhouetted against the lowering
sky.

It had begun to drizzle. There was the low boom of
distant thunder echoing like cannon across the nearby
fields, which stretched in a long, flowing line down to Old
Farnley. A storm threatened and the wind was gusting over
Hill-Top.

Audra huddled against the railings of Charlie Cake Park,
sheltering as best she could as she waited for the tramcar
from Leeds to arrive at the terminal. It was long overdue.

Shivering, she tightened the thick woolen scarf around
her neck and stamped her feet in an effort to keep them

warm. The kitchen of the cottage, with its fire banked up the chimney back, had been so cozy and comfortable she had not realized earlier just how bad it was outside. She stepped forward, glanced down Town Street. This main thoroughfare was strangely deserted; the few pedestrians who were out and about were obviously in a hurry to get home before the storm broke.

What miserable weather it is, Audra thought, and it matches my mood exactly. She drew back into the niche between the park's railings and the policeman's booth, sighing. She had chosen to leave Vincent and yet she was already missing him. How perverse I am, she muttered, not understanding herself. And then she thought: And I'm stupidly of two minds about him still. But I'm doing the right thing. I know I am. *Or am I? Am I?*

Wrapping her arms around her body, Audra tried not to think about him or to envision his face when he walked in tonight and found that she had gone, found her note. She pushed her hands under her armpits for additional warmth and went on stamping her feet. She was chilled to the bone now, and she could feel the dampness seeping through her Melton coat and the plum-colored cloche.

About twenty minutes later she heard the tram rumbling to a stop at the other side of the tiny wedge-shaped park and then the sound of voices and footsteps as people alighted. Filling with relief, she hoisted her suitcase and hurried forward, and collided bodily with a young woman who came hurtling around the corner at breakneck speed.

They both recovered their balance, started to apologize, stopped in midsentence as they recognized each other in the murky, late afternoon light. Audra found herself staring into the pretty face of the sister-in-law who was her closest friend in the Crowther clan. Her heart dropped.

"Audra! For heaven's sake, what are you doing here?" Laurette demanded and broke into warm and affectionate smiles.

"Catching a tram," Audra mumbled and began to edge away.

Spotting the suitcase, Laurette frowned. "Where are you going?"

"I don't know," Audra responded in all truthfulness, then found herself saying, "Anywhere, I suppose, as long as it's far away from Vincent."

"What do you mean?" Laurette looked at her intently, her eyes filling with alarm.

"I'm leaving him."

Sucking in her breath, Laurette exclaimed, "Audra, *no*, don't say that. You *can't* leave him."

"Oh yes, I can."

"But where will you *go*? You know you have *nowhere* to go. We're the only family you have."

Ignoring this remark, Audra improvised swiftly, saying, "I can always go to the Fever Hospital in Ripon." She nodded to herself, realizing that this was quite true. "Matron Lennox will find a place for me. I just know she will."

"Audra, listen to me! Please don't do something that you may regret. Reconsider . . . at least about leaving today; it's almost four and the weather's worse. Anyway, by the time you reach Leeds you'll have missed the last train to Ripon. Come on, love, let's go back to the cottage and talk about this," Laurette pleaded, taking hold of Audra's arm.

"Please let go of me, Laurette." Audra tried to shake off her sister-in-law's hand, but Laurette's grip was firm. "Laurette, *please!* This is ridiculous. And I certainly don't want to go back to the cottage."

"Then let's go to my mother's . . . we're only five minutes away, come on, Audra, don't be stubborn. You're shivering, your face is blue with cold and you're going to catch your death of cold out here."

"What's the point of going to your mother's house? I've made up my mind and I won't change it. *I'm leaving Vincent.*"

Laurette drew closer and put her arm around Audra's shoulders, lovingly, almost protectively. She confided softly, "Look, I'm the first to admit I was against your marriage initially, but now that you are married I do think you and our Vincent should attempt to solve your problems and—"

"How can *you* of all people say that to me!" Audra

exploded in amazement, looking askance at Laurette. "Let's not forget that *you* are in the middle of a divorce."

"Yes, I know, but that's different. You and Vincent love each other. Jimmy and I didn't, not really."

"Love is not always enough."

"But it's a foundation to build a life on, Audra, really it is."

"I've thought about this for weeks and I'm not going to be persuaded to do something against my will—" Audra broke off as a bell clanged and the tramcar rolled away down the tracks to Leeds.

Audra stared after it in dismay; then she swung toward Laurette angrily. "Now look what you've done! You've made me miss my tramcar! And there won't be another one for half an hour at least," she wailed, then burst into tears of aggravation and frustration.

The profusion of roses on the walls and underfoot and patterning the china on the Welsh dresser looked more glorious than ever on this cold winter's afternoon. They seemed to glow with the vividness of real flowers in the blaze from the fire that roared in the hearth like a furnace, and threw off tremendous heat.

All was welcoming warmth and cheeriness in Eliza Crowther's kitchen. The air was fragrant with the smell of freshly baked bread and mince pies and tea cakes cooling on the set-pot, the sharper aromas of cloves, cinnamon, nutmeg and other spices from the Indies mingling with the fruity tang of candied peel, sultanas and Egyptian dates.

Eliza Crowther had been baking, which she usually did on Friday afternoons, come winter or summer. But today she had been busier than usual. Christmas was only three weeks away and she had been making holiday fare for her large family. She moved with agility between the table under the window and the sink, where she was now placing her dirty mixing bowls and spoons, cleaning up after herself. In a short while she would have to start preparing tea for those members of her family who still lived at home, and she always preferred everything to be spic and span in her kitchen before she commenced a new task.

A woman of medium height and build, Eliza looked all of her forty-nine years. This was mainly because of her plain way of dressing, her severe hairdo pulled straight back in a bun, and her stocky body, which had thickened since the birth of her last child, Danny. But she had an attractive, pleasant face, and good bones, and her pale blue eyes were bright, lively—and coolly appraising.

And just as there was no artifice in her appearance, neither was there a jot of it in her manner. She stood no nonsense from anyone and prided herself on being a hard-working Yorkshirewoman who had her feet firmly planted on the ground. She spoke plainly and to the point, was even a little blunt at times, and she had a saying or an adage for almost everything in life and liberally peppered her speech with them.

After washing and drying all of her cooking utensils, Eliza went to the oven to check her Christmas cakes, date loaves and the huge bacon-and-egg pie she was baking for tea. Satisfied that they were coming along nicely, she returned to the table under the window; she stood screwing down the lids on the jars of the dried fruits she had just used in her cakes.

Since she was not expecting anyone at this hour, she glanced up in surprise when the front door suddenly opened.

Laurette walked in, followed by Audra. They looked pinched and cold and they were shivering.

"You're home early, love," Eliza said to Laurette. "Nothing wrong at work, I hope?"

"No, Mam, it's my early Friday. Have you forgotten?"

"Oh, I had that." Eliza looked at her daughter-in-law. "Hello, Audra."

"Hello, Mrs. Crowther."

Eliza turned back to her jars, finished replacing the last few lids. She had noticed the suitcase Audra was carrying, but she decided not to make any comment. Laurette was now pushing it into the coat closet quickly, as if to hide it. There's trouble brewing for Vincent, Eliza thought, but she said, "When you've taken your coat off, Laurette, you can mash a pot of tea, please, and you, Audra, come over to the fire and get yourself warm. You look nithered to death."

Both young women did as she said in silence.

Laurette was pleased that she had succeeded in persuading Audra to come home with her. Although she had not intended to make her miss the tram, this had served a good purpose in the end. A tenderhearted girl, Laurette had grown to care deeply for Audra. The idea of her sister-in-law wandering the streets of Leeds in this bitter weather had been more than she could stomach. If she won't go home to Pot Lane tonight, she can share my bedroom, Laurette thought, busying herself with the tea caddy. And I'm going to have a few strong words with that brother of mine at the first opportunity I get. We've spoiled him, Mam and Olive and I. And even little Maggie has always done his bidding. I bet he's not easy as a husband, or easy to live with, for that matter.

Audra, for her part, sat hunched in one of the green-moquette wing chairs, staring gloomily into the fire. She had been furious with herself for giving in to Laurette, but now she had to admit that she was glad to be inside in the warmth. The dampness had penetrated her bones and she still felt terribly cold despite the huge fire.

The kettle was hissing and steaming on the hob, as it always was in winter, and Laurette filled the large brown teapot with boiling water, then turned and put it on the table in the center of the room.

Seating herself at the table, she looked across at her mother and said, "Where're Maggie and Danny? It's well turned four and they should be home from school by now, shouldn't they?"

"No, not today. They've gone to the Parish Hall to see about the Sunday school pantomime. They both want to be in it so badly, I said they could go to try out for the parts. It's *Cinderella* they're doing this year."

"Knowing Maggie, she'll want to play the leading role and nothing else," Laurette said with a laugh. "Come on, Mam, have this cup of tea before it gets cold."

Eliza joined the two of them in front of the fire.

She took the other wing chair and, after a sip of tea, focused her attention on her daughter-in-law. "Now then, Audra lass, what's all this about? I saw the suitcase, you know. Are you running off somewhere, or moving in here?"

Audra flushed and bit her lip. But she did not reply, since she had no wish to confide in Vincent's mother.

Laurette volunteered, "I met Audra at the tram stop, Mam. She looked ever so upset and she said she was leaving Vincent, going back to work at the hospital in Ripon. But she missed her tram to Leeds when we were talking, so I made her come home with me."

"I see." Eliza sat up straighter and stared hard at Audra, frowning to herself. "What kind of silliness is this then, lass?"

"It's not *silliness!*" Audra protested indignantly, and before she could stop herself she rushed on with some fierceness, "Vincent's been behaving very *badly* in the past few months! He's not treating me properly, and there's no good reason why I should stay with him any longer!"

"He can't have been hitting you!" Eliza asserted, secure in the knowledge that her son would never strike a woman, even if severely provoked. "So what *do* you mean? Explain yourself, lass."

Knowing that she was trapped, Audra took a deep breath, said in a more even tone, "He leaves me alone a great deal these days, and you *know* he does, Mrs. Crowther. In fact, he's always out at the pub with his brothers and his friends, or at the bookie's office betting, and I don't think that's very fair of him. We might as well not be married, for all we see of each other, the little time we spend together."

Eliza sighed heavily and shook her head. "But that's the way it *is* with us, the way it *is* in our working class world, Audra. Our men toil hard, usually at manual labor, and their way of relaxing, of enjoying themselves, is to go to the pub for a pint, a game of darts, a few laughs with their mates. And what's the harm if they put a few coppers on a horse, have a bit of a flutter once in a while? Surely you don't begrudge Vincent harmless pleasures?"

"No, of course I don't. It's just that I would like to share his leisure hours; after all, I am his wife. But he goes out alone to the White Horse several nights a week, and he always disappears at weekends. He leaves me to my own devices and I'm lonely."

"Aye, I know, but as I said, that's the way it is and the way it'll always be, now that the two of you are married, settled down. It's different when you're courting, it's all sweetness and light like. But once he's got the wedding band on your finger, a man's attitude changes, Audra, and you'd better accept that. Oh aye, you had, lass. All marriages are the same, and you won't notice things so much when you have a few bairns tugging at your skirts. *They'll* occupy your time, mark my words, and you'll be glad to have Vincent out from under your feet, you'll see."

Audra's mouth tightened in annoyance. "I'm not planning on having children just *yet*, Mrs. Crowther. What I would like to do is to return to nursing, but that's another problem between us, because Vincent won't hear of me working."

Eliza was aghast. "I should think he won't!" she exclaimed in a horrified voice. "How could you ever suggest such a thing to him! It would make him feel *small*, much *less* of a man, if his wife went out to work. Whatever would people think? And what would his mates say?"

"I don't know and I don't care! Furthermore, we could really use the money I'd be earning as a nurse," Audra shot back, unable to suppress her irritation any longer. "Vincent and I had the worst quarrel we've ever had last night. It was very nasty really, almost violent. And it was about *money*. I've discovered that we're in serious debt, yes, *deeply* in debt, Mrs. Crowther, and it's Vincent's fault, not *mine*, so don't look so disapprovingly at *me*. He went off and bought things on hire purchase at Wigfalls in Leeds without telling me. He had no right to do that."

"What things?"

"The leather sofa, the wardrobe and the bed."

"And why are you acting so surprised? You knew you had those things; they're in your home, lass, aren't they?"

"Yes, but I didn't know he'd bought them on hire purchase; I thought he'd paid for them outright, paid cash. And the reason I know he didn't do so is because Vincent has missed some payments, and Wigfalls have written a nasty letter, which I opened when it came in the post yesterday. And apparently it's not the first letter they've sent him either." Audra shook her head, her expression baffled. "We need the money so badly, and yet Vincent goes out drinking and gambling as if he doesn't have a care in the world. And he refuses to let me go back to nursing. It doesn't make sense . . . his pride gets in the way of everything, and that's very stupid of him, actually."

"I'm sure there's a right good explanation why he missed a payment," Eliza replied, instantly defending her favorite child, her Stormy Petrel. "Vincent has money in the bank, I know that for a fact."

"No, he doesn't, Mrs. Crowther. He spent his savings on new clothes for the wedding, our honeymoon in Robin Hood's Bay and on other things for the cottage. I offered him my savings, and I said I would willingly sell a piece of my mother's jewelry to help clear up our debts, but he won't let me do anything to help."

"That's because he doesn't need your help," Eliza exclaimed huffily. "He probably has a nest egg tucked away somewhere, and knowing my son he'll only get angrier if you try to cut the legs out from under him. Let *him* deal with these matters, Audra, in his own way, and don't interfere. He *is* the man of the house, after all." Eliza's eyes narrowed slightly, and she went on in a sterner voice, "Anyway, I'm sure you're making a mountain out of a molehill; it's usually six of one and half a dozen of another in any marriage, and yours can't be much different from anybody else's. At least he's not chasing after other women, and you ought to be grateful for *that*. Take my advice, try a bit harder, try to understand Vincent better."

Audra stared at her mother-in-law in utter astonishment. The woman was apparently blaming her for all of their troubles and exonerating Vincent completely. She felt suddenly defeated and misunderstood. "I *have* tried . . . I know you don't like me, but I'm not a bad person—" Audra's mouth trembled, and she turned her head to one side as scalding tears stung the back of her eyes.

Eliza, startled by this statement, exclaimed, "Nay, Audra

lass, don't say a thing like that! I *do* like you, I always have, and I think you're a fine young woman."

"*Do you?*" Audra swallowed down the incipient tears. "But you haven't acted as if you like me, really you haven't, Mrs. Crowther. And you didn't want us to get married, did you?"

"No, that's true, I didn't," Eliza admitted quietly. "But only because you're from a different world to us. I was convinced you and our Vincent would end up wanting different things in life, and I wasn't so far wrong, was I?"

Audra bit her lip. "I don't know; I'm a little confused."

Eliza nodded. "Aye, you are, and that's why you shouldn't be doing owt hasty, like leaving Vincent."

"But if you feel our marriage won't work, why do you want me to stay with him?"

"We're respectable people, and one divorce in this family is enough," Eliza muttered and looked through the corner of her eye at Laurette. She cleared her throat. "Marry in haste, repent at leisure—that's what I told our Vincent. But he wouldn't listen, and I don't suppose you did either, to your friends, I mean. Well, there we are. The two of you have made your bed, so you must lie in it, regardless of whether the mattress is lumpy or not." Leaning forward, giving Audra a sharper look, she finished, "It's always the woman who makes a marriage work, never the man. Just you be remembering that, lass."

"But that's not fair!" Audra cried, her indignation surfacing.

Eliza laughed hollowly. "Whoever said a woman's life was fair? Certainly not women from my walk of life, at any rate." She laughed again, shaking her head. "Anyway, Audra, I expect things'll get better between you and Vincent once the babies start coming along and you have the little ones to love and look after."

"But I want to do something more with my life, to achieve things, and I want to be happy—"

"*Happy,*" Eliza apluttered, looking at Audra as if she had uttered an obscenity. "That's a word you'd better erase from your vocabulary, my girl, and right sharpish. Just you be thankful you've got a roof over your head, food in your

stomach and a good husband to provide for you. Happiness
is not for the likes of us, Audra, it's for the gentry, for the
rich, them as have time for happiness and can afford it. We
can't."

What a bleak outlook she has, Audra thought and turned
to Laurette. They exchanged knowing glances and Laurette
shrugged her shoulders. Then she stiffened slightly and
sniffed. "Mam, is there something burning?"

"Oh my God, the Christmas cakes and the pie for your
dad's tea!" Eliza leapt to her feet, grabbed the oven towel
and yanked open the oven door. She began pulling out her
baking tins, exclaiming to Laurette over her shoulder,
"Well, don't sit there gawping, lass, get another towel and
help me. And Audra, make a bit of space on the set-pot,
please."

Laurette and Audra sprang to her assistance and within
seconds the Christmas cakes, the date loaves and the
bacon-and-egg pie had been spread out to cool. Eliza's
critical eyes roved over them, and she nodded happily
when she saw none of them had been ruined.

"It's only me, Mam!" The door burst open and Vincent
came barging in, pulling off his cap as he did. When he saw
Audra, his brows shot up in surprise. "What are you doing
here, love?" he asked in the pleasantest of voices, smiling at
her warmly.

Last night might never have happened, Audra thought,
staring back at him mutely, marveling at his ability to shrug
everything off. His nonchalance at this moment was quite
remarkable. It annoyed her.

"She's having a cup of tea," Laurette said quickly. "We
ran into each other in Town Street, and I invited her back to
visit for a little bit."

"Oh, I see." He started to shrug out of his coat, swung to
the closet.

Laurette hurried over to him. "Here, let me hang this up
for you, Vincent," she said, taking his overcoat. "You get
over to the fire and warm yourself up. You look frozen."

She doesn't want him to see the suitcase, Eliza thought,
watching her children closely. But he's bound to see it
sooner or later. She sighed and turned back to her cakes.

"Thanks, Laurette," Vincent said, rubbing his cold hands together, striding across the room. "I wouldn't mind a spot of tea meself."

"Coming right up," his sister said and went to the Welsh dresser. Bringing a cup and saucer to the table, she lifted the teapot and poured for him.

A moment later the door again flew open and Danny ran into the kitchen, followed more sedately by Maggie, who was feeling very grown-up and important this afternoon.

"We got the parts! We got the parts!" Danny cried to the room at large, throwing his cap and scarf onto the sofa. His overcoat followed, and then he scurried over to the bird cage in the corner. "I'm home, Flyaway," he cooed. He gazed lovingly at the little bird, which Vincent had bought for him and also named.

"Danny, hang up your things at once," Eliza called to her youngest.

"I will, Mam, in a tick."

Maggie, who was taking off her own coat, said, "Oh, I'll do it, Mother."

"And what part have you got, Tiddler?" Vincent asked when the little boy came and stood at his knee a moment later.

Danny looked up at his handsome eldest brother and smiled sweetly. "I'm going to be a page boy. I don't get to say owt, but I do get to carry a luvely red velvet cushion with the glass slipper on it."

Vincent rumpled his hair. "That's grand, lad."

Maggie joined Laurette and Vincent at the table, sat down between them and grinned. "I have a speaking part though, a big part too. I'm going to be one of the Ugly Sisters."

"What perfect casting!" Vincent cried and laughed uproariously.

"You are awful, our Vincent!" Maggie screeched, punching him hard on the arm. "And if I'm ugly, then so are you, 'cos everybody says we look exactly alike." She punched him again.

He grabbed hold of her wrist, held her tightly.

"Now then, you two, stop all this roughhousing!" Eliza

cried, "your dad'll be home any minute, and he'll be wanting a bit of peace and quiet after his hard day at work."

Eliza walked over to the Welsh dresser and took down two of the largest serving platters. "And you'd better stop to your teas, Audra and Vincent. There's plenty for all of us. There's the bacon-and-egg pie, and I made a lovely jellied tongue yesterday." She peered at Audra over her shoulder. "You will stay?"

"That's up to Vincent," Audra murmured.

"Yes, of course we'll stay, Mam, why not?" He pulled out his Woodbines and lit one.

Audra sank back into the wing chair gratefully and gazed into the fire, her face abstracted.

She preferred to be here rather than alone with him at the cottage, where they were bound to quarrel. In a few minutes his brothers Jack and Bill would return from work and the atmosphere would probably turn boisterous, as it usually did when they were all together. But as rough and ready as the Crowther clan sometimes were, she knew they were good-hearted.

Often Audra did feel overwhelmed by them, and occasionally she saw them looking at her oddly. She sensed that they thought she was standoffish, and frequently they seemed wary with her. But not Laurette and Mr. Crowther. *They* were her real friends in this family, and she was quite certain they truly cared about her, just as she cared about them. They were the ones she would miss when she was back in Ripon. Despite what his mother had said, Audra was still planning to leave Vincent. She would go tomorrow.

"How could you do it? How could you go babbing to our Laurette and me Mam?" Vincent demanded furiously, the minute they arrived at the cottage in Pot Lane.

Glaring at Audra, he went on heatedly, "I couldn't believe it when Laurette took me up to the sitting room after tea, and told me how she'd stopped you from running off and leaving me. It's bloody *embarrassing*, that's what it is!"

"I didn't go blabbing to them," Audra said evenly,

holding herself very still. She was determined not to let him goad her into losing her temper as he had last night. "Laurette told you what happened. If I hadn't run into her at the tram terminal, and quite by accident, neither she nor your mother would know anything."

"Well, they *do* know, and you've gone and humiliated me again!"

"What on earth do you mean?" she demanded, drawing herself up and glaring back at him.

"First you diminish me in front of Gwen, what with all your talk of getting a job, going out to work and behaving as if I can't support you, and now you've been complaining about me to my mother and sister. Anybody would think that I'm the devil incarnate the way *you* bloody well carry on." His sudden laughter was harsh, and there was a sarcastic edge to his voice as he added, "And I thought *I'd* be the one to embarrass *you*, seeing as how you're so very much the lady. But the boot's on t'other foot, it seems to me."

"Please don't worry, Vincent, I won't embarrass you anymore. I won't be around to do so. I'm leaving you tomorrow. For good."

"Suit yourself." He marched across the little parlor-kitchen to the front door and picked up his cloth cap.

"Where are you going?" Audra demanded.

"To the pub," he replied and slammed out of the cottage without uttering another word. The door crashed behind him.

But Audra did not leave the following morning as she had threatened to do. She could not even leave their bed. Her throat was sore, her eyes were watering and she had a raging fever.

By eleven o'clock Vincent was so worried about her he sent for Doctor Stalkley, the local physician who had brought him into the world.

"Influenza, I'm afraid, Vincent," the old doctor pronounced, after he had examined Audra. "There's a lot of it going around in Armley just now. See that she stays in bed

and give her plenty of liquids. Not much else you can do,
my boy, it has to take its course."

CHAPTER EIGHTEEN

Irène Bell paused on the threshold of the dining room at
Calpher House, catching her breath in surprise.

Always a handsome room, with its cranberry-colored
wallpaper of flocked velvet and English Regency antiques,
it had a special kind of beauty this afternoon. This was due
in no small measure to the Christmas decorations which
were now in place and which had been created by Audra in
her absence.

Mrs. Bell had just returned from a two-day business trip
to London, and she stood for a moment longer, taking in the
details of the seasonal decor.

She saw that Audra had eschewed tinsel and glitter,
instead had turned to nature for her decorative theme.
Garlands and branches of evergreens and mistletoe and the
traditional hawthorn were much in evidence, tied and
swagged with burgundy velvet or gold lamé ribbons.
Crystal compotes held miniature pyramids of fruit and fir
cones and nuts, and had been trimmed with brightly
colored bows; there were masses of white candles everywhere, and two small fir trees stood guard on either side of
the fireplace. These were covered with bows and ribbon
streamers in rainbow hues, and the tubs were wrapped
with gold lamé fabric in the Victorian manner.

In fact, the entire theme had an old-fashioned, Victorian
air about it, and it was one which Irène found charming.
And as always she was impressed and admiring of Audra's
artistic talents, which she believed to be extraordinary.

I wonder how best to compensate her for this marvelous
work? Irène asked herself, giving the room a final glance
before turning away. I cannot offer her money; she'll be
insulted. She's such a proud young woman. I must find her

a very special gift tomorrow, quite aside from her Christmas present from us.

Crossing the hall in her usual energetic way, Irène Bell mounted the stairs, knowing that her child's former nanny would be in the day nursery with him, unless she had already gone home to Pot Lane.

They were sitting at the table near the fire, with a paintbox and sketching pad spread out in front of them, and they both looked up as Irène walked in saying, *"Hello, hello,"* to them.

Theophilus cried, "Mummy! Mummy! You're home!"

He ran across the floor and flung himself at her joyously. Irène bent down and kissed the top of his head and hugged him to her; then she raised her face and smiled across at Audra.

"Good afternoon, Mrs. Bell," Audra said, smiling back.

"I'm so glad you're still here, Audra. I just saw the dining room and I must thank you for the wonderful decorations; the room looks beautiful, just *beautiful*. You're to be congratulated."

A look of gratification flitted across Audra's pale face. "Thank you, but I did have a few willing helpers, you know."

Irène's brow puckered. "You did?"

"Oh yes, Mrs. Bell. Theo and Dodie, not to mention Cora."

"*Cora*. Gracious me, you are brave." Irène shook her bright-auburn head. "I don't mean to be unkind, but oh dear, that poor girl does seem to get clumsier every day. And how kind of you to include her, yes, so *very* kind of you, Audra."

Irène walked over to the table with Theo, where they both sat down.

Audra explained, "Cora's enthusiasm is worth a lot, Mrs. Bell, and she would have been heartbroken if I hadn't asked her to do something. She helped Theo to make the garlands, actually."

"That was a safe job, Mummy," Theo volunteered, earnestly gazing up at his mother. "Audra said there was no risk involved, since all Cora could break was a twig or a bit of wire. Anyway, I kept an eye on her."

"I'm sure you did, darling," Irène murmured, biting back a smile of amusement. She turned to Audra, remarked, "I just can't begin to tell you how much I appreciate your efforts. What with the cook under the weather, Mr. Agiter coming down with influenza, and the unexpected trip to London, I was quite at my wits' end earlier this week. I don't know what I would have done, if you hadn't been able to help me out with the dining room decor, Audra. We have so many dinners planned, and I must admit, I can't help wondering how on earth we'll manage without a butler at Christmas. *Oh dear.*" Irène's gay, freckled face clouded. Instantly, it cleared. "Well, never mind, *never mind*. One can't worry about such things. I shall cope somehow." Irène peered at Audra in the firelight. "How inconsiderate of me, I haven't even asked you about your health, my dear. Are you feeling better?"

"Oh yes, thank you, Mrs. Bell."

"But you look as peaked as you did on Monday, when I came down to the cottage to see you."

"I'm perfectly fine, honestly I am, Mrs. Bell."

Theo said, "Look, Mummy, Audra's been showing me how to paint a scene." He pushed the sketching pad toward her.

Glancing down at it, Irène nodded. "Very good, darling, very good indeed." Her eyes strayed to the left-hand page where Audra had painted a simple landscape for him to copy. But in its very simplicity it was absolute perfection. Irène looked at it for the longest moment, struck by its delicate beauty, the reflection of light she had captured on paper. Finally lifting her eyes to Audra's, Irène said, "This is *lovely* . . . haven't I seen something similar before?"

"Yes, I did a larger version several years ago, and it was hanging in my room when I worked here."

"Of course. And you had given it an unusual name, as I recall."

"The Memory Place," Audra said very softly, "and the painting is of the sycamore tree on the slope opposite High Cleugh . . . where my family and I used to picnic."

"Yes, I remember now." Leaning forward, Irène said in her vibrant and emphatic voice, "You are a remarkably talented artist, Audra, and I can't understand why you don't pursue your painting."

"Oh but I'm not very good, Mrs. Bell, really I'm not," Audra replied with an odd laugh that was at once both dismissive and self-deprecating. "It's just a hobby, after all."

"It could be your profession."

"Oh no, Mrs. Bell, *nursing* is my forte. You know that Matron Lennox said I was truly gifted as a nurse, a real healer."

"Yes," Irène said, very slowly. Her eyes grew thoughtful and, after a short pause, one of her perfectly penciled brows lifted inquiringly. "I presume Vincent did not change his mind and that he is still against your going back to nursing?"

"Yes, he's adamant, I'm afraid." Audra lowered her eyes, then glanced away.

"I see." Irène decided to let the subject drop immediately, understanding that she was treading on dangerous ground. She wondered if there was some sort of trouble between Audra and Vincent, other than their differences about her nursing career. The girl had seemed strangely quiet and withdrawn at the beginning of the week. But then perhaps that was due to her recent bout with flu. Perhaps she was merely a little rundown.

Audra was saying, "And speaking of my husband, I really ought to be going in a few minutes, if you'll excuse me, Mrs. Bell." She took a peek at the nursery clock. "Oh goodness, it's already five-thirty. Vincent will be home from York at seven."

"*Why* has he been to York? What's he been *doing* there?" Theo demanded, as always insatiably curious about Vincent, who fascinated him.

"Really, Theophilus," his mother chastised, "you know it's rude to ask such personal questions."

"Oh that's perfectly all right, Mrs. Bell," Audra said; then explained to the child, "He went with Mr. Varley—you know, the man who owns the building firm—and they were going to have a meeting with Mr. Rowntree . . . something about building an extension onto one of the chocolate factories."

"Ooooh! How *scrumptious!* I wish I could go to a chocolate factory. Do you think Vincent will bring you back a box of Black Magic? They're my favorite, Audra." Theo looked at her hopefully.

"I know they are, but I don't think Mr. Rowntree gives his chocolate away, Theophilus," she responded with a small smile and stood up.

"Oh Audra, please don't go," Theo pleaded, "I hardly ever get to see you these days."

Audra reached out, stroked his fair head with tenderness, filling with love for him. "That's not strictly true," she said gently, "and besides, now that you're a big boy and going to preparatory school, you don't need a nanny. After all, you are seven years old."

"I know—but you *promised* we'd be extra-special chums."

"And so we are." Audra bent forward, kissed his cheek. Theo put his arms around her neck, clung to her for a moment.

Irène Bell said, "Don't behave like a *baby*, Theophilus. You know very well Audra has other responsibilities now that she's married."

"Yes," he mumbled and let go of Audra, although he did so somewhat reluctantly.

"Shouldn't you be getting ready for the pantomime at the Grand Theatre in Leeds?" Irène now suggested, her eyes sparkling with merriment.

"Oh Mummy! *That's* my surprise! And I've been racking my brains for days!" the child shouted excitedly, jumping down off the chair. "I've been longing to see *Jack and the Beanstalk.*"

"Then run along and wash your hands and face. And Theo, please change your shirt. The one you're wearing is splattered with paint," his mother pointed out.

"Goodbye, Theo," Audra said, blowing a kiss from the doorway.

"Bye, Audra. Don't forget my party tomorrow and

please, *please* make Vincent come with you. You will, won't you?"

"I'll do my very best."

As they went down the staircase together, Irène said to Audra, "Theo does have a soft spot for Vincent, doesn't he?"

"Yes, and the feeling is mutual, I believe."

"He seems to be doing awfully well at Varley's, and that must please you."

"Oh yes, it does. Mr. Varley likes him and, of course, Vincent does have a great eye and a marvelous sense of perspective when it comes to architecture. I've told him many times that he's a born builder."

"I think it's most commendable that he's started going to night school," Irène said, turning to face Audra as they drew to a standstill in the hall. "Is he enjoying studying draftsmanship?"

"Yes," Audra murmured, not wishing to admit that Vincent had only *talked* about enrolling in the course, had never actually done so.

Studying her face closely, Irène Bell saw a flicker of something at the back of Audra's startlingly blue eyes. It was a peculiar look and it alarmed her. She's a very troubled young woman, Irène thought with a flash of intuition. Reaching out, she touched Audra's arm lightly. Her voice was low and warm as she asked, "Is everything all right with you, my dear?"

Audra hesitated.

For a fraction of a second she was on the verge of confiding in Irène Bell, and then she changed her mind. Aside from the fact that her pride and her strong sense of privacy got in the way, her intelligence told her that Mrs. Bell could not help her. Nobody could help her now.

Audra forced a bright smile onto her face. "Oh no, nothing's wrong, Mrs. Bell. Thank you for asking, but everything is fine."

"And your health *really* is all right?" Irène pressed, still not convinced.

There was a small silence before Audra nodded, almost too emphatically.

"You do look *awfully* pale suddenly," Irène insisted, frowning at her.

"It's just the aftermath of the flu, and I am also feeling a little tired now." Audra gently extricated her arm, hurried over to the coat closet. She took out her gray Melton coat and the plum-colored cloche, put them on, glancing in the hall mirror at herself as she adjusted the hat.

A moment later, as she wrapped her woolen scarf around her neck and pulled on her gloves, she asked, "Would you like me to come a little earlier on Christmas Eve? Perhaps there's something I could do to help at Theo's party, Mrs. Bell."

Irène chuckled softly. "Indeed there is, Audra. I'd be most grateful if you would keep an eye on Theophilus and nine other little terrors, at least until the Punch and Judy show starts."

No sooner had the door closed behind Audra than it sprang open again within the space of minutes.

Irène was halfway up the staircase.

She turned and her face lit up at the sight of her husband.

"Thomas darling!" she cried, "you're home early, how lovely." She sped swiftly down the stairs, across the marble hall and into his welcoming arms.

After hugging her tightly, kissing her cheek, he looked down into her face. His own filled with pleasure. "Did you have a pleasant journey back?"

"Oh yes, thank you, Thomas, and all of my news over a nice cozy drink shortly, before we go to the Grand. But first, take off your coat, and then I'll show you the decorations Audra has created in the dining room."

"I saw her leaving the house as we turned into the drive," Thomas remarked, removing his scarf. "I had Robertson stop the motorcar, and I told her he would run her home if she waited a moment for me to alight, but she wouldn't hear of it. She's always been an independent little thing, though, hasn't she?"

"Yes," Irène agreed.

She linked her arm through her husband's and led him across the floor in the direction of the dining room. "Audra doesn't look terribly well to me, and I have a feeling she and Vincent are not as happy as she would like to have me believe."

"Mmmmm. Handsome chap, Vincent Crowther. Probably ruined too, by his mother and those doting sisters of his, not to mention women—women in the past tense, of course. No, Irène, I don't imagine that that young whippersnapper is easy to live with. And then of course, he is from a different class."

"Thomas!" Irène exclaimed, drawing away, looking up at him sharply. Her eyes were dismayed. "You know I detest that sort of thing—class prejudice absolutely *incenses* me."

"Yes, but you're not going to change the nature of the English . . . it's endemic. Besides, the lower classes are just as bad as the aristocracy when it comes to that sort of thing. Snobs too, in their own way." He smiled at her somewhat wryly. "And whatever you say, background *does* make a devil of a difference, darling. Audra is a lady, and breeding will out—why it's obvious in everything she does. And unfortunately Vincent will always hold her back, hold her down, you'll see."

Thomas Bell shrugged. "But they are married, and it isn't actually any of our business."

"No, but I'm so fond of her, Thomas."

"Yes," he said.

The Bells paused on the threshold of the dining room. "*Voilà!*" Irène exclaimed, waving her hand toward the room.

For a moment Thomas Bell was startled. "Why it looks exquisite," he managed at last, obviously as impressed as his wife had been earlier.

"Very original, and quite breathtaking," Irène said and then sighed so heavily, Thomas eyed her curiously.

Irène met his direct gaze. She shook her head, and a look of perplexity washed over her expressive face. "Audra thinks she's especially gifted as a nurse, but she's not, she's simply very good and that's all. Of course, she would never believe me if I told her this, since Margaret Lennox has expressed entirely different views to her."

Swinging her eyes toward the dining room, Irène waved her hand at it again. "No, this is where her gift truly lies— in her artistic endeavors. She is an extraordinary painter, Thomas, but she can't see it, and I don't understand why she's so blind." Once again Irène sighed. "Oh Thomas, what a *waste* of talent. That's the saddest part of all."

"Perhaps it is. Poor Audra, she never had much of a chance, really. Life sort of came charging at her full tilt, and when she was so young. . . ."

CHAPTER NINETEEN

Why ever did I tell Mrs. Bell that I'm fine? I'm not fine at all. And I'm trapped. Whatever am I going to do?

These thoughts pushed all others to the back of Audra's mind as she busied herself in the kitchen-parlor of the cottage in Pot Lane, not long after she had left Calpher House.

I *should* have confided in Irène Bell, she told herself, unexpectedly regretful that she had kept her worries bottled up inside. It helped to air problems, especially if the listener was a sympathetic and understanding person like Mrs. Bell. But she had remained silent when the opportunity had presented itself, and now it was too late.

I really am on my own, Audra thought, just as I've always been on my own since I was fourteen. I have nowhere to go. No one to turn to . . . I only ever did have Matron Lennox, but even she can't help me. She can't possibly give me a job as a nurse now that I'm pregnant.

The despair that Audra had been carrying around with her for days spiraled into sudden panic, and as she put the cups and saucers on the table she saw that her hands shook slightly. Standing absolutely still in the middle of the kitchen, she took rigid control of herself. *Be calm, be calm,* she kept repeating, breathing deeply, reminding herself that panic never accomplished anything.

When Audra felt more composed, she went to look at the lamb stew for Vincent's dinner, which had been simmering in the oven of the Yorkshire range all afternoon. Satisfied that it was slowly cooking to perfection, she made a cup of tea and carried it to the fire, where she sat for a while, mulling over her predicament.

During the two weeks she had been ill with influenza, she had begun to suspect that she was pregnant. For the last few days she had been absolutely certain; a variety of changes in her body could no longer be ignored. When the cold facts had sunk in at the beginning of the week, her first thought had been of flight. She had intended to stick to her plans to leave Vincent.

But this evening, walking home from Calpher House, she had come to realize that this would be a foolish move to make when she was with child. She had no money, no job— and nowhere to run, anyway. Laurette had put it most succinctly when she had said, "We're the only family you have." *It was true*.

But to stay with Vincent? How could she? They only ever argued and bickered. Well, that was not strictly true. At least, not at the moment. He had been solicitous of her well-being whilst she had been in bed with the flu, and exceptionally kind to her, and there hadn't been a cross word between them since she had recovered.

A few days ago, he had asked her, unexpectedly and in a subdued voice, if she still intended to leave him. And she had said *yes*, and as soon as she was well enough to do so. There had been such an odd look on his face when he had turned away, and thinking about it now, she realized, suddenly, that it had been a look of genuine sadness. And she was certain there had been a hint of regret in his eyes, and that he was sorry for all of their angry words, their virulent rows that served no purpose. After all, they had started out with so much. *Oh why can't it be the way it was in the beginning?* she asked herself, and leaning back in the chair, she closed her eyes, thinking of the happy days of their courtship, fervently wishing they would come back.

A little while later, Audra sat up with a jerk, roused from her ruminations by the sound of footsteps on the flagstone path outside. The door flew open and Vincent hurried in, carrying a large bunch of holly dangling from a string.

His face brightened. He was relieved to see her sitting by the fire. These days he never knew for certain whether he was coming home to an empty house or not.

"Hello, love," he said, putting the holly on the floor, taking off his scarf and trilby hat.

"Hello," Audra responded, and she could not help thinking how handsome he looked tonight. The cold wind had brought fresh color to his cheeks, and his green eyes were alive and sparkling under the black brows. She asked, in her usual quiet way, "How was your trip to York?"

"Oh it was grand, and ever so successful, I'm happy to report. It looks as if we'll get the contract, oh yes, very definitely. Mr. Varley is right chuffed and so am I . . . it means all of our jobs are safe, well, for a bit, at least. Which is saying a lot when you look around and see what's going on in the country. Mr. Varley says we're heading for an economic crisis. . . ." He let his sentence trail off, but as he struggled out of his coat and hung it up, he added, "Oh and by the by, you can congratulate me."

Audra's brow lifted. "Why? What's happened?"

"I've been promoted. Mr. Varley made me the new foreman this afternoon. There hasn't been one, you know, since old Harry Watkins retired."

"Congratulations *are* in order, Vincent, and I am pleased for you," Audra said enthusiastically, meaning her words. "You certainly deserve it; you've worked hard enough."

"Thanks for that, love." He cleared his throat, picked up the holly and walked across the floor. "I bought this from a farm cart on one of the country roads on the way back. What shall I do with it? Shouldn't it be in water?"

"It'll be all right for a while. Put it on the set-pot. Would you like a cup of tea?"

"Er, no thanks, love." He hesitated, as if uncertain of his next move, and then he walked over to her chair, bent down and kissed her cheek. But he quickly moved away, stood with his back to the fire, warming himself.

"Thank you for the holly, Vincent," Audra murmured, looking up at him with a half smile. "It was nice of you. . . ."

"Oh it was nothing . . . do we have any beer left?"

"Yes, there are several bottles in the pantry."

He went to get one, asking, as he strode across the floor, "How's the lad, then?"

"Excited about his Christmas party, and the last thing he said to me, as I was leaving, was to be sure to make you come with me tomorrow."

"Oh, I don't know about that. . . ." Returning to the fireside, Vincent sat down in the chair opposite her, his expression reflective.

"Theophilus will be disappointed if you don't go."

Vincent stared at her in surprise, frowning, and there was a hint of bafflement in his voice as he asked, "Would you *mind* if I went? I mean, do you *want* me to go with you."

"Yes, and anyway, Theo has his heart set on it. You know the boy hero-worships you."

He nodded, took a sip of beer, said hesitantly, "Well . . . I do get off work early. Mr. Varley always shuts down at twelve on Christmas Eve."

"Yes." Audra glanced away, sat looking into the fire.

Vincent fumbled in his jacket pocket, searching for his cigarettes.

A silence fell between them.

It was the kind of companionable silence they had so often shared in the early days, and tonight they seemed to be at ease with each other in a way that they had not been for months. Quite suddenly Audra felt his eyes on her, and she brought her gaze to meet his. She held her breath. There was a look of such tenderness and love on his face it was heart-stopping.

She opened her mouth to speak and then closed it without uttering a word, incapable of saying anything at this moment, filled with a bewildering array of emotions. She glanced down at her hands. Her wedding band glinted in the firelight, so burnished, so bright, a symbol of her dreams—and hope for the future. She thought of the baby she was carrying. The child *was* the future . . . just as it was part of the past, their *past*, created out of their love and their passionate feelings and their need for each other. Deep in the inner recesses of her heart Audra understood that in spite of everything her love for Vincent remained intact and unchanged; that was an inescapable fact.

Almost as if he was reading her mind, Vincent threw his cigarette into the fire and rose. He went and knelt next to her chair, and taking her hands in his, he looked deeply into her eyes, which were huge tonight and vividly blue in her wan face.

He swallowed, said tremulously, "Don't leave me, Audra, please don't leave me. On my way home tonight I didn't know whether you'd be here or not, and my heart was in my mouth. It's always in my mouth these days . . . not knowing what to expect. And I thought, what will I do if she's not there? How can I live without her?" He paused, attempted a smile, but it faltered. "The truth is, I can't live without you, and I don't want to anyway. You see, Audra, I love you, I really do."

She knew he meant every word. There was not only a ring of sincerity in his voice, but a desperateness too, and as she returned his penetrating gaze steadily she saw the glitter of tears at the back of his green eyes.

For a moment she could not speak.

"Please don't leave me," he begged again, his voice low and emotional.

Audra touched his face gently, and then to her own surprise she blurted out, "I'm going to have a baby."

Vincent drew back, his eyes widening as he stared at her, and then grabbed her in his arms and hugged her to him. "Oh Audra, what wonderful news!" Immediately he pulled away from her. All the anxiety had been wiped off his face and he was grinning boyishly. "You can't leave me now, you know you can't! Besides, I won't *let* you. You need me to look after you, to take care of you and the baby."

"Yes," she acknowledged, knowing this was the truth.

"We'll have a better life together, I promise," he said with genuine feeling. "And I promise I'll be a better husband, I really will, Audra."

* * *

At first he was true to his word.

The kindness he had shown during her bout with influenza continued, and he was more considerate than he had ever been to her, or anyone else, for that matter. At night he rushed home from work to be with her, and he never left her side in his free time, not even on weekends, when he was accustomed to going off on his own with his friends. He fussed over her, cosseted her, and was a model husband and expectant father.

Tranquility descended on the little house in Pot Lane.

Audra was content in a way she had never been in her entire life, and grateful to have peace and quiet—and also rest. Her pregnancy was turning out to be a difficult one. The morning sickness was unusually severe, and the nausea often continued during the day; she felt out of sorts in her general health and was constantly debilitated.

In the beginning, Vincent was concerned for her and sympathetic about her condition. But it was not very long before his patience gave way to irritability and, worst of all, boredom.

Just before Christmas, when they had reconciled, they had done so lovingly and had assumed their marital relationship. But once again this had ceased. Vincent more or less understood Audra's physical withdrawal from him, since he thought that an expectant woman might not be overcome by sexual desire for her husband. What truly troubled him was her lack of real interest in him and his daily life. He found her attitude strange and hurtful.

And so not unnaturally, given his nature, he soon began to find domesticity stifling. He did love Audra, and he did want to be married to her, but he also craved the life of a bachelor. This was not because he needed to chase after other women, for indeed he did not, but rather because he missed the camaraderie of masculine company, of roistering around with his friends in the pubs and betting at the bookie's office and the race track. He had done all of these things all of his adult life and he saw no reason to change his habits.

He also resumed his constant visits to his mother's house and, very simply, he did so because he missed the hurly-burly atmosphere and the joviality of being part of a big family, particularly one filled with affection and warmth for each other as the Crowthers were.

And he did not feel guilty about his behavior in any way, mainly because Audra had become completely absorbed in the baby. It seemed to Vincent that her entire being was concentrated on the child she was carrying, and to the exclusion of all else.

He was not mistaken in this belief.

The baby represented so much to her, perhaps more than he could truly conceive or understand. To Audra, the baby was not only the fruit of their love and their first child, but the beginning of that family of her very own which she had so craved for so many years.

Terrified of endangering the baby in any way, she took care of her health so scrupulously and so obsessively that even Laurette grew impatient with her on occasions; and when she was not fussing over herself, her health and her diet, she was preparing for the great event as if this was the first child that had ever been born.

The second bedroom at number thirty-eight was turned into a nursery, with great attention paid to the smallest detail, both decoratively and hygienically. She involved almost every member of the Crowther clan, insisting that they help with the scrubbing, cleaning, wallpapering and painting of the room. And then, after she had sold a small, diamond bar pin of her mother's, she went to Harte's in Leeds, where she purchased a set of charming nursery furniture that was also beautifully made.

Vincent's sister Olive was renowned in the family and amongst her friends for the exquisite garments she knitted, and in the past year she had been teaching this practical hobby to Laurette. Audra asked Olive to help her with her own knitting, and within a short space of time she had cunningly pressed both Olive and Laurette into making clothes for the baby. The three young women knitted as if their lives depended on it, and they were a comical sight when they were together, their needles clicking, their eyes glazed in concentration on their patterns, oblivious to everything. Bonnets, bootees, leggings, cardigans, jackets, and blankets for the cot and the pram were the result of their efforts. Later Audra sewed and embroidered a variety of other baby clothes, and she crocheted two beautiful lacey shawls; it was not long before a superb layette had been created. As Audra put the tiny garments away in the bedroom chest, she carefully placed tissue paper between the layers of finely worked items, feeling very proud of this exquisite wardrobe of clothes for her unborn child.

Yet with all of her domestic activities and despite being surrounded by innumerable and often boisterous Crowthers, there were times when Audra felt more isolated and alone than ever. This was due, in part, to Vincent's defection, and because she had no real kin of her own. Try though she had to become closer to Eliza, she had been unable to do so. She was still wary of her mother-in-law and cautious in her presence. She believed that Eliza had blamed her for all of their problems months before and continued to hold her responsible, whilst exonerating Vincent. Although this was not true, nothing would have convinced her to the contrary.

On the other hand, Laurette and Audra were warm and loving with each other, and Audra enjoyed a good relationship with Alfred Crowther, who considered his son extremely fortunate to have such a fine young woman for a wife. In fact, Alfred was disapproving of Vincent's behavior and minced no words when telling him so, which he did with increasing frequency. It was Vincent's father and his favorite sister who helped Audra through some difficult moments and trying situations at this time in her life.

Oddly enough, there were no rancorous feelings between Audra and Vincent during her pregnancy, even though they were in a sense leading quite separate lives. They no longer quarreled bitterly, and even their bickering had ceased. It was as if a truce had been declared between them. They were civil, even cordial with each other—and totally preoccupied with their own problems and with themselves.

* * *

The harsh winter gave way to the most glorious spring anyone had seen in years. Blue skies and bright sunshine lifted everybody's spirits. So did the trees bursting with green buds and the appearance of the first daffodils and crocuses, shooting up early to sprinkle the dark earth with brilliant yellow and purple.

And then suddenly it was the occasion of Gwen's marriage to Geoffrey Freemantle. Audra had had to decline Gwen's request to be matron of honor, because she felt she would look ungainly in her condition.

But she and Vincent did attend the wedding at St. Margaret's Church in Horsforth on a sunny, breezy Saturday afternoon in the first week of April in 1929.

Audra had made herself a new maternity dress and matching loose coat of navy blue bouclé wool, and had bought herself a gay little hat made of straw and trimmed with midnight lace and deep blue roses. When Vincent saw her in the stunning outfit, he exclaimed at her prettiness, but Audra looked at him skeptically as she followed him out of the cottage. She felt like a small whale, and there was no question in her mind that she looked it.

As they drove to Horsforth in his Uncle Phil's car, borrowed for the occasion, Audra thought of Gwen and of the way their friendship had begun to drift during the winter months. Between her work at the Infirmary, furnishing and decorating the house in Headingley and planning her wedding, Gwen had had little time for her, for anyone else, it seemed. Also, the circumstances of their very different lives these days were slowly coming between them.

There was another problem too, in that Vincent had become even friendlier than ever with Mike Lesley, Gwen's former boyfriend. In consequence, Vincent did not want to make friends with Geoffrey Freemantle, whom he persisted in referring to as "the usurper," and even if he had, Audra knew that the snobbish doctor would have looked down on Vincent.

I'm going to lose Gwen eventually and all because of Geoffrey Freemantle, Audra thought as she sat staring out of the car window, and she filled with sadness.

Later, as she stood in the pew with Vincent, watching Gwen walk slowly down the aisle on the arm of her father, the sadness seemed to intensify, as did a peculiar sense of distance. Gwen looked so beautiful, more beautiful than she had ever been, and Audra was momentarily stunned. This was a different Gwen than the one she had known.

She wore a crinoline gown of cream lace over cream satin, a veil and a long train of Alençon lace; the veil was held in place by a coronet of waxy orange blossoms. She carried a bouquet of white roses whose petals were tinged with the palest of pinks. A diamond heart on a strand of pearls glittered at her throat and there were diamonds in her ears. Gwen was a radiant bride, blond and blue-eyed and everybody's idea of the typical English rose, and there was no question that on this very special day in her life she was absolutely breathtaking.

And I've already lost her, Audra thought wistfully. She's gone from me. Gwen's entered a new world, one I shall never know. Suddenly she was choked with tears and there was an odd ache in the region of her heart.

There was a time in my life when I had absolutely nothing and no one. All I had was Gwen, Audra thought. *And she was so good to me. I'll never forget her for that. I'll always love her and she'll always be my best friend. Not even Laurette can take her place, dear though she is and so loving and loyal.*

Gwen drew level with Audra and smiled with warmth and radiance.

Audra smiled back, looked fleetingly but deeply into that pretty face, and she said goodbye to her friend in the silence of her heart. And she wished Gwen nothing but happiness and joy all the days of her life.

Even though her sense of loss enveloped her, Audra did manage to seem carefree at the reception. This was held at The Meadow, and Audra experienced a little spurt of pleasure to be back in that house where she had spent so many happy hours. But whereas she was able to put up a good front, she noticed that the Thorntons were not so successful at this bit of deception. Audra decided she had rarely seen a family looking so glum.

She had not been in the drawing room long before Mrs. Thornton led her into a quiet corner, to speak to her alone. Phyllis Thornton immediately confided, without any preamble, that none of the family cared very much for Doctor Freemantle. Audra tried to cheer her up by saying positive things, but Mrs. Thornton was not deceived. She shook her head mournfully. "We think he's an odious man, and you don't like him either, Audra, whatever you say . . . poor Gwenny, whatever has she done?" Mrs. Thornton sighed heavily before gliding off to greet some wedding guests who had just arrived.

Audra's eyes followed her. She was filled with sympathy for Mrs. Thornton, who had always been kind to her. Vincent joined her and they went over to the buffet, where they took a selection of tea sandwiches, then moved away. Charlie found them a few minutes later, and he brought over his fiancée to meet them. She was a petite girl called Rowena, who, Audra immediately noticed, was molded from the same clay as she was. She smiled. Perhaps it was true that men always fell for the same type of woman. But she was glad that Charlie had found someone he so obviously cared about. That he was indeed smitten with Rowena was written all over his face.

After the introductions had been made, Charlie lowered his voice and pronounced Gwen's marriage to be a horrible mistake. "My parents are heartbroken, and so am I," he confided. He and Vincent were soon picking the doctor apart, and agreeing that Gwenny should have married the devoted and desirable Mike Lesley.

Why are people always so dreadful at weddings, Audra wondered at one moment. She had no ready answers for herself.

Gwen's marriage was the highlight of the spring and the early months of summer. Audra and Vincent plodded along in much the same way, absorbed and preoccupied with themselves.

Audra was on her own a lot more than ever, since Vincent was now spending two and three days a week in York.

Varley's was building the small extension onto Rowntree's chocolate factory, and Mr. Varley had put him in charge of the project. But neither Audra nor Vincent minded too much about these absences; they were both far too relieved that he still had a job.

More and more men were on the dole, and when Audra went to Calpher House she would see them standing outside the Labor Exchange at Hill-Top and her heart went out to them. They looked so without hope. And she thanked God that Vincent was not one of them.

By the end of June the building job in York was completed, and Vincent was again working locally and living at home all the time. It was a scorching Saturday morning at the beginning of July that Audra experienced her first contractions. Vincent rushed her to St. Mary's Hospital in his Uncle Phil's car, and several hours later their first child was born. It was a boy.

They had chosen his names weeks before. He was to be baptized Adrian Alfred, after their respective fathers. But right from the beginning Vincent called him Alfie and the name stuck.

Everybody loved Alfie.

He was a happy, laughing, easy-going baby with bright green eyes, dark silky hair, and a cherubic face. He hardly ever cried, and his disposition was so sweet that Vincent and Audra considered themselves to be the most fortunate of parents. All of the Crowthers petted and spoiled Alfie, most especially Eliza and Alfred, who doted on their first grandchild. But his aunts adored him too, and Audra knew there would never be a shortage of baby-sitters, whenever they were required.

As months passed, Alfie only became sweeter and happier. He gurgled and laughed and kicked his legs a lot, whether lying in his cot or his pram, and when Audra wheeled him out on Town Street, total strangers would stop her to go into raptures over "the beautiful child." He was the kind of cuddly baby that everyone wanted to pick up and squeeze and kiss. Audra soon learned to be on guard about this, forever trying to prevent it, afraid as she was of Alfie being exposed to germs.

She loved her child to distraction. Sometimes she would stop her work and go out into the little garden to look at him. As she peered down into the pram, she was certain his face lit up at the sight of her, that there was recognition in his dancing green eyes, and this made her heart leap. She had never known such happiness as this tiny person gave her.

It was obvious to Audra and everyone else that Alfie was going to favor Vincent in his looks; certainly his vivid coloring echoed his father's perfectly. Vincent loved his son as much as Audra did, and both parents were aware that their infant boy was unusually alert and bright. He was already showing signs of exceptional intelligence by the time he was six months old, and they took great delight in little Alfie and were proud of him.

In a way, the child had brought them together again.

Their relationship had improved, and there was a peaceful atmosphere in the cottage in Pot Lane. Vincent stayed home more during the week now, and when he went out on Saturday nights, Audra accompanied him more often than not. This latter development was due in no small measure to Laurette, whose own circumstances had changed—and for the better.

Vincent had played matchmaker successfully.

His favorite sister and Mike Lesley were courting. Laurette was constantly issuing invitations to Audra, and these were readily accepted. The two men enjoyed each other's company, and Vincent was quite happy to forego his Saturday nights at the pub to take his wife out with the other couple.

These four shared a love of music, in particular the popular operettas of Sigmund Romberg and Victor Herbert. Since these were currently all the rage, touring companies from London came regularly to the Grand Theatre in Leeds, and Mike was the first to buy tickets for such hit shows as *Naughty Marietta, The Desert Song,* and *The Student Prince*. Sometimes they went dancing to the Mecca, or to see the latest talking pictures, but whatever they did, they generally had fun together.

The foursome became a regular thing during the summer

and autumn of 1929, and they were all looking forward to spending Christmas together. Audra, for one, was especially happy this year. Her marriage was suddenly steady, she had a family of her own, and there was harmony in her home.

CHAPTER TWENTY

Audra and Laurette walked slowly up Pot Lane in the gathering twilight of the January day.

It was the first week of 1930. The beginning of a new year and of a new decade.

Both young women were full of good spirits and happier than they had been in years. Despite the worsening conditions in England and the world economic crisis, their own futures seemed rosy—and secure at last.

Audra was content with her life and with Vincent. And, of course, there was Alfie, her darling little baby, who grew more beautiful by the day, who was the joy of her life. Vincent continued to do well at Varley's; he had had an increase in pay and they were finally out of debt. Things had never looked better.

As for Laurette, she was filled with a marvelous sense of euphoria. She was deeply in love with Mike Lesley, and he with her, and last night they had become engaged; they planned to be married in the summer.

Although Mike was still studying medicine at Leeds University, his bachelor uncle had recently died and left him a small inheritance. This welcome little windfall had enabled them to speed up their marital plans, since it would enable Mike to support a wife until he qualified as a doctor at the end of the year. And so her head was teeming with thoughts of her wedding, her trousseau, finding a house in Upper Armley, where they wanted to live, and making a comfortable home for this man whom she so adored.

Earlier in the day, the two young women had celebrated Laurette's engagement.

Audra had insisted on treating her sister-in-law to lunch on this very special occasion. Since they only ever went to Betty's Cafe in Leeds, she had decided that a change was definitely in order, and she had been happy to splurge. It had been worth it just to see the look of surprise and delight on Laurette's face when she had led her into Turkish Delight, the charming cafe with an oriental theme in Harte's.

After lunch they had wandered around the elegant department store for a while, playing their favorite game of pretend shopping. They had looked at the exquisite couture dresses and evening gowns in the Model Room; exclaimed over fox and beaver and ermine coats in the Fur Salon; tried on chic hats in the Millinery Box; doused themselves with a variety of expensive French scents at the perfumery counter. And, all in all, they had enjoyed this harmless bit of fantasy, this brief escape from their everyday lives.

Later they had gone to Leeds Market in Kirkgate, as they usually did every Saturday afternoon. "Down to earth with a bang," Laurette had said with a wry laugh, as they had trudged around the produce stalls, looking for good buys.

Audra had also laughed as she had picked up a cauliflower and examined it. She had murmured, "Everybody's looking at us, or I should say *sniffing* us. We must really and truly *pong* after all that perfume we sprayed on ourselves."

"We probably smell like a Chinese whorehouse, as our Vincent would say."

Giggling and laughing like a couple of giddy, carefree school girls, they had plunged through the throngs of shoppers, found their bargains and left the huge market with laden shopping bags, making their way to Upper Armley on the tram.

Now, as they headed along the darkening lane in the direction of the cottage, they were both shivering in the chill wind that had blown up. During the week it had rained a lot, and the wind carried with it the pungent odor of dripping foliage, wet earth and moldering leaves. There was a dampness on the air and a mist was coming down, and both presaged more rain.

"These wet leaves are treacherous on the path," Audra exclaimed, "so do watch your step, Laurette."

"Yes, I will, and listen, Audra, thank you for a lovely day. I've really enjoyed myself, especially our lunch and browsing in Harte's. Now I'm looking forward to a nice cup of tea. I suddenly feel jiggered."

"I'm a little tired myself," Audra confessed. "All those people in the Market, I've never seen it so busy."

"I've had enough of crowds for one day . . . I'm certainly relieved we're not going dancing tonight, I don't think I'd last very long."

"My feet are killing me too," Audra said, as they went down the steps into the cul-de-sac.

Before they reached the end of the flagstone path, the door of number thirty-eight flew open and Maggie stood in a circle of light, peering out into the gloomy night. "*Audra? Laurette?*"

"Yes, it's us," Audra responded, hurrying forward. She had caught an odd note in the fourteen-year-old's voice, and a warning signal went off in her head. "Is everything all right?"

"It's our Alfie," Maggie said tensely, opening the door wider, stepping aside to let them enter. "I think he's right badly, Audra."

Audra dumped her shopping bags on the floor and flew across the room without bothering to remove her coat. She bent over the bassinet in the corner of the kitchen, staring anxiously at Alfie.

She saw at once that her baby was indeed not well. His eyes were glazed and he was obviously feverish. Pulling off her gloves, she reached out, touched his flushed cheek lightly with the tip of one finger. His little face was burning. Instantly she became alarmed. But it was not in Audra's nature to panic; also, because of her training as a nurse, plus Matron Lennox's belief that she was a gifted healer, she felt confident and certainly capable of looking after her own child when he was ill.

Straightening up, she struggled out of her gray Melton coat, tossed it on a chair, hurried to the kitchen sink to wash her hands.

She said to Laurette, "Please get me the thermometer out of the medicine chest in the cupboard near the pantry. Then clear the tea things away and put a clean towel on the table, please. I want to examine Alfie under the light and sponge him down, to cool him. Could you also bring his toilet basket, oh, and dampen his flannel for me, would you please, whilst you're at it?"

"Right away." Laurette bustled around the kitchen, doing as Audra requested.

After Audra had washed and dried her hands, she rinsed the thermometer in cold water, placed it on the kitchen table, then went to get her child. She lifted him out of his bassinet carefully and carried him to the table, where she slipped off his cardigan and romper suit, and removed his vest and his nappy. And there was gentleness and tenderness in her every movement as she handled the infant.

She took Alfie's temperature, looked up at Laurette and shook her head. "It's a hundred and four, but I'm not really surprised, he's awfully feverish. Give me the flannel, would you please, Laurette?"

"What do you think he's got?" Laurette asked, sounding worried as she brought the face cloth to Audra.

"I don't know. It could be any one of a number of children's ailments—measles, chicken pox, scarlet fever. On the other hand, I don't see any sign of a rash or spots. . . ." She let her sentence trail off, finished sponging his fat little legs, his plump little feet, then dusted him down with Fuller's Earth Powder. As she began to dress him again, she said to Laurette, without looking up, "But he does have such a *high* temperature. I wonder if I ought to give him a Fenning's Fever Powder? Or some gripe water? No, I'd better not. I think I have to send for the doctor."

Laurette nodded. "Yes, perhaps you should." She glanced at the clock. "If only Mike were here, he could examine Alfie. I can't imagine what's keeping him and Vincent."

"I can run down for Doctor Stalkley," Maggie volunteered, her voice shrill and anxious.

"Yes, I think you'd better," Audra murmured, lifting Alfie

in her arms, taking him back to his bassinet. Turning to face Maggie, she said, "But before you do, tell me everything you can about the way Alfie acted this afternoon, what time you realized he wasn't well, and any symptoms you noticed—anything odd about him."

Maggie had been worried out of her wits for hours. She had been afraid to take Alfie to the doctor's office, for fear of endangering him further; for the same reason, she had not dared to leave him alone whilst she went to fetch the doctor. Now she was not only nervous but on the verge of tears.

She said with a tremor, "Vincent and Mike went off to the football match at about one. Just after that, our Alfie started to cry, and he kept crying off and on for ages, and he was ever so fratchy and that's not like him, he's always so good. I kept going to check on him, Audra, honest I did, to see if he was all right, to see if he was wet. But his nappy was dry, and there were no pins sticking in him. Then a bit later, it must've been three or so, I saw how red he was getting. It was ever so hot in here, and I took him into the sitting room to cool him down. We sat there a bit. I was nursing him on my lap, singing to him, and he started to vomit, and in ever such a funny way, Aud—"

"Describe the vomiting," Audra interjected, stiffening.

"I don't know how to, it's difficult to describe," Maggie wailed and looked at Audra, conscious of the sudden change in her sister-in-law. Audra's acute anxiety had instantly transmitted itself to Maggie.

"Try."

Maggie gulped, racking her brains for the right words. She took a deep breath, said, "The vomit sort of came straight out of him. It was like somebody gave him a *thump* on his back and knocked it out. What was funny was that Alfie didn't heave, or do anything like that."

Projectile vomiting, Audra thought, with a stab of dread. That is what Maggie has tried so hard to describe. Oh my God. *Meningitis*. It simply can't be. Audra stood very still, knowing that it was imperative she keep a firm hold on herself, that she stay absolutely calm and clearheaded. For her baby's sake she must not permit emotion to cloud intelligence and judgment.

Swallowing her apprehension, Audra turned to the crib and peered down at Alfie. He looked so listless, and he was as flushed as before.

"Hurry to the doctor's, Maggie," Audra instructed. "Tell Doctor Stalkley that Alfie is ill, and that he must come immediately."

Maggie shot across the kitchen and snatched her coat from the closet. "What do you think's wrong with our little Alfie then, Audra? It's not serious, is it?"

"I can't be certain, but the vomiting and the high fever do worry me."

"I'll tell t'doctor about both things," Maggie said, pivoting at the front door. "And I'll run all the way there, and as fast as me legs'll carry me."

The moment they were alone, Laurette asked anxiously, "Audra, whatever is it? You've turned as white as a sheet. What on earth *is* wrong with Alfie? You must have some idea."

"I'm not sure, really I'm not," Audra replied, striving to keep her voice steady, not daring to say the name of that most ghastly illness. She had seen two children die of it when she had been a nurse at the Fever Hospital, and their suffering had been pitiful to witness.

Laurette stood up. "Well, you look awful, and I'm going to make us a pot of tea." She hurried to the sink to fill the kettle, glad to keep busy. She wished Mike were here. His presence was always comforting, and Audra had faith in his judgment.

Audra sat up slightly in the easy chair, thinking hard. She had committed a great deal of medical information to memory in the past. Suddenly, in her mind's eye, she pictured the page of her hospital textbook which dealt with meningitis. She sat staring into space, saw every word on that page quite clearly, as though someone held the book in front of her. *Meningitis: Acute inflammation of the membranes of the brain and spinal cord, or both. Also called "spotted fever," due to extensive spotting of the skin in severe cases. Symptoms: Severe headache, high fever, frequently neck and back rigidity; also twitching or convulsions. Severe vomiting is common, known as projectile vomiting due to sudden ejection of vomit to some distance; spotting of skin in severe cases; delirium, coma.*

Once more, Audra leapt to her feet and rushed over to the bassinet. Her eyes flicked over Alfie seeking signs of the symptoms she now so clearly recalled. But she saw nothing unusual. The child remained flushed, but there was no evidence of twitching or convulsions, or neck rigidity, and certainly there had been no rash on his body when she had examined him a few minutes earlier.

She let out a sigh of relief. Of course it's not meningitis, she told herself. How could it be? Anyway, Alfie's probably coming down with a winter cold, or influenza at the worst. *But his high fever, what about his high fever?* a small voice nagged at the back of her mind.

Alfie began to cry, wiping this thought right out of her head. She bent over the bassinet, reached for him.

"Hush, sweetheart, hush, my little darling," she murmured, holding him tenderly against her breast. She smoothed her hand over his dark head and across his small back, hushing him softly. Immediately, Alfie stopped crying and nestled into her. Audra walked up and down, soothing him, murmuring to him gently, and she was filled with such love for her child she thought her heart was going to burst.

And as she continued to pace back and forth in front of the fire, desperately trying to give comfort to her tiny son, she began to pray. *Oh please, God, don't let anything happen to my baby. Protect my little Alfie, please keep him safe and make him well again,* she entreated silently. And she kept repeating the words over and over again as she waited for the doctor to come.

CHAPTER TWENTY-ONE

Alfie died.

His death was so unexpected, so swift, everyone was

stunned and disbelieving. One minute he was a healthy, robust baby, laughing and gurgling in his crib, the next he was gone from them.

On that fateful Saturday evening, Doctor Stalkley had come to the cottage at once, following sharply on the heels of Vincent and Mike, who had walked in from the football match a few minutes before.

After examining Alfie, neither the doctor nor Mike believed that he had meningitis. Despite the peculiar vomiting in the afternoon, which had not recurred, his only symptom was the high temperature. "Not enough to go on," Doctor Stalkley had said. "I'll come back tomorrow morning, but meanwhile keep a close eye on him, Audra." Picking up his Gladstone bag, striding to the coat closet, he had motioned to Maggie. "Now, lassie," the old Scotsman had said, "you'd best be coming back to my office with me, and I'll give you a drop of medicine for the wee bairn."

Because the doctor and Mike had been so hopeful for Alfie's recovery from whatever it was that ailed him, Audra and Vincent had taken heart. Following the doctor's instructions explicitly, they had watched over Alfie all weekend, had not left him alone for one moment.

Audra had sponged him down frequently, to keep him cool and refreshed; she had given him the fever medicine at the prescribed times and had generally tended to him with all the skills of the professional nurse that she was. And she had hardly closed her eyes during that time.

But Audra did not care about sleep. Alfie's health was the only thing that mattered to her and Vincent. By Sunday night the entire Crowther family believed that Alfie was over the worst of his mysterious ailment. The febrile look had vanished from his eyes, and the scarlet flush had disappeared from his plump cheeks.

But on Monday morning, just before noon, the child had had a relapse.

Audra's worst fears had been confirmed.

Alfie had started to have convulsions, and the tiny spots, which looked like bright red pin pricks, had begun to appear on his milky skin. Endeavoring to control her terrible fear for her child, Audra had wrapped him in several woolen shawls and rushed to the doctor's office.

Doctor Stalkley had taken one look at Alfie and shaken his head. After a rapid examination, he had dispatched Audra to St. Mary's Hospital, just a short distance away. He promised to visit Alfie as soon as his morning office hours were over, when he started his daily rounds in the district.

Whilst she had waited for Alfie to be admitted to the children's ward, Audra had cradled him in her arms, cooing to him softly, fighting back her tears. It had been wrenching to leave him. And she had fervently wished that she was a nurse at St. Mary's, so that she could care for her beloved child herself.

Four days later Alfie came home to them in a small pine coffin.

Burdened with sorrow, Vincent dragged himself to every window in the cottage, closing the curtains to shut out the light until after the funeral, as was the custom in the North.

And then he went to comfort his wife.

Audra was inconsolable.

"Why couldn't I make him better?" she kept asking Vincent as she stood by the side of the open coffin, blinded by her scalding tears. "Matron Lennox says I'm an exceptional nurse," she sobbed, "so why couldn't I make our baby get well?"

"Audra . . . *Audra love,* nobody could have helped our poor little Alfie. It's not your fault; it's nobody's fault. Meningitis is generally fatal in small babies. Mike told me so," Vincent said quietly, "and you know that yourself, lovey."

"I should have kept him at home, nursed him myself, not left him to strangers," she cried, clutching Vincent's arm, staring at him wildly. "If I hadn't let Alfie go into the hospital, he'd be alive. He would, I just know he would!"

"No, love, that's not true," Vincent said gently, drawing her to him, smoothing her hair away from her ravaged face. "They did their very best up at St. Mary's, and they fought hard for Alfie's life. It just wasn't meant to be, Audra love."

Vincent led her out of the sitting room where the coffin stood, and took her back to the kitchen. He held her in his arms and tried to give her solace, and her tears drenched the front of his shirt, and they wept together for their child.

Eliza and Alfred came to see their dead grandchild, to share the grief of their son and daughter-in-law and do what they could to help.

Alfred, the ex-sergeant major of the Seaforth Highlanders, a tough and stalwart soldier, broke down and sobbed openly at the coffin. He was profoundly moved at the sight of Alfie, his namesake. In death, the child's beauty seemed more potent than ever and perfect in its waxlike state. Alfie looked as if he was merely sleeping. But when Alfred bent over and kissed the delicate cheek, its immense coldness struck him like a knife in the chest, and he clutched at Eliza's arm. She endeavored to comfort him, though her own sorrow was enormous.

When they joined Vincent and Audra in the kitchen a while later, Alfred looked around him, as if dazed, and asked in a shaken voice, "*Why?* Why has our little Alfie's life been snuffed out? He was only a baby, and nothing but pure joy . . . tell me why he has been taken from us so cruelly?"

No one had an answer for Alfred.

CHAPTER TWENTY-TWO

It was a golden day in late October, one of those especially glorious Indian summer days that so often occur in the autumn, just before the harsh winter sets in. The sky was the color of speedwells and luminous in the sunlight and the breeze was light, almost warm.

What a grand afternoon it is, Vincent thought, lifting his eyes, enjoying the radiance of the day. I hope this weather lasts till the weekend. Turning off Town Street, he increased his pace as he heard the church clock strike three. He was heading down Ridge Road in the direction of H. E.

Varley and Son, Builders, and he did not want to be late for his appointment with Mr. Fred Varley.

It was a Thursday, almost the end of a week that had been exceptionally hard. He had pushed his men relentlessly to finish the warehouse they were building onto Pinfold's woolen mill, and by noon tomorrow the job would be completed. No doubt that was why Mr. Varley wanted to see him, to congratulate him, and there was bound to be a nice bonus for himself and his crew.

At the thought of a little extra money, Vincent began to whistle and he stepped out jauntily. He touched his cap, smiled and nodded as he passed the vicar's wife near Christ Church Vicarage, and then crossed the road. A few seconds later he was entering the builder's office and greeting Maureen, Mr. Varley's secretary.

"Hello, love," he said, taking off his cap, giving her a broad smile. "Mr. Varley sent for me."

"Good afternoon, Vincent," Maureen replied and nodded her head toward the door. "You can go in; he's waiting for you."

Mr. Varley was speaking on the telephone, but as Vincent hove into view in the doorway, he immediately said goodbye, hung up and beckoned for Vincent to enter.

"There you are, lad, come in, come in, and sit yourself down."

"Thanks, Mr. Varley." Vincent lowered himself into the chair facing the desk. "The Pinfold job will be finished tomorrow at noon," he went on, "the lads have done right well, Mr. Varley, and I know you'll be pleased when you see the warehouse. It's a bit of good building work, even though I do say so myself."

"Aye, I'm sure it is, lad, you're a good worker, and a good foreman, the best I've ever had, in fact." Fred Varley cleared his throat. "That's why it's so hard for me to tell you this . . . I've got some right bad news for you, I'm afraid, Vincent, I do that. I'm going to have to shut up shop."

Vincent stared at him, for a moment uncomprehending. "Close down?" he said swiftly, raising his brows. "*Close* Varley's?"

"Aye, lad—as of tomorrow."

"Oh my God!" Vincent was shocked. "I don't understand," he began, and then faltered as all of the implications sank in.

"I'm going to have to go into bankruptcy, I've no alternative," Varley said.

"But why? We've had a lot of jobs in the last few months—"

"Aye, I knows we have, lad," Mr. Varley cut in. "But some of the buggers haven't paid up yet, and I've no bloody idea when they will. I've been operating on credit for a hell of a long time, Vincent, and I'm so heavily into the bank, I don't dare borrow more, and I doubt that they'd lend it to me now, anyway. I'm mortgaged up to the hilt." Shaking his head sadly, he finished, "There's no two ways about it, I've got to cut my losses. Only one way to do that . . . *close down.*"

"I can see what you mean," Vincent mumbled, his eyes troubled as he looked across the desk at his employer. He was thinking not only of himself but of the other men who would be thrown out of work tomorrow. They were all married men, too, except for Billie Johnson, the plumber's mate.

Varley said, "Naturally, I'll tell the lads meself. Tomorrow. I wouldn't be leaving owt like that to you, shirking me duty, so to speak. I shall be able to meet this week's payroll, but that's about it. No severance pay, no bonuses, nowt like that, I'm sorry to say." Fred Varley added, "When you get your cards tomorrow, Vincent, I should go up and sign on at once at the Public Assistance Board, if I was you. Better start drawing the dole as soon as you can."

Vincent nodded grimly.

"I'm hoping I'll be able to sort out this mess," Mr. Varley remarked, rising, obviously wanting to terminate this difficult conversation. "And things are bound to turn around in the country right soon. The Depression can't last forever. I intend to start afresh, you knows, and in the not too distant future, and what I want to say is this—when I do open up again, there'll be a job for you, Vincent. I do hope you'd come back to me."

Vincent also stood up. "Thanks, Mr. Varley, and yes, I

would. You've always been very decent with me, very fair
indeed. And I'm sorry your business has gone down the
drain, really sorry."

"Aye, lad, so am I. And I'm doubly sorry for you and the
rest of the men. I know how rough it's going to be on all of
you."

"I'll see you tomorrow then, Mr. Varley, Ta'rar."

"Ta'rar, lad."

CHAPTER TWENTY-THREE

Vincent Crowther sat in the recreation grounds, behind the
park in Moorfield Road, smoking a Woodbine.

He was no longer aware of the beautiful Indian summer
afternoon, and all of his earlier jauntiness had dissipated.
He was engulfed in his worries about earning a living in
order to support himself and Audra.

Only the other day he had read in the Yorkshire *Post* that
there were one million, nine hundred thousand men out of
work in England. Plus one, he muttered under his breath,
now that I'm about to join them. The idea of going on the
dole appalled him. But he would have to do so, since there
was nothing else he *could* do until he found another job.

When he had left Varley's office he had felt as if he had
been kicked in the stomach and the feeling persisted. He
had wandered into the little park twenty minutes ago,
hoping to clear his befuddled head, marshal his swimming
senses before he went home. But he was still stunned, and
just a bit bewildered. He had believed Fred Varley to be
shrewd and successful, had never once imagined that the
firm could go out of business, that Fred Varley, of all
people, would go down. Just goes to show, he thought, you
never really know about anybody.

Vincent had no idea where to begin to find work, for the
simple reason that there weren't any jobs to be had. Nor
did he have any idea how he was going to break this terrible
news to Audra.

What a blow it'll be for her, he thought, and just when she was on her feet again after little Alfie's death. He groaned out loud, then took a long, satisfying drag on his cigarette. He suddenly held it away, looked at it with a frown, asking himself how long he would be able to afford his Woodbines. And his pint of bitter. And a bet on the ponies on Saturday afternoons. A grimness settled over him. The prospects looked bleak. Bloody bleak indeed.

Rubbing his hand over his forehead, he closed his eyes, thinking about the money he had in the Yorkshire Penny Bank. Not much really. His savings would only tide them over for a month, at the most. And all he could expect to get on the dole was something like a pound a week for the two of them, perhaps a shilling or two more. Obviously he was going to have to do his damnedest to get a job, no matter what it was, or where it was, for that matter. He might well have to try other areas of Leeds, such as Bramley, Stanningley or Wortley, or go ever farther afield to Pudsey and Farsley.

"Well, well, well, if it's not the gentleman of leisure! I wish I had time to sit on a park bench in the *rec* and idly fritter away the afternoon—*and* in the middle of the week no less!"

Vincent recognized the deep, masculine voice of his friend and brother-in-law, and he opened his eyes, stared into Mike Lesley's warm and friendly face peering down into his. "Yes, that's what I am, Mike," he said with a weak laugh, "a gentlemen of leisure . . . as of about half an hour ago. Yes, I've joined the ranks of the unemployed, like the rest of me mates, and half the bleeding country."

Mike sat down heavily and frowned at his friend. "I know you're not joking, Vince. I know you *wouldn't* joke about anything as serious as this, but what happened? I thought Varley's was the one building firm in these parts that was doing well."

"So did *I*; so did *everybody*. But old man Varley just broke the news to me himself, about half an hour ago. He's going into bankruptcy."

Mike shook his sandy head slowly, his expression immediately turning dismal. "The situation's dreadful. I heard of three other companies that have gone down in the last month, and God knows where it's all going to end. But look here, Vincent, you're a skilled man, surely you'll be able to find something fairly soon—"

"Not bloody likely!" Vincent interrupted. "Even Mr. Varley has seen the writing on the wall, as far as I'm concerned, that is. He suggested that I sign on at the Labor Exchange at once."

Mike was silent. He shrugged further into his tweed overcoat, and his compassionate hazel eyes filled with concern for his best friend. He wondered if there was anything he could do to help Vincent find a job. He doubted it.

There was a momentary silence between these two young men who had gravitated to each other from the first moment they had met. They had grown even closer in the last couple of years. He was younger than Vincent, but he was blessed with great insight. If anyone understood the unusually complex man who was Vincent Crowther, then it was Mike Lesley.

Suddenly Vincent said, "How ever will I tell Audra that I've lost my job?"

"You'll tell her in the same way that you've told me, very directly," Mike said.

"She's going to be upset, to put it mildly . . . I couldn't stand it if she fell back into that awful depression. When I think of this spring, when she was so ill after Alfie died, I tremble in me boots, I do that, Mike. Audra was so odd, she was like a stranger to me."

"Yes, she *was* in a bad way," Mike conceded, "but a lot of women react as she did when they lose a child, especially when it's the first baby. They're demented for a while. And her loss was a terrible one, in that she's had so many other losses in her life already."

"Yes, she has. Poor Audra."

"Look here, Vince, my money is on your wife. Why she's got more character in her little finger than most people have in their entire bodies. She's a fighter, and she's full of Yorkshire grit and determination. I have a strong feeling that that wife of yours will take this news without flinching."

"I hope to God you're right, Mike, I do that." Vincent pushed himself up off the park bench. "Well, there's no point putting it off. I'd better get on home and tell her."

"I think you should." Mike rose and the two of them walked across the recreation grounds together.

"Do you still want to go to the City Varieties on Saturday night?"

"Of course I do!" Vincent exclaimed. "I can see no reason to change our plans. Anyway, Audra and Laurette have been looking forward to going. I wouldn't want them to be disappointed."

"Neither would I," Mike agreed.

The moment he strode into the cottage in Pot Lane, Vincent knew that something had happened—something special.

There was a record playing on the gramophone in the sitting room, filling the house with the strains of a Gilbert and Sullivan song from *The Mikado*. A vase of bronze and yellow autumnal chrysanthemums stood in the center of the table, which had been covered with a lace cloth and laid for supper with their best china. He surveyed the table, wondering if someone had been invited, but saw at once that it was set only for two. Glancing around the kitchen-parlor with quickening interest, Vincent next noticed the bottle of red wine on the set-pot; then he sniffed. His mouth began to water as he recognized the faint aroma of his favorite lamb stew coming through the oven door, which was slightly ajar. Pursing his lips, he wondered what was afoot, his curiosity truly fired now.

He had just taken off his coat and cap and hung them in the closet when the staircase door opened and Audra stepped into the kitchen. She wore a pretty, delphinium-blue blouse that matched her eyes and a dark skirt—plus the biggest smile he had seen on her face in ages.

"You look nice, love," he said, observing her appreciatively through his narrowed green gaze, half smiling as he spoke. He waved his hand around the room. "What are we celebrating then? Have you come into some sort of wind-fall?"

"You might say we've had two windfalls, in a sense. . . ." She left her sentence dangling and ran to kiss his cheek. Then she stood away from him, gave him a queer, almost smug smile and led him by the arm to the fireside. She took an envelope off the mantelpiece, waved it in front of his eyes. "First, there is this! It's a letter from that firm of solicitors in Ripon—you know, the ones who wrote to me in June to tell me that Great-Aunt Frances Reynolds had died and that she had left me something in her will. You thought it was going to be another piece of silver, or that china teapot I admired, but it isn't either thing. It's *fifty pounds*, Vincent! Wasn't that lovely of her?"

"Aye, lass, it certainly was," he said with a grin, thinking that Audra's little legacy could not have come at a more propitious time. He was about to say so, wanting to tell her that he had lost his job, get the unpleasant task over with, when she prevented this. She flung herself at him and hugged him so tightly he was taken aback.

But he hugged her in return, stared down into her face.

He saw that it was filled with laughter and her bright eyes were more brilliantly blue than ever and there was a radiance about her. "What is it, Audra? You look like the cat that's swallowed the canary. Right chuff with yourself, my girl, that's what you are!"

"Yes, I am, Vincent. I went to see Doctor Stalkley this morning and he's confirmed it to me. I'm two months pregnant; we're going to have a baby . . . next May."

It seemed to Vincent that his heart did a tiny somersault of joy. He had been praying that she would get pregnant. Another child would fill the terrible void Alfie had left, and for both of them, not just her. His grief had been as acute as hers, and he still thought about his dead son with sorrow.

Vincent drew her closer, pressed her head against his chest, stroked the crown of her burnished head. "You couldn't have told me anything better, love," he said. "I've been hoping to hear this for months, I really have. No wonder you're chuffed . . . so am I."

"I thought you would be, Vincent."

His response was to tighten his arms around her. And he decided not to spoil the special evening she had planned for them by giving her his bad news. He would tell her about Varley's going bankrupt tomorrow. That was soon enough.

Unexpectedly, and much to his astonishment, he suddenly felt optimistic about finding a job. The baby was a lucky omen.

CHAPTER TWENTY-FOUR

"Oh, Audra, what a bonny little girl!" Gwen cried, her face lighting up as she bent over the hospital bed to look at the new-born infant in Audra's arms. "She's just perfect."

"Thank you, Gwen. I think so, too, but then I'm her mother, so I suppose that's natural." Audra smiled up at her friend, who had dropped in unexpectedly to visit her at St. Mary's Hospital, then turned her eyes to the bedside table. She let them rest on the lavish bouquet Gwen had placed there a moment before. "And thank you for the flowers, they're lovely."

"Well, you always did like yellow roses, lovey. There's also this. . . ." Gwen placed a package on the bed. "It's for—" She stopped, glanced at the baby and laughed. "You haven't told me her name."

"Goodness, how stupid I am. We're going to call her Christina. Do you like it?"

"Oh I do, it's ever such a pretty name." Seating herself on the chair next to the bed, Gwen leaned forward and touched the gift. "Shall I open this for you . . . and Christina?"

Audra laughed. "Please."

"I hope you like it," Gwen murmured as she untied the ribbon around the fancy box and took off the lid. She lifted out a shell-pink dress with deeper, rose-pink smocking across the front, and held it up for Audra to see. "It's silk and it's handmade." She looked at Audra expectantly.

"Oh Gwen, it's exquisite and I love it! Christina will look

so pretty in it, but you *are* extravagant." Audra reached out and squeezed Gwen's hand.

Gwen beamed with pleasure. She leaned back in her chair and regarded Audra thoughtfully. "I must say, you do look well. Certainly a lot better than you did after you'd had Alfie—" Her voice quavered as she said his name, and she stopped, her expression chagrined. "Oh, I'm sorry. . . ."

"Don't be so silly, Gwenny, we can't avoid mentioning Alfie's name occasionally, and it doesn't upset me, truly it doesn't." Audra smiled at her reassuringly. "I've recovered from his death now, in the sense that my grief *has* lessened. It's not too painful anymore. Of course, I shall never forget Alfie and I shall always love him, but there's Christina now."

Audra dropped her eyes to the child in her arms and smiled down at her, then glanced at Gwen. "I feel quite wonderful, really. It was an easy birth, just as it was an easy pregnancy. It's odd, isn't it, that I had such a bad time with Alfie. But I hardly knew I was carrying Christina, and the delivery was over before I could blink—well, almost."

Gwen nodded her stylishly bobbed blond head. "Yes, it often happens that way." She gazed out of the window almost absently, and a wistful expression flitted across her face. "You are lucky . . . I wish I could get pregnant."

"Oh you will, just give it time."

"*Time!*" Gwen laughed softly. "It's May of 1931. I've been married exactly two years and one month." She gave a little shrug of her shoulders, added, "But then again, Geoffrey says I'm too anxious, too tense, and that I must relax about having a baby."

"Perhaps he's correct. After all, he is a doctor. And how is Geoffrey?"

"Oh he's all right." Gwen jumped up abruptly. "The nurses on this ward seem to be very careless in the execution of their duties. These roses will be half dead by the time one of them decides to bring a vase." She reached for the bunch of flowers. "I'll put them in water . . . be back in a jiffy."

Audra's eyes followed Gwen as she walked up the ward. She had changed a lot in the last two years, as Audra had known she would. *He* had changed her . . . changed the

way she dressed and spoke and walked, and perhaps even
the way she thought. And she had changed yet again since
the last time they had met. There was definitely something
odd about Gwen today, something that Audra could not
quite put her finger on. They saw each other infrequently
these days, since their friendship had continued to drift
after their marriages. And so the slightest difference in
Gwen was most apparent to Audra, the shrewd observer,
when they did meet. It has to do with her appearance,
Audra now thought, frowning. Was it her outfit? Certainly
the black linen dress and jacket were rather stark with their
lack of adornment. Also, the somber color drained the life
from her face. But no, it was not her clothes.

Puzzled, Audra let her eyes rest on Gwen as she
marched back to the bed, carrying the vase of roses. And as
she drew nearer, Audra knew, suddenly, what it was that
was so different about her friend today. *All of the light in
her eyes had died.* She's no longer happy with him, Audra
thought, if she ever was. That's why she doesn't want to talk
about him, the reason she leapt up and rushed to put the
roses in water. Oh poor Gwenny, she expected so much
from this marriage, envisioned such a wonderful life for
herself with Geoffrey, and I bet it's pure hell.

"Thank you," Audra murmured when Gwen placed the
vase on the nightstand. She scrutinized her surreptitiously.
Yes, there *was* a sadness behind those pretty pale blue eyes
and a funny little droop to Gwen's mouth which had not
been there before.

Gwen interrupted her thoughts when she announced, "I
just want you to know that I gave that young nurse a good
ticking off."

"I bet you did . . . you see how it is, Gwen; when
you're back on a ward you want to take charge . . . old
habits die hard, don't they?"

"Yes, perhaps they do." Gwen sat down, went on,
"Whilst we're on the subject of nursing, are you going back
to work for that woman in The Towers when you get out of
hospital?"

"You mean Mrs. Jarvis . . . oh yes, I *promised* her, and

I can't let her down. She's not at all well, and besides, we need the money."

A sympathetic look flashed across Gwen's face as she remarked, "It must be awful for you, lovey, Vincent *still* being out of work."

"Well, it's worse for him, really," Audra said softly, eyeing Gwen carefully, detecting criticism in her tone. "The frustration of not being able to find a job is dreadful for him, as I'm sure you can appreciate. Vincent's not a layabout, or a lazy man, you know, and—"

"I wasn't suggesting anything like that!" Gwen cried, flushing slightly.

Ignoring this comment, Audra continued speaking in an even voice, "He's out again this afternoon, doing the rounds. He's very responsible, and he follows up on every lead."

"It must rankle with him a bit," Gwen murmured. "I mean he was always dead set against you going out to work."

"Yes, he was, and don't think he's changed his mind, because he hasn't. However, that's the way it has to be just now."

"Yes, I realize that, lovey. The last time we saw each other, in March I think it was, you told me that your William had written to suggest that you and Vincent join him in Australia. Didn't that idea come to anything, then?"

"No, it didn't, and I never expected it would. Vincent might give lip service to the idea of emigrating, Gwen, but he wouldn't leave England. He grumbles, of course, about the Depression, the present conditions, and he calls the government and the politicians every nasty name he can think of, but he loves this country."

Audra shook her head slowly. "No, he wouldn't leave his mother and father and the rest of the family—they're very close-knit, you know, the Crowthers. And there was another reason—I didn't really want to go myself. Of course, I'd love to see William and Frederick again, but I don't think I'd want to live in Australia. Not anymore. It's *so* far away."

Gwen grimaced. "Yes, I know what you mean; it does

seem like the back of the beyond." Waving her hand up and down in front of her face, Gwen now exclaimed, "Phew! It has grown hot in here all of a sudden, but then it's very warm for May, isn't it?" She slipped off her jacket and hung it on the back of the chair. "Didn't you tell me that your Frederick got engaged? Is he married yet?"

Audra did not respond.

Gwen looked at her curiously. "What's the matter? Why are you staring at me like that?"

"What on earth have you done to your arm?" Audra asked, unable to take her eyes off Gwen. The dress she was wearing was sleeveless, revealing an arm that was badly swollen and dark brown with fading bruises.

With a small, embarrassed laugh, Gwen said, "Doesn't it look awful! I fell down the cellar steps the other day. Geoffrey was furious with me for being such a clumsy thing. We were going to a dance that night, and I wasn't able to wear my new dress with cap sleeves, and I paid such a lot for it in the Model Room at Harte's. Geoffrey said I could have killed myself, and he was ever so cross that I was anywhere near the cellar steps to begin with." She laughed a little nervously.

"I'm not surprised that he was angry, and you *could* have killed yourself. I remember thinking how steep the cellar steps were, when I first came to see the house. You must be more careful," Audra cautioned.

"Yes, I know." Gwen stood up, appeared restless all of a sudden and strolled over to the window. She peered through the glass, stiffened, then swung to Audra. "Mike and Laurette are coming through the hospital gates with Vincent. I'd better be going."

"But they'd all love to see you and say hello to you."

Gwen laughed awkwardly, then remarked, "I don't really want to see Mike, to tell you the truth."

"Oh you are being silly. Now that you're both married there's no reason for you to feel self-conscious."

"I know, but they're your family and I'd only be in the way. And I really should be getting back to Headingley. I've things to do . . . we're having another dinner party tonight, and that maid of mine bears watching."

"I wish you'd stay."

Gwen shook her head with a faint smile. "No, I must be off." She lightly touched the top of Christina's head, bent to kiss Audra's cheek. "Bye-bye, lovey, I'll see you again soon."

"Goodbye, Gwenny," Audra said, very quietly, knowing it would be a long time before she set eyes on her again. "Thanks for coming to see me."

Audra watched her dear old friend hurrying off down the ward and she thought: Oh Gwenny, you'll run right into Mike on the front steps of the hospital.

"How're my girls?" Vincent asked, bending over, kissing Audra on the cheek, then peeping at his daughter in her arms.

"We're both blooming," Audra said, smiling, glancing up at him quickly. She knew from his expression that he had not found any work.

Laurette came forward to greet her with great affection and warmth, then said, "Mam's sent this small fruit pie; she thought you'd enjoy it."

"I shall, and please thank her for me, Laurette."

Vincent perched on the edge of the bed, said, "We just ran into Gwen and she skittered off down the path as if we were carrying the Black Death."

"She had to get home," Audra told him. "She said something about a dinner party."

"I had a feeling she didn't want to engage in a conversation with Mike," Laurette volunteered, looking from one to the other.

"Aye, maybe you're right," Vincent said, nodding his head. "And I'm sure the feeling's mutual. What could he possibly have to say to *her*?"

Audra asked, "Where is he, anyway?"

"He stopped in to see a patient in another ward. He'll be here in a second," Laurette told her, then asked, "Can I hold Christina for a few minutes, Audra?"

"Of course you may. Here, come along, take her from me, dear."

Audra was glad to change her position in the bed, stretch a little. For a few seconds there was a quietness among the three of them, and Audra watched Laurette rocking the baby, cooing to her softly, holding her so tenderly. She suddenly said, "Vincent and I wondered—hoped actually—that you would be her godmother, Laurette, and that Mike would be her godfather."

"Oh I'd love to be!" Laurette exclaimed excitedly, "and I know Mike would too." She hesitated, then asked, "But who's the other godmother going to be? Gwen, I suppose."

"No, I have a feeling that wouldn't work somehow," Audra replied, looking at Vincent. "Do you?"

"I never did, and I'm certainly glad you've changed your mind." He grinned, glanced along the ward and added, "And here comes Mike now."

Mike made a beeline for Audra.

After kissing her cheek and squeezing her shoulder gently, he said, "No need to ask how you're feeling. For a woman who had a baby only two days ago, you look marvelous . . . I presume everything's all right, no problems of any sort?"

"No, none." Audra returned his smile, thinking yet again that he was the kindest man she had ever met. The compassion in his soul was reflected in those clear, caring eyes of his, and she knew he would become a successful doctor. His presence, his deep, warm voice, his concern engendered confidence; all were comforting. It's a gift, she thought, that sweetness of his. No wonder all of his patients love him.

Realizing that Mike was still hovering over her, looking down at her as if waiting for her to say something further, Audra remarked, "Doctor Stalkley was here earlier, and he says I can go home in a few days."

"He knows best, of course—just don't rush it," Mike warned and strode over to his wife. Resting his hand on Laurette's shoulder, he looked down at the baby in her arms and said, "She's going to be a bonny child."

"We'd like you to be Christina's godfather, Mike," Vincent announced. "Laurette's already agreed to be her godmother. So, what do you say?"

"I say yes." Mike grinned at them all. "You've just got yourself a godfather, and who's the other godmother?"

Vincent and Audra exchanged glances, and Vincent said, "I was thinking about our Olive. Audra, how do you feel about her?"

"She'd be perfect . . . yes, do let's keep it in the family."

Laurette said, "Olive will take her responsibilities as a godparent very seriously, as we will, naturally."

"Yes," Vincent agreed, "I know you'll all do your duty." He rose, went to his sister, stretched out his arms. "Can I borrow my little girl from you for a minute or two, Laurette? I haven't held her today."

Laurette gave the child to him and he stood looking down at her as he settled her comfortably in the crook of his arm, adjusted her shawl. Her skin was smooth and clear, and her features seemed quite well defined to him. Her face was not red and crumpled as Alfie's had been at birth. A feeling of awe crept over him as he continued to gaze at Christina and his heart twisted with love for her. He said, at last, "From the minute I heard from Audra that she was expecting, I felt this baby was a lucky omen. And she is, and she's going to turn out to be special."

"Very, very special," Audra added, "and I am going to give her the world."

They all looked at her in surprise.

There was a curious silence. Her words seemed to hang there in the air.

Laurette smiled, then bit her lip, not sure how to properly respond to this extraordinary statement.

Vincent walked toward the window with the baby, stood looking out, his silence pointed.

Mike's worried eyes followed him. From the tense set of his shoulders, he knew that Vincent was angered by Audra's comment. Well, it *had* sounded . . . possessive, to say the least. Couldn't she have said *we?* he thought.

Clearing his throat, wanting to bridge the awkward moment, Mike said, "That's a lovely sentiment to express, Audra."

"Oh but I mean it very seriously!" she shot back, in the strongest of voices, and pinned him with her eyes.

He had always known she had determination and guts, but now Mike saw something he had never seen before. There was a cold implacability in the set of the mouth and the thrust of the jaw, a terrible relentlessness in those extraordinary cornflower blue eyes. She not only *means* it, by God, he thought, but she's going to make it a crusade. And God help anyone who gets in her way, and that includes Vincent.

CHAPTER TWENTY-FIVE

And so it became a driving force in Audra Crowther's life— the desire to give Christina the world.

It was all she thought about from this moment on, and the struggle toward this goal, one which would last for over twenty years, began that summer of 1931.

The moment she came out of the hospital, Audra went back to work for Mrs. Jarvis, whom she had nursed for four months before Christina's birth. She had promised the old lady she would resume her duties after the confinement; this aside, they desperately needed the money. Vincent only received twenty-five shillings on the dole, a two-shilling increase per week now that they had a child. It was hardly enough to support the three of them.

The job with Mrs. Jarvis was neither difficult nor complex; it was convenient, in that the invalid lived in The Towers, only a few minutes away from the cottage on Pot Lane.

But Audra preferred hospital work to private nursing. After only a month of looking after Mrs. Jarvis, again she made it clear to the old lady that she was going to apply for work at St. Mary's. She did so at the beginning of July.

There was a vacancy at the hospital in November and Audra got the job. To her enormous delight she was assigned to the children's ward.

Audra knew that she had been given this most coveted position because of the strings Matron Lennox had pulled, the influence Mrs. Bell had exerted on Matron Fox. But this did not trouble her in the least. She had the job and that was all that mattered.

By the spring of 1932, Audra was settled at the hospital and enjoying it. Matron Fox had taken a liking to her, she was popular with the doctors, and she envisioned promotions coming her way soon. She never thought of these promotions, which she *knew* would be forthcoming, in terms of self-aggrandizement; very simply they would bring her more money, and that was why she wanted them. Money for Christina . . . for her clothes, her education, her future.

Although she could not save a single penny for Christina at the moment, she had every intention of doing so within the next couple of years. Audra had made long-term plans, since she believed this was the only way she would succeed, given her resources. She already had an idea for earning extra money, and she was going to put it into operation once she felt she was truly entrenched at the hospital. She was going to become a dressmaker in her free time.

Nursing gave Audra a sense of gratification, and she threw herself into it with her usual enthusiasm and energy, and as she went about the wards there was a new spring in her step, a smile on her face.

But things were not happy at home.

There was trouble between Audra and Vincent yet again, and their curious marriage was once more on a rocky footing.

In a way, the rift that had recently developed between them was mostly Audra's fault this time. Her entire attention was focused on Christina, whom she loved with an almost abnormal ferocity, perhaps because she had already lost one child in death.

Vincent also loved his little girl, but he had overwhelming problems of his own to contend with and, being a young and virile man, he had urgent needs as well. He wanted a relationship with his wife that was normal on every level.

Sadly, Audra was not merely preoccupied with Christina and her work, she now had no interest whatsoever in Vincent sexually.

She had stopped sleeping with him some months earlier, and this rankled. He was filled with frustration at being jobless and relegated to looking after the child. Audra's physical coldness and rejection were beginning to aggravate his growing bitterness in general.

One Saturday evening in April, after Christina had been put to bed in her room upstairs, he decided to have it out with Audra.

He bided his time until she had cleared the table and washed the dishes. But once she had settled herself in front of the fire and picked up her darning, he switched off the wireless and took the chair opposite her.

"Why did you do that?" she asked without looking up, intent on mending the hole in his sock.

"I want to talk to you, Audra, and very seriously," Vincent said, leaning forward urgently, fastening his eyes on hers.

"Oh," she said, and dropped the darning into her lap, instantly aware of his stern tone. She sat back, gave him her undivided attention.

This is exactly what he had intended. He said, "We have *very* serious problems, you and I, Audra, and it's about time we got them out in the open. No more shoving them under the rug because you—"

"Problems?" she cut in, looking at him oddly. "What do you mean, Vincent?"

"Come on, Audra, don't play daft with me. You know very well what I'm talking about. Our problems in bed, that's what. You forever turn away from me. Don't you love me anymore?"

As usual when he spoke about sex, a faint blush touched her cheeks. She exclaimed, with some indignation, "Of course I love you."

"Strange way you have of showing it. An iceberg has nothing on you."

"Oh Vincent, how unfair you are! Please don't be like this. I do care for you, I do love you. But . . . well

. . . I'm fearful of getting pregnant again. Look, you know as well as I do that another child would stretch our resources to the limit. We hardly have enough money as it is—"

"It's not my fault that the bloody country is in such a mess!" he hissed, interrupting her, throwing her an irate look. "You can blame Ramsey Macdonald and his blasted government for that! I'm not the only man out of work. There are two million eight hundred thousand of us now. And we're not simply jobless but desperate, and diminished as men because we're reduced to being on the dole—"

"You're misunderstanding me! I *wasn't* pointing a finger, Vincent. I would never do that. I *know* it's not your fault, and I also know how hard you try every day to find something. However, if we had another child it would jeopardize Christina's chances . . . don't you agree? Don't you *see* that?"

"Oh yes, I bloody well see it all right. You're planning this glittering future for her and she's not yet one year old. I sometimes wonder about you, Audra, wonder about your sanity."

He jumped up, his anger getting the better of him, and strode to the coat cupboard, grabbed his sports jacket off the hook and threw it on.

"Where are you going?" she asked, surprised that he was suddenly curtailing their important discussion, yet relieved at the same time.

"To my mother's."

"*Naturally*. And after she's sympathized with you, fussed over you, she'll give you more money to go to the pub, as she always does."

"What goes on between my mother and me is none of your bloody business," he exclaimed, glaring. "I've never asked you for a single penny and I never will."

She made no response.

He flung himself out of the house but resisted slamming the door behind him. He did not want to awaken his child.

* * *

As he walked down Town Street ten minutes later,
Vincent's temper began to cool. Nonetheless, he did not
excuse Audra's attitude; nor did he forgive her in his heart.
If anything, he held a bigger grudge against her than
before. He was not sure why, although she *had* managed to
really get his goat tonight.

If I were a rich man, he mused, married to a cold,
indifferent woman like Audra, I would take myself a
mistress. She would be beautiful, accessible and very
loving, and I would keep her in great style. Unfortunately
I'm not rich, so I can't afford a mistress.

A thought struck him. He *could* afford Millicent Arnold,
who would not cost him anything except a few good
manners, some sweet talking and a little of his persuasive
charm. Millie was not especially beautiful, but she had a
pleasant face and a gentle nature. Most importantly, she
had always had a soft spot for him, and for a number of
years, now that he thought about it.

There's nothing like a woman who truly yearns after you,
he thought. And instantly Vincent changed his plans.

He did not go to his mother's house. Nor did he stop off at
the White Horse, where he knew his brothers Jack and Bill
would be playing darts and waiting for him.

Instead he went to visit Millicent Arnold, a widow
woman at only thirty-five and childless, who, he was quite
certain, would give him a very warm welcome indeed.

Hurrying up Moorfield Road, he almost ran across the
recreation grounds and through the gate at the far side,
then sped up the ginnel that led to Rose Cottage. This was
where Millie lived alone, now that Ted was dead these past
two years. The house was in a tucked-away corner of
Armley, and this pleased him. If he was lucky enough to
become a frequent visitor, it was better that no one saw him
coming and going.

After knocking several times and getting no answer, he
turned away, disappointment filling him.

Then the door sprang open and Millie was exclaiming,
"Why, Vincent, whatever brings you to *my* doorstep on a
Saturday evening?"

"Well, it's like this," he said, pivoting, smiling down into the warm velvet-brown eyes upturned to his, "I was walking across the *rec* when I remembered what you said to me last week, you know, when we ran into each other near the library. You told me you were getting more lonesome and blue by the day. Know something strange, Millie? So am I. . . . so am I. . . ."

"Are you really, Vincent?"

He nodded, smiled his most engaging smile and leaned against the door jamb, let his eyes roam over her provocatively. He had not realized what a voluptuous figure she had. Suddenly he began to chuckle in a way he had not chuckled for years and his vivid green eyes danced.

"I was heading for the pub to meet my brothers, when I thought of you, Millicent, thought of how lonely you are, of how lonely I am." He paused. "It struck me that you might like a bit of company, and that you might be kind enough to offer a very thirsty man a beer."

Millicent swallowed, hardly daring to believe her good fortune that he had stopped by to see her. She had wanted him for years, for as long as she could remember, even when Ted was alive. She parted her moist lips, but said nothing. She simply took him by the arm and gently pulled him inside.

"Several beers, if you can drink them," she said at last, allowing her breast to brush against him, propelling him across the entrance hall.

Millie stopped abruptly, squeezed his arm and peered up into the handsome face which was now staring down at hers. A slow and languorous smile touched her lips. "And perhaps a spot of supper, too? You *can* stay to supper, can't you, Vincent?"

"I can indeed," he said, throwing his shoulders back, standing up straighter, feeling like a man again.

With great confidence, he put his arm around her slender waist and escorted her into the sitting room. And as she nestled closer to him he knew he had nothing to worry about tonight.

* * *

Vincent's daily routine did not change, even though he had plunged into an affair with Millicent Arnold.

He was discreet.

He liked Millie, enjoyed her company, basked in her affection for him, enjoyed the way she catered to his every need. And they found a great deal of pleasure and release in their long hours of lovemaking in her large and comfortable bed at Rose Cottage.

But it was a physical liaison, nothing more than that.

Vincent knew it would not last very long, as did Millie herself, and they agreed to simply let it run its course. They had also agreed there would be no recriminations on either side when one of them ended it.

All of this apart, Vincent was too responsible a man to neglect the child he adored, or to curtail his search for work simply because of a dalliance. He only visited Millie once a week, wanting to be disciplined about seeing her, and he was circumspect. He went to Rose Cottage only at night.

He continued to plod along as he had these many months.

He looked after Christina in the morning, wheeled her down to his mother's house around noon, where he had a lunchtime snack with her and Danny. And usually he left Christina in his mother's care for the remainder of the day, returning for her around four o'clock.

Almost every afternoon, and without fail, Vincent scoured the city and the outlying districts, looking for work. Sometimes he was fortunate enough to stumble on an odd job, but it was never for more than a day or two. Nothing permanent came his way.

And as the spring and summer slipped by, and autumn gave way to the winter months, Vincent Crowther began to acknowledge that nothing *was* going to turn up. The government was in the deepest and most prolonged depression ever known. England was truly on the edge of disaster, as was the entire world, since by now the economic crisis was global. In his bones, Vincent felt they were in for a long siege, and certainly there was trouble brewing everywhere; riots and hunger marches were becoming the norm.

Leeds, like the other great industrial cities, was acutely hit. The Salvation Army opened soup kitchens; other charitable organizations provided clothing and boots for the children who needed them, and also helped those who wished to leave the depressed areas to do so.

Vincent had never seen so many men on the streets—queuing up at the Labor Exchanges, loitering outside the bookies' offices and the pubs, or simply standing about in groups on street corners, looking glum and disgruntled, commiserating with each other. And there was an air of doom hanging over them all. As he looked around him, Vincent shoved aside the feelings of hopelessness that frequently invaded him these days, and dug deeper into himself for inner strength. He knew he had to keep going no matter what, and that he must keep his spirits up as best he could.

Although Vincent had never wanted Audra to go to work, he now thanked God that she was a nurse at St. Mary's. He was also grateful that other members of the Crowther clan were still working; it was a consolation to know that his parents were better off than most.

His father was with the transportation department of Leeds Industrial Co-operative Society, where he had worked for a number of years, and his job appeared to be secure. Bill was a librarian at one of the public libraries, and Jack, who was studying landscape gardening at night, had a job with the Leeds City Parks Department. Even Maggie had managed to find work in a tailoring shop in Armley, doing button holes on men's jackets.

These three did not earn as much as their father by any means, but their combined wages added up to more than most people had to live on. And so there was always plenty of good nourishing food on his mother's table and coal in her cellar, and Vincent knew that whatever happened, Audra and Christina would never go cold or hungry as many folk did in these terrible days.

As Christmas of 1932 approached, Vincent doubled his efforts to find employment, desperately wanting—and needing—to provide something for his little family over the holidays. He wanted to be able to buy a gift, however small, for Audra, a toy for Christina, and put a few luxuries on their table.

There were several big snowstorms in the early part of December and the snow settled. Many of the driveways were blocked, and late one Friday afternoon Vincent finally hit it lucky and got himself a job shoveling snow at one of the big houses nearby. Since it was already growing dark, the housekeeper told him to come back the following day at nine o'clock.

Saturday morning dawned bright but bitterly cold, and there was a biting wind. But Vincent did not care. He was so excited about earning a bit of money, nothing was going to deter him. Audra, who had the weekend off from the hospital, insisted he wrap up well. She made him put on two pullovers under his sport jacket, and, as he buttoned his overcoat, she tied a thick woolen scarf around his neck, handed him his woolen gloves.

He kissed her cheek, then said, "It shouldn't take me more than three hours at the most to clear the drive at Fell House, so I'll be back in time for lunch, love."

"I think I'll make a large pot of soup today; you'll be needing something like that after being outside in this weather," she remarked, walking with him to the door. The icy blast hit her in the face as he stepped out, and she shivered. "I'm not going to take Christina for a walk this morning; it's far too cold."

"No, I wouldn't if I were you. Ta'rar, love, see you later." He strode off down the path, turned and waved. His mood was jubilant.

Audra was very busy all that morning, looking after Christina, making the vegetable soup, doing her household chores. The time sped by.

Before she knew it, the clock was striking twelve. After setting the table for lunch, she turned on the wireless, took Christina in her arms and sat down by the fire to feed her.

When Vincent had not returned by one o'clock, Audra began to wonder what had happened to him; by two she was truly concerned. He could be tardy when he went to the pub with his brothers and friends, but never when he was working. He always came straight home from work for a cup of tea or a snack, and to change his clothes if he was going out later.

After putting Christina back in the small cot she kept in the kitchen-parlor, Audra poured herself a cup of soup but discovered she was not very hungry.

From time to time, she went to the window, parted the curtains and peered out, but there was no sign of him.

It was almost three o'clock when she heard the sharp, metallic ring of his boots on the path outside.

"I was getting dreadfully worried," she said, as he walked in and closed the door behind him. "I couldn't imagine what had happened to you."

"There was a lot of snow to shovel," he said, pulling off his cap, unwinding his scarf, slowly removing his gloves, which were hard with frozen snow. "More than I'd bargained for . . . the front driveway, two long terraces, the path down between the lawns, and the back yard."

"All those areas to clear! You must be exhausted, Vincent, and you're blue with cold. Come to the fire and get warm."

"They didn't even offer me a cup of tea at twelve—"

"My God, what kind of people are they!" She stared at him aghast.

He did not answer her.

As he came toward the fire, Audra saw something in his face that alarmed her. "Vincent," she began and hesitated. "Are you all right?" she asked, watching him carefully.

He remained silent, stood with his back to the fire, warming himself. After a moment he put his hand in his pocket, brought something out. He turned a pinched and tired face toward her and opened his trembling hand.

"This is what they paid me," he said in a voice that rang with bitterness, showing her the coin in his palm.

For a moment Audra could not believe her eyes. "Sixpence!" She was horrified. "They paid you *sixpence* for *six hours' work*. But that's outrageous . . . those people—"

She could not go on; her anger choked her.

"Yes . . ."

Audra took a deep breath, steadying herself. "Oh, Vincent, Vincent dear . . ." She leapt to her feet and hurried to him, her face grave with concern. She took hold of his arm in the most loving way. "I'm never going to let you do anything like this again. Never."

He shook his head, glanced away. After a minute or two, he turned to her. His eyes were bleak.

"There's a blight on this land," he said.

CHAPTER TWENTY-SIX

"Happy birthday to you, happy birthday to you, happy birthday dear Mam, happy birthday to you."

The second she had finished singing, Christina flew across the room, hurled herself bodily against Audra, almost knocking her over, and hugged her tightly.

Then she looked up at her mother, said, "We're giving you a birthday party, Mam. We planned it all by ourselves, and it's just for the three of us. It's a surprise."

Audra smiled down into the small, eager face lifted up to hers. "Why, how lovely, darling," she said, brushing a strand of hair away from the six-year-old's forehead, thinking how much she looked like her father today.

Although Christina had her hair and her coloring in general, she had inherited Vincent's finely chiseled features, Laurette's smokey gray eyes. She's certainly more of a Crowther than a Kenton, at least in her appearance, Audra thought yet again. This resemblance had always been marked, but it seemed more pronounced than ever lately. Christina had recently shot up, and she was going to be tall; this was another Crowther characteristic.

"Happy birthday, love," Vincent said, walking over to her, kissing her on the cheek.

Audra said with a faint laugh, "And I thought you'd forgotten it."

He grinned, took a puff on his Woodbine. "How could we? You've dropped enough hints lately," he teased.

"*Mam, please* . . . come on, come *on!* In here!" Christina cried, catching hold of her hand, pulling her away from the front door of the cottage in Pot Lane. "You've got to come in here, into the sitting room—you too, Daddy. Oh please come *on!*"

Laughing, Audra placed her handbag on the small table near the door, allowed herself to be dragged across the floor and into the next room by the surprisingly strong and determined little girl.

"There," Christina said, giving her a tiny, gentle push, "sit there, Mam, on the sofa, and you, Dad—" She glanced over her shoulder at Vincent, added, "—can sit in that chair."

"Right you are." As an aside to Audra, he said, "I think we've got the makings of an army general in this one."

Audra nodded, amused. She sat back, smoothed the skirt of her summer cotton frock and looked across at Vincent expectantly.

He gazed back at her, poker-faced; his expression revealed nothing.

Christina darted to the antique chest in the corner and returned with a number of envelopes. "Here are your birthday cards, Mam; the postman brought them just after you'd gone to the hospital this morning. I'll give them to you one by one." She handed Audra a card, then leaned forward slightly, peering at her mother, trying to see the card she held. Unable to conceal her curiosity any further, Christina asked, "Who's it from?"

"Auntie Laurette and Uncle Mike." Audra showed her the card. "Bluebirds sitting on a branch, isn't it pretty?"

Christina nodded. "If you give it to me, I'll put it on the mantelshelf . . . oh thank you, Mam." She offered Audra another envelope. "Open this *next*. . . ."

Audra noted the Australian postmark, recognized William's handwriting. "Well, we *all* know exactly *who* it's from, don't we?" she exclaimed with a little laugh.

"May I see it?" Christina came to Audra, stood with one small hand resting on her mother's shoulder, looking at the card with her. "This one's pretty too, Mam, but there's lots more yet."

The cards were slowly handed over, opened, exclaimed about and lined up with care on the mantelpiece. There was another one from Sydney, from her brother Frederick and his wife Marion; others from various members of the Crowther clan; and one from Gwen, who still remembered her birthday.

The last of the pile was presented with something of a flourish by the solemn child, who was so intent on making this a special day for her mother. "It's from us," she whispered, leaning closer to Audra, touching her cheek lovingly. "Dad picked it really, but he took me to the shop with him and I helped."

Audra ripped open the envelope and pulled out the birthday card. It was the most expensive of the lot, made of glossy paper, with a yellow silk cord slotted through it and tied around the spine. The picture on the front was of a bowl of yellow roses standing on a table near an open window, and fluttering above the bowl was a red butterfly.

"It's just beautiful," Audra said, before looking inside the card and reading the short, printed verse. Vincent had written underneath this: *Wishing you many happy returns of the day, with lots of love from your dearest husband and daughter,* and he had signed his name, and Christina had added her own signature. "Thank you, it's the loveliest birthday card I've *ever* had in my whole life," she told them, looking up, smiling first at Christina, then at Vincent.

They beamed back at her.

Christina said, "I'll get your present, Mam."

She flew to the chest, took a package from a drawer and carried it back to her mother. "This is from Dad and me," she said, smiling gravely, handing Audra the gift.

Audra slipped off the ribbon and paper, wondering what they had bought for her, filled with swelling happiness that they were making such a fuss over her birthday. She was so very touched she could hardly speak for a moment.

She found herself holding a framed watercolor. As she turned it slightly, the better to see it, her eyes widened and she caught her breath in surprise and delight. The painting was of a summer garden at sunset, and the scene was filled with golden light. There were raindrops caught on a cluster of leaves, as if there had been a brief shower before the artist had picked up the paintbrush.

The watercolor was small but quite lovely, even though it was flawed in parts and needed much more work; one side of it was unfinished and amateurish, and yet there was something distinctive about the scene, something that caught and held the attention. How fascinating, Audra thought, her eyes narrowing as they lingered on the painting. It looks curiously like my father's work.

But Audra knew that Vincent had not managed to find a very early watercolor by Adrian Kenton.

Christina's name was boldly and clearly written in one corner, but even if it had not been, she would have recognized this as her daughter's creation. As awkward and childlike as certain aspects of the painting were, Christina had managed to do one thing—capture light on paper. She had sometimes shown this ability in the past, and it was no mean feat. With this new piece of work, she had demonstrated just how much she had developed lately. The girl had displayed a remarkable talent for drawing and painting since she was four years old, but her latest endeavor proved that she was more than merely talented. She was extraordinarily gifted. Audra felt a sudden tingle of excitement at this discovery, and she filled with immense pride in her child.

Lifting her head, she found herself staring into a pair of large gray eyes worriedly fixed on her face.

"Don't you like it, Mam?" The child's lip quivered.

"Oh Christie, I do! I really do! It's simply beautiful, darling. Thank you so much." Audra brought the little girl into her arms and held her close. "I'm sorry I didn't say so immediately, I was far too busy admiring it, I'm afraid."

Christina looked into her mother's eyes, her own shining with joy. "I painted it specially for your birthday, Mam, and Dad took it to Mr. Cox's shop in Town Street and had it framed. That's why it's from the two of us . . . 'cos Daddy paid for the frame."

Giving her husband a radiant smile, Audra said, "Thank you . . . it's the best present you could have given me,

really it is. I shall treasure it always." Her bright blue eyes
held his with keenness. "And it *was* worth framing,
Vincent, wasn't it?"

"Aye, it was that. I recognized the beauty of it the minute
our Christina showed it to me." There was a proud
expression on his face as he added, "You're a right clever
little lass, love."

Christina looked pleased, then turned to her mother,
asked, "Where shall you put it, Mammy?"

"Well, let's see . . . I know *one* thing, it's going to take
pride of place in *this* house," Audra declared. "What about
here, on the mantelpiece? For the moment, anyway."

Audra rose as she spoke, crossed to the fireplace and
propped the painting on the shelf in the midst of the
birthday cards.

Turning, she asked her daughter, "And whose garden is
it? Where did you go to paint it?"

"Calpher House . . . I went up to see Mrs. Bell to ask
her if I could . . . and I went all by myself. And she said
yes, I could paint her garden for you, and so I picked that
sweet little corner near her roses . . . she kept coming
out to see how I was doing. She was ever so interested. It
was last week that I did it, Mam, and she made me come
inside when it rained and she gave me a glass of milk and a
Cadbury's chocolate finger, no *two*, and after it stopping
raining, I went out and I started all over again. I liked the
garden better then . . . it sort of glistened after the rain."

Audra nodded. "You certainly captured that feeling
beautifully, Christina, and it's the best work you've done so
far . . . you've made leaps and bounds."

The child glowed.

Vincent said to his daughter, "Now, Christie love, what
about the tea party then? Isn't it about time?"

"Oh yes! Mam, come on, and you too, Dad!"

CHAPTER TWENTY-SEVEN

It was the most splendid tea party.

Audra was not permitted to do anything.

And so she sat at the table in the kitchen-parlor, watching her husband and her child bustle around, getting everything ready. She had noticed earlier how they had both dressed up; they had turned her birthday into a truly special occasion, and she could not help but feel happy and flattered. She just wished she had had time to change out of the cotton frock she had worn to work that day, to put on something more attractive herself, but Christina had not given her the chance.

How handsome Vincent looks, Audra thought, watching her husband as he moved around the kitchen-parlor. He wore a dazzling white shirt, a burgundy tie and dark gray slacks, and he had obviously rushed home from work to shave again and to change his clothes for the tea party. She could see that he was also freshly barbered, and his black hair, brushed sleekly back to reveal his widow's peak, was still damp with water.

As for Christina, she looks adorable, Audra thought. Yes, she's the prettiest thing imaginable today.

Her little daughter had donned her best party frock of pale-blue silk trimmed with narrow bands of white lace down the bodice and on the skirt. She had put on clean white ankle socks and her Sunday-best shoes with ankle straps, made of shiny black patent leather. A blue silk ribbon was tied around her head and finished in a bow on her crown. Audra smiled to herself. Vincent had done quite a decent job of fixing the bow.

Audra sat back in her chair, now eyeing the table with interest. It was covered with their good linen cloth and set with their best china, which only came out for visitors. She saw that a linen serviette had been placed on each plate and there was a posy of yellow roses from the garden in a glass vase in the center. Again she smiled. She fancied these were her daughter's touches.

Vincent went to the set-pot and turned off the kettle, which was whistling on the gas ring. He made a big pot of tea in the silver pot from High Cleugh; Christina brought out plates of food from the pantry.

She explained, in her piping child's voice, "The teeny-weeny sandwiches are made the way you like them, Mam, and they're all your favorites . . . potted-meat spread, tomato and cucumber, and Dad bought a tin of salmon at the co-op, and we made lots of sandwiches with it."

"They all look delicious," Audra said. "You have been working hard, haven't you?"

"Dad helped," Christina said and made several more trips to the pantry, returning with chocolate biscuits, currant buns with white, sugar-icing tops, scones and raspberry jam. "Grandma made the buns and the scones for me," she explained to Audra, and ran back to the pantry one more time. "Strawberries, Mam!" she announced, depositing the dish in front of her mother. "Oh and the cream! I forgot the cream!"

"Come on, Christina love, sit yourself down now," Vincent called, bringing the teapot to the table, pouring for the three of them. "I don't know about my two girls, but I'm famished."

During tea, Audra and Vincent chatted amiably.

She spoke of her busy day at St. Mary's Hospital, where she was now a sister and in charge of the two children's wards as well as the maternity ward.

He spoke about the temporary job he and Fred Varley had, building stables onto the Pinfold mansion on Old Farnley. They were doing it together, working side by side, since Fred Varley had not been able to open up again after his bankruptcy, at least not in a big way. Varley took on small building jobs, when he could get them, and usually it was Vincent he employed to help him.

"But he'll open up shop again soon, and permanently," Vincent said. "He will that, never fear." And Audra nodded her head and crossed her fingers under the table, praying that this was true. Vincent loved his work, and things were a lot easier between them when he had a job and was earning money and supporting them himself. She had slowly come to understand that it was his frustration when he was out of work that caused some of their greatest problems.

Vincent started to talk about his brother Frank, who was in the Ninth Lancers—a cavalry regiment—and with the British Army in India. He was coming home on leave, and Vincent had decided that the entire Crowther clan should give a party for Frank's homecoming.

Christina kept her ears cocked as she always did when she was with her parents, looking from one to the other, her large gray eyes wide and missing nothing.

She was attentive to their every word as she munched on her sandwiches. Occasionally she made a remark of her own, but mostly she listened. They were both so clever, her mam and her dad. She loved to hear them talk. Her mam had such a lovely voice, so soft and musical.

She always enjoyed times like this when they were so friendly with each other, and her mother smiled a lot and her eyes got very, very blue and very bright; she didn't like it when they squabbled. Then her father went out, banging the door behind him with a crash and didn't come home until ever so late at night when *they* were fast asleep. Her mother was always cross with him for days after and looked at him in a queer way through the corner of her eye and tightened her lips.

Once, last year when she had been little and not grown up like now, her mam had waited up for her dad to come home after a row. They had shouted at each other, and her mam had screamed, "If that's the way you feel about it, then go back to your fancy woman." She had heard it all, because she had been so surprised to hear her mam shouting that she had crept out of her room, had hung over the bannisters to listen.

And for days afterward she had worried that her dad was going to go away and live with the woman who was fancy. She had wondered if *they* weren't fancy enough for him. Perhaps if they made themselves fancy, he would stay, she had thought, but she hadn't been sure how to do this.

Finally she had asked her grandma what a fancy woman looked like. Her grandma had sucked in her breath, had stared hard at her, had asked where she had heard something like that, and she had fibbed, had said, "At school." She didn't know, even now, why she had fibbed to Grandma, except that somehow she knew she should not talk about things that happened at home. Her mam never did when *she* went to Grandma's. She hardly said anything at all, and she wasn't a bit like *her mam* when she was at Grandma's house. She was different, somehow.

But in the end they hadn't had to get themselves all fancy, because her dad had not gone away. A short while after each terrible quarrel her mam and her dad were all smiles again, and loving, and forever kissing each other on the cheek and hugging. It was always like that with them.

Her father's sudden laughter brought Christina out of her reverie.

She looked at him alertly.

His expression was merry and his green eyes were all sparkly like the necklace Auntie Gwen wore when they went to tea at her house in Headingley, except that they didn't go to Auntie Gwen's anymore. And her mother was laughing too, and her eyes danced and danced with blue lights and she knew her mother was happy today.

Christina did not understand why her parents were laughing in this way; she had missed what her mother had just said. But she began to laugh too, wanting to be part of it, part of them, part of their happiness and gaiety.

Vincent, still chuckling, said, "Oh and by the way, Audra, Mike's bought tickets for the Grand Theatre on Saturday . . . it's Noël Coward's *Cavalcade*. He's invited us, so that's another nice birthday treat for you, love."

"How sweet he is, and so thoughtful."

Christina asked, "Will Auntie Maggie be looking after me when you go out on Saturday night?"

"She will that, love."

"Oh goody, Dad. We have such fun and she always lets me stay up late."

"She does!" Audra exclaimed.

"It's time for the strawberries, Mam, I'll serve," Christina cried, jumping down off her chair. "And you get to get the most, 'cos it's your birthday."

"Don't be so silly," Audra demurred. "We'll all have exactly the same amount; it's share and share alike in this family."

"No, *you* have to have the most," Christina insisted as she carefully spooned the fruit into the small glass dishes she had brought from the sideboard.

They had not had strawberries for a long time, because they were so expensive and such a special treat. And so none of them spoke as they ate them slowly, savoring every bite, but their eyes shone and they smiled at each other with their eyes. And when they had finished, they all three agreed that these were the *best* strawberries they had ever eaten . . . sweet and succulent.

But the highlight of the tea party was the birthday cake.

Christina and Vincent fussed over it in the pantry, before the child walked out, sedately, carrying it high in front of her.

And father and daughter cried in unison, "Happy birthday! Happy birthday!"

Drawing to a standstill in front of her mother, Christina said, "I'm sorry there's only one candle, Mam, but that's all that was left from my birthday cake. The others were ever so burned down."

"I don't mind, Christie. One candle is certainly better than none."

"That's what I told her," Vincent remarked, sitting down opposite Audra. "And I also said you'd probably prefer one candle to thirty."

Audra gave him a small, rueful smile. "I can't believe that I'm actually thirty years old today. Vincent . . . where have all the years gone?"

Vincent shook his head, smiled faintly. "Don't ask me, lass. I've no idea. And I'll be thirty-four in nine days . . . or had you forgotten?"

Before Audra had a chance to answer, Christina cried, "We have to have a party for you too, Dad!"

Christina knelt to say her prayers.

Audra sat in the rocking chair and listened.

Once she had finished the long ritual of blessing her uncles in Australia and every member of the Crowther clan, Christina clambered up onto her bed and slid down between the sheets.

Rising, Audra went over to her, tucked in the covers and straightened the quilt, then sat on the edge of the bed. She smoothed her hand along her child's innocent cheek and smiled at her. "It was a lovely birthday party, Christie, thank you."

Christina smiled back. Then she asked anxiously, "We can have a party for Daddy, can't we?"

"Of course we can. It wouldn't be fair if we didn't . . . you had yours last month and there was mine today— so it's his turn next." Audra leaned forward, kissed her daughter.

Plump little arms reached out and went around Audra's neck. Christina nuzzled against her mother, filling with pleasure at the familiar smell of her cool fresh skin and the scent of gardenia flower essence behind her ears. She whispered, "I love you, Mam."

"Oh darling, I love you, too. So very much. Come on, curl up and go to sleep. It's very late now. Sweet dreams, honeybunch."

"Yes, Mam. 'Night, Mam."

Christina did not fall asleep immediately.

She lay in bed watching the sky through the window. They had let her stay up way past her bedtime tonight, since it was a special occasion, and now it was very dark outside.

The sky was inky black and filled with glittering stars, oh so far away, and the moon was as round as a silver half crown and just as shiny. A full moon, her father had said, just before she had been packed off to bed.

Oh how she loved her dad. And her mam. She liked it the best when it was just the three of them . . . her mam and her dad and her. Her dad had invited Auntie Laurette and Uncle Mike to the tea party. She was ever so glad they hadn't been able to come. It wasn't that she didn't love them. She did. She loved all of her aunts and uncles and

her grandma. And Grandpa. Especially Grandpa. She liked
the way he smelled of leather and Gentleman's Hair
Pommade and eucalyptus pastilles that he sometimes gave
to her secretly, when no one was looking, and he took her
upon his knee and told her stories of many wondrous
things. She didn't mind that his big white curly moustache
tickled her when he kissed her, or that he puffed away on a
pipe that filled Grandma's kitchen-parlor with smoke and
made her eyes water. He called it, "My fine Calabash," and
he wouldn't let anybody touch that pipe of his, not even
Auntie Maggie, whom he thought the world of, so her dad
said.

But she loved her mam and her dad the most. More than
the whole world put together. They belonged to her. And
she belonged to them. She wouldn't want any other mam
and dad. Hers were special. She just knew they were.

She snuggled down in the bed and closed her eyes,
slowly drifting off to sleep. She could hear the murmur of
their voices floating up the staircase . . . soft, warm,
loving voices . . . she always felt so safe when she heard
their voices. . . .

"She's a very special child, Vincent," Audra said, settling
back against the sofa in the sitting room.

"Yes, she's clever."

"What she has is more than cleverness, more than talent
even . . . she's exceptionally gifted, Vincent." Audra let
her eyes rest on the mantelpiece where the painting stood,
propped up in the middle of the birthday cards. "Before
tea, you said you were struck by the watercolor, so much so
you decided to have it framed."

"Aye, no two ways about it, I was impressed." Vincent
glanced at the painting Audra had done years before of the
Memory Place, then let this eyes wander to the back wall
where a landscape by Adrian Kenton hung. "Our Christina
gets it from you and your father, Audra—her artistic talent,
I mean."

"Yes, she does. But she's going to be a much better artist
than I am when she grows up . . . and she'll probably be

better than my father too. The indications are already there."

"There shouldn't be any doubt in your mind anymore about who your father really was, Audra." He gave her a slow smile.

"Oh, there isn't, and I don't suppose there ever was actually. I knew my mother would never do anything to hurt my father whilst he was alive. It was not in her nature to do anything shoddy. I think I've always known that she and Uncle Peter only ever became involved much later, after she was widowed."

Vincent nodded and reached for his glass of beer. He was glad that they had laid that old ghost finally.

They were both silent for a while, each lost in diverse thoughts.

The June evening had turned coolish, and Vincent had put a match to the fire whilst Audra had been putting Christina to bed. Now she sat staring into the flames, thinking of the child who lay asleep upstairs: the very gifted child, the child she had always known was going to have a glittering future.

Suddenly, Audra leaned forward, startling Vincent as she exclaimed, "Yes, we must do it!"

"Do what?" he asked, looking at her curiously.

She did not answer this question directly; instead she said, "I've been helping her the best I can for the last couple of years, and I'll continue to do so, but there's only so much knowledge *I* can impart, since I'm self-taught."

"Yes," he said.

"She'll have to go to art school when she's sixteen. They won't accept her at Leeds College of Art before then. Later she'll have to go to London. To study at the Slade—no, better still, at the Royal College of Art."

"How are we going to pay for all this?" he demanded, his voice rising sharply. "We'll never be able to afford an education like that for her, not even if the Depression ends and I get a permanent job. It'll cost *thousands*."

"Yes, I know, but we'll do it," she replied, very firmly. "We must, Vincent, we must!" There was an eagerness in her voice, an excitement he had not heard for a long time.

"Christina must be given every chance," Audra rushed on. "I won't have her cheated just because of a lack of money. She has a gift . . . it must be trained. She is going to be a brilliant painter, a great artist, Vincent."

"Well," he said slowly, his voice sinking, "I just don't know . . ."

Audra sat up straighter and gave him one of her penetrating stares. "There can be no hesitation on our parts, Vincent, none whatsoever. We must strive toward this goal, whatever the sacrifice. Christina must have that chance. And I, for one, am going to make sure she gets it!"

CHAPTER TWENTY-EIGHT

"I don't know what to do about Audra anymore, Mike, I don't really. I'm at the end of my tether," Vincent said in a shaky voice.

He jumped up and strode over to the window, where he stood looking out, narrowing his eyes against the bright April sunlight.

Mike said, "Yes, I'm aware how worried you've been." The young doctor frowned, conscious of his friend's anxiety, as well as his frustration at being jobless. Vincent's emotions were close to the surface these days, and the set of his shoulders indicated to Mike just how tense and distressed he was this morning.

"What can I do to help—" Mike began, but broke off as the sitting room door swung open.

Laurette backed herself into the room, carrying a tray. She turned and marched over to the fireplace. "Sorry I took so long with the coffee," she said brightly, "but I had to check on the Sunday joint and the roast potatoes. . . ." Laurette paused in midsentence, suddenly noticing Mike's troubled face, Vincent's rigid stance.

"Oh," she said quickly, "am I interrupting something? I'd better take my cup of coffee back to the kitchen and leave you both in peace."

"No," Vincent said, spinning around, coming back to the seating arrangement near the fireplace. "It's not anything you can't hear." Lowering himself into a chair, he took out his cigarettes, lit one.

Laurette passed around the cups of coffee, then sat down, looking at Vincent expectantly, waiting for him to continue. For a moment Laurette observed her brother.

Vincent sat staring into the fire morosely, his face brooding as he smoked his cigarette.

Finally, hoping to draw him out, she asked, "Where did you say Audra and Christina have gone today?"

"To Fountains Abbey," he said without looking up. "Another painting lesson in the country, a field trip, as Audra calls it." At last he turned his face to Laurette, and added, "But you know she always takes Christie out to paint, on her Sundays off from the hospital."

"Yes, and I think it's admirable the way she's exposing her to paintings in the big houses like Temple Newsam and Harewood. Audra's giving Christie a good grounding, Vincent, and she'll be well prepared for art school."

Vincent nodded but made no comment.

Mike remarked, "You said you didn't know what to do about Audra anymore. Let's talk about it . . . it does help to get it off your chest, and that's really why you came to see us this morning, isn't it?"

"Yes, that's true, Mike." Vincent cleared his throat. "It's Audra's health that I'm worried about. She's pushing herself harder than ever these days, stretching her strength to the limit. You both know what her schedule's like . . . she's working damned hard at the hospital and taking on additional duty, whenever she gets the chance, for the extra money. Then, when she comes home, she's looking after us, cooking, cleaning, washing and ironing. And she's tutoring Christie in art. And when she's not doing that, she's toiling at that bloody sewing machine Mrs. Bell gave her, doing alterations and making clothes for people. The work aside, she scrimps and scrapes, does without herself, in order to save every penny she can for Christina's education."

They both looked at him attentively, their faces sympathetic.

Vincent shook his head slowly. "It's this relentless pursuit of money that troubles me, and I'm powerless to stop it. Helpless, really." Unexpectedly, Vincent's voice shook again. "I daren't interfere, daren't say a word . . . when I have in the past, she's bitten my head off. . . . I was hoping *you'd* talk to her, Mike, you know, as a doctor. She'd listen to you."

"I doubt that, Vince," Mike answered, his tone gloomy. "Of course, I'd be willing to try, but I'd be wasting my breath. And so would Laurette, as close as she is to Audra. No one, nothing is going to stop Audra. She's single-minded and she's stubborn."

"Aye, I know that only too well," Vincent muttered. "All this started years ago when Christina was first born. I told Audra at the time that she was propelled by a terrible driving force within herself, and I was right." He ran his hand over his weary face. "There's nothing wrong with being ambitious, wanting the best for a child, I realize that. But what Audra's been doing these past few years—well, it's bloody abnormal if you ask me."

Laurette said, "I'm not sure if abnormal is quite the right word, Vincent—" She hesitated, searching for the correct expression to convey the sudden thought that had struck her. Then she said, slowly, carefully, "What we're witnessing is an act of will, and one so selfless, so powerfully motivated it's . . . well, it's just *awesome* to watch."

"Bloody frightening, you mean," Vincent said harshly. He took a deep breath, tried to soften his voice. "Look, Laurette, I want the best for our Christie, I really do. But there's a limit to what people in our circumstances can do. Audra's reaching for far too much for the lass. And anyway, it's not fair to the child; she has no little friends, no fun. I love Audra. . . ." He paused, cleared his throat. "I don't want her to collapse, to get sick. I'm only trying to protect her."

"I don't think she'll pay any attention to any of us, as I said, but I *will* have a talk with her tomorrow, Vince," Mike promised. "I'll be up at the hospital to see patients, and I'll find an opportunity to say something to her. I'll insist she has a general checkup, just as a matter of routine. At least that might ease your mind."

"Oh it will, Mike, it will. Thanks ever so much."

Laurette smiled at her brother, patted his arm. "Try and relax a bit, love; it'll be all right."

Vincent nodded, put another cigarette in his mouth, struck a match.

"Will you stay for Sunday lunch?" Laurette asked. "It's roast lamb, new potatoes and spring cabbage—all the things you like."

"No, thanks though. I said I'd meet our Bill and Jack for a drink at the Traveler's Rest at Hill-Top; then I'll probably walk back to our mam's with them, have a spot of lunch there." Vincent eyed his sister, said in a careful tone, "I don't want you to say anything to Mam, but our Bill is thinking of going into the Merchant Navy."

Staring at him, her eyes widening, Laurette said, "She's not going to like that! Not with our Frank already in the army."

"I know she won't." Vincent turned to his brother-in-law. "There's going to be a war, Mike. The writing's on the wall, what with Hitler on the march, invading parts of Czechoslovakia in March and now, just last week, the man was making impossible demands on Poland—"

"I was reading about that in the *Sunday Express* before you came in," Mike interrupted. "The man's getting greedier than ever, territorially speaking, demanding that the Free City of Danzig be ceded to Germany. It seems we've pledged to support Poland in this new crisis; so has France."

Their troubled eyes locked.

"It's an uneasy peace we have at the moment, Mike, and it won't last long . . . we'll be at war with Germany before the end of the year, mark my words."

"Don't say that!" Laurette exclaimed, looking from her brother to her husband. "Will you . . . will you both have to go if there's a war?"

"Yes," Mike said.

CHAPTER TWENTY-NINE

"What a lovely morning it is," Audra said, walking to the open door of the cottage in Pot Lane, standing on the doorstep, looking out. She lifted her eyes. "And the sky's so cloudless, Vincent."

"Yes, it *is* a bonny day," Vincent agreed, joining her in the doorway. He followed her gaze. It was directed to the bottom of the small garden where Christina sat sketching, and he smiled with pleasure at the sight of his child. "And much too nice to stay inside . . . I think I'll come with you this afternoon—if you'll have me, that is."

Audra looked at him in astonishment. "But you always go to the White Horse on Sunday at lunchtime—" She broke off as her laughter bubbled up and her eyes grew bright with happiness. "But we'd love it if you came with us. We're not going far, only to Temple Newsam. I want Christie to study some of the paintings there, in particular the Old Masters."

Vincent put his arm around her, squeezed her shoulder, stared down into her face. He saw the tiredness behind the sudden radiance filling her face at this moment, and his heart tightened. She was still pushing herself too hard, despite Mike's friendly lecture in the spring, and she worried him a lot. But she would not listen to him; his words seemed to make no impression on her. She continued to toil as she always had.

Vincent said in a rush, "Listen, love, I've got a idea, a wonderful idea. Let's get ready and go to Temple Newsam *now*. Well, in about half an hour or so. You know, make a day of it, Audra. We could take a picnic with us . . . that'd save you struggling over a hot stove, cooking Sunday lunch before we go. Come on, what do you say?"

Audra nodded her head, smiling. It was not often that he ventured out with them on these Sunday art excursions, and she was delighted. She looked over her shoulder at the

clock on the mantelshelf. "It's ten past eleven already
. . . but oh *yes*, why not!" Swinging to face the garden,
shading her eyes against the sunlight, she called, "Christie,
Christie, come inside, please. Your daddy's coming with us
to Temple Newsam, and we're taking a picnic lunch with us
and I need you to help me."

"Oh!" Christina cried and leapt to her feet, excited that
her father was going too.

"Let's start making the sandwiches first," Audra said,
bustling over to the pantry.

"Can I do anything to help?" Vincent asked.

"Not really, but you might put the wireless on. It would
be nice to have a bit of music this morning."

"Done," he said, striding to the set, twiddling the knob.
"Ah, here's a nice bit of music . . . why it's the *Blue
Danube*, Audra. Fancy that—the first dance we had
together at the Parish Hall, all those years ago."

Turning her head, she gave him the sweetest of smiles;
then she frowned as the music stopped abruptly. "Oh dear,
don't tell me that the wireless is broken again."

"*We interrupt this program to bring you an important
message from the Prime Minister,*" a BBC announcer was
saying.

Vincent and Audra stared at each other, neither of them
moving as the voice of Neville Chamberlain flowed out of
the set, telling them and the rest of the country that Hitler
had invaded Poland and England was now at war with
Germany.

"*Now may God bless you all and may He defend the
right.*" The Prime Minister's voice, so grave and somber,
was replaced by the national anthem, and the familiar
strains of "God Save the King" reverberated around the
kitchen.

"It's September the third today," Vincent muttered,
glancing at Audra through troubled eyes. "I've been
expecting a war, but it's come sooner than I thought it
would."

"Yes." Audra lowered herself into the nearest chair,
feeling weak in the legs as the implications of the Prime
Minister's message sank in.

Christina looked from her mother to her father, her eyes puzzled. "What does it mean? What's going to happen, Dad?"

"We're going to be fighting the Germans, but don't you worry, pet, everything's going to turn out all right in the end."

"What shall we do about Temple Newsam?" Audra suddenly said. "Perhaps we'd better not go today, after all."

"Oh Mam, don't say that," Christina cried, "not when Daddy said he'd come with us."

Christina's face was so crestfallen and she sounded so let down, Vincent could not help exclaiming, "Oh what the hell, let's go, Audra. It'll probably be the last chance we get to do something together like this for a long time."

"That's true," Audra said hesitantly.

Eagerly, Christina asked, "Can we go then, Mam?"

"Yes—run upstairs and change your frock. Your daddy will help me to finish preparing the picnic."

"Shall I wear my yellow cotton frock with the primrose pattern?"

"If you like, dear."

When they were alone, Vincent said, "I don't know when the recruiting offices will open—tomorrow or Tuesday, I expect." He paused. "But I'm going to volunteer as soon as they *are* open for business."

"Yes," she said, "yes, I knew you would, if war came."

"Aye, like every Englishman worth his salt. God knows, I don't wish war on any of us; it's going to be hell on earth, but maybe I can now stand up and be a man."

She stared at him in amazement. "You've always been a man to me, Vincent."

Vincent Crowther joined the Royal Navy on Tuesday, and by the end of the week he had been sent to the big naval barracks at Harwich to start his basic training.

The cottage in Pot Lane seemed quiet and empty without him. It was the first time they had been separated since their marriage, and Audra soon began to realize just how much she missed him.

They had an odd marriage in some ways, she was the first to admit that, but in spite of their quarrels and differences, they loved each other. And they had this glittering prize who was their daughter Christina, and it was she who bound them together irrevocably.

And so as she went about her work at the hospital and at home, Audra thought about Vincent and worried about him and wondered how he was getting on in the Royal Navy.

Soon his letters started to come on a regular weekly basis, and she and Christina sat and pored over them and talked about him lovingly, and they could not wait for his first leave.

Because of his absence, Christina had to look after herself during the day when Audra was working at St. Mary's. "I don't mind, Mam. I can manage, honestly I can," the girl kept telling her, and this was the truth. Christina was exceptionally grown-up for an eight-year-old, mostly because of her intelligence and the practical domestic training she had been given by her mother, but also because she had been surrounded by adults all of her life.

In particular, she was close to her Auntie Laurette, and when Audra was on night duty, Christina now slept at her aunt's house. Mike Lesley had enlisted in the Medical Corps, and since she was alone, Laurette was happy to have her niece for company. With Mike's departure, Laurette had gone back to work. Wanting to do her bit for the war effort, she had taken a job as secretary to the managing director of an engineering firm in Armley which was now making bombs.

Every day, when her mother was at work, Christina went to her grandmother's for lunch, as she had done since she was a baby and had been taken there by her father in her pram. Eliza's cheerful kitchen with its plethora of roses had always rung with laughter and the jollity of her boisterous family. But now it was deathly quiet.

Bill had joined the Merchant Navy, Jack had gone into the army, and Maggie had enlisted in the ATS—the Auxiliary Territorial Service. She had first gone to a training center near Reading for a month's basic army training, then on to a huge camp in Shropshire, where she was learning to use antiaircraft instruments. Hal, Olive's husband, was in the Royal Air Force, and only Alfred and Danny, who was just sixteen, remained at home.

The Crowthers were suddenly a family of women, except of course for Alf and his youngest son, whom they all knew would go when he was old enough, and they drew closer as England mobilized for war.

Barrage balloons and searchlights, air raid sirens and the "all clear" signal, blackout curtains at every window, identity cards, air raid shelters and gas masks—all became quite commonplace. So did food rationing, clothing coupons, petrol rationing and shortages of every kind, and air raid drills conducted by members of the Civil Defense. Mr. Trotter, the local air raid warden for Pot Lane, became a familiar and friendly face to Audra and Christina.

As trying and as difficult as these times were, Audra kept to her regular routine of years' standing, and she insisted that Christina do the same. Aside from her school work, the tutoring in art continued, and Christina was expected to work at it with dedication every day.

But they had their little pleasures too, and in particular they loved going to the pictures to see the latest films from America, as well as those made at home. They were also rabid fans of the radio and listened to everything from the news to comedy and musical programs. It was the cinema that always won out, though, and they went once a week, sometimes twice, usually accompanied by Laurette.

One Saturday afternoon in late October of 1939, Audra, Laurette and Christina were having tea in the kitchen of the cottage, before going to the Picturedrome to see the latest Robert Donat picture, *Goodbye, Mr. Chips*.

Laurette, who was a real fan and read a lot about films and film stars, had been telling them about the movie, relating something of the story.

"Don't tell us any more," Audra exclaimed. "Otherwise you'll spoil it for us."

"Oh sorry," Laurette apologized, and, changing the subject, she went on, "What *I* can't wait to see is *Gone With the Wind*. I've been reading about it in *Picturegoer Magazine* and it sounds wonderful. Vivien Leigh looked so beautiful in last week's issue, and Clark Gable! *He's* just gorgeous."

Audra grinned. "If Mike heard you, he'd be jealous—" She glanced over her shoulder at the sound of knocking on the front door.

"I'll go," Christina cried, slipping off the chair, excusing herself from the table, running to open the door. "Oh hello, Mr. Trotter," she said, staring up at the air raid warden.

"Hello, love, is your mam in?"

"Yes, Mr. Trotter." Christina opened the door wider. "Please come in."

Jim Trotter took off his metal helmet, stepped into the house. "Good evening, Mrs. Crowther," he said, smiling warmly at Audra. "I'm ever so sorry to trouble you, just when you're having your teas, but I stopped by to have a word with you about Miss Dobbs in the corner cottage."

"What about Miss Dobbs?" Audra asked, regarding the older man curiously.

"Well, you see, it's like this, Mrs. Crowther, she never comes to the air raid drills, and I don't know what's going to happen to her when there's a real air raid, I don't really."

Audra frowned. "She'll join us in the bomb shelter at the bottom of the garden, Mr. Trotter. My father-in-law built it for us and Christina and I have made it relatively comfortable and—"

"Oh but she won't *go* into the air raid shelter, Mrs. Crowther," Jim Trotter exclaimed, interrupting her. "I've just had a word with Miss Dobbs about that and I got a real flea in me ear for me trouble, I can tell you."

"Oh," Audra said, giving him a baffled look.

"You'll never believe what she said to me," Mr. Trotter went on.

"No, I don't suppose I will," she said. "What did Miss Dobbs say?"

"Well, she sort of looked at me funny like, as if I'd landed from another planet, and shouted, 'Go and sit in that hole, yonder down the garden, sit *under* the ground. Not likely, lad. I'm going to be in the ground a long time when I'm dead, so I'll be staying up here as long as I'm alive, and if I get hit by a bomb, I get hit by a bomb.' Them's her exact words, Mrs. Crowther."

Audra tried hard, but there was no way she could keep her face straight. Christina and Laurette also began to laugh.

Jim Trotter looked at them all askance, then addressed Audra. "It's no laughing matter, Mrs. Crowther," he said indignantly.

"No, I know it's not," Audra gasped, "but I sort of share her sentiments about sitting in a hole under the ground."

"I sincerely hope you don't, Mrs. Crowther!" There was sudden alarm on Jim Trotter's face. "I'd be very upset indeed if I had two of you in this yard being *difficult*."

Audra nodded, biting her lip, unable to speak. She was finding it difficult to suppress her laughter.

Trotter went on, "What am I going to do about Miss Dobbs? I mean, I'm responsible for everyone in these houses on Pot Lane."

Understanding, all of a sudden, why he had come, Audra said as soberly as she could, "I'll do my best to get Miss Dobbs to come into the shelter with us when there's a raid, Mr. Trotter. But I can only try; I can't force someone against their will."

"Thank you very much, Mrs. Crowther, I'm grateful for your cooperation. Good evening." The warden took his leave quickly.

As his footsteps faded away down the path, Audra managed to compose herself. "Poor Mr. Trotter . . . he always seemed to like me, but I don't think he's going to feel quite the same way about me ever again. Oh dear . . ."

"Don't be silly," Laurette said. "You were right when you said we had to keep a sense of humor in these awful times. If we didn't, I think we'd all go mad."

The English had mobilized for war, and then nothing very much had happened on the home front.

In fact there was such inactivity in the air and on the land that this period soon became known as the "phony war."

At sea, though, war had started almost at once in

September; in October the battleship *Royal Oak* was
torpedoed as she lay in Scapa Flow, supposedly in safe
harbor and secure from German attack. And by the middle
of November something like 60,000 tons of British shipping
had been sunk by the dreaded and deadly magnetic mines.

Every time Audra picked up a paper or listened to the
wireless, her heart filled with fear. The news of the war at
sea was never anything but disastrous, and she worried
about Vincent all the time now that he had been assigned to
a destroyer and was somewhere out there at sea. Every
letter she received from him brought a sigh of relief, as did
his letters to his mother.

Although he did not get leave for Christmas of 1939, he
did come home in January of 1940 on a seventy-two-hour
pass from Hull, where his ship was docked after a stretch
patrolling the North Sea.

Audra had asked for time off from the hospital, so that she
could be with him for his entire stay, and Matron Fox had
been happy to give it to her. And so she was waiting for him
at the cottage on that cold and drizzly Thursday afternoon,
wearing the delphinium-blue blouse he liked so much and a
dark gray skirt.

The moment he walked through the door, she saw how
proud he was to be in the Royal Navy, to be wearing the
uniform. He held himself very straight, with his shoulders
thrown back, and looked taller than ever, and there was a
new air of assurance about him, a confident look in his
bright green eyes.

Audra flew across the floor to him, and he hugged her
tightly, held her away, looked deeply into her eyes and then
gave her a long and loving kiss on the mouth.

"It's nice to be home, love," he said, finally releasing her.

"And it's nice to have you back! I've missed you; *we've*
missed you."

"Yes, it's been the same for me."

A few minutes later, as they sat drinking their cups of tea,
Audra gave him all the news about the Crowther clan and
his brothers and Maggie, who were away in the service.
Then in a soft voice she told him how worried she had been
for months on end.

"All I read about are naval disasters, Vincent. Aren't we ever going to have a victory?"

"We did have one, in December, Audra!" he exclaimed, looking at her fiercely. "Don't tell me you've already forgotten that three British cruisers scuttled the German battleship *Graf Spee* during the Battle of the River Plate?"

"No, I haven't, but I was thinking of something closer to home—"

"The *Graf Spee* had eluded the British Navy for months, and sinking her was a tremendous feather in our caps . . . don't think it hasn't had a demoralizing effect on the Jerries, because it has." Vincent's face glowed. "Winston's right pleased, I can tell you that."

Audra smiled indulgently. "Don't tell me you're on a first-name basis with the First Lord of the Admiralty," she teased. "Does Mr. Churchill *know* that you are?"

Vincent grinned. "We all call him Winston, behind his back, of course. We all love him—that's why." He leaned forward with a certain eagerness. "Do you know how the Admiralty announced his return last September? I mean, announced it to the entire British Fleet."

Audra shook her head. "How could I?"

After taking a long draw on his cigarette, he said, "Just the words *Winston is back!* But it was a hell of a bloody compliment to him . . . a joyful salute. Aye, he's a great man, Churchill is, lass. He ought to be Prime Minister. He probably will be too; *everybody's* dissatisfied with Chamberlain."

"Wouldn't you be upset to lose . . . *Winston* as First Sea Lord?"

"Yes, but I'd rather have him at the helm of this country than anybody else, I bloody would—" Vincent broke off, glanced around as he heard the door open.

"Daddy!" Christina dropped her satchel and sped across to him without taking off her coat and hat. She flung herself into his outstretched arms. They hugged and hugged each other, and then Vincent pulled away and asked, "How's my little poppet?"

Christina stared up into his familiar, much-loved face, and burst into tears.

"Now then, what's all this, love?" Vincent asked, pulling her back into his enfolding arms, smoothing his hand over her hair gently.

Christina's shoulders shook and she gasped for breath as she clung to him. "I—I—thought I'd never—never—see you again," she sobbed. "I've been so worried, Daddy. I thought your ship would get sunk."

"Aren't you the silly duck egg!" Vincent laughed and chucked her under the chin. "Nothing's ever going to happen to me, little Miss Muffet. Come on, take your coat off and let's go to the table and have the nice tea your mam's made. Then later we'll walk down to see your grandma." He leaned into her, his eyes twinkling and said in a half whisper, "And tomorrow I'm taking you and Mam to the pictures in Leeds. You'll like that, won't you?"

Christina nodded her head, her eyes shining.

Audra smiled as she watched the two of them together. He had always been a loving father to Christina; she could never take that away from him.

Vincent's leave came to an end all too quickly.

Audra got up at five o'clock on Sunday morning, to make breakfast for him whilst he shaved and dressed.

Eggs were a precious commodity, very scarce, but Audra had managed to get hold of two. She had cooked one for Christina's tea the day before, and now she fried the second for Vincent, along with a tomato and a small piece of bacon which Eliza had given her.

When Vincent saw the egg on his plate, he was upset. "Oh you shouldn't have," he said, frowning at her. "You should have kept it for yourself. Come on, take half of it to eat with your toast."

Audra prevented him from dividing the egg. "Thanks, but I'm not very hungry. Please eat it, Vincent; you won't get anything else for hours and hours. You told me the troop trains are running slowly, and you've no idea what time you'll get back to Hull today."

"That's true." Nevertheless, he ate the egg reluctantly,

and he wished she had kept it for Christina, if she did not want it for herself.

Neither of them said much during breakfast. They were both aware that he was going back to fight a war, and they had no idea when they would see each other again. It could be months on end, maybe even years.

As the clock struck six, Vincent stood up. "I'd better be going. My train's at seven."

"Yes."

As he put on his regulation navy topcoat, picked up his sailor hat and brought his kit bag to the door, he said, "I kissed Christie before I came down for breakfast. . . . I don't want to go upstairs again; I might wake her. Say goodbye to her for me."

Audra nodded, too choked to speak. She came to him in the doorway, stood on tiptoe to kiss him. He kissed her in return, held her tightly for a moment longer.

"Please be careful, Vincent," she managed to say in a tight voice.

"I will, don't fret, love. I'll write. . . ."

A second later he was gone.

Suddenly she was standing alone in the kitchen.

She ran to the window, parted the curtains, watched him hurrying down the path in the remote light of the January dawn.

Instinctively her hand came up to her heart, fearing for him, fearing for his safety. Come back to me, she whispered in the silence of the empty room. And Audra stood there for a long time after he had disappeared from sight, facing an irrefutable fact. Her love for Vincent Crowther was undiminished, despite all of their troubles and problems over the years.

CHAPTER THIRTY

Spring came, bringing with it an end to the "phony war."

Audra sat glued to her wireless in the evening, whilst

Christina did her homework or sketched and painted. And the more Audra heard, the more she became alarmed for her husband and the rest of the family and friends who were fighting the enemy.

Events were moving so rapidly she could scarcely keep track of them. On April 9 Hitler invaded Denmark and Norway. Denmark fell at once, but the valiant Norwegians fought back heroically and appealed to Britian for help. Immediately naval and military forces were dispatched.

For the next three weeks Audra behaved like a sleep-walker, doing everything automatically, as if by rote. She knew from the news on the radio that Vincent's destroyer was amongst those ships which had sailed to assist the Norwegians. She was frozen with fear and for once her optimistic nature seemed to desert her completely.

The news grew more grim by the day; and every time she picked up a newspaper her heart lurched.

The Luftwaffe all but demolished the British forces as they tried in vain to help the Norwegians, but by the end of the month most of the British had been evacuated. Vincent's ship finally limped back into British territorial waters; miraculously he was safe. The losses to the forces were enormous, and it soon became clear to Audra and the rest of the country that the failure to heed Winston Churchill's warnings in the past had been disastrous.

"Thank God he's finally been made Prime Minister," Audra said to Laurette as they sat close to the wireless on the evening of May 13. That morning Churchill had given his first speech as Prime Minister to the House of Commons. In a few minutes he was to address the nation.

"Vincent has always said that Churchill is the only man to lead us out of this mess, and I know he's right," Audra said.

Laurette nodded. "I agree, but even so, I think we're in for a long siege."

"Still, we have a *real* leader now—" Audra stopped, tapped Christina on her shoulder and motioned to the radio, then brought her finger to her lips.

The three of them sat perfectly still, straining to hear every word, mesmerized by the extraordinary voice and rhetoric of Winston Churchill bringing hope and courage and inspiration to the English people.

Audra and Laurette were buoyed up that evening, but as the days passed Audra knew that her sister-in-law had been correct. They *were* in for a siege, and it would be both long and deadly.

First there was the hell of Dunkirk.

Thousands upon thousands of British and Allied troops were stranded on the beaches of France, cruelly caught between the sea and the advancing German army. England held its breath. And then only through acts of desperate heroism were they rescued by a motley armada of British destroyers and cruisers, pleasure launches, rowboats, trawlers, yachts and even barges. Civilians had answered Winston Churchill's plea for everyone who had a vessel to pitch in and help the Royal Navy get the boys off the beaches. In doing so they saved lives by the hundreds of thousands—and gripped the imagination of the whole of England and her allies with their extraordinary valor.

The great epic of Dunkirk was an inspiration to everyone, and when Audra went around the general adult wards in the hospital, which she was now supervising, she saw how high morale was amongst her patients. Men and women alike took hold of her hand, and with tears in their eyes they spoke of their pride and their patriotism, and mentioned Churchill with reverence and love.

Audra herself had immense faith in Winston Churchill, this man who had said to them only a few weeks before: "*I have nothing to offer but blood, toil, tears and sweat.*" She understood words like that only too well, and she also understood that Dunkirk was only the beginning. . . . Churchill had warned the British people on June 4 that a terrible storm would soon break over them to test them all. And it did.

France fell.

Suddenly England stood alone.

And in August the might of the German Luftwaffe was flung against the country in bombardments that were to continue for months to come.

The Battle of Britain had begun.

At first the bombings were centered on London and the southern counties, but they soon became more widespread, and many of the industrial cities and airfields in the midlands and the north became prime targets.

Audra was cutting roses in her garden one Saturday afternoon when the drone of planes and the harsh and relentless rattle of machine-gun fire broke the silence of the sultry day.

Her head flew up with a jerk. As she squinted against the sun, she saw desperate aerial combat raging in the blue summer sky immediately above her house and her precious little world.

To Audra it was a horrifying and shocking sight, this dog fight between the Royal Air Force and the Luftwaffe. That it could happen over England in the middle of the day stunned her. She was momentarily rooted to the spot as she continued to stare up into the sky. Then one of the planes exploded in a great burst of flames and began to fall.

"Mam! Mam!" Christina cried, flinging down her brush and palette, running up the flagstone path.

The girl's voice roused Audra, galvanized her into action. Grasping Christina's hand she raced her child back along the path and into the air raid shelter.

"I thought we'd better come in here for a few minutes, just in case of falling debris," Audra said, giving her nine-year-old child a reassuring look. She forced a bright smile. "I suppose we could have gone into the house, but I seem to run for the shelter these days."

"It was such a lovely afternoon, and it happened so suddenly, Mam, didn't it?"

"Yes." Audra stared at the corrugated-iron wall of the shelter, an abstracted look crossing her face as she murmured in a saddened voice, "Hearts at peace, under an English heaven."

"That's Rupert Brooke, from the book your mother gave you long ago, isn't it, Mam?"

Audra nodded. "Yes, it is, and as I looked up into our lovely English sky a few minutes ago, Christina, and saw those planes going at each other hammer and tongs, that

line of verse flashed through my mind, and I couldn't help
wondering just when our hearts *would* be at peace again."

A flicker of fear touched Audra's blue eyes, and she
added, "It might easily have been Theo up there . . . he
is so young, only nineteen. But then, all of our Air Force
boys are young. Oh, I pray that Theo is safe, Christie, I
pray for him every day."

"Yes, Mam, so do I, when I pray for Daddy and Auntie
Maggie and Uncle Mike, and all of my uncles and
everybody who's fighting for us."

It was not long after this incident that the Germans
stepped up their bombing raids on England, and although
London was the chief target, Leeds was one of the northern
cities that came in for heavy pummeling.

Audra and Christina now found themselves living in the
air raid shelter almost every night. But they were the only
occupants. Audra had been unable to persuade old Miss
Dobbs to join them; the family in the third cottage in the
cul-de-sac had closed it up for the duration and moved to
the country to stay with friends.

If Laurette was visiting them when the banshee wailing
of the sirens started, Audra insisted that she spend the
night with them in the shelter. She would not allow
Laurette to walk home to Moorfield Road during a raid,
even though the sky was brilliant with seachlights. Audra
believed in following regulations, and they had been
warned by the Civil Defense to stay inside.

The shelter was now well equipped with cots, blankets
and pillows, candles, paraffin lamps, a kerosene stove for
heat, and a first-aid kit. Audra had stacked up tins of food,
and every day she and Christina carried bottles of fresh
water down to the shelter in case of emergency.

But in spite of the bombings, the perpetual fear, the
worry about Vincent and the rest of their family and
friends, and the hardships in general, life somehow went
on.

The newspapers were full of talk about the German

invasion of England in late August, but the English seemed
to take this with their usual imperturbability.

Audra's attitude seemed to sum up the universal feeling
when she said to Christina one day in late August,
"Invasion or no invasion, you're starting at Miss Mellor's
Private School for Girls when the winter term begins in
September. You've got to have an education, whether the
Germans land here or not. Besides, as Winston Churchill
said, we'll fight them in the hedges, if we have to, and
demolish them to a man."

"You mean I *am* going to Miss Mellor's School after all!"
Christina cried excitedly, breaking into smiles.

The two of them sat on the upper deck of the tramcar
going into Leeds, and Audra turned to look at her. "Of
course you are. Why do you sound so surprised?"

"Well, you haven't mentioned it lately, even though I
passed the entrance exam. I thought you'd changed your
mind."

"Now why on earth would I change my mind, dear?"

"I thought Grandma might have said something to you,
Mam."

"*Grandma?*"

"Yes. I heard her telling Grandpa that you oughtn't to be
sending me to a private school, that Christ Church was
good enough. She said you had big ideas for me and that
they'd only lead to trouble. I thought she'd said the same to
you and that you'd listened to her."

"That'll be the day," Audra replied with a hint of acerbity.
"And just as a matter of interest, what did Grandpa say in
response to Grandma's comments?"

"He said you were wise to reach for the stars, that he
admired you for it, and then he told her I was going to be a
great artist one day."

Audra smiled to herself. "Your grandfather is quite right,
Christie."

Christina tucked her arm through her mother's companionably. "Is that why we're going to town, Mam? To buy my
school uniform?"

"Yes, it is, and I'm thrilled you're going to start at Miss
Mellor's, Christie. They have an excellent fine arts pro-

gram, and I've had several long chats with the art teacher. She knows all about our plans, and she'll prepare you well for Leeds College of Art."

"And then after that I'll go to the Royal College of Art in London, won't I, Mother?" Christina looked into Audra's face, her gray eyes bright with anticipation.

Audra could not help laughing. "Of course, I promised, didn't I? But they won't accept you until you're twenty, you know. We've a long way to go yet."

Christina and Audra had always been close, but they drew closer than ever during the war years. With Vincent away at sea it was just the two of them, and although they saw Laurette at least once a week, they were mostly on their own.

The glittering future she had planned for her child occupied Audra most of the time. When she wasn't scrimping and scraping to pay for Christina's education, she was finding ways to expand the child's mind in other areas as well as in art.

Wartime conditions being what they were, there were not many plays coming to the theater in Leeds. But when something new did open, Audra always tried to get tickets for them; she took Christina to classical music concerts and to the opera whenever a company came to the Leeds. But these pleasures aside, books and especially the English classics were also part of Audra's cultural program for her daughter, and Christina acquired a love of reading early in her life.

As always, films were the mainstay of their entertainment during the forties, and they both derived a great deal of pleasure from their Saturday night jaunts to the local cinema. Usually Laurette accompanied them, for she and Audra had become dearer friends than ever, bound by so many common bonds and family ties, but mostly because of their love for each other.

As the war years dragged on, leaves were few and far between, and neither Vincent nor Mike came home more than once between the summer of 1941 and the winter of 1942.

Both women worried a lot about their husbands and about the rest of the Crowther family who were in the services. But they were women of strong character, and they learned to live with constant air raids, life in the shelters, rationing, shortages and hardships, and the terrible fear of losing loved ones. And they did so without complaint, always endeavoring to look to the future, to the day when Britain would win the war and life would return to normal.

In October of 1944 Audra had a wonderful piece of good luck. Margaret Lennox, whom she had always idolized since her days in Ripon, was appointed matron of Leeds Infirmary. And almost immediately she telephoned Audra at St. Mary's to offer her the position of sister in charge of the main surgical ward. Audra accepted the job over the telephone, and without having to think twice. The money was more than she was presently earning, the job a challenge. Also, Audra had always dreamed of working with Matron Lennox again.

It did not take Audra long to settle into life at Leeds General Infirmary, even though it was a vast and hectic hospital and not as cozy and intimate as St. Mary's had been. But she found the work stimulating, and satisfying, and as she plunged into it with her usual energy and concentration, she realized that it was helping to keep fear at bay.

To Audra's vast relief the beginning of 1945 brought good news of allied breakthroughs all over Europe. The tide was turning, and there was no longer any question who was going to win the war. It was only a matter of time.

Soon Audra was reaching for the newspapers and switching on the radio with eagerness rather than dread. By the spring she had started to take heart, as had the whole of Britain, and on May 7 the Germans surrendered unconditionally at Reims in France.

Suddenly the war in Europe was over.

Audra and Christina could hardly believe it. They

laughed and they wept as they embraced each other fiercely in the cottage in Pot Lane.

Two days earlier, Christina had celebrated her fourteenth birthday, and now she said to Audra, "But this is my best birthday present, Mam, knowing that it's over and that Daddy's safe."

"Yes, it is, darling," Audra replied. She glanced at the collection of framed photographs lined up on the sideboard: Vincent, her brother William in the Australian Forces, Mike, Theo Bell, Maggie and Vincent's brothers Frank, Jack, Bill and Danny, and Olive's husband Hal. How smart they looked and so proud in their various uniforms.

She turned to Christina and said, "They're all safe, thank God! How lucky we've been . . . luckier than most."

CHAPTER THIRTY-ONE

Audra Crowther was so concentrated on what she was doing in the next few years she hardly ever had time to pause, except to look at her lovely and gifted daughter.

But one day she found herself staring into the mirror on her dressing table—and taking stock.

It was a warm day in July of 1951, and later that afternoon Christina was graduating with honors from Leeds College of Art. It was a most important occasion in her daughter's life as well as her own and Vincent's, and so not unnaturally she wanted to look her best.

Audra leaned closer to the glass, inspecting her face.

There were a few faint tell-tale lines around her eyes, and the stubbornness and resoluteness that had always marked her face seemed more pronounced than ever. But aside from these little flaws, if they could be called that, and a hint of gray at her temples, she decided she did not look too bad for forty-four.

Her light brown hair, cut short and framing her face in a flattering style, was still thick and luxuriant; her creamy complexion was as flawless as it had always been, and the blueness of her eyes had not dimmed over the years.

And I've kept my slim figure, she added, reaching for the bottle of foundation lotion. Usually she only had time to dab a powder puff on her nose and put on a trace of lipstick, before dashing off to Leeds Infirmary, where she still worked and was now a senior member of the staff. But today she was going to take her time and do a proper job of making herself up, and to this end she had borrowed some of Christina's cosmetics.

After smoothing on the foundation, she powdered her face, dusted off the excess, added rouge to emphasize her high cheekbones, then used brown mascara on her lashes, before outlining her mouth with pink lipstick.

Satisfied that she had done the best she could, Audra sat back and regarded herself. She was momentarily startled by her own reflection. The makeup had brought out her best features and highlighted her eyes and her skin. Her face had taken on a fresh look, seemed more vibrant and alive. Pleased with the effect she had created, she brushed her hair, smoothed it into place with the comb and then, as a final touch, she added a dab of her favorite gardenia perfume behind her ears.

Standing up, Audra walked across the bedroom to the wardrobe and took out the tailored navy-blue silk dress she had made for herself last week. It was a perfect copy of a Christian Dior afternoon dress she had seen in *Vogue* magazine earlier in the year, and she had clipped out the photograph, as she always did when she saw a style she liked, whether it was for herself or for Christina.

After placing the dress on the bed, she took out her navy bag, white fabric gloves, the small navy straw hat trimmed with a single white rose and the pair of navy court shoes she had bought yesterday.

Once she had slipped on the dress and shoes, Audra returned to the dressing table and sat down again. She put on her hat, added the marquisite earrings Vincent had given her for Christmas, her mother's engagement ring, and her watch, and then she slid open the drawer and took out the box containing Laurette's pearls.

Lifting the lid, Audra stared at them, admiring them. There was only a single strand, but the pearls were of good quality. Mike had bought them for Laurette at Greenwood's, the finest jewelers in Leeds, not long after the end of the war, and her sister-in-law had so loved them.

Audra sighed, touched by a sudden fleeting sadness for her darling Laurette, who had died three years ago. It had been sudden; she still hadn't quite recovered from the shock. None of them had. Laurette had looked so well in the spring of 1948, but she had fallen sick that summer and by November they were burying her. It had been cancer. She was thankful that Laurette had gone quickly, that her suffering had not been prolonged. She missed her so very much. There would always be a void without Laurette—and for all of them.

Remembering the time, Audra sat up straighter in her chair. She took the pearls from the box and fastened them around her neck, looking in the mirror again, touching the necklace, smiling softly to herself. And she let go of the sadness, let go of the painful memories of Laurette's passing. The last thing *she* would have wanted was for her to be sorrowful on a day like this. Laurette had always been so terribly proud of Christina.

Rising, Audra went to the bed, picked up her gloves and bag and hurried down the stairs. She dropped her things on the hall table next to the telephone and paused, glanced at the grandfather clock, wondering what had happened to Vincent. He had said he would be home by one-thirty and it was already one forty-five.

Aside from the shock and anguish they had suffered with Laurette's death, the last few years had been good to the Crowthers. They no longer lived in the cottage in Pot Lane. They had moved into this much larger house in Upper Armley in 1949. It was not far from Charlie Cake Park, and it had three bedrooms, a dining room, a sitting room, and a big, family-style kitchen-parlor, where, as usual, everyone seemed to congregate. The rooms were spacious and there was a light, airy feeling about the house in general.

In particular, Audra loved the long back garden. She had planted it with rose bushes and delphiniums and a variety of other flowers, and with its smooth green lawn stretching down to two shady trees at the bottom, it was a paradise in the summer weather. Audra derived much enjoyment from it, and from her flowers and the small vegetable plot she had started near the high back fence beyond the trees.

Vincent was more prosperous. Immediately after he was demobilized, at the end of the war, he had gone into partnership with Fred Varley and his son, Harry. And finally, after talking about it for so many years, he had enrolled in night school in Leeds, to study architecture and draftsmanship. He no longer worked outdoors on the building sites, but ran the business with Fred; he did most of the planning, drawing and paperwork. Varley and Crowther was a small company, but they were kept busy with local building projects and Vincent was earning a decent living, and he was able to support his family himself. The money Audra earned at the Infirmary went into the bank for Christina's education and her clothes.

The war had changed Vincent Crowther.

His turbulent character and restless ways had been tempered by the death and destruction he had witnessed in the navy. He still liked to go to the pub on weekends, and he continued to bet on the horses, but he no longer indulged himself in romantic flings with other women.

Not that his relationship with Audra had changed. But after twenty-three years together they were used to each other. It was an enduring marriage, it seemed, and they shared a bond, one that truly welded them together: their immense pride in their daughter, who had turned out to be very special indeed.

Audra was thinking about Christina and the clothes she still had to make for her as she filled the teapot and carried it over to the table. There were only ten days left before they went to London to get Christie settled in the little studio flat. Well, she would have time to cut and sew at least one more dress in that time, and the remainder of her clothes for college would have to be sent by parcel post.

"Sorry I'm late," Vincent said, barging in through the back door in a great rush. "There was such a lot of traffic between here and Pudsey, I thought I'd never get here—"

He cut himself short, stared at her through narrowed eyes. "What have you done to yourself, Audra?"

"I haven't done anything," she exclaimed, stiffening, giving him a defensive look. His tone had sounded critical.

He held his head on one side and studied her thoughtfully. "It must be the hat, or maybe it's the new dress—"

"Oh for heaven's sake it's the makeup," she muttered. "I'm wearing some of Christie's foundation lotion and rouge."

"I like it," he said, grinning at her. "You look nice. Ever so nice, love. You should wear makeup more often."

Audra half smiled and then glanced away quickly. She felt suddenly self-conscious under his unexpected scrutiny. Vincent had not looked at her like that in years. She said, "Do you want a cup of tea now? Or later, after you've changed your shirt and suit?"

"Later. I won't be but a few minutes." He hurried out.

Audra remained standing near the kitchen table, staring after him, thinking how well he looked.

Vincent had hardly changed over the years, hardly aged at all. Last month he had celebrated his forty-eighth birthday, but he appeared to be much younger. There wasn't a gray hair on his head and his face had retained a certain boyishness, and the smoothness of his cheeks and brow, along with his fresh complexion, only underscored his youthfulness.

She took a chair, sat waiting for him to return, thinking about him, wondering if he ever had love affairs these days. Years ago she had suspected that he saw other women, even though there had never been gossip, nor had she had any proof. But their relationship had been so bad at times she had supposed he found solace for his woes in more welcoming arms than hers.

A deep sigh escaped her, and she shook her head, mildly irritated with herself. She was having such strange thoughts today. First she had been on the verge of tears, dwelling on Laurette, missing her, and now here she was brooding over all sorts of imponderables about Vincent. And as if it made any difference now.

"Let's have that cup of tea, Audra," Vincent exclaimed,

coming back into the kitchen. "We haven't got much time to waste."

He sat down opposite her and reached for the teapot. "Did our Christie get off all right?"

"Yes," Audra said. "She left at noon. She said she had several things to check in the college gallery—the exhibition, I expect. She always fusses about having the proper kind of light on her paintings—you know what a perfectionist she is; everything has to be exactly right."

"Just like her mother," he said with a laugh. "Come on, love, get your bits and pieces together and let's be off. We don't want to miss the ceremony; it's something you've been looking forward to for the last twenty years."

Audra smiled. "That's absolutely true. And so have you."

Later, as they were driving into town, Audra suddenly put her hand on Vincent's knee and squeezed it.

He glanced at her through the corner of his eye. "What?"

"I *know* that one day Christina will be as famous as those other two great Leeds College Art students, Barbara Hepworth and Henry Moore."

Vincent nodded. Who was he to argue with her? She had always been right about their daughter thus far.

Christina
1951 to 1965

CHAPTER THIRTY-TWO

Christina loved the little flat in London.

It was in a tall, narrow house in Chester Street, not far from Belgrave Square. The house belonged to Irène Bell, and Christina and her mother had stayed at the flat several times in the past when they had come to London on their educational trips, to visit the many galleries and museums. And so she already knew it well.

Irène Bell was renting the flat to Audra for four guineas a week. Audra thought it was a bargain at the price, and indeed it was, but Christina knew that Mrs. Bell hated charging her mother rent. She would have much preferred to let her have it for nothing. But as she had explained privately to Christina, that was not Audra's way of doing things. "Your mother's too shrewd," Irène Bell had said. "If the rent doesn't seem right to her, she'll be suspicious." Christina had agreed, and together they had arrived at a suitable figure.

The flat was on the top floor of the house, was in fact converted attics with a living room, bedroom, bathroom and kitchen. It had its own front door and was a self-contained little dwelling within the house.

Originally, Irène Bell had created the studio flat at the top of her house for her daughters to live in at different stages of their lives. It had been a *pied-à-terre* for them and later for Theo, when he had been studying law at Cambridge and came to London on weekends occasionally. Theo, who was thirty and a barrister with chambers in the Temple, had recently married, and he and his wife Angela occupied the town house. Sometimes Irène Bell came to stay with her son and daughter-in-law, but only rarely. She was in her seventies now, and since Thomas Bell's death three years before, she rarely ventured far afield. She liked to hold court at Calpher House, and have her children and many grandchildren visit her there.

On the day that Christina and Audra had arrived from
Leeds, the Bells' house in Belgravia was deserted. Theo
and Angela were away on holiday in France, but Mrs. Bell
had given Audra a set of keys and told her they should make
themselves at home.

This they had done and now, at the end of the first week
in London, Christina was settled in the studio under the
eaves. Her easel, spare canvases, paints and brushes had
been unpacked and put away, as had her books, her other
possessions and her clothes.

These filled the large closet in the bedroom and every
time Christina looked inside she was impressed with the
spectacular selection of outfits her mother had made for
her.

The measuring, cutting, pinning, sewing and pressing
had gone on for the last eight months, but it was only when
she saw everything hanging there together that she realized
what an extraordinary undertaking creating this stylish
wardrobe had been for her mother.

"I'm going to be the best-dressed girl at the Royal
College of Art," Christina said to Audra late on Friday
afternoon as she took a pearl-gray silk dress from the closet,
held it against herself, stared in the mirror.

"I should hope so," Audra said with a light laugh,
watching her from the doorway of the bedroom. "I certainly
worked hard enough."

"Oh Mummy, you did! I *know* you did. Thank you for all
of my lovely clothes, for all the time and effort you put into
them, and the money you've spent. You're a wonder,
Mother, you truly are."

"I don't know about that," Audra said, hastily brushing
aside the thanks and the compliment. But nevertheless she
looked pleased as she came into the bedroom and sat down
on one of the twin beds.

Christina swung around, still holding the silk dress
pressed close to her lithe body. "What do you think about
this for the theater tonight, Mummy?"

Audra nodded her approval.

Christina flashed her a vivid smile, hung the dress on the
top of the closet door and said, "I'd better find the right

shoes and bag . . . the black patent, I think. And perhaps I'll take the gray silk Dior shawl Grandma gave me for my birthday, just in case it gets cool later."

"I doubt that's going to happen," Audra said, "it's been awfully hot today. In fact, I think we're in for a heat wave this weekend."

"Don't say that, Mother!" Christina made a face. "Not when we've planned to go to Windsor Castle for the day on Sunday. I don't fancy the idea of sweltering in the scorching August sun all day, as we tramp around the grounds."

Audra smiled as she leaned back against the pillows, watching her daughter take out her accessories for the evening, thinking how striking she was to look at.

Christina's light brown hair of childhood had turned years ago to a deeper, richer chestnut, and in the summer it was always shot through with reddish golden streaks from the sun. Her resemblance to her father was marked, and although she was not strictly beautiful, she had an arresting face with clear, chiseled features and a lovely complexion like Audra. Her huge gray eyes, so soft, so smokey, were Laurette's eyes, and Christina had inherited the Crowther height; she stood five feet seven in her stocking feet. This pleased Audra. She had always hated being short.

Her attractive appearance and her obvious artistic gifts to one side, Christina had turned out to be an exceptional young woman in other ways. Everyone agreed on that. Despite Grandma Crowther's predictions that the private school and Audra's big ideas would lead to trouble, this had not been the case. Christina had not grown up to be difficult, rebellious or a snob; nor had she turned on her parents, preferring her college friends to them. Quite the contrary, in fact. She was a loving daughter, who adored Audra and Vincent in much the same way as they adored her, and, as she had done when she was a child, she enjoyed their company, believed *them* to be special.

Audra Crowther had done her job well.

Apart from providing Christina with the best of everything within her power, she had given the girl the best of herself. She had taught Christina the proper human values, instilled in her a sense of honor, duty and purpose.

Drawing on her own genteel upbringing, Audra had reared her to have consideration for others. But perhaps most importantly of all, Audra had given Christina something else of incalculable value—a feeling of self-worth. And so she was remarkably secure.

Though frequently uncommunicative and undemonstrative with Vincent, which had always been at the root of the trouble between them, Audra had been able to express her love for her child verbally and with a show of physical affection. Yet with this unconditional love had come discipline, and from both her parents. Vincent, in particular, had been very strict with Christina when she had been a teenager and especially about boys.

Yes, she does have a certain kind of grace, Audra commented to herself, continuing to observe her daughter as she moved around the bedroom. But she's not perfect by any means, and of course who is? Christie does have Vincent's quick, rather violent temper, and his expensive tastes, his love of clothes and the finer things of life. And she can be impetuous. But, withal, she's not a spoiled girl. Audra smiled. How many times had Eliza said, "You're spoiling that girl, Audra, and so is Vincent. You'll both live to regret it . . . oh yes, spare the rod and spoil the child." An echo of her mother-in-law's voice reverberated in her head.

"You're looking pensive, Mummy. Is something wrong?"

Audra sat up with a start. "No." She laughed wryly. "To tell you the truth, I was thinking about your grandma. She always said my plans for you were far too elaborate and high flown. And la-di-da . . . That was her favorite expression for anything that had to do with me when you were little."

"Don't I know it. She's old-fashioned and so class-bound, poor old thing. But she means well, Mummy, and she's always been very loving with me." Christina grinned. "But then I'm the only child of her darling Stormy Petrel."

"*Stormy Petrel?*"

"Yes, that's what she called Daddy when he was first born, and when he was a little boy. Didn't she ever tell you that?"

"No. But then your grandma and I have never been

close, never seen eye to eye on anything much, and certainly her ideas about a woman's place in the world have always gone against the grain with me."

"What do you mean?"

"Your grandma has always believed that women should . . . well, be subservient to men. Long before you were born, she was horrified when I said I wanted a nursing career. She told me it was my duty to settle down and have babies and toe the line and cater to your father."

"I can understand her saying that, Mother. I don't think she approves of my coming to London and attending the Royal College of Art at all. She seems to think it's a waste of money. When I went to say goodbye to her and Grandpa the other day, she clucked and said something about it being a terrible expense, when I was bound to give up my art to get married and have babies the moment I met the first suitable young man."

Audra smiled faintly. "That sounds like Eliza. . . ." She paused reflectively, and then after a moment she fixed her bright blue eyes on Christina. "You know, Christie, I am glad you're ambitious, that you want a career for yourself, as well as those other things in life. You can have them all, you know, you really can. In fact, there's nothing you can't have if you try hard enough, work hard enough and strive toward a goal. And never, never limit yourself—"

Christina interrupted, smiling at Audra, "Just as you've taught me to . . . and I remember very well what Grandpa said that September you sent me to Miss Mellor's, when Grandma was doing her usual bit of grousing. He told her you were right to *reach for the stars*. He's always admired you for that, Mummy." The phone rang and Christina turned to the small desk and reached for it.

"Oh hello, Daddy. How are you?" There was a short pause as she listened carefully; then she looked across at Audra, nodding and smiling. "Yes, Daddy, I understand." There was another pause. "Yes, we went to lunch at Fortnum's, and then we spent the afternoon at the Tate looking at the Turners." Christina laughed at a remark of her father's, then finished, "Let me get Mummy for you now."

Audra rose and went to take the telephone from her

daughter. "Hello, Vincent. Is everything all right?" she asked and immediately fell silent as Vincent spoke to her in a rush of words.

Christina slipped out, smiling to herself. She crossed the minuscule hall and went into the kitchen that adjoined the living room; after putting the kettle on the gas, she took endive, lettuce and tomatoes from the refrigerator and began to wash them.

A few minutes later, Audra joined her in the small galley-style kitchen. "Let me help you," she said.

"There's not much to do, really." Christina glanced over her shoulder and remarked. "Honestly, Daddy's getting to be such an old fuss pot. I can't have a conversation with him at the moment without him telling me to watch me step, and he keeps saying, 'Think on, love, think on.' I don't know what's got into him lately."

"Well, you're *still* his little girl, and he's a bit worried about you being out on your own, I suppose."

"Mmmmm," was Christina's only reply as she began to peel a tomato. Suddenly she giggled and said, "Gosh, you're going to have a *huge* phone bill, Mum, when you get home. Daddy's hardly been off it this week." She began to giggle, and her eyes were mischievous. "I do believe he's courting you again."

"Don't be ridiculous!" Audra exclaimed.

That evening Christina took Audra to see her favorite actress and actor—Vivien Leigh and Laurence Olivier.

They were starring in the Festival of Britain's production of Shaw's *Caesar and Cleopatra* and Shakespeare's *Antony and Cleopatra*, each play being performed on successive nights.

This was Christina's big surprise for her mother.

Audra knew they were going to the theater, but she had no idea what they were going to see, and she was thrilled when Christina told her their destination as they sat on the bus.

"There's no point in seeing one play without the other, so

I bought tickets for both nights, Mummy, and we'll be coming back tomorrow."

"Oh darling, how extravagant you are, just like your daddy," Audra said, but her face glowed with happiness.

"This is a theatrical *first*, Mum. I know we're in for a splendid evening in the theater, one we're not likely to forget," Christina remarked, filled with pleasure that she could do something nice for her mother.

Audra could hardly contain her excitement as they took their seats in the theater, and she reached out and squeezed her daughter's hand, whispered, "Thank you, Christie, for thinking of this very special treat for me. . . . I know I'll never forget it."

Before either of them realized it, Audra's second week in London came to an end.

It had been a wonderful time for them both. Apart from getting Christina settled in the flat before she started her courses at the Royal College of Art in September, they had been able to share some happy days together. They had been to see other plays and to the pictures, which they always enjoyed; they had visited museums and as many art galleries as they could cram in.

Vincent had given Audra some money before they had left Leeds and told her to take themselves out to dinner on him, and this they had done, booking a table at a little bistro called Chez Jacques. There had been days when they had simply pottered around the little flat and gone for walks through Green Park and down by The Mall, or window-shopped in Bond Street and browsed around Hatchard's, Audra's favorite bookstore. But every minute had been precious to mother and daughter, and Audra would never forget her two weeks with Christina at this time in her daughter's life.

"My stay in London has been so special," Audra said as they sat in the taxi going to King's Cross railway station, on Friday morning at the end of her stay.

"And for me too, Mummy," Christina replied and instantly became silent. She suddenly realized how much she was going to miss her mother, and it also registered, forcibly, that from today onward she was going to be on her own.

They were both a little sad as they walked down the platform toward the train for Leeds, and just before Audra boarded, Christina hugged her, said in a tremulous voice, "I'll never be able to thank you enough, or repay you for everything you've done for me, Mummy. You've been the best, the most wonderful mother in the world."

Audra stared at Christina, a look of surprise crossing her face. "But I only did my duty," she said.

Audra had told Vincent not to meet her at Leeds City station and being as frugal as always she took a tram back home to Upper Armley.

From the moment she let herself into the house she was conscious of the quietness; she was stunned by it, really. As she put her suitcase down in the hall and took off her hat, she felt the tears she had suppressed throughout the day begin to brim in her eyes. All of the sunshine has gone out of my life, she thought, groping in her pocket for her handkerchief.

Vincent also felt Christina's absence when he came home from work that evening. But he did not say anything to Audra, aware of her sadness. Instead he chatted about her trip, endeavored to draw her out about it, believing this would lift her out of herself. And it did for a while.

But after supper, as they sat drinking their coffee in front of the fire, she retreated into herself. So did he, and they were lost in their own thoughts for a short while.

Suddenly, Vincent felt that he had to talk to her about his feelings, and he looked across at her and murmured, "It's odd, isn't it, not having our Christie around? So quiet, Audra."

"Yes."

Vincent sighed softly. "Well, lass, she's gone from us now. I don't suppose she'll ever come back here—to live, I mean."

Audra frowned at him. "I don't want her to, Vincent. If she did that, what would it have all been about?"

"Aye, that's true. You said you'd give her the world when she was a baby in St. Mary's Hospital, and you have, love."

Vincent sipped his coffee, then took out a packet of cigarettes. He toyed with them for a few minutes, before putting them down on the coffee table. He fixed his eyes on her. "We've been through a lot, Audra, you and I."

"Yes, we have." She met his gaze. A curious thought struck her, and before she could stop herself, she said, "We've been tested, I think."

He stared at her intently.

"But we've come through all right. We have, haven't we, Vincent?"

He nodded, then cleared his throat. "I was thinking that you might like to go away with me next weekend . . . now that we're alone there's no reason why we can't do that, is there?"

Audra was flabbergasted. "Where to? Where would we go?"

"Robin Hood's Bay?"

"Why?"

"Because that's where we went on our honeymoon—" Vincent paused, took a deep breath. "It's not too late for us, is it, Audra? Couldn't we start all over again, as if this was the beginning?"

"Perhaps it is," she said.

CHAPTER THIRTY-THREE

Although she missed her parents and was frequently homesick, Christina soon settled into her new life of independence.

She was exhilarated by the excitement of London and all of the attractions it offered, but because she was aware of the supreme effort which had been expended by Audra to bring her to this point in her life, she was an assiduous student.

Christina had no intention of falling into bad ways, neglecting her studies and so risk disappointing her mother. This aside, she was a hard worker by nature and ambitious.

From the first day she started in September, her classes at the Royal College of Art in Kensington were challenging and stimulating, and she threw herself into her work with enthusiasm and dedication.

It was at this time—the early fifties—that the college was starting to be known as the art mecca of the world, and it was teeming with gifted people; tutors and students alike, and in all departments, from figurative and landscape painting and sculpture to textile, costume and scenic design.

From the day she had applied for entry into the college earlier that year, had submitted her best work, then been interviewed and accepted, the tutors at the college had been aware of her extraordinary gifts as a landscape painter. Since her childhood, Christina had seen everything in terms of light, and her paintings seemed drenched with it, whether it was the golden light of a sunlit summer day, the cold, pewter-colored light of a Yorkshire sea in a winter storm or the brilliant luminous light that suffused the Dales in spring. Because of the quality of her work and her dedication to it, Christina was soon a favorite with her tutor, as well as other members of the staff, who all saw in her the ideal student.

Being an open, outgoing and friendly young woman, Christina was also popular with her contemporaries, and within her first couple of weeks at college she quickly made a number of friends of both sexes. But the one she gravitated to the most, and who was her special favorite, was a girl of her own age called Jane Sedgewick.

Jane was ebullient, good-natured and something of a madcap. Pretty and dashing, with flaxen hair and eyes the color of pansies, she was one of the most engaging girls Christina had ever met.

They were painting together in one of the big studios on

a particular afternoon in September when she completely endeared herself to Christina.

Unexpectedly, Jane began to camp it up. Adopting the stance of a tragedienne, she cried dramatically, in a voice of mock despair, "My work looks like the devil's brew compared to yours. Alas, alack, woe is me." She paused, brought her clenched fist up to her chest and rolled her eyes to the ceiling. "I have no alternative but to kill myself. But before I put an end to this sweet young life . . . grant me one last favor."

"Of course, what is it?" Christina asked, playing along with her, laughing at her histrionics.

"Come and have coffee with me after class."

Still laughing, Christina accepted the invitation. A little later they wandered off down by the side of the Victoria and Albert Museum, chatting animatedly on their way to a coffee shop nearby. And neither girl knew that this was the beginning of an extraordinary friendship, one which was to last all of their lives.

Over several cups of *espresso* they learned more about each other. After Christina had told Jane something about herself, it was her turn to listen and she did so attentively. She was startled to discover that Jane was the eldest daughter of Dulcie Manville and Ralph Sedgewick, a husband-and-wife acting team equally as famous as the Oliviers, in their own way. And then she thought: But that explains her theatricality.

The Sedgewicks had appeared in countless films made by Gainsborough Pictures in the forties, and Christina and Audra had seen all of them at the Picturedome in Armley.

She told Jane, "Gosh, my mother will be *thrilled* to hear that I know you. She's a great fan of your parents, and so am I. In fact, when she was here in August, we went to see them in *Lovers' Quarrel* at the Haymarket. We laughed our heads off; it was simply marvelous, the best comedy we've seen in years."

"How would you like to meet the old folks in person?" Jane asked. "Do come and stay with us this weekend. We'd love to have you."

Christina stared at her in surprise. "But are you sure it's

all right? It is a bit last-minute, isn't it? I mean for them. Today's Thursday, Jane."

"Oh that's no problem; we have a jolly old crazy household. Come on, *do* say yes. We'll have some fun, and the grounds are pretty, so you can paint if you want to. Mind you there's only one problem—" Jane made a sour face. "My siblings, the little monsters, are positively *revolting*, but I suppose we don't have to bother with them. So, will you come?"

"Why yes, I will, thank you very much," Christina said, smiling. "It's a lovely invitation."

Christina and Jane drove down to Kent the following afternoon in Jane's beaten-up MG sports car painted a vivid yellow.

The Sedgewicks owned an old country house called Hadley Court in the pretty village of Aldington. Not long after they had left the village behind, Jane slowed down and pointed to a beautiful Tudor manor, long and low with leaded windows, set behind large iron gates and just visible from the road.

"That's Goldenhurst, Uncle Noël's house," Jane explained. "He's my godfather and quite a dear. On Sunday morning we'll be going over to his house for drinks and a slap-up Sunday lunch. It'll be quite mad, of course; he always has the most scandalous and outrageous people as house guests. But at least we'll have a giggle and escape the *revolting* monsters for a while."

Christina gave her a puzzled look. "What's wrong with your brothers and sisters?"

"They're little beasts. You'll soon see."

"And when do your parents come down to the country?"

"After the Saturday night performance. They flee the theater still wearing their makeup and race down here at breakneck speed, arrive at midnight. That's when you'll meet them, *if* you can stay awake to have sandwiches and coffee with them at that hour."

Jane swung the MG into a long driveway that twisted and turned up to the house, and Christina fell in love with it the minute she saw it. In a way, the architecture reminded her of High Cleugh, which her mother had often taken her to see when she was a child. They had had picnics on the slope near the Memory Place, and her mother had told her about the house where she had grown up. And later she had gone back to the slope above the River Ure and painted High Cleugh as a gift for Audra.

Hadley Court was a rambling old place with odd-shaped rooms, great fireplaces, flaring windows and lots and lots of character. The grounds were pastoral and romantic-looking, with weeping willows and a lily pond and randomly planted flowers that gave it an Old World air. Later when Christina strolled around the gardens, her fingers itched to put their misty green beauty and the soft southern light of Kent on the canvas she had brought with her.

As Jane had promised, the weekend was a lot of fun.

But Christina did have a few surprises, and she soon discovered that her new friend had a tendency to exaggerate.

The revolting siblings, as Jane called them, were not revolting at all; nor were they little beasts. Hadley and Lyndon, eleven-year-old twins, were tow-headed, freckle-faced boys who were cherubic and well behaved. Jane insisted that this was because she had terrified them into toeing the line that weekend by making all manner of dire threats against them. Their sister, nine-year-old Poppy Louise, was an enchantress with huge pansy-colored eyes like Jane's and bright red-gold hair. And she captivated Christina with her winning smiles and fanciful child's chatter.

As for Dulcie and Ralph Sedgewick, they were gracious and charming to her and made her feel like a member of the family immediately. They were not a bit as she had expected them to be, not at all theatrical or showy. They were both cultivated and witty. Ralph, in particular, was most amusing. Christina quickly decided that it was Jane who had all the flamboyance in this family.

Uncle Noël turned out to be Noël Coward, and Christina was rendered speechless when she walked into the living room at Goldenhurst on Sunday and found herself being introduced to Laurence Olivier and, shortly thereafter, to Vivien Leigh.

When she finally managed to get Jane into a corner, Christina whispered, "What do you mean outrageous and scandalous house guests! You might have warned me!"

Jane giggled and rolled her eyes. "But it wouldn't have been any fun if you'd known Larry and Viv were coming." Her face sobered, and she took hold of Christina's arm, staring anxiously into her face. "You're not angry with me, are you? I couldn't bear it if you were."

Christina said, "No, of course I'm not, Janey," and gave her a reassuring smile.

After this first weekend, Christina became a regular guest at Hadley Court and a constant visitor to the Sedgewicks' flat in Mayfair. Dulcie Manville Sedgewick had taken a great liking to Christina and thought her to be a wonderful influence on her rather scatterbrained daughter.

Being an only child, Christina reveled at being in the midst of the loving and amusing Sedgewick family, and enjoyed meeting the celebrated personalities who populated their parties—show-business folk, writers, journalists and politicians.

Yet this exciting and glittering world, as captivating as it was, did not unduly dazzle Christina, and her feet were always planted firmly on the ground, her dedication to her painting intact.

And as always she was devoted to her parents, most especially to Audra. During the next nine months her mother came twice to stay at the little studio flat in Chester Street, and Christina often went up to Yorkshire for weekends, and always during the holidays when the college was in recess.

Christina knew that her mother lived for these times when they were together and that she derived enormous vicarious pleasure as she listened to anecdotes about the Sedgewicks and her other friends, the parties and elegant dinners she attended.

Audra's pride in her daughter knew no bounds. Christina's record at the Royal College of Art was brilliant, and her popularity and success in social circles was gratifying, another reason for Audra to rejoice. She knew, at last, that she had kept the vow she had made to herself years ago. She had given her daughter a far better life than she herself had known. And she was satisfied that her own life, and everything she had done for Christina, had been justified.

Christina's first and second years in London were full of numerous challenges and new experiences, and were productive periods for her. Only one thing marred her happiness—the knowledge that her mother was still working.

Although Vincent was a partner in Varley and Crowther and doing quite well, he was still not earning enough to carry *all* of the family's financial burdens. Audra had continued nursing at the Infirmary essentially to support Christina's life in London. It was she who paid Christina's tuition, rent, and gave her an allowance, bought the fabrics for her clothes, and other clothing. Christina was acutely aware that without these commitments her mother would be able to cease her endless toil and have a much easier life.

And so at the end of her second year at college, Christina cautiously suggested getting a part-time job to help out. Audra was furious and adamant in her refusal to even consider such a thing, believing it would distract Christina and interfere with her studies. But she had not bargained for her daughter's stubbornness and determination. Christina was as strong-willed as Audra, and she resolutely set out to curtail the flow of money from Leeds to London.

She did not dare get a job, but she did adopt a more frugal way of living, and she cut down on overhead by moving in with Jane. Her best friend had been asking her to share her flat in Walton Street for ages, and since it was owned by Jane's Aunt Elspeth, who had lived in Monte Carlo since her marriage, the rent was nominal. "Oh, just give me a pound a week," Jane had said when Christina had asked her what her share would be.

Christina also decided she must start making her own clothes. Whilst this step might not save money exactly, it would take the job off her mother's back. She was egged on by Jane, who knew she had a great flair for designing. In fact, Christina had inherited Audra's cleverness with scissors and a needle; also, she had stood at her mother's knee for years, watching her make beautiful garments for themselves as well as for other people and technique had brushed off. In no time at all she had revamped some of her old dresses and created a couple of new ones, and she was inordinately pleased with herself.

Audra was not. However, she finally came to admit that the sewing was not injuring her daughter's work at the Royal College of Art. Grudgingly, she agreed that the hand-painted dresses and jackets and the starkly tailored suits had elegance and originality.

Christina found time to make a hand-painted blouse for her mother in the autumn of 1953, and she took it with her when she went to Leeds for the winter holidays.

Audra was thrilled when she opened the box on Christmas Day and immediately exclaimed over its beauty and the wonderful mingling of the blue delphiniums on the paler blue silk.

"But you shouldn't have," she chastised mildly. "All this sewing is taking you away from your studies."

"No, it isn't," Christina said with a laugh, hugging her. "I wanted you to have something beautiful, something that I had painted and made for you, Mummy."

That particular December was a happy time for the Crowthers. They had a simple family Christmas and in January Christina returned to London to resume her classes at the Royal College of Art.

She launched herself into her final courses with the immense enthusiasm and the extraordinary dedication she had previously shown, knowing that she would be graduating in August. She wanted to do well not only because of her own sense of pride, but for her mother.

CHAPTER THIRTY-FOUR

Vincent saw Christina before she saw him.

She had alighted from the London train at the far end of the platform and he caught flashes of her as she dodged in and out between the other passengers now hurrying toward the exit turnstile.

How young and lovely she looked in the belted camel coat and the very high-heeled court shoes she always wore. She stepped out briskly, her shoulders thrown back, her head held erect; there was something very confident about her, and this pleased him.

She would be twenty-three next month. He could hardly believe it. It seemed like only yesterday that he had been pushing her around in her pram. She had grown up to be a good girl, with a good head on her shoulders. He trusted her implicitly. When she had first gone to live in London, he had worried about her, been concerned about her judgment of situations and people, and particularly men. And then one day he had wondered why he was fretting. They had brought her up properly; she knew the difference between right and wrong. He had stopped worrying that instant. Yes, their daughter was a credit to them.

Suddenly Christina caught sight of him, waved, increased her pace, her face illuminated by the brightest of smiles.

Vincent hurried forward, smiling and waving himself. They came to a standstill in front of each other.

"Hello, Daddy," she cried, dropping her suitcase.

"Hello, pet," he said, beaming at her, reaching for her.

They embraced, laughing, then stepped away, staring into each other's faces. It was Good Friday afternoon and they had not met since Christmas and, as they usually did after an absence, they took stock of each other.

He looks a bit tired, older, Christina thought, surprised. Her father rarely showed his age.

She's more radiant than ever, Vincent thought, and his heart tightened imperceptibly. He knew she was going to be upset when he told her about Audra and that her radiance would be diluted somewhat. He wondered when he should tell her. Well, certainly before they got to the house.

"Come on, love," he said, lifting her suitcase, taking her arm, hurrying along the platform with her. "Your mam's waiting for you, and as anxiously as always."

"I can't wait to see her either. Where are you parked, Dad?"

"Just outside the station, and I'll have you home in no time at all."

As Vincent drove them up Stanningley Road in the direction of Upper Armley, Christina chatted to her father about her plans for the Easter holidays. "I thought I'd spend the weekend at home with you and Mummy, and then if it's all right with the two of you, I'd like to go off on one of my field trips to paint for a few days."

"That's fine, Christie. Where were you thinking of going?"

"Originally I had the Lake District in mind, but I want to do a seascape and I was toying with the idea of going to the East Coast . . . Whitby, Scarborough, Flamborough Head, somewhere around there. What do you think?"

"All of your childhood haunts, eh? Well, you could do worse than to pick one of them, but what about up near Ravenscar? There are some very dramatic views from the cliffs, and there's a nice hotel nearby. We like you to be comfortable when you're off on these field trips, you know."

"You both spoil me," she said, laughing. "I wish Mummy could get a couple of days off from the Infirmary to come with me. It'd do her good, don't you think, Daddy?"

Vincent was silent. He pulled the car onto the side of the road and braked, turned to face his daughter. "There's something I have to tell you—"

"What is it?" she cried, cutting him off, knowing at once that something was terribly wrong from the tone of his voice, the concern in his vivid green eyes. "It's Mummy, isn't it?"

Vincent nodded. "I'm afraid it is, love."

She reached out, clutched at his arm, stared at him, anxiety filling her face. "What's the matter?" she demanded.

"Your mam's been ill, gravely ill, Christie. She collapsed three weeks ago with viral pneumonia. She was in the Infirmary for over two weeks . . . there were complications at first; the doctors were worried about her lungs. Don't look so frightened, love, she's fine now. She's recuperating at home."

Christina was momentarily stunned.

She sat staring at her father for a few seconds, and then she exclaimed, with a flash of anger, "Why didn't you let me know? How unfair of you, Dad, to keep me in the dark. I should have been with her and certainly last week, once she was at home." Her angry stare intensified, and she added furiously, "You should have told me!"

"I didn't dare go against your mother's wishes, Christie love," Vincent said quietly. "I didn't dare upset her, and I would have if I'd sent for you. She didn't want you to be worried. You know what your mam's like."

"I don't understand you, I don't really," Christina cried, shaking her head in perplexity. "I can't imagine why you listened to Mummy. And anyway, who *has* been looking after her since she's been at home?"

"I have," Vincent said, turning on the ignition, glancing behind him before pulling out. "I took a week off from work. We're not very busy at the moment, and I had some holiday time due me, anyway."

"I could have come up last week," Christina snapped, her annoyance unabated. "I was just marking time in London, waiting to come home. I didn't have any special classes at the college."

Vincent realized that it would be wiser to remain silent. With their similar temperaments they could quarrel very easily, and that was the last thing he wanted today. He put his foot down on the accelerator and concentrated on his driving.

Halfway up Ridge Road, he glanced at her quickly out of the corner of his eye and said in the softest but firmest of

voices, "I hope you've calmed down, our Christie. I don't
want you barging into the house full of belligerence and
upsetting your mother."

"God, Dad, you're impossible at times! How could you
even think I would do such a thing?"

Audra's eyes looked bigger and bluer than ever in her
face, which was drawn and chalky in color and reflected her
suffering of the last few weeks. It lit up at the sight of
Christina standing in the doorway.

"Hello, darling," Audra said in a weak voice, half pushing
herself up on her elbows as Christina sped to her bedside.

"Oh Mummy, Mummy darling," Christina whispered,
kneeling down, taking Audra in her arms tenderly, embracing her. "You should have let Daddy send for me," she
murmured against her mother's hair, "you really should
have." Releasing her, she sat back, regarding her carefully,
wanting to assess her true condition.

Audra lifted her hand, touched Christina's face. "You
have your studies and they're more important than anything else right now."

Although Christina did not agree with this, believing that
her mother's health came first, she nodded her head.
Rising, she went to the bay window, pulled a chair closer to
Audra, sat down.

Vincent came in, hovered near the foot of the bed. He
said to Audra, "How do you feel, love? Are you all right?
Comfortable?"

"Yes, thank you, Vincent."

"I'll go and put the kettle on," he said.

Christina leaned forward after her father had left the
room, said in a cheery tone, "Well anyway, I'm here now,
Mummy, and for the next week I'm going to look after you.
I'm going to pamper and spoil you in the way you deserve."

A frown creased Audra's brow. "At Christmas you told me
you were thinking of going off on a field trip to the Lake
District. I hope you haven't changed your mind because of
me."

"No, no," Christina said quickly. "My tutor doesn't think it's necessary. I have plenty of finished paintings in hand."

"It'll be nice to have you here for the whole week," Audra murmured, settling back against the pillows, her face suffused with sudden contentment. "How's Jane?"

"As sweet as always, Mummy, and she sends you her love."

"I'm glad you have her for a friend and that you're happy sharing the flat in Walton Street with her. It's such a charming, cozy place." Another smile flitted across Audra's thin face. "Tell me everything you've been doing . . . you know how I love to hear about your exciting life in London."

"Yes, I will, but first I'm going downstairs to help Daddy . . . would you like to have something to eat with your cup of tea?"

"No, I'm not hungry, darling, but thank you."

Christina ran downstairs, wanting to alert her father that she had changed her plans before he blurted something out in front of her mother.

She found him in the kitchen unwrapping a slab of butter. He looked up as she came in. "Oh there you are, love. I bought some hot-cross buns at the confectioner's earlier. I thought I'd butter one for your mam."

"She said she's not hungry, Dad."

"Oh but she'll eat this," he said confidently. "She always likes a hot-cross bun at Easter, you know that. It's sort of a tradition with her, from her childhood at High Cleugh . . . having one on Good Friday." He sliced the bun in half and began to spread the butter on it. "You may think your mother looks haggard, but she's a lot better, Christie, she really is, and very much on the mend now."

Christina nodded. "Look, I just wanted to warn you not to say anything to her about my field trip to the East Coast. I'm staying here to look after Mummy for the entire week."

"Oh but she won't like that, it'll upset her—"

"I've already told her, Dad!" Christina interjected firmly. "So *please* don't say anything. I just told her my tutor didn't think it was necessary."

"Very well then." He glanced up and his eyes filled with

love for his only child. "You're a good lass, Christie, and it'll be a real tonic for your mother to have you here for a while. Better than any medicine."

It was a busy week for Christina.

She took over the running of the house; she cleaned and shopped and cooked and ironed, and looked after her mother with efficiency and the greatest devotion.

When the Easter weekend was over, she insisted that her father return to work, and he did so, although he protested vociferously about her bossiness to her mother. She heard him say to Audra as she passed their bedroom one morning, "I always warned you we had the makings of an army general in that one, and I knew I was right. She's just proved it to me. And I'll tell you something else, I wouldn't like to work for *her.*"

Christina had smiled as she had gone about her chores. She knew very well from whom she had inherited her bossy nature: her father.

Nursing her mother, pampering her and catering to her every need gave Christina a great deal of satisfaction. But as the week progressed it struck her that her mother had been making a stupendous effort to be bright and lively for her benefit.

It was now becoming obvious that this effort had been a terrible strain. Toward the end of the week Audra looked drained of all strength, and Christina's concern grew.

On Friday, her last morning at home, she was upset when she saw that her mother had only picked at the breakfast she had made for her. The scrambled eggs and bacon were untouched, the toast only half eaten, the peach unpeeled.

"Mummy, you've got an appetite like a sparrow! I shall be sick with worry once I've left."

"Don't be so silly, dear. I'm not hungry at the moment, that's all it is; and don't forget, I have been quite ill, Christie. My appetite will improve when I get my energy back, when I'm up and about again."

"I think I'd better stay at home another week."

"Absolutely not, I won't hear of it. There are your studies to think about. You mustn't neglect them, and this *is* your last term."

Christina sighed and lifted the tray, placed it on a nearby chest. She came to the bed and sat down, took hold of her mother's hand. "Can't you try and eat the peach if I peel it for you?"

"No, but thank you." Audra squeezed her hand. "It's been lovely to have you here, darling, but now you must get back to your life in London, the college, your friends," she said, smiling deeply at her daughter.

Christina smiled back; then her smile slipped.

In the bright sunlight of the April morning her mother's face was clearly illuminated, and for the first time in years she saw Audra with stunning objectivity. And as her eyes remained fixed on that wan face that was so very dear to her, Christina was appalled.

She thought: How she's aged in the last three years. She's not quite forty-seven, but she looks like an old woman today.

Her mother's life of sacrifice and struggle flashed through her mind with such breathtaking clarity Christina was suddenly filled with an aching sorrow. And then her heart clenched with feelings of tenderness and compassion for this small, fragile-looking woman who stood ten feet tall in her eyes.

Unexpectedly choking up, Christina leaned forward and embraced her mother, not wishing her to see the emotions unexpectedly overwhelming her.

And as she clung to Audra it became clear to Christina that she could not permit her to continue living her life in this way. I can't, I simply can't, she said to herself. All of this work and sacrifice and struggle for *me* must come to an end.

I myself will end it.

CHAPTER THIRTY-FIVE

Later that day, as she sat on the train going back to London, Christina could not expunge the image of her mother's worn face from her mind.

Furthermore, she knew that it would continue to haunt her for a very long time.

As she sat staring morosely out of the train window, she asked herself what she was going to do. One thing was certain . . . she could not allow her mother to go on supporting her after she had graduated from the Royal College of Art later that summer.

Christina sighed heavily and leaned her head against the window. It would take years to establish herself as a landscape painter, to make a name for herself, to start selling her work and earn a living. She was well aware of that, as every young artist was these days.

And so was Audra. How many times had she said in the last couple of years: "Don't be concerned, Christie. You just continue to paint your beautiful pictures and let me worry about the money and where it's coming from."

Remembering these words sent a wave of coldness through Christina, and she shivered involuntarily. That was the crux of the problem—well, at least part of it—her mother's determination to support *her* until she was famous and her paintings were in great demand.

Christina shivered again and goose bumps speckled her arms. It was as if somebody had walked over her grave. Was her mother going to have to continue working at Leeds Infirmary until she was a very old woman, in order to pay *her* rent, buy *her* clothes, put food on *her* table, pay for everything she needed in *her* life?

No, Christina said under her breath. *No*. I won't let her be a drudge anymore, to earn money for *me*. I won't. I will end it, just as I vowed I would this morning. But how? And what am I going to do? She huddled in the corner of the seat and closed her eyes. Whatever am I going to do? How will I solve this dilemma? she asked herself.

The wheels of the train turned and turned and turned relentlessly, and they seemed to pound this question into her brain. By the time the coach was pulling into King's Cross Station, she had a splitting headache and felt slightly faint. She wondered if she was coming down with the flu.

And it would be raining, Christina thought miserably as she glanced out of the window and then pulled her suitcase down off the rack above her head when the train came to a final shuddering halt.

A few seconds later, as she hurried along the platform, she decided to take a taxi home to Walton Street, even though being careful with money was now uppermost in her mind. It was absolutely imperative to Christina that she get back to the flat quickly. She needed to be enveloped in its peacefulness and solitude. She had some hard thinking to do tonight, some hard choices to make.

In the past when she had come back from Yorkshire after the holidays, Christina had been disappointed if Jane was not already ensconced in Walton Street and waiting for her. But as she let herself in tonight she was pleased that her friend was not returning from Hadley Court until Sunday evening.

Christina had to wrestle with her problems, to find a solution to each one of them. Before she settled down to do this, she rang her father in Leeds to tell him she had arrived safely. "Don't disturb Mummy," she said, after a brief chat with him. "Just give her a big hug and a kiss from me." After hanging up the phone, she unpacked her suitcase, then ran a bath.

She soaked in a hot tub for a good fifteen minutes, emptying her head of everything, endeavoring to relax, and as soon as she felt a little of the tension easing out of her aching muscles, she stepped out of the bath and dried herself hard.

Later, wrapped in a toweling robe, she sat curled up on her bed, drinking a cup of Nescafé with cream and sugar. Slowly her eyes began to roam around her room . . . there was one of her paintings on each wall, and her gaze finally settled on her latest, which she had called *Lily at Hadley*. It was an oil of the lily pond at Hadley Court, and it abounded with many shades of green . . . the murky green-blue of the pond water, the lighter, softer green of the spongy moss trailing over the edge of the pond, the polished, glossy green of the floating lily pads. The only other colors were the sharp, pure white of the single lily, its petals beautifully defined and glistening with drops of crystal dew, and the color of the light, a narrow corridor of radiance that filtered through the junglelike foliage in the background of the painting. The light held a hint of yellow, appeared to shimmer with sunlight as it touched the water, then spread out in a spraylike effect, became diffused over the lily itself.

Christina put down the cup of coffee on the bedside table and turned on her side, pressed her face into the pillow. She found it unbearable to look upon that painting, or on any of her paintings for that matter. All of her joy in her art had been suddenly snuffed out, extinguished by her immense pain.

Too high a price had been paid for it.

Audra's years of punishing, brutal toil . . . her health . . . all the little luxuries and comforts she might have bought for herself . . . a holiday occasionally . . . a new outfit.

A lump formed in Christina's throat. How long had she seen her mother wearing the same navy blue reefer coat? Winter after winter, for years and years. The tears came then, pouring out of her eyes, and she wept for her mother and for all of those lost years in Audra's life when she had been slaving away in order to give *her* a future. And she cried until there seemed to be no tears left inside her, and finally she dozed.

Christina felt as if she was falling . . . falling through dark space, and she snapped her eyes open, half sat up with a start, coming awake. She wondered where she was for a moment, feeling disoriented, and then she realized she was lying on her bed in the Walton Street flat. She glanced at the alarm clock. It was almost one in the morning. She had slept for hours, an exhausted sleep.

She turned out the light, fell back against the pillows and

closed her eyes. Her mind turned on her dilemma yet
again. It struck her that getting a job to support herself
whilst she painted would be easy enough, but that was not
the real issue. *What was crucial was the debt she owed her
mother.*

This sudden revelation was so enlightening it brought
her upright in bed again. And as she stared out into the
darkness of the room she understood then what had been
troubling her for hours: *the debt she owed her mother.* That
was it. And she must repay it.

If I do not, it will weigh heavy on my conscience all the
days of my life, she thought. And that I could not bear.

CHAPTER THIRTY-SIX

"Listen, Crowther, I know something's been troubling you
for weeks, and tonight we're going to talk," Jane announced
aggressively, pouncing on Christina the moment she
walked into the flat.

Christina stared at her, closed the door, then allowed
Jane to take her arm, to propel her into their living room.

After gently pushing her dearest friend down onto the
sofa, Jane took the chair opposite. "I am right, aren't I,
Christie?" Jane pressed. "Something *is* terribly wrong, isn't
it?"

"Yes," Christina admitted. "I *have* been wrestling with a
problem, a number of problems really, and I've wanted to
talk to you, to unburden myself, but . . ." Christina
paused, shook her head slowly, looked out the window, a
faraway expression touching her lovely eyes.

Jane sat watching her, waiting patiently now, understanding that Christina was finally going to confide in her. She
was filled with relief. Her friend had not been at all like
herself for the past two months, ever since she had
returned from Yorkshire after the Easter holidays. She had
been subdued, distracted, irritable and gloomy by turn,

and every time Jane had approached her she had denied
there was anything amiss.

Finally, Christina spoke. "First, I must apologize, Jane,"
she said, giving her a loving look. "I know I haven't been
easy to live with and that I've been snippy at times. I'm
sorry . . . forgive me?"

"Don't be so silly, there's nothing to forgive. But if it
makes you feel any better, yes, I do forgive you."

A fleeting smile crossed Christina's face. She went on,
"I've been struggling to make some decisions, and I didn't
want to talk to you until I had."

Jane returned Christina's long thoughtful look but made
no comment.

"I've decided to give up my art," Christina said softly.

"You can't be serious!" Jane shouted, sitting bolt upright.

"Yes, I am."

"I won't let you!" Jane bellowed.

Christina shook her head vehemently. "You can't stop
me. And anyway, listen who's talking. *You* told me six
months ago that *you* were going to give up *your* art to
become a scenic designer. I distinctly remember you telling
me that you had no intention of starving in a garret in the
faint hope that somebody would buy one of your paintings
one day. In fact, you went on to add that art lovers who had
money to spend bought only big-name artists, such as
Renoir, Van Gogh, Monet, Picasso, et cetera, et cetera, et
cetera."

"But you're better than I am!"

Christina ignored this remark. She said, "Several classmates—Jamie Angers, Danielle Forbes and Patricia
Smith—are going into other areas of art—textile design,
interior design, costume and scenic design, like you are."

Jane repeated, "But *you* are better than *we* are." Her
deep-violet eyes swept the room, and she waved her hand
at two of Christina's paintings hanging on the walls. "Look!
Just look! How can you give *that* up?"

"Very easily," Christina said, her voice so low it was
hardly audible. "Since it's costing a woman's life."

"*Whose life?*" Jane cried.

"*My mother's.*"

Christina did not give Jane a chance to respond to this. She began to speak slowly and carefully, and she explained everything to Jane, recounting the history of Audra's background, the years of hard work and sacrifice on her behalf. And when Christina had finally finished, Jane had tears in her eyes.

And Christina continued, "You see, Jane, I don't believe I could convince her to stop working, even after I graduate later in the summer. She'll insist on supporting me until my paintings start selling. She's stubborn, implacable really. I could get a job, earn a living whilst I paint, and send the money she sends me back to her. And I suppose I could eventually convince her that I can stand on my own two feet, and so put an end to her toiling. But none of that is quite good enough for me, Janey."

"I don't think I'm following you, Christie."

"It's simply not enough for me to say to her: *Thank you, I can look after myself now, Mother.*" Christina shook her head. "No. I have a terrible need, a compelling need, to bring ease and comfort to her life. I want to give her the kind of luxuries she's never known. And the kind of luxuries I'm thinking about cost money . . . oodles and oodles of money. As a struggling artist it would take years and years to earn enough to give her those things. I don't have time; I want her to have them as quickly as possible, whilst she's still young enough to enjoy them."

"But how are you going to make your pots and pots of money?" Jane asked, looking at her in bafflement.

"I'm going into business—that's where the money is . . . and I mean *business* with a capital B. I'm going to become a fashion designer, but I aim to be a rich and famous fashion designer—and very very quickly."

"But how are you going to get started?"

"Actually with your help."

"*My help.*"

"Your mother's really, if you'll give me your permission to talk to her about this project."

"Of course you can talk to her. But how can Mummy help?"

Christina leaned forward, sudden enthusiasm filling her

eyes, extinguishing the worry of earlier. "She's constantly after me to make her one of my hand-painted silk dresses, and she told me only a few weeks ago that she could sell them like hot cakes to her friends, if only I had a secret hoard of them tucked away somewhere. She was laughing when she said that—about her friends, I mean—but I bet some of them would be interested in buying from me. You know, at that party your mother gave for her American agent, both Polly Lamb and Lady Buckley were admiring of my hand-painted silk jacket. They both wanted to know where I'd bought it. Don't you see, Janey, my hand-painted evening clothes are very original, my *exclusive* design, and they *would* be a beginning. Later on, I could make my tailored suits . . . everyone so admires those."

"You're right!" Jane exclaimed. "You *must* talk to Mummy, get her measurements, and then design the dress for her. And I'm sure she won't mind if you approach her friends, especially those who were so interested at the cocktail party."

"Oh, I am glad you agree! However, there's a slight problem." Christina threw Jane a worried glance. "Do you think your mother would give me half the money in advance? You know, pay half the price of the dress before I deliver it? And get her friends who order dresses to do the same? If they did, it would help me immensely. I could use the money to buy the fabrics and the special paint I need."

"Of course Mummy will pay up front, and she'll jolly well make sure her friends do too." Jane sat back, looking confident, then screwed up her mouth in a thoughtful way. "But that's not the real solution, Christie. If you're going into the fashion business and want it to become *big* business, then you must have working capital."

Christina laughed hollowly. "Don't I know it . . . however, I'm afraid I don't have a bean to my name."

"Oh but I do!" Jane announced gleefully. "I have the five thousand pounds that Granny Manville left me, and the money's just sitting there in Lloyds Bank earning a bit of interest that's worth tiddlywinks. I'm going to lend you my five thousand pounds!"

"Jane, that's truly a wonderful gesture, but I couldn't possibly borrow money from you," Christina protested.

"You're going to take it . . . I shall *force* you to take it. If you have a bit of decent capital behind you, the business will grow much faster, and things will run better. You could take on a seamstress, maybe even two, and also find small premises."

"Yes, you're right. As a matter of fact, I had made those sorts of plans," Christina remarked, standing up, walking over to the fireplace. She ran her hand over her mouth, pondering for a moment. "Of course, I hadn't intended to branch out like that until next year, when I'd already made a little money." Christina directed her steady, smokey gaze at Jane. "If you lend me your five thousand pounds, I could do it sooner, that's true. So—thank you, I accept your offer, and I'm very grateful, Janey darling." She went over to Jane's chair, bent down and hugged her.

Jane immediately sprang to her feet, hugged Christina in return, her face wreathed in smiles. Then she thrust out her hand. "Shake, partner. I'll draw the money out of my savings account tomorrow morning first thing, and *voilà*, you'll be in business!"

They stood in the center of the floor, shaking hands and grinning broadly at each other.

Jane said, "And I'll help you any other way I can, rustle up business—" Jane broke off and her face fell.

"What's the matter?" Christina asked.

"How on earth will you break this news to your mother? She'll be devastated when you tell her that you're giving up painting. Oh my God, Christie, she'll be dreadfully upset."

"Yes, I know," Christina agreed, sounding suddenly gloomy. "Don't think I haven't wrestled with that problem for weeks, because I have. And I've come to the conclusion that it's better I don't tell her anything at all right now. Once I've graduated in August, I shall let her think that I'm painting away, and about four or five months after that, let's say around Christmas, I'll tell her I've sold some of my work and that I can start supporting myself."

"Do you think she'll believe you?" Jane asked.

"I hope so, Janey, I sincerely hope so."

CHAPTER THIRTY-SEVEN

Artistic talent was not the only thing that Christina had inherited from Audra.

She had her mother's penchant for hard work, her physical stamina and energy, her stubbornness and her determination to succeed at whatever she did.

And all of these characteristics came into play in the first six months she was in business, and they were fundamental to her extraordinary success in this relatively short period of time.

Christina also discovered that she had a good head for business, something she had not realized she possessed, and this too played a large role in her rise to stardom in the world of haute couture.

Even so, perhaps her greatest strength was her gift for translating art into fashion, in the form of the exquisite, elaborately painted evening gowns and coats and jackets which were to become her lasting trademark and which would always be in demand throughout her career.

Jane said to her one afternoon, "Fortuny became renowned for his pleated-silk Delphos gowns, Chanel for her cardigan suits, Dior for his New Look and Balenciaga for his perfect cutting. *You* are going to be known for your translation of art into couture, for your incredible paintings on silk. Those gowns will soon become classics, just like Poiret's beaded evening gowns. People are going to keep your dresses for years and years to come, Christie, my pet."

Christina accepted this compliment from her friend and partner, knowing that she was speaking from the heart. Then she suddenly broke into laughter and exclaimed, "I shall also be remembered for my ability to work eighteen hours a day, seven days a week, for weeks and weeks and weeks on end."

"Yes, that's true," Jane admitted, grinning at her. "You *have* worked like a galley slave these last few months, but let's face it, the effort was worth it. We're inundated with orders—" Jane gave Christina an amused look. "When I told Mummy you were toiling in the salt mines these days, she said that surely I must mean the gold mines! And listen, talking of the orders piling up, shouldn't we try to find another seamstress?"

Christina nodded. "Yes, and the word is already out. Elise and Germaine are asking around amongst their friends in the French community, and I'm sure they'll dig somebody up pretty quickly."

"I hope they do; otherwise *we'll* be the ones sitting at the sewing machines, not to mention the handwork. Which would be all we need after painting the damn things!"

Christina said, "Listen, I'm very grateful to you for helping with those mandarin sleeves on the two chiffons for Mrs. Bolton." She eyed her friend with amusement. "You've got pink paint all over your nose . . . still, you really do do the best butterflies in town."

Jane giggled, felt her nose. "I'm glad to help. I just wish I could do more in the business for you. I feel sort of useless to you most of the time. . . ."

"Don't be silly; you're invaluable, Jane! You work on the accounts, do a bit of everything really, and furthermore, without you there would be no business. Don't let's forget your five thousand pounds."

"It's a good investment, Crowther. Aren't I the shrewd one, backing *you*." Jane rolled her eyes villainously, then went to empty the coffee pot in the small kitchen adjoining the office.

Christina leapt to her feet, stretched and walked over to the window, stood looking out into the backyard behind "the factory," as she called their premises. She had found it in August, not long after graduating from the Painting School of the Royal College of Art. Previously a green-grocer's shop and living quarters, the building was located at the far end of the King's Road; and aside from its reasonable rent, she considered it to be perfect for her needs for several reasons.

There was a great deal of natural light coming in through the windows, which was essential for the painting of the fabrics and the sewing of the garments; then again, the space was more than adequate, even allowed for growth, since the living quarters attached offered plenty of room for additional staff if and when they were required.

The shop part, where vegetables had been sold until very recently, had been transformed into a small reception area. Here clients could wait to be measured and fitted. Christina and Jane had painted all of the interiors white, except that for the reception room they had used a soft pearl-gray paint on the walls here and had hung a cafe curtain of gray watered silk across the window fronting onto the street. It prevented pedestrians from looking inside, offered a degree of privacy to the waiting clients. Dulcie had given them an oriental rug, several chairs, a table and a lamp, all castoffs from Hadley Court, and with the addition of a couple of potted plants and some of their own drawings on the walls, the girls had created a cheerful effect.

The living room behind the shop had been turned into a general office; upstairs, one bedroom had become the sewing room, a second smaller bedroom was the fitting room, while the third and largest bedroom was the studio where Christina worked. It was here that she painted the fabrics for the evening clothes, and where Jane and a couple of their former classmates helped her out at times by painting sleeves. Since the major artwork on the gowns and coats was signed by Christina, she would permit no one else to do this.

Now, as she stood staring out of the window on this gray March afternoon in 1955, the hand-painted fabrics were very much on her mind. She swung to face Jane and said, "Listen, I know we're making a great deal of money with the evening clothes, but I do think I have to start designing other garments and expand the line."

"I've been expecting you to say that . . . the painting is very time-consuming, Christie. I think you *must* always make the hand-painted clothes, they are your trademark after all, but perhaps you can cut down on them a little."

"Yes, and I'll start designing the tailored suits and dresses your mother admires so much . . . she's a good judge of what will sell, Janey."

"That's true, and talking of my mama, I had better love you and leave you," Jane murmured, rising to her feet. "She'll be mad if I'm late for my appointment with her and Gregory Joynson, and I do have to dash home and change first. So, Crowther, aren't you going to wish me luck?"

"Of course I am, and I know he'll like your preliminary costume designs . . . they are out of this world."

Jane gave her a sly wink as she picked up her handbag and coat. "It's a good job the star likes them, isn't it? Thank God for my mother, the actress, who is such an advocate of nepotism." Pausing at the door, Jane added, "And don't stay here burning the midnight oil, Crowther, you're starting to look tired."

"No, I won't. See you back at Walton Street later."

Once she was alone, Christina went upstairs and turned on all of the powerful overhead lights which she had had installed in the big studio so she could work at night. She looked at the fabric she had finished painting that morning and nodded her head in satisfaction.

The painting was of white calla lilies on black chiffon, and she had worked on the large piece of fabric before she had started to design the actual dress. This she planned to do tomorrow, and she would design and cut the dress to fit the painted motif. She often adopted this method; other times, she would create the syle of the dress or gown or coat, make the *toile*, cut the front and back panels and then paint her flowers within the framework of the garment. She never limited herself, always left herself open to her art, and in a sense she let the art dictate the style of the piece of clothing. For this reason none of her hand-painted clothes were ever alike.

Christina checked several other fabrics, then returned to her office downstairs, where she sat down at her desk. Pulling a piece of writing paper toward her, she started a letter to her parents. She always wrote them once a week and phoned every Sunday without fail, and her weekly letter was due today.

She sighed to herself as she filled the pages with lies . . . lies about the paintings she was selling . . . lies about her social activities . . . lies about her life in

general. She had to invent because she had no personal life
at all at the moment, and no boyfriend either, since her last
rather lame romance with a fellow student had fizzled out,
like the others in the last few years.

Putting her elbow on the desk, resting her head on her
hand, Christina racked her brains for something exciting to
make up, to recount to her mother. Audra so loved hearing
about her dazzling social life with Jane and the Sedgewicks
and the other celebrated people she met at their parties.

Leaning back in the chair, she put down the pen,
thinking suddenly of Dulcie Manville. What a good friend
she had been, and how sweet she had been to her parents
when they had come to London for her graduation. Jane
had moved out of the Walton Street flat, had gone back to
her parents' Mayfair home for a few days, so that Vincent
and Audra could stay with her. They had enjoyed being
with her, and their trip had been an enormous success all
around.

The Sedgewicks had given a party for Jane and her to
celebrate their graduation. Dulcie had seemed taken aback
when she had met her father, and now Christina smiled to
herself as she remembered Dulcie's reaction. She had taken
her to one side and remarked, "You might have told me
your father looked like Robert Taylor, Christie. My goodness, if he were an actor, his face would be his fortune, my
dear." Later that evening, when she had repeated the
comment to her parents, her father had looked tickled to
death, but her mother had seemed put out, even irritated,
and she had known then that her mother was terribly
jealous of Vincent.

Those two, Christina muttered under her breath, reaching for the pen again. I'm always on a roller coaster ride
with them, and they're either at each other's throats or in
each other's arms. She thought of her parents with a sudden
rush of warmth and affection. She loved them both very
much, and she had always tried to walk a line between
them, doing a balancing act in a sense, endeavoring not to
take sides, not wishing to hurt either one. And I think I've
succeeded, she added to herself as she attempted to finish
her letter of lies. But they're only white lies, she thought.

It was nine o'clock when Christina finally left "the

factory" and headed down the King's Road in the direction of Sloane Square. Her thoughts still lingered on her mother as she walked along at a brisk pace. She had managed to convince Audra not to send any more money, by vehemently insisting that her work was now selling well. But what troubled Christina was that Audra was still working at Leeds Infirmary. "She won't listen to me, lass," her father had said when she had tackled him about it during the Christmas holidays. "Your mother's always had a mind of her own, and I'd be the last one to make her change it." Audra had not listened to her, either, and she had eventually let the matter drop.

Well, at least I have the satisfaction of knowing she is keeping the money she earns for herself, Christina thought, dropping the letter in the box at the post office in Sloane Square. It's a huge relief to know she's no longer working simply to support me.

Ever since she had given up her landscapes, Christina had not thought too much about this move. As far as she was concerned, her decision was irrevocable, and she did not harbor any regrets. Carving a niche for herself in the world of high fashion, and in a big, big way, had now become the most powerful motivating force in her life. Christina believed that only by making money, vast amounts of it, could she repay her immense debt to her mother by surrounding her with comfort and every luxury imaginable. And she hoped soon to be able to do this.

Now, as she hurried along Sloane Street, tightening her headscarf against the March wind, Christina thought of the large order for clothes she had received from the actress Miranda Fowler. The star was leaving in three months for New York, where she was to appear in a Broadway play, and had asked Christina to make as many evening clothes as she could for her.

How ever will I get them finished in time, Christina wondered, as she let herself into the flat on Walton Street. And over a sandwich and a glass of milk she started to make notes that night, focusing on the designs with her usual concentration.

* * *

In the next few days it seemed to Christina that inspiration dwelt in her fingertips.

Her sketching pad was soon filled with the first early drawings for the Miranda Fowler wardrobe, and ideas flowed out of her without cease as she visualized the clothes in her fertile imagination. Forms, shapes, styles, colors, flower formations, fabrics, embroideries . . . all jostled for prominence in her head. Within ten days she had edited her initial ideas and sketches, selected her favorites, completed the drawings and started to pick the materials she would use.

For several days chiffons, silks, satins, brocades, crepes and georgettes swirled around her in a dizzying array of colors. Slowly these, too, were edited down until she had settled on silk, chiffon and georgette for the evening dresses, heavy satin for evening pajamas and a long evening coat, brocade for two jackets to wear with silk pants.

When the actress came to have her measurements taken, she was delighted with the drawings and fabrics; Christina explained that if she was to create a full wardrobe of evening clothes for her, not all of them could be hand-painted. The new client said this was acceptable.

Christina worked around the clock, whilst the two French seamstresses sewed like demons to finish the wardrobe for the celebrated musical comedy star. Several weeks after she had commenced work on the clothes, Christina hired another Frenchwoman, a friend of Germaine's, called Lucie James. Lucie came highly recommended, and aside from being an excellent needlewoman, she had a fine reputation as a cutter and had worked at the Balenciaga salon before the war and her marriage to an Englishman in 1938. Lucie had previously worked for Mr. Michael, the couturier with a salon in Carlos Place. It did not take Christina long to realize that she had a real find in Lucie. She knew Lucie would take some of the burdens of cutting the garments away from her, which meant she could devote herself to the painting.

It had been a supreme effort on all their parts, and a monumental achievement, to have the clothes ready by the date Miranda Fowler had specified. In point of fact,

Christina was a little ahead of time, and early one warm evening toward the end of May, she took Jane upstairs to see the rack of clothes in the studio.

Flipping the switch, flooding the studio with light, she pulled the sheet off the rack and cried, "The unveiling . . . ta-da ta-da! And before I show you each elegant and exquisite creation, let me just say this . . . once Miranda Fowler has paid me, I'll be able to finally repay you your five thousand pounds. Isn't that wonderful news, Janey?"

"Yes, it is, but there's no real hurry," Jane said, and then she went into raptures over the stunningly beautiful outfits.

When the two girls had returned to the office, Christina said, "Look, I'm taking my three lovely women to dinner tonight, a special treat for them, for all the hard work they've put in. Why don't you come with us, Janey? After all, you're part of the family."

"Oh that's lovely of you, but I really am whacked," Jane said. "I've been pushing myself hard on those costumes for the play, and I've got to solve the problem with those blasted ruffs tonight. They won't stay stiff, and starch is so scratchy against the actors' necks. Oh God, why does my mother have the urge to play Elizabeth Tudor?"

Christina laughed at the look on her face, and pointed out, "It might do you good to come with us . . . it would take your mind off those ruffs."

Jane shook her head. "Thanks, but no thanks. I shall do some work, make a fried-egg sandwich and go to bed early." She eyed Christina dourly and her pretty young mouth twisted in a grimace. "Romantic life we both lead these days, isn't it?"

"We'll make up for it when we're both rich and famous."

"You bet we will," Jane said with a leer. "And listen, Crowther, don't come banging and clattering into the flat tonight. I really meant it when I said I intend to go to bed early."

"You can sleep late tomorrow—it's Saturday."

"Fat chance of that." Jane picked up her briefcase. "Have a lovely meal, darling."

* * *

It was a few minutes after eleven when Christina walked down Walton Street that night, after taking her three employees to dinner.

She was suddenly feeling weary.

It had been a hard few months and for the first time in ages she had relaxed during the evening, had finally let go; the rich meal at Ox on the Roof restaurant and the red wine had also had an enervating effect on her. She could not wait to get undressed and climb into bed.

Remembering that Jane had said she was going to sleep early, Christina could not help wondering why all of their living room lights were blazing. As she drew to a stop in front of the house where they lived on the top floor, she looked up at the windows, frowning to herself.

I expect she's forgotten to turn them off, she muttered, unlocking the street door, climbing the steep flight of stairs to their landing.

Christina was fumbling with her key chain, standing outside the door of the flat when it suddenly flew open.

Surprised, she jumped and glared at Jane. "Honestly, you scared me—" she began and stopped when Jane grabbed her arm.

Jane hissed, "Your parents are here. And your mother is absolutely *furious* . . . she can't take her eyes off your paintings hanging on our walls."

"Oh my God," Christina whispered back, blanching. "How stupid I am."

CHAPTER THIRTY-EIGHT

The coldness in her mother's startling blue eyes blinded her.

She hesitated in the doorway. All of her strength ebbed out of her and she was gripped by a terrible internal shaking.

Her parents sat together on the sofa. They both looked as if they had turned to granite.

No one spoke.

Somewhere behind her in the hall, Jane hovered nervously.

She could move neither forward nor backward. She had turned to stone like her parents.

At last she found her voice. "Hello, Mummy, Daddy . . . this is a surprise."

"Apparently so," Audra responded in an icy tone that matched her eyes.

Christina swallowed.

Vincent glared.

Audra suddenly sprang up, startling them.

She began to move around the room rapidly, pausing briefly at each one of Christina's paintings, saying their names in a clipped, cold voice, "*Elms in Winter . . . Sky at Gunnerside . . . Houghley Beck . . . Edith's Delphiniums,* and through the open door of your bedroom—" She snapped off the end of her sentence, pivoted to face Christina, and glaring at her, she finished, "I can see *Lily at Hadley.* You told me you had *sold* all of these paintings. You lied to me, Christina. *Why?* And how are you managing to live? How are you paying your bills? Something is wrong, very, very wrong here. I demand to know what's going on at once! *At once, do you hear me!*"

Christina moved forward, galvanized by her mother's angry words, knowing she had to get this over with once and for all.

She drew to a stop next to Audra. She took a deep breath. "Mummy, I have something to tell you, something I've been wanting to tell you for ages. . . ." She looked down at her mother, so fragile, and she was instantly intimidated by the force of Audra's personality, the indomitability reflected in her face. She could not go on. Her nerve failed her.

Audra's bright blue eyes impaled hers. "I'm waiting, Christina."

In a great rush of words, Christina blurted out, "I've given up my painting. I've become a fashion designer. I decided it wasn't worth it, being a struggling artist. You see,

I wanted to make money. My clothes are lovely, beautiful really; I know you'll like them—"

"You gave up your art to become a *dressmaker!*" Audra gasped, stunned, stupefied. She gaped at Christina. All of the color drained out of her face and her eyes were stark with incredulity. "You gave up your art!" she repeated. "You threw away your great gift for creating beauty for . . . a *commercial* venture. I can't believe it! I just can't believe it!"

Audra shook her head from side to side as if denying this awful knowledge.

She suddenly cried, "And after all I did for you! After all I did to give you your art! Oh my God, when I think of all my years of grueling work and sacrifice and scrimping and scraping, and going without to give to you, and giving and giving of myself until I had nothing left to give, and always putting you first, always putting you before your father, neglecting him—"

Audra was unable to continue.

She turned to Vincent. A look of excruciating pain mingled with overwhelming sorrow settled on her face, and her eyes, dark with hurt now, filled with sudden tears. "Oh Vincent—" She reached out for him blindly, the tears falling unchecked, blurring her vision.

He was by her side in a flash.

His arms went around her, and he held her protectively against his body, one hand patting her shoulder, comforting. He looked down at her and he sighed, ever so lightly, and then he lifted his head.

Vincent leveled his gaze at his daughter. He stared as if seeing her for the first time.

Christina flinched under his hard, cold scrutiny. Her mouth began to tremble.

Disdain flashed onto Vincent's handsome face, and his eyes were steely green and uncompromising. "You've just broken your mother's heart," he said in a voice that shook.

Without another word he turned his back on Christina and led the weeping Audra from the room.

Christina stared after her parents speechlessly. And then

she ran forward, caught up with them in the hall. "Daddy . . . wait," she cried, reaching out, grasping his sleeve.

He shook her hand off, a certain harshness in his movements, and glanced over his shoulder. "Don't *you* Daddy me," he snapped. "I've had enough of *you* for one night, Christina. I never thought I'd live to see you hurt your mother so cruelly."

Christina recoiled at his words, and she remained rooted in the doorway of the flat as her mother and father crossed the landing and went down the stairs together.

From behind her, Jane whispered, "Oh God, Christie, that was simply ghastly. Are you all right?"

When Christina did not respond, Jane put her arm around her dearest friend and drew her inside. She pushed the front door closed with her other hand, walked Christina through the hall and into the living room, pressed her down onto the sofa.

Christina began to shake uncontrollably, and she looked at Jane helplessly. "I must go after them," she began and immediately burst into tears.

"Oh darling, don't, don't," Jane murmured, her voice consoling as she lowered herself onto the sofa and took Christina's hand in hers. "You can't go after them, and it wouldn't do any good, not tonight." Jane gave her a quick hug and rose, hurried out.

She returned a moment later with a large handkerchief. "Here, wipe your eyes," she said, giving it to Christina, "and I'll get us a drink. I think we could both use a brandy."

After mopping her eyes and blowing her nose, Christina accepted the cognac from Jane, took a long swallow. She said, "Perhaps I'd better ring them in a little while. They must be staying in the studio flat at Theo's; they have *carte blanche* to stay there any time they—"

"Oh no, they're at a hotel," Jane interjected and grimaced. "Oh botheration, what an idiot *I* am! I should have asked your father which hotel, when he mentioned it."

"Oh Jane . . ." She fell back against the sofa, her misery growing more acute by the moment. "I simply assumed they were at the house in Chester Street; now I'll *never* find them this weekend."

"Perhaps they'll phone you tomorrow," Jane said, her face brightening at this thought. "Oh yes, I'm sure they will."

"I doubt it very much. Mummy is devastated and my father's furious with me." Christina rubbed her hand over her weary eyes and asked, "Tell me what happened this evening."

"They arrived at about ten-fifteen. I'd gone to bed earlier, but the phone kept ringing. The calls were stupid too . . . first Gregory Joynson called to complain that one of my costumes for Mummy clashed with a pillow on the stage—he's such a nit. Then she rang up, worrying about those damned Elizabethan ruffs. I'd no sooner hung up on her, when Harry Manderville phoned to invite us to some stupid arts ball next month. In sheer desperation I finally took the phone off the hook. I promptly fell asleep. The next thing I knew, the intercom was buzzing for all it was worth. It was your father, telling me they were downstairs. Naturally, I asked them to come up—what else *could* I do? Besides, I was half asleep, and I didn't even think of the paintings."

"Oh Jane, I don't blame *you* for anything!" Christina exclaimed. "Of course you had to ask them upstairs. But did they say why they were in London? They don't usually take it into their heads to come up to town, not just like that."

"Your father apparently had the brilliant idea of bringing your mother to London to see you—as a special treat. They wanted to surprise you; that's why they didn't let you know they were coming."

"If only they had . . . we could have taken the paintings down, stored them at the factory, and they would never have been any the wiser."

"Only too true," Jane agreed and threw Christina an apologetic look. "I must admit, I do feel a bit responsible. If I hadn't had the phone off the hook, they would have got through to me . . . you see, they had been trying earlier. When it was constantly busy, they went to have supper somewhere, tried to ring us again later. They were worried and decided to come over when the operator told them the line was out of order. Oh hell, if only I'd spoken to them, I could have reassured them that everything was all right, prevented them from coming here until tomorrow, and certainly I could have done the necessary and removed the paintings."

"Oh Jane, please don't feel responsible. *Please*. If I hadn't taken the women out to dinner, I would have been here myself. Life is always full of *if onlys* and *buts* and *maybes*. You know that as well as I do."

Christina's eyes roamed around the living room, and she remarked quietly, "I suppose my mother spotted the paintings right away."

"Do you have to ask! Of course she did; you know she doesn't miss a trick, and who *could* miss these? They're larger than life. I realized immediately what a couple of fools *we'd* been, and I rushed to the kitchen, put the kettle on . . . I felt violently sick, and the only thing I could think of doing was making them a cup of tea. It was a jolly strained hour too, being here with them, waiting for you to return."

"Did she ask you a lot of questions—about what I was doing?"

"Not one, and neither did your father."

Christina looked at her watch. "I keep telling myself they'll ring, but that's just wishful thinking on my part. I know they won't."

"They will tomorrow, you'll see."

Christina nodded, knowing Jane was only trying to make her feel better. She also knew her friend was wrong.

Christina could not sleep.

She did not even try. She lay in bed thinking about her mother and waited for the morning to come.

At seven o'clock she snapped on the bedside lamp, drew her telephone book toward her and found Mike Lesley's number. During the dawn hours it had struck her that if anyone knew where her parents were staying, it would be

Uncle Mike. She dialed the Leeds number quickly, now that it was a reasonable hour to telephone him.

"Doctor Lesley here," he said, answering immediately, sounding wide awake.

"Hello, Uncle Mike. It's Christie."

"Yes, I know. Good morning, dear."

"I'm sorry to disturb you so early, but I thought you might know which hotel Mummy and Daddy are staying at. We had a bit of an upset last night and—"

"Yes, your father told me all about it a short while ago."

"*Oh.* So you must know where they are."

"Yes, they were staying at Brown's, Christie. But your father called me about half an hour ago, and they were just checking out to drive back to Yorkshire. You won't reach them now."

"Oh damn," she exclaimed, "and I was hoping to see them this morning, to explain . . ." Her disappointment choked her, and she left her sentence dangling.

Mike said, "Perhaps it's just as well they've left, Christie dear. I think you'll be far better off talking to your mother later. In a few weeks, when she has calmed down."

"Oh no, I don't think so, Uncle Mike. I have to talk to her in the next *day* or two. She was so distressed last night and terribly hurt. Didn't Daddy explain everything to you?"

"Yes, he did, Christie."

"So you know that I've given up my painting, that I've become a designer?"

"Yes."

"And you don't approve either?"

"It's your life, Christina, and you must live it as you see fit . . . and I'm sure you have your reasons for doing what you've done, good reasons."

"Oh Uncle Mike, I do, I do. And I must make Mummy understand them. You see, I couldn't let her go on supporting me, I really couldn't. I have to take care of myself from now on. The fact that she was still slaving at the Infirmary to give me financial help was just intolerable to me. I have a real talent for fashion designing, and I saw a chance to make a success out of it, to make money. Not only money for me, but money for my mother. I do want to repay my great debt to her."

"Oh Christie . . ." There was a silence at the other end of the telephone and Mike sighed heavily. He said softly, "Your mother didn't do what she did looking for a reward, Christie. Her reward is her pride in you."

"That may be enough for Mummy, but it certainly isn't enough for me, not by a long shot. I want her to have so much more—I want her to have the best of everything money can buy actually, and I won't rest until she has it!"

"No, I don't suppose you will," he said with dawning comprehension. "There's too much of Audra in you. But I wonder if *she* will ever understand that you are repeating the pattern."

"What do you mean?" Christina asked, tightening her grip on the receiver. "I'm not following you, Uncle Mike."

Mike Lesley did not answer this in a direct way. Instead he said, "Years ago your father came to talk to me about your mother; he was worried about her health, you see, worried about the way she was working, pushing herself to the limit. It was the spring of 1939. I remember the year very well, because war broke out that September. Anyway, your father said that what your mother was doing to ensure that you had a glittering future was abnormal. Laurette said she didn't think that abnormal was quite the right word. And then she told your father and me that we were witnessing an act of will. Yes, an act of will so powerfully motivated and so selfless it was awesome to witness."

Tears sprang into Christina's eyes and she blinked, brushed them away with her fingertips. She said, "And it was exactly that, wasn't it?"

"Yes, my dear. And now you are committing your own act of will, and your mother won't be able to stop you, just as your father was never able to stop her."

"But why do you say she won't understand, Uncle Mike?"

"Because she'll never accept the fact that you've given up your art in order to pay your debt to her. She would find that absolutely preposterous. And if you tell her that this is the reason why you have gone into business, her answer will be very simple, Christie. She'll insist you go back to painting pictures because she doesn't want the best that money can buy."

Christina was silent. "Yes," she said after a short pause, "perhaps you're right. But I have to do what I believe I have to do."

It was his turn to be silent.

Waiting, Christina heard him sigh deeply at the other end of the phone.

"So be it," he said at last. "And God bless you, Christie."

CHAPTER THIRTY-NINE

"I want to go big, and I really mean *big*," Christina said. "And I want to do it at once. *Now!*"

Startled, Jane stared at her, removed a couple of pins from her mouth and waved them at Christina. "I do wish you wouldn't make your important announcements when I have these between my teeth. I almost swallowed them."

"Oh sorry."

Jane grinned. "Okay, so you want to go big. I'm all ears; tell me more, Crowther."

"I fully intend to in a minute," Christina replied, walking across the studio to the corner where Jane was working on a costume for Dulcie.

It was a scorching hot July afternoon, and in an effort to beat the heat Jane had tied her pink cotton shirt under her bust to reveal a bare midriff, exchanged her skirt for a pair of white cotton shorts, discarded her shoes and stockings, and swept her long, wheat-colored hair on top of her head.

Christina could not help thinking how pretty her friend looked, despite the somewhat messy hairdo, makeup that had streaked and lipstick that had been chewed off. Her admiration and deep affection for Jane Sedgewick welled up in her. How lucky she was to have her friendship.

"How about a glass of lemonade?" Christina asked, putting the tray she was carrying down on the table, unscrewing the cap of the bottle. "You must be parched, Jane; it's sweltering in here."

"I know, I think we have to buy another fan. And thanks, I will have some of that stuff." Jame stepped away from the dressmaker's dummy, eyed the Tudor-style theatrical costume she was working on, then swung around, sat down on a stool nearby and took the glass of lemonade from Christina. "So go on," she said, "tell me about your plans. Knowing you, I bet you've got them all worked out."

"Sort of," Christina admitted and perched on the end of the table. "We've been in business for ten months and we've done extremely well. But we could sell twice as many clothes if we could produce them. I think we should expand, go big, as I just said."

"How?"

"Hire more cutters and seamstresses, as well as office staff, and take showrooms in the West End."

"That'll cost money. Even if you keep my five thousand pounds in the business, that won't be enough, Christie."

"I know. I need about fifty thousand actually."

Jane whistled. "As much as that! *Gosh!* But yes, I think you're right."

"I know I am," Christina asserted. "I've worked it all out on paper. Aside from the salaries, we'd have to carry plenty of stock—fabrics, other supplies, and then of course there would be the rent of the showroom. I've looked at several in the last week, and they're expensive, especially those in Mayfair, which is where I feel we should be."

"You do mean *big* when you say big, don't you?"

"Yes, and *fancy*. About the fifty thousand, Jane, I think we could borrow it from the bank, even though neither of us has any collateral, if your mother would be our guarantor—you know, guarantee the loan or the overdraft, if that's what it's going to be."

Jane shook her head, frowned hard, and bit her lip. "No, I don't think that's a good idea—going to the bank, I mean. I'd rather borrow the money from Mummy, and I think she'd give us at least half. I know Aunt Elspeth would cough up the rest, because she once asked me if you needed money for the business. So I know she'd go for it, and she is a great fan of you and your clothes."

"Jane, that would be wonderful if they would do it . . . do you honestly think they'd take a gamble on me?"

"Yes, I do. Besides, backing you is hardly a gamble, and we all know that."

"I'd prefer to make it a loan, repayable with interest, of course, if that'd be all right with them. We don't need too many partners, do we?"

"No, you're right there. Not that Mummy or Aunt Elspeth would interfere, but still, I agree with you, I prefer they lend us the money." Jane jumped off the stool.

"Let's go down to the office and phone Mummy now," she cried, full of tremendous enthusiasm for Christina's latest scheme. "I know she's at home learning her lines, and once we've spoken to her, I'll call Aunt Elspeth in Monte Carlo. Oh this *is* exciting, Christie, and I know they'll jump at it. You'll see . . . by next week we'll really be rolling. Rolling in a *big* way, just like you want, heading for the *big* time."

Jane skipped and danced across the studio, did a Highland Fling when she reached the doorway, and then tripped down the stairs singing, "We're heading for the big time, the big time, the big time."

Christina followed more sedately, laughing at her friend's exuberance and keeping her fingers crossed, praying that Jane was right.

She was.

Dulcie Manville and her sister Elspeth D'Langer provided the extra working capital Christina Crowther needed to expand her haute couture business and move to the West End.

Elspeth flew from France four days after receiving Jane's phone call. She and her sister and the girls had several meetings with Dulcie's solicitors. It was during these meetings that Dulcie and Elspeth decided that Christina needed more cushioning in case of unforeseen emergencies. And so they increased their loan to one hundred thousand pounds, by putting up fifty thousand each.

This was the amount Christina finally deposited in her business account at the bank before the month of July was out, after the necessary papers had been drawn and duly signed by everyone.

In a sense the hard part started *after* this.

Christina found she had to split herself in two.

By day she was the businesswoman. She interviewed office staff; she saw seamstresses, cutters, needlewomen who did only hand sewing and embroidery work, and hand pressers, and as always she hired on the very best in every area. Lucie James, whom she had promoted to head of the workrooms, had good advice and suggestions to make. Lucie had a great many friends in the French community in London, and it was she who introduced Giselle Roux to Christina, suggested she be taken on as head *vendeuse* in charge of the showroom. Giselle, like Lucie, was married to an Englishman, and had lived in London since 1952. An elegant and sophisticated woman in her thirties, she had been a *vendeuse* at the Pierre Balmain salon in Paris, and was experienced and responsible. Christina left the hiring of the other saleswomen to Giselle, trusting her judgment completely. And when she wasn't interviewing, and hiring staff, Christina was looking at possible showrooms, tramping through buildings throughout the West End of London, and growing more and more discouraged.

Just when she had given up hope of ever finding the right building, she stumbled on a small but elegant town house on Bruton Street in Mayfair.

The real estate agent showed her around the house on a muggy, drizzly Saturday morning late in August, but despite the weather, Christina saw at once how airy the rooms were, especially on the upper floors.

She rented it immediately, knowing it was ideal. The house was in good condition, needed little work.

There was plenty of space, on six floors, for offices, workrooms and a studio for herself, plus two large reception rooms which opened off a central hall and would be perfect for the showrooms.

These were on the second floor of the house, had high ceilings, fireplaces, tall French windows opening onto little balconies, and their dimensions were spacious. As she walked between the two light-filled rooms, Christina visualized how charming and elegant they would look, decorated entirely in her favorite soft shades of gray and white, with thick carpeting and shimmering crystal chandeliers dropping from the ceilings.

By night she shed the role of businesswoman, became the creative artist.

Long after everyone had left the factory on the King's Road, Christina worked on her designs for her first collection under the Christina label. It was a summer collection and she planned to present it to the public and the press at the beginning of 1956. She had only five months to create the sixty-five outfits she wanted to show, and so she knew she had her work cut out for her. This was her first collection proper, since in the past ten months she had simply shown clients sketches and fabrics, and then made the garments to measure for them.

Designing an entire line of clothes with a distinctive underlying theme was tremendously challenging to Christina, and it was the excitement, the sheer exhilaration of such a huge creative effort that fed her natural energy, kept her going at an extraordinary pace. For aside from designing the outfits themselves, she had to design or select the accessories to go with them. To her, each dress or suit or coat was not finished until it had been properly accessorized down to the last detail. She saw it as an entity.

Although Christina was thrilled that she was now being launched in the way she wanted and deriving a great deal of artistic satisfaction from her work, one thing marred her happiness. This was her estrangement from her mother and father.

After their terrible upset in May, she had telephoned them often and had been up to Yorkshire to see them, and she had written regularly. Her father had warmed up a little, but her mother was still cold and so distant that Christina had decided to take Mike Lesley's advice. In consequence, she did not divulge her real reason for giving up her life as an artist—her overwhelming desire, her genuine need, to give her mother a life of total comfort and ease as a way of repaying her debt to her.

Christina harbored the belief that she and her mother would be reconciled one day soon. She knew Audra loved her far too much to remain angry with her for very long. She also hoped that her father was already exerting some influence.

In the meantime, she was going to do her damnedest to make them proud of her.

CHAPTER FORTY

Christina stood in the hallway that linked the two reception rooms, looked first to her right and then to her left.

Each room was a replica of the other: pearl-gray walls and matching carpet, white-painted fireplaces, French crystal chandeliers and wall sconces, and antique Venetian mirrors.

The two rooms flowed into each other beautifully, just the way she had planned. She nodded in approval, appreciating the cool, calm feeling produced by the pearl gray and the hint of white. This essentially monochromatic scheme was unrelieved by any other color—and purposely so. Christina did not want anything to distract from her clothes or compete with them. Even flowers were barred from these two rooms, appeared only in hallways of the Bruton Street house.

Turning, Christina glanced at the floral arrangement on the Louis XVI console in the hall. It was composed entirely of white flowers and once again she nodded, knowing it was exactly right, perfect in this particular spot.

Moving forward, she hurried into the larger of the two rooms and looked around for the umpteenth time on this cold January day, checking every detail.

A runway now divided the room in half, and on either side of it stood rows of little gilt chairs. Christina experienced a tingle of excitement, feeling the thrill of it all. In less than an hour her first couture collection was going to be presented to the world. She took a deep breath and clasped her hands together, sudden apprehension tugging at her as she thought of the clothes she had designed.

"Mademoiselle—"

She swung around to see her head *vendeuse* hovering in the doorway that led out to the dressing rooms in the back, where the models were getting ready for the show which was due to commence at three.

"Giselle!"

"I came to wish you *bonne chance*, Mademoiselle, good luck," the Frenchwoman said, smiling at her warmly.

"Thank you, Giselle," Christina replied, also smiling, then she gave her a hard stare. "The collection *is* all right, isn't it?"

The head *vendeuse* brought her fingertips to her lips and kissed them, then blew the kiss into the air. "Not all right, Mademoiselle, superb, simply *superb*. When I was at the House of Balmain, I always told Monsieur that when there was the great excitement in the workrooms there would be the thunder in the chairs—" She paused, waved her hand at the golden rows and added confidently, "And at the House of Christina we have the excitement in the workrooms—so be assured there *will* be the great applause out here."

A young assistant dresser poked her head around the door at the far end of the room. "Sorry to interrupt, Miss Christina, but Madame Roux is needed."

"Excuse me, Mademoiselle," the head *vendeuse* said and hurried out.

Christina walked over to the fireplace and stood with her back to it. She looked down the entire room, through the hallway and into the adjoining room, her eyes following the first runway and then the second. And in her imagination she visualized the models walking, turning, swirling, halting, posing, showing off her clothes to their best advantage. She loved each garment she had designed and she could only pray that everyone else would. She asked herself how she had done it, how she had finished this collection in so short a time, and she had absolutely no idea whatsoever. Blood, toil, sweat and tears, she said under her breath, thinking of Winston Churchill's memorable line from the war years when she had been a child.

Turning around, she stared at herself in the Venetian mirror above the fireplace. She had thought she looked tired and pinched earlier, and she had put on more rouge than she normally wore. But it seemed to have been absorbed into her skin. She was pale again. Perhaps it was the black suit that was pulling the color from her face. She always needed more makeup when she wore black.

Christina stepped back, regarded herself, holding her head slightly on one side, studying the suit. Beautifully cut and tailored, it was a masterpiece of engineering. Its only adornment was a white gardenia pinned on one shoulder— the white gardenia that she had chosen to become her own special motif, her trademark.

Lifting her hand, Christina smoothed her hair.

It was then that she saw them reflected in the mirror, standing in the doorway, looking uncertain, hesitant.

For a split second she thought it was her imagination playing tricks. But of course it was not. She turned slowly, opened her mouth to say something. No words come out. She simply stood there, staring, unable to move.

Her mother took a few steps forward and then stopped abruptly. Audra said, "We had to come . . . we couldn't stay away. Not today."

"Oh Mummy—"

"Christie darling—"

Both women moved at the same time. They met in the middle of the floor.

Audra looked up at Christina and her bright blue eyes filled with tears. "I've missed you so much. . . ."

Christina reached out, put her arms around Audra, hugged her mother to her as if never to let her go. "Oh Mam, I've missed you too; you'll never know how much."

Suddenly Vincent joined them, and he put his arms around them both, and they all three cried a little, then laughed. And finally Christina stepped away and looked at her parents, and her happiness was reflected in her shining eyes, her joyous smile.

"I'm so glad you came, so very, *very* glad. It means so much to have you here." She broke off, then looked deeply into Audra's face and asked, almost in a whisper, "Have you forgiven me, Mother?"

"There's nothing to forgive, Christie," Audra answered, her voice gentle, loving. "I was angry and upset with you, and dreadfully, dreadfully hurt. But I realize now that I was wrong to cut you off in the way that I did. As your Uncle Mike said to your Daddy and me quite recently, you had to do what you had to do." A lovely smile touched Audra's mouth. "I may have given you the chance to have a better life, but I cannot live that life for you. I came to realize this, and I knew that I had to make my peace with you, darling."

Christina bent forward and kissed Audra's cheek. "Today is going to be the best day for me, now that you and Daddy are here."

Turning to Vincent, she took his arm, squeezed it affectionately, reached up and kissed his cheek. "Thank you for bringing her, Daddy, and for being here yourself. I love you both very much."

Vincent put his arm around Christina's shoulders. He said, "We love you too, Christie, and when your invitation came with your little note, I told your mother we couldn't miss this important day in your life."

CHAPTER FORTY-ONE

Christina Crowther became a superstar in the international fashion firmament overnight.

Success was so instantaneous, orders so overwhelming, she knew within the first twenty-four hours that additional space had to be found, extra help hired, more fabric ordered—and at once. There was no time to waste.

Elise, Germaine and Lucie handled all of these details, with speed and efficiency, whilst Giselle Roux and her small showroom staff coped with clients who came flooding in through the doors of the Bruton Street house.

Christina's private clientele bought extensively from the collection, as did innumerable new customers, but there were some gigantic orders from stores which not only staggered Christina but also the more experienced Giselle.

The buyer from Bergdorf Goodman in New York was so dazzled by the clothes she took almost the entire collection, as did the buyer from the Haute Couture Salon at Harte's in Knightsbridge. It was she who announced to everyone that Christina was the fashion discovery of the decade, and pointed out that there hadn't been such a sensational success and a stampede like this since Christian Dior opened his own salon in 1947 and introduced his now-famous New Look. Giselle concurred, said, "It *is* the same, *vraiment*, Mademoiselle, truly, it is." Christina believed her.

These orders represented hundreds and hundreds of thousands of pounds. Christina had become very big business in one leap from the former greengrocer's shop on the King's Road to the elegant town house in Mayfair. It was a gigantic leap.

The cause of all the excitement and furor was the collection Christina had called the Flower Line. And indeed it was exactly that, with the theme of the flower running throughout.

The evening clothes were exquisite and extraordinary, featuring all manner of flowers from the exotic orchid to the simplest kind of blooms. When her first big collection had been conceived months before, Christina had realized she could not paint every evening garment personally. It was far too time-consuming. And so she had hired several clever artists to copy her paintings, insisting on perfect duplication.

But she had also had some of her own flower paintings hand-screened onto fabrics, and these prints on romantic, floating chiffons and georgettes were as much of a sensation as the hand-painted garments. Evening and cocktail dresses made from these prints would become huge sellers and remain popular forever, earning her millions of pounds and millions of dollars over the years.

Other evening gowns of heavier-weight silk had a single

but dominant flower motif. This might be on the skirt at the back and front, on the bodice and the one shoulder; sometimes it was repeated on the skirt and the bodice. But this single flower was always heavily encrusted with jeweled embroidery and was like an enormous piece of jewelry, in point of fact. These evening gowns were also snapped up instantly, with no questions asked about the price.

All of Christina's evening clothes in the Flower Line were lavish and very feminine, and they caused most people to gasp in delight when they first set eyes on them. Colors ranged from white and delicate pastels to vivid red, yellow, sapphire and summer black, which Christina had always advocated.

The flower theme was preserved all the way and reappeared in the day wear, this time in the actual contour of the clothes.

Suits, coats and dresses boasted a slender skirt, but from the waist up, the tops were slightly oversized, as were the shoulders, but these were softly rounded, not squared off. The shape of all these garments suggested a flower on a delicate stem.

The day wear was austere in some instances, immaculately cut and tailored, often with an architectural feeling, and it was undeniably chic.

Fabrics were light and included silks, cottons, linens and light wool crepes. Colors were clear, often sharp, with many pinks and mauves and lovely English blues, and greens that ran from bright emerald to the softer lime. And each garment, whether for day or evening, was perfectly accessorized for the total look Christina insisted on presenting.

Apart from her acceptance by the public, Christina had become the darling of the press. They loved her. The fashion editors from *Vogue*, *Harper's Bazaar* and *Queen* were sophisticated women who had seen it all. None of them was readily fooled and they could as easily spot a phony as they could recognize and applaud geniune talent. They knew at once that Christina was no flash in the pan, that she would go from strength to strength.

As for the popular newspapers, they adored her too.

She was wonderful copy for them. A new discovery who was all the rage, young, immensely talented, good-looking—and from an ordinary background, a girl from the provinces. This made her specially attractive to them, since their readers could identify with her, and certainly with Vincent and Audra, who had been much photographed with her at the unveiling of her collection in January.

Christina enjoyed her success, basked in it a bit. But her feet continued to be firmly planted on the ground, and she understood deep in her heart that the best part of it all was the pride her parents had in her. She would never forget the expressions on their faces as *she* had watched *them* watching the gorgeous models parading down the runway, to the sound of the thunderous applause, under the glittering lights.

And as Jane said later that evening, after the three Crowthers had been to dinner with the three Sedgewicks, "They were beside themselves with happiness and pride, Christie. I thought they were going to burst at the seams during the show, and I do believe your father had tears in his eyes at one moment." Christina had smiled and nodded, and then she had repeated her mother's lovely words to Jane.

The words continued to echo in Christina's head weeks later. Audra had come up to her at the champagne reception after the show, had given her a half apologetic smile, and said, "This is a lot more than dressmaking, Christie. *This is art.*"

Although Christina had promised to go with Jane to the French Alps for a winter vacation in February, in the end she was only able to have a long weekend with her at the ski resort. There was too much activity at the fashion house and she could not neglect her flourishing business.

But the four days she did spend in the Alpes d'Huez with Jane were relaxing and the two girls had great fun. There were plenty of attractive admirers around to take them for cocktails in the evening or fondue suppers and sometimes dancing afterward at one of the rustic Alpine bars.

Christina did not ski and she had no intention of even trying, but she enjoyed watching the athletic Jane whiz down the slopes. Her friend was a crack skier and an expert skater. And on Sunday afternoon, as Christina sat at the open-air rink, her eyes were glued to Jane in admiration as she floated and pirouetted across the ice.

It was then that a thought struck Christina . . . the thought that women needed clothes which were relaxed and loose, to allow for ease of movement and comfort. And several new ideas for her winter collection began to germinate. This prescience, this ability to forecast coming trends, would prove to be another secret of her success. For it was her vision that lifted Christina Crowther from the ranks of the merely talented designers into the stratosphere of the truly brilliant.

The ideas which had come to her at the ice rink in the Alps immediately went onto the drawing boards in her studio at the top of the Bruton Street house, when she returned to London. Christina was aware that her winter collection had to be in production by May if it was to be ready for showing in September of that year. And so she kept her head down working hard all through the remainder of February and into March, as did Jane.

Jane's career as a costume designer was flourishing.

The clothes she had designed for her mother and the rest of the cast in *Elizabeth Regina* had been highly acclaimed, and she had gone on to do the costumes for another West End production. During the spring of 1956 she was busy at work on the entire wardrobe for a film soon to be shot at Elstree Studios, and once this was completed she was planning to go to New York for several months. She had recently signed a contract to design the costumes for a Broadway show, a musical that was apparently going to be spectacular. Not unnaturally, she considered this to be a great challenge and was looking forward to her sojourn on the other side of the Atlantic.

But in spite of all their work, the two friends managed to

have a busy social life, and in many ways this was the most
hectic spring and summer either of them had ever
experienced.

At the beginning of May, Ralph Sedgewirk invited them
to come and stay at the villa he and Dulcie had rented in
the South of France for the month of June.

"Do let's go," Jane said. "We both need a holiday, but
especially you, and Beaulieu-Sur-Mer is such a pretty
place. And listen, Crowther, after we've had a few days of
rest and recuperation, we can take a car and drive up to
Grasse, so you can investigate that perfume idea."

"Of course!" Christina exclaimed. "What a wonderful
suggestion that is, Janey. And I'd love to come. I'll ring your
father tomorrow, to thank him and accept."

For the next few weeks Christina turned her attention to
the perfume she wished to market under the Christina
label. Her name had already acquired cachet on both sides
of the Atlantic, and she knew that a perfume was an
inspired idea.

This had actually been the brainstorm of Giselle Roux,
immediately after the immense success in January. "You
must have the *parfum*, Mademoiselle," the head *vendeuse*
had told Christina. "That has always been the tradition with
the grand *couturiers* . . . Dior, Chanel, Balmain, Balenciaga, Givenchy. Yes, yes, you must do it, you must; it is
important, Mademoiselle."

"But how would I go about it?" Christina had asked. She
had seized on the idea at once, seeing its tremendous
possibilities.

"First, Mademoiselle, you must consider the fragrances
. . . the ones that give you pleasure . . . the special
scent of *les fleurs*, your favorite flowers. Perhaps the
rose . . . the lily of the valley . . . the jasmine. Then
you must go to Grasse, Mademoiselle. Here is the center of
the French *parfumerie* industry, and here they will create
for you the special Christina *parfum*, Mademoiselle."

Christina had thanked her head *vendeuse*, and had
promised to look into it. She had been far too busy
designing her winter collection to follow through immediately, although she had mentioned it in passing to

Jane. But she had put it at the top of her list of important future projects.

Now with the trip to the South of France coming up in June, Christina asked Giselle to make arrangements for her to visit some of the men who created the scents, who were working in Grasse. The head *vendeuse* had written off at once to a contact in Paris.

"*Gardenia!*" Christina said to Jane as they sat in the rented car driving to Grasse, during the latter part of June. "It must be gardenia. That's the one fragrance that I keep coming back to . . . it's very evocative . . . perhaps because my mother always wore gardenia scent when I was a child. It was called Gardenia Flower Essence and Mrs. Bell used to buy it for her at Harrods as a gift."

"I like the smell of gardenias too," Jane replied, "but you've got to come up with a better name. You can't call it just *gardenia*. That's far too mundane. You must find a fancier name."

"Blue Gardenia," Christina suggested.

"No, there was a movie with Alan Ladd called—"

"That was *The Blue Dahlia*," Christina shot back, grinning. "Listen, Janey, I *do* like Blue Gardenia. It has a nice ring to it, and my mother does have the bluest of eyes. . . ."

Jane smiled. "Then Blue Gardenia it must be. Actually, I like it, too, especially since you're naming it for your lovely mum." Jane suddenly began to sniff the air blowing in through the car windows. "Gosh, I can smell the flowers already. We must be nearly there," she said, slowing the car.

"Yes, we are," Christina exclaimed. "Look, there's Grasse in the distance. I'd better keep my eyes open for the hotel when we get into the town . . . we're staying at a place Giselle recommended—Le Regent."

Christina and Jane spent three days in the lovely town of Grasse, which was situated in the Alpes Maritimes high above Cannes. It was a charming spot, ancient and totally surrounded by field upon glorious field of flowers and magnificent rose gardens. Fragonard, the great French painter, had been born here, and there was a Fragonard Museum, which of course the girls gravitated to the first chance they had. They also spent time going around the splendid Gothic cathedral, and visiting the many famous gardens.

But mostly they visited the various perfumeries, sniffing scents and talking to the chemists. In the end, Christina settled on two fragrances which would be created specially for her, to be marketed the following year. One would have gardenia as its base, the other roses, and their names would be Blue Gardenia and Christina, respectively.

CHAPTER FORTY-TWO

"I don't think I've seen Hadley Court ever looking quite as beautiful as it does tonight," Christina said, turning to Jane's father, smiling at him. "The flowers and candlelight inside the house create such a magical effect, and the gardens out here . . . why, they are *ethereal* in the reflected light from the house."

The famous actor, tall, rangy, with the look of a professor about him, followed her gaze across the lawns of his country manor house in Aldington in Kent.

"Yes, the gardens do have a special quality, especially when viewed from this terrace . . . they're like a black-cloth on the stage tonight, almost too perfect to be real. But I don't suppose there is anything quite as lovely as an English summer evening, after a day of truly glorious weather," Ralph said, his mellifluous voice echoing on the warm air.

His was one of the most celebrated voices on the English stage, and Christina never tired of listening to it.

Ralph continued, "You said *magical*, Christie, and I do believe the entire evening has had a touch of magic to it, everything has gone so beautifully. And out here, now, it's so balmy, and there's not a whisper of that frightful wind we often get down here. Yes, we've been lucky; it's been perfect July weather for Janey's party."

Turning to look at Christina directly, Ralph Sedgewick adopted a fatherly manner toward her, asked, "Have you enjoyed yourself, my dear?"

"Oh yes, I have, Ralph, thank you very much. It's been a simply gorgeous evening, but I am a little sad that Jane's going off to New York for four or five months—I'm going to miss her terribly. Oh gosh, that sounded so selfish! I know you and Dulcie are going to feel it too, when she's gone."

"Yes, we are," he admitted, "but I'm hoping we might be lucky enough to do a play on Broadway whilst she's there. David Merrick wants us for a new comedy, so our American agent tells us. Anyway, Christie, aren't you planning to go over to the States for a visit in October? At least I think that's what Dulcie said to me?" He made this sound like a question. "Or am I mistaken?"

Christina suppressed a smile of amusement. Ralph's absentmindedness was an old joke within the Sedgewick family, and Jane was forever saying the only thing her father could remember was his part in a play.

"No, no, you're not wrong, Ralph. I do hope to be going over to America then," Christie told him. "My clothes have done well in New York, and Bergdorf Goodman have invited me to show my winter collection, after it's opened here in London, of course."

"Congratulations, Christie, that's wonderful." He squeezed her arm, smiled at her through warm hazel eyes. "I must admit, I am extraordinarily proud of you and my little Janey . . . you've both done wonderfully well since you graduated from the Royal College and—"

"There you are!" Jane cried.

Christina and Ralph swung to face her.

She glided through the French doors and out onto the terrace, her feet barely touching the ground. She was exceptionally happy tonight and she looked ravishing. Her Christina gown was made of tulle and lace, and it had a bouffant skirt decorated with lover's knots picked out in silver and pearl sequins, and it floated around her like a soft hazy pink cloud shot through with iridescent lights.

"I've been looking all over for the two of you. What a couple of fuddy-duddies you are, standing there, nursing your drinks . . . and *gossiping*, I've no doubt," Jane said. "What am I missing? No, don't bother to tell me. You should both be inside, dancing and whirling around the floor."

She grinned at them, tucked her arm through her father's. "I must say, Daddy, that's a really super band you found. They've got a fabulous beat, and they've got everybody really going at it, jiving it up. Come on, let's go inside and shake a leg," she finished gaily, her voice and her face filled with her infectious girlish laughter.

Ralph gave her an indulgent look. "I'm afraid I'm a little too old for that sort of thing," he announced. "And it's jolly warm indoors; that's why Christina and I came out here in the first place, to get a breath of fresh air."

He swung to face the gardens again, put his brandy balloon down on the stone wall of the terrace, reached into the pocket of his dinner jacket and took out a gold cigarette case.

After lighting a cigarette, he asked, "Where's your mother, by the way? Don't tell me she's jumping up and down like a mad thing . . . not in this heat, I hope, and at her age."

Jane giggled. "Honestly, father of mine, you do make Mummy sound old. She's only fifty-one, for God's sake. But no, she's not dancing, she's talking to Miles, who arrived a little while ago. And all on his little *own* too—" Jane paused dramatically, rolled her eyes and made an ugly face.

"Miles is here!" Ralph sounded and looked extremely pleased.

"He certainly is," a light, amused, masculine voice said from the direction of the French doors.

"Miles, old chap! How wonderful that you could make it after all!" Ralph hurried forward, his hand outstretched.

The two men clasped hands, beamed at each other. They had only recently become friends, but they had liked each other immediately.

Miles said, "So sorry I wasn't able to get here in time for supper, Ralph, but I got caught up in town . . . nothing I could do about it really . . . *you* know how it is . . . in *my position*. . . ." He allowed his voice to trail off, as if suggesting he had been detained by important government business that could not be discussed. Top secret sort of stuff. Miles knew he had no need to explain his tardiness. Politicians were generally excused for this little social sin, if not for anything else they did.

Now he glanced at Jane, whom he had already greeted inside the house, and acknowledged her again with a slight nod.

Ralph asked, "Are you quite positive you don't want something to eat? I know the buffet is still being served, Miles. Certainly I must get you a drink. What would you like?" Ralph came to a stop as he realized that Miles's attention was focused behind him.

Ralph swung around, apologetic. "How frightfully rude of me, Christina, my dear. Don't hang back there. Do come and meet Miles."

"Yes, you must meet Miles," Miles said, stepping out into the middle of the terrace.

Jane said, "Excuse me, I'm going to get a myself a glass of the old bubbly."

Christina moved forward slowly, conscious of the blue radiance of the eyes fixed so intently on her. There was a sudden constriction in her chest.

As he watched her approach, Miles Sutherland thought he had never seen such a lovely young woman. Her chestnut hair was swept up on top of her head to form a crown of curls. It was an odd style, reminiscent of the 1940s, and yet it suited her. She was dressed in a simple gown. Chiffon. Pale gray, Grecian in style. One shoulder bare. She wore a choker of beads and earrings that matched. Gray stones, resembling those huge gray luminous eyes that seemed to swamp her face. Opals? Moonstones? He wasn't sure.

He smiled, sensing a certain shyness in her, wanting to put her at ease.

Ralph cleared his throat. "Christina, may I present Miles Sutherland, one of our most brilliant politicians, as I'm sure you're aware. And Miles, this is Christina Crowther, Jane's dearest friend and flat mate, whom we consider to be a member of the family, actually."

"How do you do," Christina said.

Miles took the cool, tapering hand in his and held it tightly. Slowly he increased the pressure of his fingers, not wishing to let go of it. He knew at once that he wanted her. He aimed to have her.

"I'm very pleased to meet you," Miles said finally, and reluctantly released her hand, adding, "I've heard a great deal about you—from my sister. She wears your clothes."

"Your sister?" she repeated, feeling like an imbecile for not knowing who his sister was.

He said, "Yes, Susan Radley."

"Lady Radley?" she asked and felt even more foolish.

He smiled, as if amused. "Yes." He glanced at Ralph, said, "I wouldn't mind that drink, old chap. If you would show me where the bar is, I'll—"

"No, no, stay where you are, Miles," Ralph insisted. "What would you like to have?"

"Scotch, I think, with a splash of soda. Thanks, Ralph."

Ralph Sedgewick looked at Christina. "You haven't touched your cognac, my dear. Would you prefer something else perhaps?"

"Please . . . a glass of champagne would be nice." She suddenly wished Ralph would not go away and leave her with this man who continued to stare at her with his curiously hypnotic eyes.

They were alone on the terrace.

Miles smiled a lazy sort of smile, gave her a searching look, as if answering a question in his own mind, then took out a packet of cigarettes. He offered her one silently. She shook her head.

After striking a match, drawing on the cigarette, he said in that same amused, superior voice, "Your newspaper photographs don't do you justice, don't you know . . . they make you look much older too . . . and tell me, how do you manage to cope with our national press? I find them a bit pesky myself, at times."

Christina ignored the backhanded compliment he had paid her, said carefully, "I find the press—wonderfully well, thank you very much. They're certainly decent to me, but then I'm not a brilliant politician who's always making national news."

"*Touché.*" He laughed, moved closer to her and leaned against the stone balustrade, his posture nonchalant. He said, "That choker you're wearing . . . are those moonstones?"

"No, they're just gray glass beads, but I like the milky effect they have, that's why I bought them."

"Do you ever wear opals?"

She shook her head.

He stared at her, his gaze speculative, appraising, bold. She found herself returning his stare unblinkingly.

He said at last in a low, quick voice, "You should, you know. Opals would look lovely against that extraordinary skin . . . with those extraordinary eyes. . . ."

Christina was startled. She could not answer him. Her legs needed support. She sat down on the balustrade.

Miles Sutherland could not tear his eyes away from her. She touched him in a way that he had not been touched in years and he felt curious stirrings within himself. And his physical desire for her was hot and urgent.

To Christina's immense relief Ralph walked out onto the terrace carrying their drinks.

She sat sipping her champagne, listening to the murmur of their voices as they spoke at length about British politics. But she was not really hearing anything at all. She was studying Miles Sutherland, wondering what it was about the man that so unnerved her. Was it his great presence? Force of personality? Charisma? She was not certain. He was not the most handsome man she had ever met, but he did have an attractive face, lean, intelligent, composed of uneven planes and angles. His hair was a dark blondish brown that had a hint of gray at the sides. Slim in build, he was not much taller than she was, only about an inch or so in fact.

It was his eyes, of course, that so mesmerized. They were a lovely clear blue that reminded her of an English sky on a summer day.

The two men continued to talk for a while, and she

listened, let his voice roll over her, absorbing it, committing it to memory. It was full of nuances and inflections. She pictured him speaking in the Commons.

And suddenly Miles was standing in front of her, saying goodnight.

"It was so nice to meet you," he said in an indifferent voice.

Christina slid off the balustrade, took his hand, shook it briskly. "I enjoyed meeting you," she said, forcing cheerfulness.

Later, when she was in bed, she wondered why she was feeling so disappointed and let down.

CHAPTER FORTY-THREE

Jane exclaimed, "What a nerve he's got, strolling in here, trying to seduce you!"

"He didn't stroll in," Christina corrected. "He phoned me at Bruton Street. And he's not trying to seduce me."

"Oh yes he is."

"Don't be so silly, Janey . . . over lunch?" Christina began to laugh.

"*After* lunch," Jane cried fiercely. "The French call it a *matinée*."

"This is London, not Paris, remember?"

Jane chewed her inner lip nervously. "My God, Mummy would have a fit—she'd be absolutely furious if she knew; after all, you met him through us down at Hadley."

"You're not going to tell her?" Christina sounded horrified.

"Of course, I'm not." Jane looked at her askance. "God, you can be stupid at times, Crowther . . . and you'll certainly be *bloody* stupid if you go out with Miles Sutherland."

"*Why?*"

"Because he's dangerous. Emotionally dangerous. I just know it in my bones."

"You're the one who's being stupid now, and far-fetched. How can he possibly be dangerous to me?" Christina demanded.

"He's married, for one thing."

"Estranged, separated. Everybody knows that. It was all over the newspapers ages ago."

"But he's not divorced, Christie."

"I don't know why you're acting this way, Jane, I really don't. Miles seems to be a nice man, and I'm sure he's decent and honorable too."

Jane let out a guffaw. "I bet he's a cad."

Christina gaped at her. "I don't know what's got into you today, making such sweeping statements."

Jane stared at her dearest friend. "Okay, let's go over a few facts. Miles Sutherland is good-looking and charming and cuts quite a swathe at parties, I'll grant you that. But let's not forget that he also cuts quite a swathe in the House of Commons and that he is a brilliant and ambitious politician."

"I'm not sure I understand what you're getting at, Janey."

"Oh for God's sake, Christina, don't be so bloody dense! There happens to be a woman in his life already, a woman called Candida Sutherland, who is his wife and the mother of his three brats. Who just happens to be the daughter—actually the only child—of one of Britain's foremost industrialists. She's got pots and pots and *pots* of money, and if—"

"I *know* all that."

"And you can be damned sure that Miles Sutherland *knows* which side *his* bread is buttered on, my darling. Oh yes. When a man's a Member of Parliament and a leading light in the Labor Party, with a spectacular career unfolding, his wife's money comes in very useful indeed. Do you think he's going to jeopardize all that—"

"Jane, stop this!" Christina spluttered. "You're being absolutely preposterous." She let out a funny little laugh and eyed Jane curiously. "The way *you're* talking, anybody would think we're having a wild affair when—"

"I bet he'd love that! Miles Sutherland looks very randy to me."

"—when I hardly know the man. Besides, he's only invited me to lunch."

Jane looked at her through narrowed violet eyes. "When a man like Miles Sutherland invites a woman like you to lunch, he has only *one thing* on his mind and it's certainly not buying you a decent meal."

"I am going to have lunch with him, Jane, no matter what you say," Christina asserted in a firm tone.

"I wish you wouldn't . . . you just won't be able to cope with it."

"With *what?*"

"His bloody fatal charm and smooth talk and all that sort of codswallop. Don't forget, he's a politician and they've got the gift of gab, Mummy says."

"I can take care of myself, Jane."

"No, you can't."

Christina said slowly, almost reflectively, "My mother had a friend once—Gwen. *Auntie* Gwen I used to call her when I was little. They were very close when they were young women, nurses at Ripon Fever Hospital. But Gwen never did like Daddy much, which naturally made Mummy furious, and then Gwen married some twerp called Geoffrey Freemantle. Geoffrey sort of came between them too, as my father had, in a way."

Christina paused, took a deep breath. "And I just don't want that to happen to *us*, Janey, I really don't. So let's make a pact right now. Let's agree that men will *never* come between us. Let's try and be above all that sort of thing. What do you think?"

"Oh Christie darling, of course I agree with you completely! We mustn't let the men we get involved with make one single ripple between us."

Later that evening Christina and Jane went to Le Matelot in Belgravia for dinner.

They both liked the little bistro with a nautical theme

and casual ambience. It reminded them of their trip to the South of France the month before.

As they sipped their glasses of white wine, waiting for the first course, Jane asked, "What happened to her?"

"Who?" Christina looked puzzled.

"Your mother's friend—Gwen."

"Oh gosh, Janey, that's quite a sad story really. Her life wasn't very happy with the Geoffrey person. He turned out to be a wife beater, for one thing."

"My God, how awful!" Jane exclaimed, looking horror-struck.

"Yes, it was." Christina leaned her elbows on the table, said, "When I was small Mummy began to suspect there was something odd going on there, at least that's what she told me when I was grown up. You see, poor Auntie Gwen was always having these terrible accidents . . . falling down the cellar steps, or some such thing, and it began to worry my mother. At first she thought Gwen had an illness—you know, a brain tumor or something like that—and then it finally dawned on her. And she tackled Gwen about it, but of course Gwen denied it, and that's when we stopped going to see her."

"And what happened to Gwen in the end?" Janey asked.

"During the war she came to see us. Unexpectedly. I remember it very well because she brought me some pretty glass beads. I must have been about ten or eleven at the time. Anyway, she came for tea and stayed the evening, and after I'd gone to bed she apparently told my mother everything. I think she must have been at the end of her rope by then. Eventually Mummy persuaded her to move back to live with her parents, although I believe *that* took a lot of doing." Christina sat back, took a sip of wine.

Jane said, "Go on . . . I'll kill you if you don't finish the story."

"My mother talked to Gwen's brother, Charlie," Christina explained, "and he told the husband that he'd better not come near Gwen again. And he didn't."

"And she got a divorce."

"No, but the Geoffrey fellow was killed during the war. He wasn't in the forces, but he was here in London on some business, in 1944 I think it was, and he was killed during a bombing raid."

"And where's Gwen now? What happened to her in the end?"

Christina smiled, and her eyes lit up. "Her story had a happy ending really, Janey. She married my Uncle Mike in 1952. He was a widower by then and very lonely. It was my mother who persuaded him to join them for dinner with Gwen. You see, years before *they'd* gone out together. I suppose you could say they picked up where they left off."

"Hardly that," Jane said with a laugh. "But I *am* glad her life finally turned around . . . poor woman." After a short pause, she said, "Christie, about Miles—"

"What about him?"

"When are you having lunch with him?"

"Friday—the day after tomorrow," Christina said.

Jane sat back and grimaced, eyeing her friend with concern. "That's the day I leave for New York, and since I'm booked on the ten o'clock flight, you'd better call me later in the day and tell me what happens. I shall be all ears!"

Christina burst out laughing. "Oh Jane, you are impossible. Nothing's going to happen . . . but I'll phone you anyway to make sure *you're* all right, that you've arrived safely in little old Manhattan."

"Do you find Miles so irresistible, Christie? I mean, are you madly attracted to him?" Jane probed.

"He's quite attractive," Christina murmured, wanting to sound as noncommittal as possible, not daring to confide her true feelings to Jane.

He canceled the lunch at the last minute.

"I'm so frightfully sorry to do this," he said in an apologetic voice when he telephoned her on Friday morning, "but I can't meet you today as we arranged. Something's come up . . . it's all become *rather* complicated. Do forgive me, Christina. Another time perhaps?"

"Oh," Christina said, gripping the receiver much tighter, sitting down behind the desk in her studio at the Bruton Street house.

"I say, I have a much better idea!" Miles exclaimed, as if something brilliant had just struck him. "Why don't we have *dinner* next week? I see from my calendar that I'm awfully jammed with luncheon engagements . . . what about having dinner with me on Tuesday evening?"

"I'd love to, Miles, but I can't," Christina said, genuinely regretful. "I'm going to Paris on Monday."

Disbelief echoed in his laughter. "Paris in July. You're going to find that all the Parisians have fled. There'll be no one there but American tourists."

"I'm going on business," she explained softly, feeling her disappointment about the canceled lunch so acutely her throat was tight.

"Business or pleasure, it's still one of my favorite cities. When do you plan to return?"

"In about ten days."

"Then I shall give you a ring in . . . let's say two weeks? Is that all right, Christina?"

"Yes, that'll be lovely, Miles."

After she had hung up, she stared at the phone for a long time. It troubled her that he aroused such strong feelings in her.

CHAPTER FORTY-FOUR

Although she no longer painted landscapes, Christina still saw everything in terms of light.

And the first week she was in Paris, it seemed to her that every single day was filled with a luminous light that was glorious. As she went from the Ritz Hotel, where she was staying, to her various appointments, she would look up and marvel at the shining sky flung high like a canopy of pale blue silk above this most beautiful of cities.

The weather was perfect, mild, sunny and without the mugginess that had made London so unbearable before she had left. Yet despite her appreciation of the radiant skies, the sunlight shimmering on the river Seine and leaking through the leafy green cupolas of the trees, and casting its soft golden glow on the wide boulevards and ancient buildings, Christina had no desire to put what she saw on canvas.

The day she had given up her painting she had vowed she would not hanker after it, or have regrets, and she had not.

In some ways, it was a relief for her not to have to strive to top the world's most renowned painters, which was something her mother had somehow always believed she could do. It would be impossible for anyone to better J. M. W. Turner, that greatest of all the nineteenth-century English landscape artists, who had captured light on canvas with such brilliance. Or Van Gogh or Renoir or Monet, who had done something of the same.

And in all truth, Christina enjoyed her work as a fashion designer. It was a constant challenge, and she was savoring the business side as well as the creative endeavor it involved.

And not unnaturally, the extraordinary acclaim she was receiving gave her great pleasure, whilst the money she was earning was more than gratifying—it was positively thrilling. She knew that by the end of the year she would be able to repay her loans to Dulcie and Elspeth. But most important of all, her mother had finally retired from Leeds General Infirmary and had agreed to accept a check every month from her. It had been a battle, but *she* had won in the end, thanks in no small measure to her father, who had run interference for her. He had understood how much it meant to her.

This week, as she had gone from her appointments with the perfume manufacturer to meetings at the fabric houses, and generally attended to her business, she had managed to find time to go shopping for gifts for her parents. For her mother she had found butter-soft kid gloves and a silk scarf and several blouses; for her father, silk ties and voile shirts and an elegant cigarette lighter. Jane had not been left out, and she had bought her dearest friend a glamorous silk evening shawl from Hermès in a mixture of the pretty pinks Jane loved.

Christina thought of Jane now, as she walked slowly across the Place Vendôme toward the Ritz Hotel early on Friday evening at the end of her first week in Paris. It didn't seem possible that Jane had left for New York only last Friday. It felt so much longer.

She missed her a lot, but then they had been inseparable for the last five years, so that was only natural, she supposed. Jane was the best friend she had ever had, and the only close friend really. Her mother had kept her so busy with her painting when she was growing up there hadn't been much time for playmates when she was little, or chums when she was a teenager. It had always been painting lessons and field trips and museums and galleries and being force-fed art, art, art. Now that she looked back, she realized that she had spent most of her growing-up years with Audra, until she had left for the Royal College of Art in London.

Christina smiled to herself as she went through the doors of the Ritz, remembering with some affection the little Hôtel des Deux Continents where she and Jane had stayed on several trips to Paris in their college days. It had been a far cry from this elegant edifice where Hemingway had once hung out and movie stars and princes stayed. She wished Jane were here with her on *this* trip, staying *here* . . . what fun they would have together.

Her suite was in the other wing of the Ritz, at the Rue Cambon side of the hotel, and she had to traverse a long gallery of shops to reach the smaller of the two lobbies. But she did not stop to browse as she usually did; she was far too anxious to get up to her suite, take off her shoes and order a pot of tea. It had been a hectic day and she had walked a lot, since most of her appointments had been close to each other.

The *concierge* smiled pleasantly as he handed her the key to her suite, and told her no, there were no messages, in answer to her question. Smiling back, murmuring her thanks, she swung around, took a step toward the elevator.

It was then that she saw him.

She stopped dead in her tracks, staring.

His eyes were riveted on her. He rose from the chair, walked toward her in easy, graceful strides.

She was dazzled by the blue radiance of his eyes.

As he drew level with her, he said, "*Hello.*"

"Miles." After a pause, finally finding her voice, she managed, "What are *you* doing here?"

The small, amused smile she remembered so well tugged at one corner of his mouth. "I'm staying here," he said. "I always stay at the Ritz when I'm in Paris."

"Oh."

He put his hand under her elbow purposefully and escorted her to the elevator. They did not speak riding up, and he followed her out at her floor; when they reached the door of her suite, she fumbled with the key and, in her nervousness, dropped it.

He picked it up, put it in the lock, turned it, held the door open for her, then stepped inside after her. He leaned against the door watching her move ahead of him, so willowy and lithe. She had the most gorgeous legs. Why hadn't he noticed that before now? But how could he have known it? She had been wearing the long gray Grecian gown at Hadley. He knew one thing, though. The heat was in him again, as it had been the night he had first set eyes on her at the beginning of the month. That was why he was here, wasn't it?

Strolling across the foyer toward the sitting room, Miles leaned against the door jamb, still watching her, fascinated by her. He couldn't wait to take her in his arms, to make love to her. He would like to do that right now, at this very moment. Yet he knew he could never make a move like that. He was a gentleman, and he did not want to frighten her by pouncing on her in a predatory manner. She struck him as being naive and inexperienced, at least where men were concerned. Beyond all of these things, though, he wanted to get to know her a little better, to savor her and enjoy the anticipation of his ultimate possession of her.

Christina placed her handbag and document case on a chair and pivoted so suddenly she startled him.

She said, "It's not a coincidence, is it?"

"Of course it isn't, Christina."

He moved into the room, came to a stop next to her and took her hand in his, held on to it tightly, crushing it between his fingers. He looked at her deeply, his face close to hers, their eyes on a level. He said, "I decided I didn't want to wait two weeks to take you out to dinner. That's why I'm here . . . to have dinner with you. Tonight—I hope? You are free?"

"Yes." She searched his face, her brows drawing together in a pucker. "Don't you have business here too? I mean, you didn't fly from London to Paris simply to have dinner with me . . . surely not?"

"I most certainly did."

"Oh." She felt the sudden rush of heat to her face and there was that tight feeling in her chest again. She wanted to look away but she found that she could not. His eyes held hers in the same mesmerizing way they had at Hadley Court.

Miles smiled an odd little smile and let go of her hand, walked over to the window and parted the curtain, looked down into the gardens below. Swinging to face her, he said lightly, "If it weren't July and the tourist season, I'd take you to Maxim's tonight, but since it is, and since I didn't bring a dinner jacket, which is obligatory masculine dress on Fridays, shall we dine in the gardens here at the hotel?"

"Anywhere you wish. Yes, here would be lovely, Miles."

"Then I'll meet you downstairs in the American Bar at—" He pushed up his cuff, glanced at his watch. "Eight o'clock? Is that all right with you? It does give you an hour to change and dress."

"That's plenty of time, thank you."

He came across the room, paused as he drew alongside her and looked deeply into her face for the second time in a few minutes. He took her hand, kissed her finger tips, then said, "Of course I came to Paris because of you. Believe it— it's true. You see, I haven't been able to get you off my mind since we met at Hadley."

He was gone before she could say a word in response, striding across the sitting room, through the foyer and out of the suite. He did not look back as she somehow thought he might.

The door clicked softly behind him.

She was standing alone in the middle of the floor.

She blinked, for a moment unable to absorb everything that had happened in the space of . . . what? Fifteen minutes, at the most? He had followed her to Paris as soon as he could get away . . . he had been in the lobby waiting for her to return this evening . . . and of course he had more on his mind than buying her a decent meal, as Jane had so succinctly put it. But then so did she.

She had not been able to stop thinking about Miles Sutherland for the past two weeks, and her disappointment over the canceled lunch had been so acute it had lingered for days. Walking through into the bedroom, unbuttoning her black linen dress, Christina let her mind rest on Miles.

He was unlike any man she had ever met. And he *was* a man. Not like the students she had gone out with, or the young fellows she had dated in the last couple of years.

Miles Sutherland was, after all, a man of the world. A little shiver ran through her as she slipped out of her dress and went to the armoire, thinking about Miles. She shivered again, remembering how intensely and passionately he had looked at her as he had held her hand, then kissed her fingers. She had thought, for a moment, that he was going to take her in his arms, and she had felt weak with desire for him. Her excitement and anticipation about the evening accelerated. And as she gave her attention to the clothes hanging in front of her, she could not help wondering what sort of evening it would turn out to be.

Her hand settled on a cocktail dress made of a chiffon that was striated in a mèlange of lilacs and mauves that bled into each other and faded to the softest of grays. Sleeveless, it had a ruched bodice and a very low vee neckline at the front and the back, and a full gathered skirt.

She knew how alluring she looked in it. She wanted to be as irresistible to Miles Sutherland as he was to her.

A few minutes later, as she pinned up her hair before taking a bath, she peered at herself in the bathroom mirror. She saw his face in her mind's eye so vividly and felt his presence so strongly he might have been standing behind her looking at her in the glass.

"Oh Miles," she said out loud. "I haven't been able to get you out of my mind either."

CHAPTER FORTY-FIVE

His heart quickened at the sight of her.

She stood poised at the entrance to the bar, wearing a dress the color of lilacs in the spring, and the choker of milky-gray glass beads encircled her throat and her hair was upswept in a coronet of curls as it had been on the night he had first met her in Kent.

He was on his feet at once and halfway across the small bar before she saw him, and when she did a smile struck her face and she came forward in a rush, and as they met he caught a faint whiff of her perfume, something light and fresh and green-smelling, which evoked sunny summer meadows.

Neither of them spoke. They looked at each other, their eyes locking for a split second.

And then he took hold of her arm and drew her toward the table in the far corner, where the bottle of Dom Perignon sat in a bucket of ice and his cigarette was smoldering in an ashtray next to the glass of good Scotch whisky he had been fortifying himself with before she arrived.

They sat down opposite each other, and he stubbed out the cigarette and lifted his head and smiled at her, very deeply, and she smiled back at him in the same way.

In one sense, he was glad to have the table between them. It was a welcome barrier since it prevented him from doing something foolish, like taking her in his arms and kissing her and so making a spectacle of himself in public. And anyway, he wanted to look at her, study her face, reinforce the image of her that had been etched in his mind for several weeks.

"You were drinking champagne at Hadley, so I ordered a bottle," he said. As he spoke he heard the tightness in his voice and he was amazed. The tension had been building up in him since he had decided to come here to Paris, and the last hour of waiting for her to change and join him had become unbearable. "Is that all right with you?" he went on, trying to relax, motioning to the waiter to come and open the bottle.

"Why yes, thank you, Miles, it's lovely," she said, "and I only ever drink white wine or champagne, never hard liquor. Anyway, champagne *is* so festive and this *is* a special occasion, after all."

"It is?" He looked at her alertly.

"*Absolutely.*"

"Why?" he asked, fishing. He leaned over the table ever so slightly.

"Because it's not often that I get taken out to dinner by a celebrated English politician . . . and one who flies across the English Channel, no less, in order to do so."

He saw the merriment in her eyes, the laughter bubbling under the surface, and he felt the sudden, unexpected laughter in himself, realizing that she was teasing him, and he thought: Thank God she has a sense of humor.

"The flight was well worth it," Miles replied, letting his eyes rest on her appreciatively, "just to have the view from where I'm sitting—it's quite lovely."

"Thank you."

The waiter poured the champagne. Miles tasted it and nodded, and the waiter filled their flutes. Miles raised his glass. Clinking it against hers, he said, "To our first evening together."

"Yes—and to our dinner. It's probably the most expensive you've ever had to buy, if you include your airfare and the hotel room here. Unless, of course, you do this kind of thing frequently, then I realize it must be nothing exceptional at all."

He stared at her intently, wondering if she was insinuating something about other women, but he saw at once there was no innuendo behind her words. Her expression was guileless.

Then her laughter rippled on the air between them, light, amused.

Miles took in her merry face and dancing gray eyes and he burst out laughing too. The laughter helped to ease his tension, though not much. He had wanted her for two weeks, had fantasized about making love to her so many times he had worked himself up into a terrible state. Now that he was finally with her, he was focused entirely on her, and his whole body was taut with his desire to possess her. He knew he would explode before the night was out if he did not make love to her.

Christina sipped her champagne, eyed him quizzically, asked, "Miles, what would you have done if I'd had another date tonight?"

He sat back, took a cigarette, struck a match, the bright blue eyes still crinkling at the corners with laughter. "That possibility had occurred to me, I must confess."

He leaned across the table in an intimate manner, explained, "I would have invited you to dine tomorrow or Sunday, and if you'd had engagements for those evenings, I would have asked you out to lunch or suggested that we have drinks on one of those days. And in the end, I would have probably settled for a cup of tea, or breakfast, or a walk in the *bois* or whatever you'd agreed to do with me. You see, I did want to get better acquainted with you, Christina, and I can be very, very persistent."

"Yes, I know."

"You do?" He raised an eyebrow. "*How?*"

"From what I've read about you in the newspapers over the past few years. You seem to have a reputation for stubbornness and determination . . . you certainly keep going after the Tories, keep *them* on their toes in the House of Commons, don't you?"

He grinned, drew on his cigarette. "That's the duty of members of the shadow cabinet . . . to keep the opposition off balance, you know."

Miles leaned back in the chair, studied her face thoughtfully. "I meant what I said at Hadley—those photographs I've seen of you in the papers and magazines definitely do *not* do you justice. Far too grainy in the papers particularly, and they make you look older." He paused, then asked, "How old *are* you, Christina?"

"I was twenty-five in May."

He was surprised. He had thought she was about twenty-seven or even twenty-eight. Not that she looked it, but there was her enormous success as a *couturière* to consider; also, she had a certain reserve in her manner, a caution, a prudence almost, and these things suggested maturity to him somehow. *Twenty-five.* She was so young really, just a girl.

Miles said, "I'm much older than you—I'm thirty-eight."

"Forty."

He threw back his head and roared.

Christina sat back, gazing at him, her eyes filling with mischief.

"Well, well, well, how's that for a small display of male vanity? And how did you know my real age? I don't think I've ever seen it mentioned in the newspapers, at least not lately."

She had gone to the library and looked him up in one of the political reference books, but she had no intention of admitting this. So she lied, "I think Jane must have told me."

"Oh yes, of course, my sister is very friendly with Dulcie. But then you know that, since it was Dulcie who introduced Susan to you—and your gorgeous clothes." He poured more champagne into their glasses. "You've done awfully well in your career as a fashion designer and become quite a celebrity too—and all in a very short few years. I admire women of accomplishment and brains. . . . I want to know all about you and how you did it, Christina. Will you tell me?"

"Yes, if you really want to hear."

"I most certainly do."

She kept her recital succinct, recounting her years of growing up in Yorkshire, meeting Jane at the Royal College of Art, and then she told him about her decision to become a *couturière.* But she did not reveal her real reason for giving up painting, preferred to let him think that she had done so because fashion designing was her first love.

Fifteen minutes later she finished. "There, you have it all

in a nutshell." She reached for her glass, took a long swallow of champagne.

"It's been a meteoric rise. I salute you," he said, giving her a look of sincere admiration. He had enjoyed listening to her. She had a pleasant, well-modulated voice, and suddenly he was curiously soothed. Perhaps this was because he knew she was his captive for the next few hours, and a lot could happen in that time.

Christina smiled at him, said, "Now it's *your* turn to tell me all about *you*, Miles." What she had read in the reference book had been scanty, and she wanted to know as much as possible about him.

"There's nothing very exciting to tell," Miles said, with a shrug, a small smile. "I was born in London. Grew up there and in Suffolk. Went to Eton, Oxford, studied law, practiced as a barrister for a short while. Preferred politics, you know. Won my first election when I was twenty-seven. Became a Member of Parliament and have managed to keep my constituency in Manchester over the years. Very loyal voters, fortunately. My parents are still alive, thank God, and I have just the one sister. No hobbies, no interests really, other than politics. I do love them, they're my life, actually." He stubbed out his cigarette, lifted his glass. "That's *my* potted biography. Rather a dull chap, wouldn't you say?"

She shook her head. "Quite the contrary," Christina answered and thought: But he didn't mention his wife.

As if he had read her mind, Miles brought his head closer to hers, fixed her with a hard stare and his voice was low, suddenly intense, when he said, "Oh, and by the way, I'm separated from my wife."

"I know you are."

"Jane told you?"

"No, I saw an item in William Hickey's column in the *Daily Express*—when you became estranged."

"But that was two years ago." He gave her an astonished look. "Isn't that odd—we've both read so much about each other and remembered it." He stopped; his mouth twitched with hidden amusement. "Do you think it signifies something special?" he asked in a teasing tone.

"Yes, that we both have excellent memories for the rubbish we read in the gossip columns."

Miles grinned, enjoying her more than ever, then reached out, took her hand in both of his. "Oh I think it's more than that," he said.

"What do you mean?"

"I'll tell you later." He motioned to the waiter, reached inside his jacket for his wallet. "I think perhaps we ought to go out to the gardens for dinner. I don't want to lose the table."

CHAPTER FORTY-SIX

The tension that had eased out of him in the bar took hold of him again during dinner.

It happened so unexpectedly he was startled, and to his amazement he thought his hand was going to shake and so he put down his fork, sat back, looked across at her.

There was a hurricane lamp on the table between them, and in the flickering light of the candle her face had taken on a mysterious cast, and as she moved slightly a shadow obscured her mouth. He wanted to kiss that mouth, crush it under his own, take her to him, love her with all the strength of his body. He wondered why they were squandering their time here in the restaurant.

Christina reached for her glass of Montrachet, took a sip, regarded Miles over the rim, feeling the potency of his presence more than ever. Aside from being charismatic, he was an elegantly dressed man and this pleased her. She studied him surreptitiously, thinking how well he looked in the chalk-stripe gray suit and the pale blue shirt that emphasized the color of his eyes.

Suddenly she saw those mesmeric eyes change, darken, as if he was troubled, and a fretful expression flicked onto his narrow, intelligent face and his mouth tightened noticeably.

What was wrong? Did he now regret his actions? Was he

sorry he had flown to Paris after all? Dismay lodged in the pit of her stomach. What if he said a polite goodnight to her at the end of the evening and left it at that? Perhaps she had imagined that look in his eyes at Hadley Court and earlier this evening in the bar. Perhaps it was all wishful thinking on her part. She didn't want him to leave her alone after dinner. She wanted to be with him. *She wanted him*.

Before she could stop herself, she leaned forward, asked, "Is there something wrong, Miles?"

"No, of course not," he exclaimed, rousing himself, pushing aside his erotic thoughts of her. He picked up his glass, drank, then asked, "Whatever made you think there was?"

"You look distressed—" she blurted out and stopped, stared at him, saw the amusement crossing his face.

"Did I?" He put his glass down, took a packet of cigarettes out of his pocket. "Do you mind if I smoke?" He looked at her inquiringly. She shook her head. Then he went on, "I'm afraid I'm not very hungry."

"Neither am I."

"So I notice," he murmured as he glanced at her plate. She had merely toyed with the veal medallions as he had himself; she had barely eaten a mouthful.

Now Miles lifted his head. His eyes settled on her eyes. And he saw something in them that brought him up with a start. There was a new awareness of him in them and a sexuality reflected there as well. He had always known she was interested in him. He had seen that quickening curiosity mixed with speculation illuminate her face at Hadley Court. But was she feeling *exactly* what he was feeling? Could it be that she desired him as much as he desired her?

Miles bent forward and said in the quietest of voices, without preamble, "When you get to know me better, you'll soon discover that I can be brutally frank, but at least you'll always know exactly where you stand with me. I want to be frank now, to say this to you . . . let's not be juvenile about tonight. We're both adults and you know as well as I do why I came to see you in Paris." He reached across the table, gripped her hand tightly. "I want to be with you,

Christie, to hold you in my arms, to make love *to* you and
with you. Do you want me in that way?"

"Yes, Miles, I do," she whispered.

"Then I don't think we should torture ourselves any
longer. Let me get the bill and we'll get out of here."

He took her in his arms the moment they entered her
suite, pushing the door closed with his foot.

Drawing her to him roughly, he brought his mouth down
hard on hers and kissed her passionately, parted her lips,
pushed his tongue in her mouth, began to savor hers. Then
he tightened his hold so that she was welded against the
hardness of his growing erection and ran his hand over her
shoulders and her back and onto her buttocks.

Her arms were around his neck and she was returning his
kisses with an ardor that was as fervent as his, and she let
her tongue slip under and over his, and she felt a shiver run
though him.

Christina thought she was dissolving into Miles, becoming part of him, and she held on to him tightly, afraid that
her legs were going to buckle. And then unexpectedly he
broke away from her and lifted her up in his arms and
carried her into the bedroom.

The bed was huge and the sheets gleamed whitely in the
corridor of light streaming in from the sitting room. He laid
her on it, took off his jacket, flung it on a chair, kicked off his
shoes.

As he took a step toward the bed she opened her arms to
him, and he saw the intensity and longing on her face and
his heart leapt with anticipation and excitement. He
slipped off her sandals, tossed them on the floor, lay down
on the bed next to her. Again she opened her arms to him
and he came into them, embracing her, pressing her tightly
to his chest.

"Christie, oh Christie," he said against her neck. "I want
you so much. I've ached for you since the night I saw you
on Ralph's terrace."

"Oh Miles, I know. I want *you*, I've longed for
you. . . ."

He raised himself on one elbow, looked down into her

face, touched her cheek gently. He gave her a searching
look, murmured, "Oh darling, if only you knew how much
you've haunted me." He kissed her. It was a long, slow,
melting kiss. She yielded her mouth up to his demands. He
sucked her tongue into his mouth, and he felt the ecstasy of
their prolonged kiss shoot down to the pit of his stomach.
Every one of his senses strained toward her. Possession of
her was the only thing that mattered to him at this moment.

With one hand, he caressed her face and her throat, then
slid his fingers down the vee of her dress to touch her
breast, and he experienced a thrilling sensation as he
realized she was not wearing a bra.

He bent his head over her, parted the neckline, slipped
his hand under her breast, lifted it out of the dress, took the
hardening nipple in his mouth. He drew up her chiffon
skirt, trailing one hand along her leg, finding the silky feel
of her stocking erotic, and when his hand came to rest on
the bare flesh of her thigh, he raised his head, sighed
deeply, then put his mouth gently on hers. His fingers came
to their final resting place between her legs, and as they
crept inside the silken panties he felt the moistness of her,
knew that she truly yearned for him as passionately and as
anxiously as he yearned for her.

Against her ear, he whispered, "Take your dress off,
darling," and immediately he stood, began to shed his
clothes.

Christina did the same, feeling quite unselfconscious in
front of him. She was undressed first. She lay down on the
bed, let her eyes rest on him as he came toward her. Miles
had a lean, taut body, without an extra ounce of flesh on it,
and she felt that athletic hardness, the strength of it, as he
took her firmly in his arms and wrapped his long legs
around her.

His hands went up into her hair, pulling out the pins, and
once her hair was flowing freely around her face, he slipped
both his hands up into it once more, held her head very
tightly between them, started to kiss her face and her neck
and her mouth.

But he stopped abruptly, said in an urgent voice that was

low and thick with desire, "I've got to have you now, I can't help it. I'm sorry. I've got to be inside you, Christie."

"Yes, yes, I know."

He braced himself above her on his hands, looked down into her face, experiencing the most overwhelming feelings for her. And instantly he saw the radiance that filled her face, saw the joy and desire for him in her marvelous eyes, and he knew everything he needed or ever wanted to know.

Christina reached up to touch his hair, then smoothed her hand along his tense cheek, looked up into his eyes, her gaze penetrating. "Oh Miles," she sighed, "oh Miles."

He lowered himself on top of her, pushing his hands under her buttocks, and drew her closer to him. And as he entered her he felt a rush of intense heat searing through his whole body, reaching up to touch his heart and then his mind. He plunged deeper into her, quickly, expertly, and she moved against him and they found their own rhythm immediately, their entwined bodies rising and falling together. And he thought triumphantly: *I knew it. I knew it would be perfect with her, that we were meant for each other, that we would be as one.*

And Christina, clinging to him, thought: *I never realized it could be like this. I want all of him, every part of him. I want to be bound to him always, to be in his arms always. I belong to him now. He has made me his tonight. Irrevocably and completely his.*

Suddenly Miles felt a great wave of strength and passion surging through him unchecked, and he could no longer restrain himself, and unable to hold back he cried against her tumbled hair, "Oh my darling my darling, I'm so sorry I can't help it I'm coming oh please come to me my darling."

"I will, I will, Miles! Oh Miles!"

"Christie, *now*. Oh my Christie! Oh my God!"

The match flared in the semidarkness of the room as he lit a cigarette, inhaled deeply, then turned to her and said softly, "I'm sorry, that was too quick. It'll be better next time."

"Don't be so silly, Miles . . . it was wonderful, you're wonderful."

"Ah, but you're prejudiced, my love."

"Well yes, I am, but nevertheless what I just said *is* true." She smiled at him.

Miles smiled back. It was a tender smile, and he put his arm around her, pulled her closer, so that her head rested against his chest.

"May I ask you a question, Miles?"

"Of course."

"What did you mean when you said that our reading things about each other in the newspapers and remembering them signified something special?"

"It suddenly struck me in the bar earlier that perhaps we'd been unconsciously drawn to each other before we actually met at Jane's party."

She smiled against his chest. "I think I was."

"So was I . . . I do believe," he admitted.

Christina confessed, "When I saw you come out onto the terrace at Hadley, I got a terrible pain in my chest, a tightness that was really quite awful, and I felt very wobbly all of a sudden."

Miles smiled. She was so open and ingenuous. Relatively few women would have told him something so revealing at this stage in the relationship. But he was glad she had. It confirmed his opinion that she was straightforward and an innocent despite her sophisticated circle of friends. He liked this about her. He was pleased she was untarnished by other men.

"If it makes you feel any better, Christie, I had a strong reaction to you, too. I knew I had to see you again." He drew on his cigarette. "And I really was most frightfully annoyed when I had to cancel lunch at the last minute."

"So was I . . . well, disappointed really, Miles . . . when did you decide to come to Paris?"

"Earlier in the week. Fridays are generally quiet in the Commons, are usually devoted to uncontroversial issues and private bills, and I knew I could get away early, so I booked a flight—"

"And obviously rang up Bruton Street to ask where I was staying."

"I did."

"I'm surprised my secretary didn't tell me."

Miles chuckled. "I said I was calling for Susan Radley, that she wished to send you flowers and needed the name of your hotel in Paris. I explained you weren't to be told, since the flowers were meant to be a surprise. And I thought to add that I was the florist."

Christina laughed. "Aren't you the crafty one," she teased. "And why didn't you want me to know you were coming to Paris? Obviously you *didn't*, from what you've just said."

"I wanted to surprise you."

"How did you know I wasn't meeting someone here? A special man? A lover?"

"I hoped and prayed you weren't." Stubbing out the cigarette, Miles bent over her, kissed her brow, whispered, "Are you glad I decided to hop over?"

"Yes, Miles, very glad." Her arms went around him and they kissed quietly, and then Christina placed her hands on his bare chest, looked up at him and gently pushed him away. "Are you going to stay through tomorrow too?"

"Oh yes, indeed I am. In fact, I'm going to stay all weekend. I'm not leaving until early on Monday morning, my sweet." The lazy smile touched his mouth and he took hold of her shoulders, forced her down onto the pillows. Kneeling over her, he began to stroke her breasts and then her stomach, murmuring, "Now lie still, don't say a word, I want to make love to you in a very special way. . . ."

They got up at midnight and went out.

Miles loved jazz and he took her to one of his favorite old haunts, the Mars Club, just off the Champs-Elysées. It was dark and smokey and intimate, and they sat squashed close together on a red plush banquette, holding hands, and he drank warm Scotch and she sipped icy white wine. And between sets he talked jazz, told her about Bix Beiderbecke and Charlie Parker and Fats Waller and Django Reinhardt

and Louis Armstrong. And from time to time he would kiss
her cheek unexpectedly, or squeeze her knee and smile into
her eyes, and as the minutes ticked by, Christina fell more
and more in love with Miles Sutherland.

Later they went off to Les Halles, the old produce
markets, to have the famous onion soup at one of the little
cafes, and as they spooned it up hungrily and ate the
toasted French bread and runny cheese that floated on top,
he spoke of his childhood, of growing up in the rambling
old country house in Suffolk that had been his family's home
for centuries. And she listened attentively, relishing every
word, enjoying hearing about his youth and his father and
mother, and it was almost six in the morning when they
returned to the Ritz, holding hands and laughing, still wide
awake and excited about discovering each other.

Miles opened the door of her suite and followed her
inside.

"You're not going to throw me out?" he asked, removing
his jacket, loosening his tie, slipping off his shoes. "I *can*
sleep here with you, can't I? Please don't banish me. . . ."

Her answer was to smile at him, a long, slow smile, and
to offer him her hand. He took it in his and together they
walked into the bedroom.

Miles closed the door and locked it, and he took her in
his arms, whispering her name over and over again as he
lifted her in his arms and carried her to the bed. And they
made love once more and slept and made love, and that's
the way it was for the rest of the weekend.

CHAPTER FORTY-SEVEN

"No two ways about it," Miles said to Christina on Sunday
night, "I've got a really horrendous week ahead of me."

They were having dinner at La Coupole on the Left Bank
and she looked at him, put her fork down on her plate. He
hadn't sounded serious at all during the weekend. Now he

lid. "What do you mean?" she asked, reaching for her glass of wine.

Miles leaned closer. "Hugh Gaitskell is going to be coming down hard on Anthony Eden because of the trouble with Nasser and the Suez Canal. I'm going to be really slogging it out with my opposition, especially as one of Hugh's protégés. But then I suppose the entire shadow cabinet is going to be on the attack. It's such a terrible mess."

"You don't really think there's going to be a war in the Middle East, do you?"

Miles nodded and his face became instantly grave. "I'm afraid so—Egypt—because of the Canal problems. But let's not discuss it tonight. When will you be coming back to London, Christie?"

"Not until Saturday. My lawyer Maître Bitoun needs me here to conclude everything with the perfume manufacturer."

Miles took hold of her hand and he gave her a mischievous look. "Shall I come back next weekend . . . to be with you here?"

"Oh Miles, could you?" Her face flushed up and her eyes sparkled. "That would be wonderful, wouldn't it?"

"That's what I think," he said and grinned.

After dinner they walked for a while, and then they took a rackety old cab, the only one they could find, back to the hotel. "I swear to God he's three sheets to the wind," Miles muttered in her ear as they sat on the back seat holding hands while the driver weaved his way across Paris.

Later that night in bed, as he held her in his arms, Miles said in that low, intense voice of his, "I'm afraid I'm getting rather entangled with you, Christie."

"And I with you, Miles."

"I know I shouldn't, that we shouldn't, but I just can't seem to stop myself, or *you*, I suppose."

"Why shouldn't we get involved?" Christie asked, drawing closer, wrapping one leg over his body, tightening her arms around him.

A deep sigh rippled through Miles and for a moment he

did not respond; then he said, very quietly, "I've nothing to offer . . . she'll never divorce me. . . ."

"I don't care."

"You might one day, Christina."

"Why won't she? Divorce you, I mean?"

"I've not been able to fathom it, actually. You see, she doesn't want me, but she doesn't want anyone else to have me either."

"Do I? Have you, I mean? Do I have just a tiny little half inch of you?"

He smiled. Now it was her turn to fish. He had been doing that almost the entire weekend in a variety of different ways, at times feeling as foolish as a lovesick schoolboy.

Miles said, "Yes, you do . . . just a tiny little half inch of me, as you said." He bent over her, kissed her hair. "However, I think too much of you to play games with you, darling. I want this, want us, want you. Yes, I *damn well* do want what we've started this weekend to continue . . . selfishly I want it. But if we do continue, it would have to be clandestine. That's not fair to you. If Candida ever found out, she would create a frightful scandal. I couldn't afford that . . . there's my political career—don't you see?"

"I do. But *I* want *us* too, Miles. *I want you*. Look, we can be careful. We don't have to go out . . . be in public. I don't mind it being secret."

"You'll mind one day, Christie."

"Oh no, I won't, Miles."

He made no response. He held her close in his arms and eventually they both fell into an exhausted sleep.

Miles left for London the next morning.

He thought about this last conversation a lot in the ensuing week, as he went from his flat in Knightsbridge to the House of Commons, and about his other business. And over and over again he asked himself if he ought not to take matters into his own hands and simply terminate their relationship. Miles Sutherland was a responsible man and bore no resemblance to the cad Jane Sedgewick had

onjured up in her girlish imagination. In point of fact, he
as just the opposite. He was a man of honor, a man of
ommitment. He longed to be free of his neurotic wife; he
ad no interest in her money or her father's money, since he
as a man of private wealth himself.

End it now, before it gets out of hand, he kept saying to
imself, but then he would telephone Christie at the Ritz in
ie evening, as he had said he would, and the sound of her
oice drove any thoughts of rational action right out of his
ead. He wanted this woman in a way he had never wanted
woman before. He was hopelessly involved with her
hether he wanted to be or not. *He could not change the
.ay he felt*.

And so on Friday afternoon he flew back to Paris.

The minute Miles walked into her suite and saw Chris-
ina, he felt his heart skip a beat and his spirits lift, and he
new that *he* would never be the one to put an end to their
ve affair. She was like air and light and sun to him.

Christina had second-guessed him. Before he even got a
hance to say he did not wish to go out to a restaurant to
line, she informed him that she had ordered smoked
almon, Brie cheese, French bread and fresh fruit, and that
hey were about to have a picnic. "In bed," she said gaily,
aughing as she brought him a glass of Scotch with ice and a
plash of soda, mixed exactly the way he liked it.

After they had sipped their drinks, Miles put his hand in
is pocket and brought out a small red leather jewel case.
These are for you, Christie. Opals . . . remember how I
aid you should always wear opals the night we met?"

"Oh Miles, they're beautiful!" she exclaimed, "exqui-
ite." She glanced up at him, her eyes shining. "I've never
een anything with such fire. . . ."

"Yes, and they're going to look superb on you. Come,
et's see."

He led her to the mirror and she fastened the earrings
n, and admired them, and he admired her wearing them
nd they laughed, enjoying being together again. And then
he ran into the bedroom and returned with a package.

"This is for you," she said.

He was grinning with pleasure as he tore off the paper.

"Oh my God, you *really* shouldn't have!" He shook his head, looking down at the Cartier gold cigarette case in his hand. "Now, my girl—"

She silenced him with a kiss.

Much, much later when they made love, it seemed to Miles that he had never touched her before. Every part of her body seemed fresh and new to him, and more beautiful than ever. And at one moment, at the height of his passion, as he soared above her in ecstasy, he cried out, "I love you, Christie! I've fallen in love with you!"

"And I love you, Miles! Oh my darling, I love you so much!"

It was a rapturous affair.

They were obsessed with each other. This was not a question of one loving the other more. They were crazy about each other. They were deeply and intensely involved on every level. It was her first real love affair; although Miles was worldly and had had other affairs, he realized that this was the first time he had ever been truly in love.

At one point that weekend, Miles had the brilliant idea of coming to Paris every Friday. He felt safer here, free from prying eyes. And so they made their regular weekend trips through August. "But we must start going to another hotel," Christie said at the end of the month. "We can't continue to stay at the Ritz . . . we're becoming a couple, in quotes, and people are beginning to notice us."

And so they stayed at the George V and the Prince des Galles and the Lancaster and the Raphael. It became a joke for a while, but then Miles decided they had better stop flying in and out of Paris anyway, because that was becoming noticeable too.

"We're going to have to find a little hideaway somewhere in England," he said to Christie on their last trip to Paris. "Why don't you get on to it next week, my sweet?"

CHAPTER FORTY-EIGHT

It was pouring.

There was a high wind that blew the rain against the windows, and the sound was like hundreds of nail heads striking the glass.

But in the library of the small country house in the Cotswolds all was warmth and muted light and tranquility on this cold day in early November.

Christina was stretched out on the sofa, listening to the rain. It was oddly soothing, and she felt herself drifting with her thoughts, enjoying the aimlessness of this lazy Sunday afternoon.

She stole a secret look at Miles, as she constantly found herself doing. She loved him so much, more than she had ever believed it was possible to love a man. Her career mattered to her and she worked hard. But he was her whole reason for being now.

She existed for the weekends. These were the best times . . . being alone together in this charming and secluded house just outside Cirencester, which she had found quite by accident at the beginning of October. It was available for six months, and since it was furnished they had had nothing to do but buy groceries and move in.

They were involved in an extremely secretive affair. But she didn't care. She didn't need other people, only Miles. They were together whenever he was free during the week; they couldn't go out, so they usually stayed in at the Walton Street flat. And also, since he was often preoccupied with the goings-on in the Commons, the weekends were the most relaxed. They did very little . . . read and talked . . . and went for walks . . . she loved cooking for him, taking care of him, sharing his thoughts, his feelings, his extraordinary passion and his vibrant sexuality. And his tenderness. He was such a mixture.

He sat opposite her in a chair by the fire, engrossed in

The Observer. The rest of the Sunday papers were
scattered at his feet, discarded after he had plowed through
them doggedly, muttering and cursing under his breath,
sometimes laughing out loud, or exclaiming "*Damnation!*"
and then grinning at her sheepishly, and explaining and
sharing. Always sharing everything.

His face was tense at this moment. She knew he was
worried about the situation in the Middle East. They were
engaged in hostilities with Egypt because President Nasser
had nationalized the Suez Canal. Britain and France and
Israel had bombed Cairo, and Miles was still fuming in
private, and driving points home in the Commons.

As if he suddenly became aware of her eyes on him, he
looked across at her over the top of the paper, asked, "What
is it, Christie?"

"Nothing, darling," she replied, sitting up, swinging her
legs to the floor. "Just admiring you."

"Aha!" he exclaimed and eyed her wickedly. "In that
case, if you so admire me, shall we climb the stairs together
for a little sweet dalliance on this quiet Sunday afternoon?
What better thing is there to do than make love on a wet
day?"

"Honestly, Miles, you are impossible!"

"That's not what you said to me last night . . . you were
full of compliments last night."

Her response was to walk over to him, take the paper out
of his hands and sit down on his knee. She leaned into him,
kissed him on the cheek. "Well, you were terrific last
night."

He smiled his faintly amused little smile, took off his
horn-rimmed glasses and rubbed his eyes. "I think I've had
it with the papers . . . I wouldn't mind some air. Shall we
go for a walk? You're the only person I know, other than
myself, and apparently the Queen, who likes to walk in the
country in the rain."

"Yes, come on, let's go, Miles." Christina jumped up,
then offered him her hand.

Miles held her in his arms, looking down at her, watching

the play of lights on her face. He loved her far too much, he sometimes thought.

Christina opened her eyes and stared up at him. Then she smiled. "You're spoiling me . . . you're always making love to *me*, Miles. . . ." She touched his cheek lingeringly.

"Mmmm, that's quite true," he said, and pushed her farther down in the bed, and wrapped his legs around her. "I *am* turning into an unselfish sort of bloke, aren't I? But we can always correct that, or rather, you can, you know. I'm very available right now."

He brought his mouth to hers, kissing her slowly, sweetly until the heat began to soar through him, charging him up, making his heart race, his passion soar. He felt her hands in his hair, on the back of his neck, smoothing down over his shoulders. He wanted her. He seemed to want her more and more every day. He could never get enough of her.

His voice was low and thick with emotion as he said, "Kiss me, Christie, oh please kiss me, my darling."

She sat up and knelt over him and stared into his face intently. She had grown to so love that face. It could block out everything, the image of it filling her mind absolutely until she was overwhelmed by it.

She ran her hands over his chest and down onto his flat hard stomach. His skin was as smooth and as dry as polished marble, glistening pale gold here and there where the half light shone on the fine blond hair on his lithe body. She moved to kneel between his legs and felt an involuntary quiver run through him as she put her hands on his thighs.

Christina looked up at Miles and saw that he was gazing down at her, his eyes a reflection of her own, awash with desire and love. Her throat tightened and her heart was clattering as she bent toward him, her mouth anxiously searching out the center of his passion just as his own had searched for hers a short while before.

He groaned as her mouth made contact with his body. "Oh God, Christie, what do you do to me?"

She filled her mouth with his sex, her lips lingering lovingly on him.

Now Miles was truly hers, spread out before her, immobile and breathless, offering himself up to her, a gift of love. And she was possessing the very core of him, his life's essence, his soul, and at that moment he belonged entirely to her.

He ran his fingers through her thick and tumbled hair, and caressed her shoulders, then brought his hands down to clasp hers gently resting on his stomach. He clenched his fingers around hers in a tenacious hold. An aching moan trickled from his throat.

She lifted her eyes and saw a fleeting flash of anguish smudge out the bright blue of his eyes, so that they became dark and flaring.

Suddenly Miles moved, put his hands around her face, lifted it up. He leaned down to her, kissed her sweetly, and then gently pulled her up the bed to him. He said, "I want you, Christie, want to be inside you. I must be enveloped in that lovely warmth that is you, my darling."

Suddenly he was on top of her, floating over her, and she was drowning in the midnight blueness of his eyes. He entered her almost roughly, and she began to quiver as she felt the rock-hard thrust of him. It was as if they ignited each other, moving in a rhythm that soon began to attain greater intensity. His passion seemed to spiral up and up, and she met its flight, rising higher and higher with him, at one with him. There was no separation anymore.

Miles opened his eyes and looked at her and cried harshly, "Oh God! Oh you! Oh I—" He crushed his mouth on her, devoured her lips, her tongue.

"I want all of you," he whispered against the hollow of her neck. "All of your essence, all of your breath, all of you!"

Christina felt as if he had reached up and touched her heart. And then, as if from a long distance, she heard his name being called. But it was she who was shouting, "Miles! Miles! I love you!"

They clung to each other with a kind of desperateness, were welded together in an embrace that was primal and full of need. His mouth sought hers briefly, and as he drew all of her strength into him, he rushed headlong into the core of her.

And she heard him cry, "Christie! Christie! I love you I love you I can't live without you don't ever leave oh my God I'm coming come to me my love."

He lay motionless with his head on her shoulder.

Christina felt dazed. She looked down at his translucent face and her tears welled up. What was it about his face? This face that so moved her, touched some inner spring of memory so poignant it made her want to cry at times.

Miles opened his eyes. "What happens to us when we're together like this?"

"I don't know. I think we float off somewhere. At least I do. Haven't you noticed that in me, Miles?"

"No, but then I'm wherever it is you are, Christie."

"Have you ever been there before? With anyone else?"

"No." He cleared his throat, said softly, "I think I know what happens to *us*, darling . . . when the sex act is so perfect, as it is with us, then that combination of the most intense physical pleasure and ecstasy, along with complete mental and emotional connection, makes the experience transcendental. We're transported to a higher level of consciousness."

"Yes, Miles, I think we are."

He stroked her hair, turned her face to his, murmured, "Set me as a seal upon thine heart, as a seal upon thine arm, for love is strong as death—" He paused and frowned. "Now I've gone and ruined it because I can't remember any more."

"Jealousy is cruel as the grave," Christina supplied.

"Yes, that's it. What comes next?"

"I can't remember either, but I know a bit of the next verse. Many waters cannot quench love, neither can the floods drown it. You see, I know my Bible too."

"Yes . . ." Miles was hesitant and then he said, "Christie, there's something I haven't told you. . . . I did something when you were in New York for your show a couple of weeks ago. . . ."

When he did not finish his sentence and because he sounded so serious, grave even, she sat up swiftly, stared at him. "What did you do?"

Miles also sat, reached for a cigarette on the bedside table, and lit it. He took a long draw, and then looked at her, said slowly, carefully, "I did something I vowed I would never do ever again. I went to see Candida. To ask for a divorce."

"And?"

"The answer was *no*. Many *no's* were flung at me, along with a variety of threats about creating a scandal if I broach it again." He exhaled. "I went to see her because I want to marry you, Christie. I don't want this creeping around corners, being unable to take you out with me. I want you as my wife." He shook his head sadly. "But it seems that's not to be."

"I don't care," she exclaimed, coming into his arms. "It doesn't matter. Nothing matters, Miles, as long as we can be together."

CHAPTER FORTY-NINE

"What's the matter, darling?" Miles asked, walking across the living room of the Walton Street flat. "Don't you like the necklace?" He looked down at her, narrowing his eyes, trying to ascertain why she appeared to be so upset.

Christina's hand went up to her neck and she touched the lacy cobweb of delicate chains set with diamonds and opals, then lowered her eyes to look at it. "Miles, it's the most beautiful gift I've ever had. I love it."

"Then why such a long face, Christie?" He lowered himself onto the sofa next to her and took her slender, tapering hand in his. "Is it because I can't spend Christmas with you? Because if it is, I'll try to do something about cutting the holiday short. Look, I have an idea, I'll spend the day with you on Christmas Eve," he said, improvising apidly. "Than that evening I'll drive down to Suffolk in rder to have dinner with the boys and my parents. I'll pend Christmas Day with them, come back to town for Boxing Day with you, and—"

"Miles, no, I won't permit you to split yourself in two like that, or change your plans at this late date. Besides, it would be impossible for me to change mine. My parents would be so unhappy if I didn't go to Yorkshire. They've been looking forward to it, and I haven't seen much of them lately, you know that."

"Candida isn't going to be there, if that's what you're thinking. She really is going to take Monica up to Scotland. They're to stay at her father's shooting lodge with him." Miles shook his head in puzzlement. "I'll never know why she suddenly said I could have the boys, I really won't."

Christina sat staring ahead at the fireplace.

Miles lifted his hand, turned her face to his. "That is the God's honest truth, darling. Candida won't be at Broxley Hall." When she remained silent, he exclaimed, "You do believe me, don't you, Christina?"

She heard the anxiety in his voice and saw the alarm on his face, and she squeezed his hand. "Oh Miles, I know very well you'd never lie to me, it's not in your nature."

Miles looked deeply into her face. Her emotions were always explicit in her eyes. They usually told him everything. He saw that she was still perturbed but decided not to press her for the moment. They would not be seeing each other for a week, the longest they had been apart in the last six months. He had wanted it to be a very special night and he had no intention of spoiling it.

Almost as if he had telegraphed this thought to her, Christina pushed a bright smile onto her face and jumped to her feet. "Darling, fling a couple of logs on the fire and open the champagne, and let's settle in for a really gorgeous evening. I'm going to get your presents . . . after all, this *is* our Christmas tonight."

"Righto," he said, standing, smiling at her. He pulled her to him, kissed the hollow in her neck. "I do love you so much."

She extricated herself gently and ran to the bedroom,

turned in the doorway. He was standing watching her intently. She blew him a kiss.

Miles was fiddling with the cork in the champagne bottle when she came floating back into the room, her arms full of packages. "Those are not all for me, are they?"

She grinned at him and carried them over to the fireplace. "One more trip, and that's it."

He shook his head, laughing with her, and his heart was full of love. There was no woman in this world quite like his Christie.

"You've always hankered after this," she said, walking toward him, carrying a large parcel wrapped in brown paper. "And I especially want you to have it. And it's with all of my love, my darling."

He took the parcel, knowing it was one of her paintings. Since he had admired them all, he did not know which one this was. He smiled at her. "Thank you, Christie. I know it's one of your paintings from the shape . . . which one is it?"

"Open it and see for yourself." She stood with her back to the fire, watching him as he carried the package to the sofa and tore off the paper. When he had the painting in his hands, he held it up and exclaimed, "Oh Christie, *Lily at Hadley* . . . oh Christie, how generous of you to give me this particular one. I know it's your favorite. Thank you." He put the painting against the sofa, came over and hugged her tightly.

Christina saw that he was pleased, and this pleased her. She said, "It only became my favorite *after* we met at Hadley Court . . . and that's why I want you to have it, because it will always remind you of me."

His smile slipped, and he frowned at her. "Are you going away?"

"No, silly. Why do you ask that?"

"It was the way you said *remind me of you* . . . as if I'd need reminding of you when you're always going to be with me."

"Of course I am, Miles. Now, how about a glass of champagne before you open the rest of your presents."

He went to pour the drinks. "I had a Christmas card and

a scribbled note from Ralph and Dulcie. I understand they're going to stay in New York for a while, what with that picture coming up in Hollywood and the possibility of a Broadway play. And what have you heard from Jane lately?"

"She was grumbling about the little monsters going over to New York for Christmas when she called me yesterday at the office. But otherwise she doesn't have much news. She is going to do the costumes for the new Hal Prince play on Broadway and she said she'd be staying on for another six months."

"Good for her. Jane's a talented girl." Miles brought their drinks and they clinked glasses. "Happy Christmas, my sweet."

"Happy Christmas, Miles."

They sat in front of the fire, slowly demolishing the bottle of Dom Perignon whilst Miles opened his gifts one by one, thanking her profusely, exclaiming over the books and jazz records, the ties and the silk dressing gown.

But it was the pair of sapphire cuff links that stunned him. "They're quite extraordinary," he exclaimed at last, holding them in his hand, admiring them. "You're far too extravagant."

"Listen who's talking," she said, coming to kneel next to his chair, looking up at him adoringly. "Do you really like them?"

"You know I do."

"So do I . . . they match your eyes."

He smiled and put his hand in his pocket, brought out a small box. "And this is another Christmas present from me."

It was a ring, a large opal ring surrounded by diamonds. It matched the necklace he had given her earlier, and the ring was equally exquisite.

"Thank you so much, Miles. How lovely it is." She slipped it on her right ring finger, held her hand out, looking at it.

Miles said, "Wrong hand, darling." He pulled the ring off and put it on her left hand. "Let's just say I prefer to see it there—" He broke off, staring at her. Tears swam in her lovely gray eyes and her lip trembled. "Christie, whatever is it?"

She shook her head, brushed her eyes with her hand, swallowed. "Miles . . ."

"Yes, darling, what is it? Whatever's wrong?"

Christina looked at him carefully. Her eyes held his. "I'm pregnant."

She saw the instant flash of happiness and pride in his eyes, the sudden delighted smile he couldn't suppress and which revealed so much. And then his face was wiped clean like an empty slate. "Oh Christie," he said and shook his head slowly. "Oh, Christie . . ."

And she could not fail to miss the dismal tone, the misery in his eyes, the worry which was now enveloping him. She knew him far too well. "But you were pleased a second ago!" she cried, taking his hand. "I know you were!"

"Of course I was, but—" He was unable to continue. Miles swallowed, and deep within himself he knew that he had never loved her so much as he did at this moment.

She said, "I wasn't going to tell you tonight. If you hadn't taken the ring off my right hand and put it on the other, I wouldn't have."

"I'm glad you did . . . we're in this together. You can't carry such a burden all alone, Christie."

"I didn't want to worry you, not with Christmas just around the corner. I didn't want to spoil it for you . . . you don't get to see the boys enough as it is."

He touched her cheek. "You're always so thoughtful, my lovely Christie." He sat back in the chair, then said, "Well, this does present us with a problem, doesn't it, darling?"

She nodded. "Miles, I don't want to have . . . an abortion, I just don't. I realize a baby would be difficult for you to handle, but I was thinking—"

"Christie, a baby wouldn't be difficult, it would be *impossible*. I don't want you to have an abortion either." His brow furrowed. "I just don't know what the solution is right at this minute."

"Why couldn't I have the baby, Miles? Who would know it was yours? Only you and I . . . I'm healthy financially, I can take care of everything, and—"

"I'm not sure that would work," he interrupted swiftly. "What if something leaked out . . . my political career . . ."

"Yes, I know, there are so many things to consider, aren't there?"

"When did you find out?"

"Four days ago."

"You should have told me before. I can't bear to think how dreadfully worried you must have been, Christie. It was wrong of you not to confide in me."

"I didn't want to upset you before Christmas."

"How pregnant are you?"

"Six weeks."

He brought her into his arms and held her close, stroked her head. "We'll think of the proper solution," Miles murmured. "Try not to worry, darling. We'll cope with everything after the holidays."

CHAPTER FIFTY

Although Miles had told her not to worry, Christina did little else for the next twenty-four hours as she prepared to go to Yorkshire to spend Christmas with her parents.

She worried about Miles. She worried about herself. She worried about the baby. Or more precisely, she worried about what to do about the baby.

Christina knew that Miles Sutherland loved her with all of his heart and that he did not want her to have an abortion. She also knew deep within herself that he wanted the baby, wanted *their* child. Yet she was too pragmatic a woman not to understand that there was his political career looming over their heads.

He had once said to her, not in the heat of passion, but quietly on one of their long walks in the country, "You're my life, Christie." But this was not strictly true. His political career was his life. And she could never ask him to give it up for her. To live openly with her. To have their baby.

If she did ask him, he would consider it, might even do it. But one day he would regret it, and she would regret it even more. To ask this man whom she loved so desperately to sacrifice his career would mean that she did not love him at all.

Politics and Miles Sutherland were too intertwined ever to be separated the one from the other. Miles would wither away without his constituency, his political cronies, the House of Commons and his life in that combative and exciting arena. Winston Churchill had once said he was a child of the House of Commons. So was Miles Sutherland.

And I am on the horns of a dilemma, I really am, Christina thought the following evening as she walked in from the Bruton Street fashion house at eight o'clock. Miles had left for Broxley Hall in Suffolk that morning, as loving and as concerned as he had been when she had broken the news. She had finished her Christmas shopping and then gone to her office to sign checks, give out Christmas gifts, and to attend the Christmas party Giselle had given for the staff.

Now here she was with nothing to do but worry until tomorrow morning, when she was taking the Pullman to Leeds. After hanging up her coat, she put a match to the fire that Mrs. Green, the char, had laid earlier, then hurried into the kitchen. She was not particularly hungry but knew she ought to eat something, so she opened a can of tomato soup. As she waited for it to heat on the gas ring, she made herself a sandwich from the smoked salmon left over from last night's dinner.

Ten minutes later Christina took her light supper into the living room and ate it in front of the now blazing fire. Her mind turned over various possibilities. She could have the baby and perhaps risk losing Miles. She could have an abortion. She could disappear, move to a foreign country, have the baby and live abroad for the rest of her life. Miles could visit her from time to time.

She jumped up and began to walk up and down the room. How stupid I am, she thought. None of those possibilities would work. There is only *one* solution: Miles has to force Candida to give him a divorce so that we can be married. Of course! Why hadn't she and Miles thought of it last night? Only because they were not both browbeaten into believing there never would be a divorce. But perhaps something could be worked out after all. Christina returned to the chair by the fireside and relaxed for the first time in several days.

Resting her hands on her stomach, she thought about the baby. *Their* baby. *His* baby. It thrilled her to think that part of Miles was now growing inside her. She was going to have the baby. She was going to marry Miles. It was going to work out.

The shrilling telephone made her jump in surprise. She went to answer it.

He said, "Hello, my love, how are you?"

"Miles, I'm wonderful. I've just had a brilliant idea."

He laughed into the telephone. "So have I. But tell me yours first."

"You've got to go to *you know who* again and make her give you your freedom."

"Well, I always knew I loved you for a reason, and it's obviously your brains! And great minds do think alike, it seems. I thought of the same thing this evening, and I couldn't wait to get through dinner to ring you. I *will* see Candida again, Christie, as soon as she's back from Scotland. We'll sort this out, you'll see. Everything's going to be all right."

"I feel so much better suddenly. Christmas isn't going to be so difficult after all."

"No, and we'll be together next week. Listen, darling, are you sure you don't want me to ring you in Leeds?"

"Perhaps you'd better not. I don't want to have to start explaining who you are. You know what parents are like."

"I do, my sweet. I love you, Christie."

"I love you, Miles."

"Where to, miss?" the cabbie said, after he had stowed her suitcase in the cab.

"King's Cross, please."

"Right you are, miss."

Christina sat back, smoothed the skirt of her coat and glanced out of the window. It had started to snow. Just small flurries, but it seemed to be settling. She wondered if it would be a white Christmas, whether it was snowing in Yorkshire.

She looked at her watch. She had plenty of time to catch the ten-thirty restaurant car going to Doncaster, Leeds and Harrogate. The best morning train on the Northern run, it went on up to Edinburgh. Scotland, she thought, her mind turning to Candida. Miles would get his freedom. They would marry. She would have their baby. She let her hand stray onto her stomach. It was flat. Nothing showed yet. But in a few months she would look pregnant. She would have to start thinking about designing herself a wardrobe of maternity clothes. . . .

Neither the cab driver nor Christina saw the huge truck go into a skid on the slippery road which was wet with snow and drizzle. The truck slammed hard into the passenger door of the cab and sent the vehicle spinning across the road and into a lamp post.

Christina was flung off the seat. She hit her head on the glass partition in front of her and landed on the floor in a crumpled heap. She was unconscious when they got her out of the mangled cab and put her in an ambulance bound for Middlesex Hospital. Miraculously her injuries were minor, mostly a light concussion and bruises. But an hour after being admitted to the emergency room she lost the baby.

CHAPTER FIFTY-ONE

Christina felt empty and desolated for weeks after she lost the baby. Miles was devastated too, and he was kind and loving to her, but it took her a long time to heal.

Slowly she began to pick up the threads of her life, put aside her sadness about the miscarriage. Her work was demanding and it helped to keep her going. It wasn't just the loss of the baby which troubled Christina in the early part of 1957. She had also come to believe that she and Miles would always be hampered by a wife who refused to divorce him. Under normal circumstances they could have lived openly together, but a politician was far too vulnerable, especially a man like Miles, and they would never be able to take that step.

He had gone to Candida again in February and asked for a divorce. Once more he had been refused. And he had come back to Walton Street looking defeated and humiliated. Christina's heart had gone out to him that night.

As he had sipped the Scotch and soda she had handed him, he had said, "I literally went down on my bending knees and begged. That woman's made of stone."

And then at the end of the month the bombshell had dropped. His sister had told him that they had been seen together in the Cotswolds. Even their weekend house, always so comforting and reinforcing for them both, suddenly became a prison. Their relationship seemed to grow more secretive and restrictive than ever.

For the first time since they had fallen in love, she and Miles began to quarrel. Small, insignificant quarrels admittedly, but nevertheless, the harmony, the tranquility they had always enjoyed together had gone slightly askew.

In April Christina was sure of only three things: Miles would never be able to rid himself of Candida, except perhaps through death; his political career came first; and she could no longer support the way she herself was living. Her life was built around him, his needs, and the circumstances of his work and the life he had had before they had met. It was impossible for her to continue.

It became clear to Christina in July of that year that there was only one solution to her predicament. She had to leave England for an extended stay in the United States. Only by putting distance between herself and Miles could she ever hope to break off the relationship. She loved him so much she knew that if she stayed in London she would never have the strength or the will to give him up. And she had to give him up to save her own life. The pain she was experiencing was now too great a price to pay for stolen moments. Also she wanted all of the things he had always said she would want one day: a normal life, a husband, children . . . and dignity. She could no longer bear to crawl around corners with Miles. And having to hide in the country had become the last straw.

She did not consult with him about her plans, nor did she confide in him. She knew he would never let her go. It would have to be a *fait accompli* when she told him. Her first step was to make Giselle Roux head of the House of Christina on a temporary basis for the next year. She gave her parents the keys to the Walton Street flat and told them to use it once a month. Her secretary Liz was given another set of keys to deal with the post and other day to day matters, since Christina did not want to give up the flat and neither did Jane. And she put plans in operation to start up a New York branch of the House of Christina. She had plenty of money to finance this project and a long list of loyal American clients. And finally, she had her dearest friend Jane, who was waiting impatiently for her to come. Christina had confided in Jane long ago, and when she had decided to break with Miles she had taken her close friend into her confidence again.

The last person she told was Miles.

"You looked so beautiful tonight, Christie," Miles said, as he sat down in the Walton Street flat and took the glass of white wine from her. "Cool as the proverbial cucumber," he said, giving her a glance that was both loving and appraising.

She hurried into the kitchen on the pretense of getting ice, suddenly overcome by her love for him. He looked good tonight, dressed in a light beige summer suit. Pale colors always sat well on him. She understood, as she filled the ice bucket, that she could not spend the evening with him as she had planned. She had to tell him at once. Immediately. It was too unnerving for her to be with him.

He said, as she went back into the sitting room, "I've always liked you in lime green, Christie, but you should be wearing my opals with that dress." He frowned. "I haven't seen them on you lately. Don't you like them anymore?"

"Yes, I do, Miles, I love them. But they are so valuable, I keep them locked away." She cleared her throat, sat down on the edge of the chair and looked across at him. She said as steadily as she could, "Miles, there's something that I have to tell you."

He was instantly aware of her grave tone and knew at once that something was dreadfully amiss.

"I'm going away, Miles. I can't live here in England any longer," Christina said. He tried to interrupt her, but she held up her hand. "No, Miles, you must let me finish, you really must. *You* can't go away, you're a Member of Parliament, but *I* can and I'm going to New York. Tomorrow. For at least a year."

"But, darling, why, for God's sake, *why?*" he demanded furiously, his face white, his eyes stark with shock.

"Because our life together is insupportable, Miles. I love you, I love you so very, very much, my darling, but I can't continue. I must put distance between us in order to start a new life for myself, don't you see?"

"I'll go and ask Candida again!"

"It won't work, Miles. You know that as well as I do. She'll never divorce you. I must go to save my own life."

He was on his feet and across the room, pulling her up and off the chair and into his arms. "I love you, Christie. You're my life. For God's sake, please don't leave me."

"I'm not your *whole* life, Miles . . . only a part of it. You have your political career and you have your children, but mostly you have your career. It won't be easy for you, but you'll be all right—" She could not continue. She slipped out of his arms, moved toward the fireplace.

He stared at her. He thought the world had just come to an end. *His* world had.

Christie said, "Miles, if you love me, you'll let me go, you'll set me free. . . ." Tears spurted from her eyes. She couldn't control them. "If you love me as much as you say you do, you'll give me this chance, never get in touch with me, never see me again. You'll let me be in peace."

"Christie," he cried desperately, "please, my darling, we'll find a way, we'll find a solution."

She shook her head. "There is only one way for us now, Miles. *You must let me go.*"

A million thoughts rushed through his head. So many things he had never told her, never shared, so many loving words he had never spoken, so much he still had to give her. He loved her with every fiber of his being. And because he did, he had to give her this chance she asked for. Too late now to do it all differently. Too late now with her.

Miles took a shaky step toward her and then stopped. He could not go and kiss her. He did not dare.

"Goodbye, my darling," he said, and stumbled out of the room. And as he ran down the stairs, he was blinded by his tears and he knew he would never love like this again.

She wept all the way across the Atlantic.

Jane met her at the airport, took one look at her and bundled her into the waiting limousine.

"Thank God they invented dark glasses," Christie said, trying to be light and normal with Jane, and then promptly burst into tears again.

Jane took her in her arms, patted her back and told her to cry it all out, and Christina sobbed all the way into Manhattan as Jane made sympathetic and loving noises.

The tears were endless. But somehow she managed to go about her business, to lose herself in her work. It was work she loved and it helped to keep grief at bay. And she *was* grieving for Miles, she knew that. She also understood somewhere in the hidden regions of her heart that she would always grieve for him. He had been her first real love and they had loved each other so very much.

But as the weeks turned into months she became more controlled, and one night she actually fell asleep without shedding a single tear.

The next morning at breakfast, she said to Jane, "I think I'm on the mend. I didn't cry myself to sleep last night."

"I'm glad, Christie," Jane said quietly. She had understood from the beginning that Christie was truly suffering, and that she was broken-hearted, and so she had been kind,

supportive, and continued to be so. Nor had she ever said
one mean thing about Miles. Now she murmured, "But it
has been a long time, you know."

"What do you mean?" Christie asked, stirring her cup of
tea, giving Jane an inquiring look.

"It is the first week of December, and you arrived here in
July. Six months of tears! My God! That must be some
record."

Christina began to laugh.

So did Jane, and she said, "Now I know you're really on
the mend, Crowther. And perhaps you'll help me plan my
Christmas party . . . our Christmas party."

"Are we having one?"

"We are . . . I want you to meet this actor chap, Simon;
you'll approve I hope, because I'm actually thinking of
marrying him."

"How long has *that* been going on?" Christina cried.
"Haven't I noticed the actor chap around here, or what?"

"Oh no, he's new . . . and adorable."

"Actors make lousy husbands, Janey."

"Are you throwing aspersions on my father?" Jane
demanded a little indignantly. "Mummy wouldn't like
that."

"Ralph is different," Christina said.

"So is Alex Newman."

"I thought you said his name was Simon."

"It is, Christie. Alex Newman is for you."

Christina held up her hand. "Oh no . . . I'm not ready
for men yet!"

But she had not bargained for Alex Newman.

She realized that he *was* different from the moment she
met him. He had a distinction that set him apart, and that
had nothing to do with his good looks or his charm.

Jane brought him over to be introduced and Christina
had no idea as she shook his hand that he had already
decided to marry her as he had looked at her from across
the room.

He was charming to her all evening, and attentive to her

needs throughout the party. He made her laugh a lot and she enjoyed his dry wit and found herself taking to him. But when he asked her out the following evening, she shook her head. "Thank you so much, but I don't think so."

"Aren't you ready yet?" he asked quietly.

She drew back slightly. "What do you mean?" She wondered if Jane had told him something about her problems, her unhappiness, and then realized her friend would not have done a mean thing like that.

"Don't look so affronted," Alex said, smiling. "Instinctively, I feel that you've been hurt recently. By a man. And I thought that perhaps explained your reluctance to accept my invitation to dinner." He grinned at her rather boyishly. "Obviously it's me you don't like."

"Oh but I do like you, Alex, a lot," Christina said. "And yes, I will come out with you tomorrow night."

He smiled and went to fetch them both an after-dinner drink, and they sat by the fire for a long time, chatting about innumerable things, and found they had common interests.

Alex said, "I understand from Jane that the House of Christina is ready to be launched early next year, so I guess that means you'll be living here permanently?"

"Oh no, I don't suppose so," Christina said quickly. "The London house needs me, and so I imagine I'll commute back and forth across the Atlantic. I gave myself a year to get everything rolling properly here."

"I see. But your business will be bigger here, won't it? Eventually. I would have thought you could sell twice as much in New York as you do in London."

Christina looked at him with interest, knowing that he was a banker, and for the rest of the evening they talked about business. And later, after everyone had left and she was helping Jane to clear away the glasses and plates, she found herself thinking about Alex Newman and his fascinating marketing ideas.

As she and Jane washed the crystal glasses, Christina suddenly said, "I did like Alex. You were right, he is a lovely man and different."

"And rich," Jane said, grinning at her. "Not that that makes any difference to you."

"No, it doesn't. And don't get any ideas, Janey Sedgewick, I'm only interested in him as a friend. I liked his ideas about business, and he says he'll be happy to help me any time."

"I'll bet he will," Jane cried, rolling her eyes and laughing. "And apart from being charming, good-looking, rich and intelligent, he's also single."

"He sounds like Mr. Perfect," Christina remarked. "So why isn't he married?"

"I believe he's divorced."

Christina shook her head and seemed to shrink into the wall, and she turned away, walked back into the living room.

Jane ran after her at once. "Oh Christie, darling, I'm so sorry. I didn't mean to upset you."

"You didn't, Janey, really. I don't think I'm ready for other men yet."

"But go out with Alex tomorrow. He's so nice, and I know he's taken to you. Please, for me."

And so Christina met Alex Newman for dinner at Le Pavillon the following evening. She did not know then that he would be the one to heal her wounds and make her whole again.

CHAPTER FIFTY-TWO

"Mommy, why won't you tell me what we've bought Grandma for her birthday? I want to know!"

Christina looked down at her six-year-old daughter and said, "Ssshhh, Kyle, don't shout in the middle of the street."

"But why won't you tell me?" Kyle wailed.

"Because you can't keep a secret, and Daddy and I daren't risk confiding in you, since it is such a special gift.

We're afraid that you'll blurt it out, and then it won't be a lovely surprise for Gran."

"Oh Mommy, I won't," Kyle protested indignantly. "I'm not a baby like Auntie Janey's Clarissa."

Taking hold of the child's hand firmly, Christina walked her across Grosvenor Square in the direction of South Audley Street. It was a bright June day in 1965 and Audra would be fifty-eight years old this week. She and Alex were giving a small dinner for her tonight at their flat in Eaton Square, and Kyle had been a pest for days, badgering her about the gift.

"Please tell me, Mommy!"

"I'll make a deal with you, Kyle," Christina murmured, curbing her exasperation. "If you don't mention it again in the street, I'll tell you when we get home—is that agreed?"

"Oh yes, it is."

They walked on in silence, much to Christina's relief. She was preoccupied with her business and wondered whether to stop in at Bruton Street for a few minutes to talk to Alex and Giselle about the winter collection now being produced. She decided against it. Her parents, Janey and her husband Simon, and the Sedgewicks would be arriving around six-thirty, and it was already four. Better perhaps to get back to Eaton Square.

She was thinking about her dress for the evening when she saw him getting out of a chauffeur-driven car ahead.

Her step faltered for a split second, but she went on walking at the snail's pace Kyle always adopted.

He swung away from the car, turned his head, looked down the street in her direction. He saw her immediately. He stopped in the middle of the pavement, stood stock still, as if immobilized by shock, and she realized he was waiting for her.

And then he began to walk, very slowly, toward her, his eyes riveted on her face.

How extraordinary, he hasn't changed at all in eight years, Christina thought. A little grayer at the temples, but he looks exactly the same as he always did. He was famous now. The Labor Party had won the last general election in 1964 and he was a minister and very important in the

British Government. Some said he would rise to be Prime
Minister one day. Candida had divorced him six years ago
to marry some impoverished Frenchman with a grand title,
a duke or a count, she wasn't sure. Occasionally she saw his
name linked to various women in the columns, but he had
never remarried.

As they drew closer Christina's heart began to thunder in
her chest and her mouth went dry.

"Hello, Christina," he said softly when they finally stood
in front of each other.

"Miles—" She could not say anything else for a moment.
She was blinded by the blue radiance of his eyes, deafened
by the noise in her chest. At last she managed, "It's lovely to
see you after all these years."

"Yes . . . eight years, Christie, a long time."

"Yes. Congratulations, Miles . . . on all of your wonderful successes, becoming a cabinet minister."

"And yours, Christina. I see your name wherever I
look—perfume, clothes, sunglasses, lingerie, hats—" Miles
was overcome. He held himself still, afraid that he would
grasp her arm, drag her with him to some place, any place,
where they could be alone, where he could take her in his
arms and tell her how much he still loved her.

Neither of them could move on, or tear their eyes from
each other. Time stood still for them both.

A thousand memories flooded her mind, and as she
looked at him she knew he was remembering so many
things himself.

"Mommy."

The child's voice broke the spell.

Miles looked down. He cleared his throat. "I'm Miles.
What's your name?" he asked in his resonant voice, offering
her his hand.

She took it, smiled up at him, her little cheeks dimpling.
"I'm Kyle."

"How old are you, Kyle?"

"I'm six."

He lifted his head. "Oh Christie—"

She saw the pain in his eyes and the sudden glitter of
tears. And there was such yearning on his lean, intelligent

face, she knew then that he had never stopped loving her and that he was thinking of their child, the one she had lost. And she knew too that he had never remarried because of her.

Christina's eyes brimmed. "Miles, oh Miles," she said and her voice trembled.

"Don't," he said, sounding as shaky as she, putting his hand on her arm. "Oh please don't, my dear, it's hard enough for me to bear. Take care of yourself, Christie . . . goodbye, Kyle."

He pivoted and walked back to the house where his car was parked, and sprang up the steps. And she waited until the door had closed behind him before she started to walk again.

"Why are you crying, Mommy?"

"I'm not."

"Yes, you are."

"It's the wind in my eyes."

"There isn't a wind, Mommy."

"I'm taller than you, and up here there's a wind."

"Oh."

"Let's find a taxi," Christina exclaimed, brushing her wet cheeks with her fingertips, hurrying her daughter forward.

"You promised to tell me about Grandma's present when we got home," Kyle said immediately as they entered the flat in Eaton Square.

Christina looked down at her, nodded. "Yes, Kyle, that's quite true, I did. However, I didn't say what *time* I would tell you. You'll know when Grandma knows—later this evening."

"That's not fair!"

At this moment, Nanny Fraser, the lovely Scotswoman who looked after Kyle, appeared in the entrance foyer and scooped Kyle up and off to the nursery.

Christina went down the hall and into her bedroom, dropped her handbag on the bed, and crossed to the adjoining bathroom. She locked the door, turned on the taps in the washbasin, found a hand towel and buried her face in it. And then she leaned against the wall and sobbed and sobbed until there were no tears left inside her. She wept for the child she had lost, the love she had lost. And she wept for Miles, and for his loneliness and for the tragic circumstances of his life and for all that he had missed with her.

And when she was finally calm, she washed her face and went out to the bedroom to redo her makeup and dress for her mother's birthday dinner. Earlier that day she had selected a mauve silk dress and matching mauve silk shoes, and all of the opals that Miles had given her. They went so well with the lilac colors. And now as she held them in her hands, she thought how odd it was that she had chosen to wear them tonight, had taken them out of the safe that very morning. She never before had bumped into Miles in all the years she had been traveling back and forth between London and New York.

Once she was dressed, Christina left the bedroom, hurried in the direction of the living room to inspect it before their guests arrived. In the entrance hall she heard Kyle's shrill voice echoing from Alex's study and she walked across to it, stood in the doorway. And Kyle was saying, "And after he left us, Mommy started to cry."

Alex looked up, smiled. But his eyes were momentarily perplexed as he came toward her. "Hello, my Chris-Chris," he said. "You're looking beautiful tonight. Very beautiful."

She met him halfway, stretched out her hands to his, looked up into his face, loving him with her eyes. She was so glad she was married to this man.

He kissed her cheek, turned to his child. "Hey, little poppet, shouldn't you run along and get changed? Grandpa and Grandma will be here any minute."

Once they were alone, Alex took her in his arms and held her very tightly. He said against her luxuriant hair, "So you finally ran into Miles Sutherland, and after all these years."

"Yes." There was a small silence. She said, "I felt so sad for him, Alex. That's why I cried after he left; it was for no other reason."

"I realize that, Christie. I suspect he's a lonely man, in spite of all the glory and the power."

"Yes." And then she murmured, "It really is the only reason, you know."

Alex held her away from him, smiled and shook his head. "Do you think I don't know where I stand with you after seven years of marriage?"

"Was it Miles?" Jane asked, looking at her intently. "The man whom you ran into this afternoon?"

Christina nodded and pursed her lips. "So she's told you as well, the little monkey . . . she's told your parents too, I think."

Jane squeezed her arm. "Don't be annoyed with her, Christie darling. You know what children are like, and anyway, no one's paid any attention."

Christina laughed hollowly. "Want to bet?" She drew Jane closer to the window and edged her out onto the terrace of the penthouse. "My mother came up to me a little while ago, and asked me who we ran into this afternoon, who the man was. Then she had the nerve to ask me if I was happy with Alex."

"You are, aren't you?" Jane suddenly looked worried. "You don't still hanker after Miles, do you?"

"Oh Christ, Janey, how can you of all people ask a question like that? You know how much I adore Alex. I have the best marriage in the world, the best of everything." Christina took a sip of champagne, eyed Jane carefully and said, "Now it's my turn to ask you a question, one that's been on the tip of my tongue for years . . . what did you ever have against poor Miles? You were always so down on him."

Jane gave her a small shamefaced smile. "I think I was rather attracted to him and furious because he never paid me a blind bit of notice. And then when he started chasing after you I was worried, Christie. I really thought you were going to be hurt." Jane dropped her voice. "And you were."

"Not irreparably, I wasn't."

"Thank God." Jane walked to the edge of the terrace, looked down at the leafy gardens in the center of Eaton Square, then turned. "Everything's all right with Simon

and me again, Christie. It was all a storm in a teacup last
week . . . well, you were forever cautioning me about
marrying an actor."

Christina smiled, took hold of her arm, drew her back
toward the French windows. "I knew it would be fine. Now
I think we'd better go inside. I know Alex wants me to say
my little piece to Mummy, and then we'll give her our
present, so that we can pack Miss Tattle Tale off to
bedibyes."

Alex cleared his throat and said, "Could we possibly have
a little quiet, please? Christie has something to say."

Everyone stopped talking and Christina walked into the
center of the room, leading Kyle by the hand. The child,
wearing one of her best party frocks, was carrying a gift-
wrapped box.

Christina smiled at her guests and then her eyes settled
on Audra. She said, "I had an idea last year, Mummy, and I
confided it to Alex. He loved it as much as I did . . . it
was an idea for this year's birthday present for you . . .
from the three of us. It comes with all of our love, and we
hope you're going to enjoy it as much as we believed you
would when we bought it for you a few months ago."

Kyle looked up at her mother and Christina nodded.
"Yes, go along, Kyle, give our gift to Grandma."

"Here you are, Gran," the child said, offering her the
box, and then she put her arms around Audra's neck and
kissed her cheek. She leaned against her grandmother,
said, "Please hurry up and open it, Gran, 'cos they didn't
tell me what it is . . . Mommy says I can't keep secrets."

Everyone laughed.

Audra, her face flushed with happiness, untied the blue
ribbon, pulled off the crinkly silver paper and lifted the lid.
She stared inside the box and then frowned. "What is it?"
she asked, throwing Alex and her daughter a puzzled stare
as she took out the old iron key. She glanced at Vincent
sitting next to her. "Do you know what this key's for?" she
asked her husband.

Vincent shook his head, although he knew very well. He

had been in on the secret right from the outset and was very much a part of it all.

Christina said, "It's the key to your new house, Mummy . . . yours and Daddy's. Alex and I have bought High Cleugh for you. That's your birthday present . . . your childhood home."

Audra opened her mouth. No sound came out. She looked at the key in her hand, then at Vincent, and she pushed herself up off the sofa unsteadily. She had paled and her eyes were exceptionally bright as she went to her daughter and son-in-law. She shook her head, glanced once more at the key.

"I never thought I would ever hold this key in my hand again . . . thank you, Christie and Alex, thank you so much for giving me back that house. " She reached out and took hold of Christina's arm, afraid that her legs were about to give way under her. The tears welled up and she leaned into her daughter and whispered, "Oh darling, thank you, thank you." And then Audra smiled and she went on smiling all night.

Christina rested her head against Alex's bare chest and listened to him breathing lightly, smoothing her hand along his arm.

"Do you think Mummy enjoyed her birthday dinner, and that she's excited about owning High Cleugh?"

Alex smiled. "Yes, to both of those questions. In fact, I think excited is far too mild a word . . . how about ecstatic or overwhelmed?"

Christina laughed, wrapped her legs around him. "Oh Alex, it was a lovely evening, thanks for helping to make it possible."

He said nothing, stroked her hair, held her head against him tenderly. He loved his wife so very much. He had from the first moment he had set eyes on her in New York, at that party of Janey's. He had looked across the room at her and his heart had jumped and he had known he was going to marry her. Suddenly he wished his child had not carried home tales about this afternoon's encounter. He would have preferred not to know that Christina had run into Miles Sutherland. All that had been over so long ago, but he hated the thought that she had seen him again. Miles had caused her so much pain in the past. Then he chastised himself for being so selfish. It was better he knew, just in case Christie wanted to spill out her thoughts. She had never told him much about Miles, but he had known in Paris on their honeymoon that the man had had a deep effect on her and that she had loved Miles. But then he had loved another woman before Christie. Everyone came with a history and a past. But he didn't suppose Christie would say much to him about the British politician. She was secretive about Miles, and yet she told him her thoughts and feelings on everything else. They *shared*—that was one of the reasons they had such a good marriage; it was also the reason why they worked so well in business together. They were the best team. He had taken the House of Christina and made it into an international business worth billions. She had the artistic talent, he had the business acumen and by licensing her name she had become bigger than ever.

"Are you happy with me?" she asked suddenly.

"You know I am, my Chris-Chris."

"Are you sorry I can't have any more children? Would you have liked another child, Alex?"

"No, Kyle is quite enough," he said, and then groaned in mock horror. "Imagine two like her."

"Be serious."

"I am . . . it's fine the way it is, darling. As long as you're happy, Christie. You are, aren't you?"

"Yes, I am. Are you sorry we never had a son? You know, a son as in son and heir. . . ."

"No, and anyway, we have a daughter and heir, and that's sufficient for me." He sensed her smile and he bent over her, moved her head slightly, brought his face down to hers.

He found her mouth with his and kissed her softly, slid his tongue alongside hers. And slowly and gently he began to make love to her, touching her breasts and stroking her body, letting her know how much he loved her and telling her in a thousand different silent ways that *he* would never hurt her.

And with delicacy and expertise he brought her to new heights of passion, and as she stiffened and began to spasm he took her to him, entered her swiftly, and made her his. Not only for tonight, but for always.

EPILOGUE

❧❧

Kyle, Audra and Christina
1978

EPILOGUE

"I don't want to paint dresses like she does, I want to paint pictures," Kyle said to her grandmother.

Audra flinched at these words. There's nothing like getting to the heart of the matter, she thought, but oh the brutality of the young. She said, "I know you've wanted to paint, to be an artist, for the last couple of years, Kyle dear, but I'm not sure you've gone about this in *exactly* the right way—with your parents, I mean."

"It's not Daddy, he doesn't care whether I go into the stupid business or not. It's *her!*"

"Now look here, Kyle, I won't allow you to speak about your mother in that tone of voice. You *are* being unfair, you know."

Kyle threw Audra a half apologetic look, but her mouth settled into sulky lines. "Anyway, I can't imagine why I'm defending Daddy, he's always on her side. He always has been. For as long as I can remember it's been the two of them against me . . . even when I was little I felt left out. They were the best team. That's what they always said, and it *was* just the two of them, Gran. I wasn't included."

Audra looked at Kyle in astonishment and sighed heavily. She wanted to shake her granddaughter, and if they hadn't been in the restaurant of the Carlyle Hotel, having coffee after lunch, she would have done so. "You're quite wrong, Kyle, in that assumption. I can distinctly remember when you came to England in 1965 . . . you were walking around, singing, 'We're the best team, the best team, Mummy and Daddy and me.' I remember it so well because it was the year your parents bought High Cleugh for me. You were six. And your parents have never shut you out. *Never.* You've been included in everything. They've been wonderful parents and they love you very much."

"They love each other more than they love me."

"Don't be so ridiculous," Audra snapped, genuine anger

surfacing. "Of course they love each other—they've never been anything *else* but very much *in* love, as a matter of fact. And you should thank your lucky stars they have, Kyle. What do you want to be? A child of a broken marriage?"

"I didn't mean it that way," Kyle answered swiftly, a chagrined expression flickering on her face. "It's just that I'm so upset, Grandma. I hate the fashion business and everything about it. I don't want to design clothes and sit behind a desk and do trunk shows and cope with imbecilic models who starve themselves to anorexic death and primp and pile ten pounds of icky goo on their faces every day. I want to paint what I see."

Her young face suddenly lost its petulant look, became gloriously alive, and all of her rebelliousness seemed to fall away from her. Kyle sat forward eagerly, and her dark eyes shone. "I want to paint landscapes and seascapes, like I did last summer when I was in Yorkshire with you, Gran. Oh it was lovely, being there at High Cleugh, going to Robin Hood's Bay and the Dales, and sitting with my easel and being quiet and putting beauty down on canvas, as I saw it my particular way . . . through my own special angle of vision. I was so happy last summer with you, Grandma. Happier than I've ever been. And then I had to come back here to New York and go out with Mom on the road. Stupid trunk shows. I hate them. And I detest the Fashion Institute."

Audra reached out and took the girl's hand. "I know things have been difficult lately, dear."

"I'm getting so that I can't function properly anymore, I'm so frustrated and unhappy." Kyle took a deep breath. "All it would take to make me happy is to be allowed to go to the Royal College of Art in London for a couple of years and then become a landscape painter. But she'll never understand *that*. All she's interested in is making money."

Audra's eyes welled with tears. "Oh Kyle, that's not true," she said and stopped, found her bag on the banquette, opened it, groped for her handkerchief.

Kyle was distressed and she squeezed her grandmother's arm. "I'm sorry, Gran, I didn't mean to sound nasty. I'm

orry too if I've hurt your feelings; after all she is your
daughter."

"And she's your mother, Kyle, and the best mother in the
world," Audra exclaimed. "Take my word for it. She only
wants the best for you. Why, she'd give her life for you. I've
been on your side all along, but I'm not going to be much
longer if you play the spoiled child, and speak of your
mother in this unkind and disrespectful way." Audra fixed
her piercing blue eyes on Kyle. "Do I make myself clear?"
she asked in a stern and reprimanding voice.

"Yes, Gran," Kyle replied meekly. She had always been a
bit afraid of Audra.

"Very well. Now listen to me, and you'd better listen
very carefully . . . and perhaps when I've finished you'll
understand your mother's motivations, understand *her*,
understand why she loves her business so much. All right?"

Kyle nodded.

"Your mother was a landscape painter, and she sacrificed
her art for the business. She once had what you want so
badly right in the palm of her hand. And she was brilliant,
Kyle. But she gave it all up for *me* . . . to make money for
me . . . to give *me* the comforts and luxuries she thought
I was entitled to have." Audra grasped Kyle's hand, held on
to it tightly. "I'll tell you about it . . . Christie should
have told you, but she hasn't . . . so I shall tell you now."

Kyle gave her grandmother her entire attention, and as
Audra continued to speak much of the anger and irritation
with her mother which had been building for the past year
dissolved. And when Audra had finished, Kyle's eyes were
moist too. "What an extraordinary thing Mom did for you,
Gran. I wish she'd told me." Kyle bit her lip. "Do you think
she misses painting? Do you think that's why she doesn't
have much of her own work around in the New York
apartment and the house in Connecticut? I mean, you have
most of it at High Cleugh, and Aunt Janey has some.
Perhaps she doesn't want to be reminded too much about
what she gave up."

Audra winced. Kyle's excruciating honesty was unnerving at times. "Perhaps she misses it . . . I don't really
know. We never speak of it. We never have actually, not

even in the beginning. But I've been wrong, Kyle. We
should have talked, she and I." Audra settled back against
the banquette, looking reflective. I was always afraid of
saying the wrong thing, of upsetting her, Audra thought.
Yes, I was wrong and in so many ways.

"I don't know what to do, Grandmother," Kyle muttered.
"I feel awful. I've been mean to Mom for months and
months. I must have hurt her dreadfully."

Audra patted her hand. "You won't have any problems
with your mother. . . . I know my daughter very well.
She loves you so much. She'll accept your apology and
forgive you at once."

"Do you think so, Gran?"

"I *know* so." Leaning closer, Audra smiled for the first
time in days. "I think I've come up with a compromise for
the two of you. I've been racking my brains all week, and I
think I have the solution, Kyle darling."

"Oh God I hope so, Grandma. What is it?"

"I'm going to talk to your mother again when we get back
to the apartment. If she's still insistent that you go into the
business, I'm going to ask her to give you a sabbatical.
Mind you, Kyle, you've got to promise to give her three
years in the business later, if she gives you three years now,
allows you to come back to London with me next week.
We'll apply at once to the Royal College, and in the
meantime, until you're accepted, you can live with me at
High Cleugh and paint to your heart's content. So . . .
what do you think?"

"Gran, it's brilliant! Brilliant!"

"Do you agree to keep your end of the bargain?"

"Yep. I do! I do!" Kyle's face glowed.

When they left the Carlyle Hotel, they walked down
Madison Avenue a short way.

It was a pretty Saturday afternoon at the end of May and
the lovely weather had brought many people out to gaze in
the windows of the elegant boutiques and browse in the art
galleries.

"I think I'd like to go up to Park Avenue and take a cab

back to the apartment," Audra said, reaching for Kyle's arm. "There are too many people about now."

"Are you all right?" Kyle looked at her grandmother worriedly.

"I feel a bit tired suddenly."

Kyle hailed a taxi on Park Avenue and helped Audra inside, and within ten minutes they were alighting in front of the apartment building on Sutton Place where the Newmans lived.

"Now let me do the talking," Audra insisted firmly as they went up in the elevator. "Keep that busy tongue of yours still for once. And when I've said my piece, you can apologize to your mother for your recent behavior. And you must do that, Kyle, whatever happens. Understand?"

"Yes."

Audra was disappointed when they let themselves into the hall.

The huge apartment was deathly quiet and seemed deserted. She knew Alex had had a luncheon engagement to keep, but she had expected her daughter to be home. Then Audra heard footsteps echoing in the marble gallery adjoining the foyer.

Suddenly Christina was standing there, smiling at them, looking impossibly young in a pair of blue jeans and a white silk shirt and lots of heavy gold jewelry. And she was positively radiant. The worry and anxiety and rage which had been etched on her face for the past week had completely washed away. She was like a new person. Or rather, like her old self.

"Hello, you two," Christina said brightly, coming forward eagerly, smiling. "Did you have a nice lunch? A good talk?"

"Yes, thank you, we did, Christie." Audra narrowed her eyes, wondering what had wrought the change in her daughter.

"I am glad, Mummy," Christina said.

"I'd like to talk to you," Audra announced rather abruptly.

"Then let's go into my study." Christina spun around and walked down the long gallery in the direction of her den.

Kyle looked at her grandmother inquiringly. Audra

shrugged in answer to the unasked but obvious question. They were both puzzled by the marked difference in Christina and hurried after her, riddled with curiosity.

She stood in the center of the study, waiting for them. "What do you want to talk to me about, Mother?" she asked.

Kyle went and perched on the arm of the sofa, and Audra sat down in a chair. She said, "Christie, I think I've come up with a solution to Kyle's—"

"Just a minute," Christina exclaimed, holding up her hand. "Before we get into that, I want to tell you about the plans I've made for your birthday next week, Mummy. Your seventy-first birthday—"

"Really, Christie," Audra interjected crossly. "I'm not interested in my birthday. I've better fish to fry this afternoon. Kyle is much more important than—"

"I *insist* on discussing this first, Mother," Christina cut in, her voice strong and firm. "And I also want to give you two of your gifts today."

Audra was furious and her mouth tightened. But she knew better than to interrupt.

Kyle was also annoyed but controlled her own flaring temper. Whatever her grandma said to the contrary, her mother *was* impossible.

Christina walked to the fireplace and stood next to it, resting one hand on the mantel. She said slowly, carefully, "My first gift to you, Mummy, is the thing I know you truly want the most in your deepest heart . . . a granddaughter living in England and studying at the Royal College."

Audra and Kyle stared at Christina and then at each other. They were stunned.

"I've done a lot of soul searching in the last few days, and I know how wrong I've been about Kyle—" Christina glanced at her daughter, smiled warmly. "Kyle must have her chance to follow her own lodestar. As you put it to me years ago, and then again the other day, a child is only ever lent to you. And so I want her to do whatever she wants with her life . . . it *is* hers, after all."

Audra stared speechlessly at her daughter.

"Mom! Mom! Do you really mean it?" Kyle shrieked,

jumping off the sofa, running to Christina, grasping her arm.

"Yes, darling, I do. I shouldn't have tried to push you into the business against your will."

"Oh Mom, I've been rude and cruel and impossible. I'm so very *sorry*. Can you ever forgive me, Mom?"

"There's nothing to forgive, Kyle. I simply want us to be friends again and I want you to have what makes you happy."

"Mom!" Kyle flung her arms around Christina and kissed her, and they pulled away and looked at each other and laughed and hugged again.

Audra, watching them both, thought: Thank God, thank God. Everything's going to be all right after all.

Christina exclaimed, "And now for your second birthday present, Mother. I'll just go and get it for you." She hurried across the floor.

"Why do *you* think she changed her mind, Gran?" Kyle asked the minute they were alone. She was flushed and excited, could hardly contain herself.

"I've no idea. But your mother's always had her feet on the ground, had a lot of common sense, and perhaps she finally realized as I once did, that you can't live somebody else's life for—"

"Hello, Audra love."

Audra turned her head sharply at the sound of the familiar voice, and surprise widened her eyes. She pushed herself to her feet and went to him, saying, "Vincent, my goodness! However did you get here?"

"By Concorde," he said and swung his handsome silver head to Alex, who stood behind him beaming. "This son-in-law of ours arranged everything. He came to meet me at the airport early this morning, sneaked me in here while you were asleep, then took me out to lunch after you'd gone off with Kyle." Vincent smiled at her. "Alex and Christie wanted to surprise you. I've come for your birthday, love."

"And it *is* a surprise," Audra exclaimed, standing on her tiptoes, kissing his cheek. He smiled at her and as he put his arm around her, drew her closer, Audra murmured, "Oh it's so good to see you. I've missed you this past week, Vincent, I really have."

"And I've missed you, Audra." Vincent glanced across at Kyle. "Now, love, what about a kiss for your grandfather?"

She flew to him. They embraced in the middle of the floor and then, arms linked, they walked over to the sofa and sat down. They had always been the best of friends, and had spent a lot of time together when she had come to England as a child.

Audra turned to Alex. "Thank you for bringing Vincent here, Alex, it was such a lovely gesture. And now that I think about it, my birthday wouldn't have been the same without him, it really wouldn't . . . we've always spent it together for exactly fifty years."

Alex put his arm around his mother-in-law, the other around his wife. "It was Christie's idea," he said.

"No, it wasn't, it was yours," Christina contradicted, smiling up at him, her luminous gray eyes shining with love.

Alex bent down, kissed Christina's brow, said, "It doesn't matter who thought about it—as long as it makes everyone happy."

"Yes, that's true," Audra agreed.

She looked across at Vincent and Kyle sitting on the sofa, allowed her eyes to rest on her granddaughter. Then she turned to Christina. "Kyle is the fulfillment of life's purpose . . . my life and yours. *She* reaps the benefit of all that we sacrificed for each other, and that's not such a bad thing, is it?"

Christina looked down at Audra. "No, it's not, Mother, it's really quite wonderful."

Reaching out, Audra took Christina's hand in hers, and her bright blue eyes were radiant with happiness as she added, "And in letting her go you have kept her for always."

ABOUT THE AUTHOR

BARBARA TAYLOR BRADFORD has had a notable
career in journalism, both in England and the
United States. Since writing *A Woman of
Substance*, she has devoted herself to writing
only fiction. Her most recent novel, *Hold the
Dream*, was on the *New York Times* hardcover
best-seller list for nineteen weeks. She lives in
New York City with her husband, Robert.

SPECTACULAR ENTERTAINMENT ALL SUMMER LONG!
SUMMER SPECTACULAR FREQUENT READERS SWEEPSTAKES
WIN A 1988 Cadillac Cimarron Automobile or
12 other Fabulous Prizes

IT'S EASY TO ENTER. HERE'S HOW IT WORKS:

1. Enter *one* individual book sweepstakes, by completing and submitting the Official Entry form found in the back of that Summer Spectacular book, and you qualify for that book's prize drawing.

2. Enter *two* individual book sweepstakes, by completing and submitting two Official Entry Forms found in the back of those two Summer Spectacular books, and you qualify for the prize drawings for those two individual books.

3. Enter *three or more* individual book sweepstakes, by completing and submitting—in one envelope—three or more Official Entry forms found in the back of three or more individual Summer Spectacular books, and you qualify not only for those three or more individual books but also for THE BONUS PRIZE of a brand new Cadillac Cimarron Automobile!

Be sure to fill in the Bantam bookseller where you learned about this Sweepstakes . . . because if you win one of the twelve Sweepstakes prizes . . . your bookseller wins too!

SEE OFFICIAL RULES BELOW FOR DETAILS including alternate means of entry.

No Purchase Necessary.

Here are the Summer Spectacular Sweepstakes Books and Prizes!

BOOK TITLE	PRIZE
On Sale May 20, 1987	
ACT OF WILL	A luxurious weekend for two (3 days/2 nights) at first class hotel, MAP meals—(transportation not included) Approximate value: $750.00
MEN WHO HATE WOMEN & THE WOMEN WHO LOVE THEM	Gourmet food of the month for 6 months N.Y. Gourmet Co. Approximate value: $750.00
VENDETTA	Schrade Collector's Knife set Approximate value: $750.00
On Sale June 17, 1987	
LAST OF THE BREED	Sharp Video Camera and VCR Approximate value: $1,600.00

WHITE DOVE (available in US only)	Lenox China white coffee service Approximate value: $750.00
THE MOTH (available in Canada only)	
THE BE (HAPPY) ATTITUDES	Set of DP workout equipment Approximate value: $1,000.00

On Sale July 15, 1987

THE UNWANTED	Bug Zapper and Samsonite Chairs—Table—Umbrella—Outdoor Furniture Approximate value: $1,300.00
A GRAND PASSION	Cake of the month plan Approximate value: $800.00
110 SHANGHAI ROAD	$1,000 American Express Gift Certificates Value: $1,000.00

On Sale August 12, 1987

HIS WAY	Disc Player with library of Sinatra discs Approximate value: $1,000.00
SUSPECTS	Home Security System Approximate value: $1,000.00
PORTRAIT OF A MARRIED WOMAN	Minolta Auto-Focus Camera Kit Approximate value: $750.00

OFFICIAL RULES

1. There are twelve individual sweepstakes, each with its own prize award. There will be twelve separate sweepstakes drawings. You will be entered into the drawing for the prize corresponding to the book(s) from which you have obtained your entry blank, any one or up to all twelve. Submit your completed entry on the Official Entry Form found in this book and any of the other participating books ... mail one or up to all twelve completed sweepstakes entries *in one envelope* to:

Frequent Readers Sweepstakes
PO Box 43 New York, New York 10046

2. NO PURCHASE NECESSARY TO ENTER OR WIN A PRIZE: Residents of Ohio and those wishing to obtain an Official Entry Form (covering all 12 sweepstakes) and the Official Rules send a self-addressed stamped envelope to: Frequent Reader Sweepstakes, P.O. Box 549, Sayreville, NJ 08872. One Official Entry Form per request. Requests must be received by August 14, 1987. Residents of Washington and Vermont need not include return postage.

3. Winners for each of the 12 sweepstakes will be selected in a random drawing to be conducted on or about October 19, 1987, from all completed entries received, under the supervision of Marden-Kane, Inc. an independent judging organization. If any of the 12 consumer winners selected have included completed Official Entry Forms from three or more books, or have included completed Official Entry Forms from three or more books, or have entered 3 or more sweepstakes on the Alternate Mail-In Official Entry Form (See Rule #2) they are qualified to participate in a separate BONUS DRAWING to be conducted on or about Oct. 19, 1987 for a 1988 Cadillac Cimarron. In the event that none of the twelve individual sweepstake prize winners qualify for the BONUS PRIZE, the bonus prize will be selected from all completed sweepstakes entries received. No mechanically reproduced entries accepted. All entries must be received by September 30, 1987 to be eligible. Not responsible for late, lost or misdirected mail or printing errors.

- -

ACT OF WILL
OFFICIAL ENTRY FORM

Please complete by entering all the information requested and
Mail to: Frequent Readers Sweepstakes
P.O. Box 43
New York, N.Y. 10046

NAME _____

ADDRESS _____

CITY _____ STATE _____ ZIP _____

BANTAM BOOK RETAILER WHERE YOU LEARNED ABOUT THIS SWEEPSTAKES

NAME _____

ADDRESS _____

CITY _____ STATE _____ ZIP _____

Completed entries must be received by September 30, 1987 in order to be eligible.

ISBN-0533-26543-1